Accidentally in Love

BELINDA MISSEN

ONE PLACE. MANY STORIES

This novel is entirely a work of fiction. The names, characters and incidents portrayed in it are the work of the author's imagination. Any resemblance to actual persons, living or dead, events or localities is entirely coincidental.

HQ
An imprint of HarperCollins*Publishers* Ltd
1 London Bridge Street
London SE1 9GF

1

This edition published in Great Britain by
HQ, an imprint of HarperCollins*Publishers* Ltd 2020

Copyright © Belinda Missen 2020

Belinda Missen asserts the moral right to be
identified as the author of this work.
A catalogue record for this book is
available from the British Library.

ISBN: 9780008331047

MIX
Paper from
responsible sources
FSC™ C007454

This book is produced from independently certified FSC™ paper
to ensure responsible forest management.

For more information visit: www.harpercollins.co.uk/green

Printed and bound in Great Britain by
CPI Group (UK) Ltd, Croydon, CR0 4YY

All rights reserved. No part of this publication may be reproduced,
stored in a retrieval system, or transmitted, in any form or by any means,
electronic, mechanical, photocopying, recording or otherwise,
without the prior permission of the publishers.

This book is sold subject to the condition that it shall not, by way of trade
or otherwise, be lent, re-sold, hired out or otherwise circulated without
the publisher's prior consent in any form of binding or cover other than
that in which it is published and without a similar condition including this
condition being imposed on the subsequent purchaser.

Chapter 1

'Urgh. Yuck. Hair in my lip gloss.'

My best friend and colleague, Lainey, pulls globby strands of blonde hair away from her mouth. She puckers and plumps and adjusts her blouse one last time. 'Okay, all right, I'm good.'

I lift my camera and adjust the zoom, lowering it – and my shoulders – just as quickly.

'Now what?' she cries.

'I'm just waiting for the bus to pass.' I gesture at the giant red mass beetling along Embankment on the opposite side of the Thames.

'Really?' She turns to shout at it, and we fall about laughing, much to the annoyance of passers-by. It's London's South Bank in the middle of summer, she's lucky her background isn't a sea of tourists. They've so far been gracious enough to give us a wide berth.

'Surely you don't want it to look like you have a TFL special protruding from your ear in your photo, do you?' I ask.

She chortles. 'It *would* make a great talking point.'

After the bus disappears and a water taxi is out of focus, I snap off a handful of shots and hope they aren't awful. I'm so out of practice with this photography lark that I've got the camera

1

set to 'automatic' and all my extremities crossed. I don't have time to worry about focal length and shutter speed today. I try for a few different angles, forcing Lainey into some uncomfortable-looking poses and, when I'm satisfied I've got enough photos, I wave her over to look.

'Nope, not that one.' She swipes at the two-inch display as if it'll make her photo disappear. 'I look like I've just done a double-shift at the London Dungeon.'

'What?' I shriek in disbelief. 'You do not. Don't be awful about yourself. You look fine.'

Nobody could accuse Lainey of looking like a horror movie villain. Ever. From the moment I met her, in our first year at Sheffield Hallam University, she's carried herself with ballerina grace and the style of a golden era Hollywood starlet. Her hair, usually held in an impeccable ballet bun, is free-flowing today, with no thanks to the muggy summer breeze. It's the kind of warmth that feels like breathing tepid water and I'm not a fan.

'What about this one? How do I zoom?' She jabs at the + button I point to. 'That's better. More professional, less crazy eyes.'

'What did you want these for again?' I ask.

Lainey grimaces. 'LinkedIn.'

'What? You're leaving? Really?'

'Figure it's time to put myself out there,' she says quietly. 'Look for something that pays a bit better. I'd launch my own social media business, but what with the brand-new mortgage—'

'And a wedding coming up.'

She grumbles. 'Don't remind me.'

When she's not posing for an updated profile photo, Lainey normally occupies a desk on the same floor as me at Webster Fine Art Gallery on the South Bank. While I'm with the curating team, she's smack-bang in the middle of the social media hub, updating, sharing, engaging the community, and enticing visitors through our doors with fresh and ever-changing content. She's so amazing at what she does that I have no doubt she could sell art to even the most hard-nosed critic.

'Wait, is that why you weren't in today?' I look up at her, twinkling brown kohl-rimmed eyes betraying the horrible lurgy she reportedly had on the phone this morning.

'Shhh.' She presses a finger to her lips. 'I got a sick note. It's legitimate.'

'In light of that, you need to get out of here before old Mr Webster spots you.' I throw an arm around her neck and hug her tightly. My phone pings as I pull back; an appointment reminder. 'I'm apparently on a tea break, and I have a meeting with Rockin' Roland in twenty.'

'A meeting?' she asks. 'About what?'

I pull a face. 'I'm hoping it'll be to tell me I've got the senior curator job.'

When the clock struck midnight on the first of January this year, I braved the chill of a London night to raise my thumbprint-smeared martini glass to the sky. Fireworks bloomed in convex perfection through it and, in that moment of inebriated clarity, I promised myself two things would happen this year. I don't so much call them resolutions as I do revolutions, because that's what we're doing: revolving around the sun. Ask Julian Lennon, he'll tell you.

The first of those revolutions was to level-up at work. After five years slaving away as an assistant then junior curator, cataloguing and keeping records, planning and budgeting, I'd landed on my feet as one of the gallery's two curators, designing my own programmes and acquiring new art.

Sure that I was destined for bigger things and all that, when Roland announced last month that he was leaving for a stint at an Irish museum, I threw down my application quicker than a winning hand at poker and bailed out of the room with explosions in the background, billowing hair and perfect slow motion.

Well, not exactly, but you get the picture.

'Good luck with that.' She almost scoffs. 'You know, I caught the three of them in the tearoom the other day. Roland, Steve and that brown-nose Charles.'

'Oh, please call me Charlie,' we mock in unison before sniggering.

On his first day in the office eighteen months ago, he'd made sure to tell all of us to call him Charlie, as if the affable nickname would make the shitty attitude vaporise.

'Standing about with their dicks in their hands, no doubt,' I say. 'You know, we were supposed to have a strategy meeting, me, Steve and Roland. As it turned out, I got an email about half an hour after they'd finished, telling me they caught up in the hallway and decided we didn't need a full meeting but here are the Cliff Notes if you need them.'

'If you *need* them,' she mimics Steve's nasal whine. 'Yeah, well, conversation fell off a crag the moment I walked in the room, but it was all covert looks and nudge, nudge until I left.'

'They make me so angry.' I lift my chin in the direction of the gallery and we begin walking. 'I don't know what I'm going to do if I don't get this role.'

Lainey gives my camera a nudge. 'Why don't you do something with your photography? You've always taken amazing photos.'

'That never really took off though, did it?' I said. 'I mean, it was fine as a hobby in university. I didn't have bills to pay then, but you've got to grow up and get an adult job some time.'

'Adults,' she scoffs. 'Are we boring? We are, aren't we? Mortgage dwellers with a solid nine-to-five and a rosé habit.'

'That's a bit grim.' I wince, stuffing my camera back into my bag. 'What I'd really love is my own gallery, something small like that place near Embankment.'

'The one that did the Kennedy exhibition? I love that place,' she coos at the memory. 'Let's go back there soon.'

4

'Absolutely,' I say, pulling to a stop just by the doors of the gallery. They swish open with a wave of air conditioning. 'Speaking of habits. Dinner tonight?'

'Hello, yes, always. I'm going to go get us a table right now, in fact.'

'Even better. Fingers crossed we'll be celebrating.'

'Good luck.' She hugs me again and offers a small wave as she melts into the crowd by Jubilee Gardens.

Slinking back to my desk, a family photo catches in the corner of my eye. A pre-digital age selfie of my father, brother and me at Disneyland Paris. I wonder what they're both up to right now. I'd likely know if I opened Adam's emails, but I've been too preoccupied this afternoon with Lainey's photos and waiting on data from one of our researchers, Sally. I need her document before the weekend kicks in, otherwise I'll be spending another Saturday night writing exhibition notes with only Netflix and a bottle of wine for company, like all good social animals.

As always, I'll answer Adam later. He never expects a response straightaway.

'Katharine, are you ready?'

Roland, my boss, pokes his head out of his door and waves a beckoning hand. He's the only one in our small team who's been blessed with an office, not that it's much to write home about. The windows look like they haven't been cleaned since Theresa May was Home Secretary, the carpet is weak tea beige, and it smells like toilet lollies.

I cross the office knowing all eyes are following me like a stage spotlight. Guess I'm not the only one who knows I have a meeting today. It's a little intimidating if I'm honest. The door closes behind me with a soft click.

Situations like this don't normally faze me. Roland's attitude is less wanky art gallery manager and more everyone's-best-friend-Bob-Ross. I've spent more time in the last five years schmoozing with million-dollar corporate sponsors and doing

5

more overtime than I care to admit, so I can talk the talk, but he's fiddling with things on his desk like they'll never quite line up properly. And is that sweat beading on his forehead? Gross.

It's also not often that I apply for his job, either.

I have the nous and the experience, which certainly helps, but it's nothing without the art. While photography gave me a place to belong as a teenager, somewhere to explore ideas and feelings, as I got older, I began to experiment with different streams. I've dabbled in sketching, oils and watercolours. And, even though photography remains my one true love, I'm constantly amazed by the texture and depth, the layers that are built up to create a story on a canvas.

Regardless of my efforts, I could never quite convince a gallery to show my photography. A lot of conversations ended with 'It's fantastic, but …', or the less brutal 'We just don't have the room.' So, I set my sights on curation instead. Sure, I wasn't creating work as such, my own art fell by the wayside of busy adult life, but I was creating experiences and sharing my love of art with the world, all while being able to pay my bills at the end of each month. It was the perfect match, and one I wanted to nurture throughout my career. Long story short: being senior curator would be a dream come true.

Looking around the office while Roland finishes nesting, my eye catches on faded prints that have been passed down through generations of senior curators. If this becomes my office, they'll be out the door and replaced with photography, or an original Romantic period painting if ever I could afford one (I say as I laugh into my empty bank account). The desk looks like it was built around the same time as the museum, during the peach tubular metal fascination of the mid-Eighties, back when Springsteen was The Boss and a DeLorean was the only way to travel.

'Sit, sit,' Roland urges as he throws himself into his own chair.

Air wheezes from the asthmatic cushion. 'How's your day been? Good?'

'Busy,' I say, blowing my cheeks out. 'I've been downstairs with the design team this morning, looking at their plans for the exhibition that opens next month. They've got everything under control, the displays are coming together nicely. They were working on the entrance piece today. In fact, I'm ecstatic with the way things are progressing. I'm planning on writing up the didactic panels this weekend.'

Didactic panels are those little squares next to artwork in museums, and they can be more painful to get right than a thesis after a bottle or two of cava. So much information to impart, so little space.

'Excellent.' Roland laces his fingers and hunches over his desk. 'Tell me, have we talked about the fundraiser a few weeks ago?'

My mind wormholes back to that night, to the exhibition space that had been transformed into a sleek, polished concrete, dimly lit function room. Soft blue and purple lights embedded in the floor made us look properly fancy, as if our best outfits and napkin swans hadn't already.

The finest pieces from each department had been painstakingly moved and displayed away from the trajectory of wine glasses and greasy finger-foods, and team members worked the room using our best manners and extensive art knowledge to woo potential corporate sponsors. Now, though, I'm left with the frightening realisation that maybe I'd done something wrong, and that's why I'm in here. I run through all the conversations I had and try to pinpoint anything crucial. Wait. I didn't have a full tits-out experience no one told me about, did I? I'm mortified at the thought.

I shake my head and try to gather some moisture in my mouth. It doesn't happen.

'Let me be blunt: we smashed it out of the park.' Roland reaches for a thick legal pad. 'I had a cheeky vino with the powers that be at lunch today and they've greenlit our Van Gogh exhibition for next year. They say there's enough folding stuff to see us through to the end of next year. We're all ridiculously excited about it, especially me, because I won't be here having to do the hard work.' He snorts a derisive laugh.

'That's excellent.' I nod, feeling myself lean closer. Is he about to tell me what I want to hear? I mean, this is all good news, isn't it? We've made our money and my exhibition suggestion has just been greenlit. 'Though I'm a tad confused as to why we didn't just have a team meeting for this?'

'Oh, right. Yes.'

He mashes his computer mouse into the mat so hard dust floats from the monitor. Pushing fire-engine-red thick-rimmed glasses back up his nose, he squints at the screen. 'I have one email here … here it is. "*We were particularly enthused by Katharine's knowledge of classics—*" they mentioned you specifically "*—and are one hundred per cent sure the exhibition will be a success.*"'

My insides bubble in the effervescent wonder that, for once, something might be going right. I bite my lip and try to repress a smile. 'Ah, that's wonderful. I'm so pleased.'

'Don't be so coy.' Roland finger-guns me. 'That's incredible feedback. You're a bloody star, you are. A credit to any team.'

'That's very kind, thank you.'

Wait? What? Any team?

Please, just bloody tell me already. I've chiselled away at this job for years. It's been the Rodin on my CV; long and arduous but ultimately worth it. After all the work I've put in, the scratchy-eyed overtime and dinners sucking up to rich people who, despite what they think, know very little about art, and books I've spent late nights memorising, I was secretly confident I was a shoo-in for the position. So why the gut feeling that I was being put on the rack?

But I can't stop here. After compliments like that, I decide I've got nothing to lose. I need an answer.

'Roland, tell me about this lunch meeting,' I probe. 'Did they talk about plans beyond Van Gogh? What can I expect to be working on after that? Is it the Women in Renaissance exhibition maybe? I adore that period, and it would be a great win for the museum.'

'Okay.' He wriggles uncomfortably, like he has an itchy bomb in his pants. I'd allow myself to entertain that idea if it weren't for the fact I might laugh in his face. 'I'm really glad you asked, because there's been a lot of chatter about who'll be filling my role and what the office is going to look like—'

'And?' I cut over the top of him, too excited to care for rigmarole or patience. Now is good. My heart is beating against my ribs like a muffled xylophone. Flight of the bumblebees, maybe.

'Management went through each interview: yours, Steve's, and the other applicants. They looked at responses, qualifications, roles within the team, work that needed to be done, and matched it all up against the criteria matrix, et cetera and so forth.'

He swallows. Hard. And he isn't making eye contact, instead looking anywhere *but* at me.

I roll a hand in the hope that the breeze I create will hurry him along. I know I ticked all the boxes on all their checklists; I'd studied the job ad profusely, made notes and carried index cards around the entire week before my interview. Hell, Lainey was even roped into no less than six mock interviews. Nobody could tell me I didn't meet the qualification criteria – I hold a Masters in Curating and Collections, something Roland likes to throw out to the investors like it's a dangling carrot. If that isn't enough, then poke me with a fork because I am *done*.

'They've decided to run with Steve.'

He says this with such finality that it's like dropping a brick from a height. For a moment, I can hear nothing but my own blood racing through my ears.

'Steve?' I ask, knowing how incredulous I sound. Not even sorry; I can't help it.

Roland fumbles, for what I don't know. 'W-w-well, y-yes. He's got the experience of his stint at MoMA, and he does consistently great work.'

'He was at MoMA for ten whole days,' I deadpan before mumbling, 'And that was including the jetlag.'

As I say this, I can see Roland's frame shrink back. He knows this is bad, and not at all the answer I was expecting. I also suspect he knows this makes no sense either, other than the preferential treatment of friends, but no more words come. My mouth gawps like a sunbathing goldfish.

'All right then.' I nod and purse my lips.

What else am I supposed to say? I can't argue, because it would only make me look bad. Assertiveness is often dismissed as aggressiveness in women, and it's no different here in the art world than it is in any other corporate office. Roland's leg starts bouncing, and a sinking feeling sets in. This is about to get worse. I'm acutely aware that there is now complete silence in the office behind me; no radio, no chatter, nothing.

Until laughter erupts outside. I glance sideways to see Steve hovering over the desk of one of the other male curators, a sly look trained my way. He knows that I know, and he knows exactly what he's doing. Right now, I want to grab him by his scrawny designer-shirt-clad shoulders and shake the smug out of him. But I can't. Instead, I bite the inside of my cheek so hard I can taste the iron tang of blood.

I am furious in a way I don't think I have ever been before in my life. I wasn't even this angry when I was nineteen and my brother borrowed my clapped-out Ford Escort and deposited it into a brick wall.

The next few minutes don't register, not really. Breath coming in short spurts, I get up from the seat as calmly as I *think* I can, and yank the door open so hard I'm surprised the hinges are still intact. Walking into the open-plan area from Roland's office, I reach for the first empty box I can find and drag it over to my cubicle.

Family photos and postcard artworks are tacked on the walls of my desk partition, a designer ceramic pot that found a new life as a pen holder is slumped in the corner, and a folder of plans that has been dropped on my keyboard during the time it took for Roland to drop his bombshell leaves my computer trilling its disapproval. A tiny brass plaque with my name engraved sits above my monitor as if to taunt me.

I tear everything down and toss it into the ratty box. There's no rhyme or reason, and I'm far from gentle with any of it. When I'm done, I reach into my messenger bag and feel around for my next target. From the corner of my eye, I can see the room at a standstill. Roland is pleading with me to come back into his office and talk, but he's an underwater mumble in a raging torrent of anger.

What am I even doing? Who the hell knows? All I can tell you is that I am not putting up with this anymore. I am not being overlooked in favour of jobs for mates, not anymore. I am not smiling and nodding while I watch the incompetent leap-frog over me. Again. I am not working nights and weekends and overtime just to be kept in a holding pattern. I have had *enough*. Time to draw a line in the sand.

And I draw it in Taylor Swift-red lipstick. Before I can talk myself out of it, I grab a sheet of paper from my in-tray and scrawl 'I QUIT' across it in big bold letters, the lipstick crumbling and mashing as I go. Grinning at Roland, who I can't quite hear over the siren call of blood in my ears, I hold my sign aloft like I'm about to announce a wrestling match.

The office erupts into a cacophony of noise. Roland shouting for me to stop breaks through the hoots and hollers. I push past him, head held high until I pause below the glowing Exit sign and clock my sight on Steve. One hand on the emergency exit door, I raise the other up in line with my face and indulge in one last act of pettiness, showing him my middle finger. The drum of my chest is replaced by the clacking of heels as I flee down the stairwell, and, somewhere behind me, I'm sure I can hear the faint clatter of clapping.

Chapter 2

Above my head, the shining face of Big Ben lights up against the dusky sky, reminding me that as of 5.09 p.m. on a muggy Friday in July, I am now unemployed. A busker croons by the Westminster tube entrance, but I'm not sure his upbeat Ed Sheeran covers are going to cut it tonight. I don't need castles on hills or to sing at the top of my lungs. The exhilaration of leaving the office is beginning to wear off, so I need food and drink and the company of a good friend to help unravel the humiliated knot in my stomach.

When I finally stop and take stock, I realise that I am absolutely, bottom of the well without a ladder terrified. I could barely afford to live in London on my wage, let alone without it. Sure, I've got some savings stashed away, but they won't last forever. Hell, they probably won't last until the change of seasons.

A summer breeze tickles the backs of my wobbly legs as I hoist my messenger bag higher on my shoulder and scramble to stop my small box of junk cascading out of my arms and onto the pavement. It's not like it's an Aladdin's cave of treasure, but it is mine and I'd rather keep it that way. I jab at the pedestrian crossing, once, twice, three times in quick succession while my mind runs over the last excruciating thirty minutes of my life.

'Hurry up!'

The woman next to me glares at me with all the patience of a lottery winner waiting on a cheque. Ironic, really. She probably wouldn't be too excited if she were me, though I don't say that aloud. In a pocket I can't reach, my phone continues to vibrate. It has since my heels hit the street.

A Hop-On Hop-Off bus rolls over Westminster Bridge and through the intersection, the flash of camera phones turns the top deck into a mobile disco. It's joined by a swarm of Deliveroo cyclists trying to beat everyone through the intersection. As they pass, the last of them chiming wildly on their bell, the lights change, and I join the throng as we pull each other across the street. It's a regular Friday evening synchronised swim.

I muddle my way through the crowd. It's not as simple as it looks when everyone's clambering up and down the steps for the tube and I'm not. I find myself unusually irritated with the slow movers and the tourists who bottleneck because they need to work out the best vantage point for just *one more* photo of Big Ben.

I get it, I really do, but he's under scaffolding and I need to be somewhere. Leave him (and me) in peace.

Slipping through all that, I turn into Parliament and head for the Red Lion. With its dark façade of railway tiles, glittering signage, and bushels of flowers, it brings a bit of old-world charm into every Friday evening. I glance in the windows quickly as I approach.

'Hungry, miss? Table for one? Two?' A waiter catches my eye.

'Two, thank you.' I smile politely. By the time he pulls his notepad from the pocket of his apron, I'm already pointing out Lainey, who's perched at a bench for two in the back window.

With an arm outstretched, he lets me wind my own way through the maze of diners to where my friend sits, already looking cosy with a bottle of white.

I've known Lainey going on sixteen years now. Outside my family, she's the longest, dearest friendship I've had. We met one fly-riddled, sticky afternoon after an all you could handle beer and pizza bender organised by the student union. I'd sat myself down on a grassy hill and peeled off my shoes and socks just to feel something cool under my feet and photograph some of the boxy modern architecture.

With a harrumph, she flopped down beside me and shook out a bag of liquorice while muttering about boys who couldn't take a hint and how, under no circumstance, did she want to go and look at the Def Leppard plaque at the spoon factory. When I chimed in about how it reminded me of a boyfriend I'd recently broken up with, it set us on the start of our long trajectory of broken hearts and happily ever afters.

After university, she decamped to London, heading straight from undergraduate into working for a smaller gallery. I stayed in Sheffield to complete my master's before landing an assistant role at Webster Fine Art. When a position in my office opened up a few months later, I sent her the job ad, she applied, and we'd worked together ever since.

Tonight, even with her day off, she looks like the poster child for corporate office perfection, whereas I'm sure I left the office looking like the love child of Beetlejuice and Alice Cooper.

Her smile slips as she takes one look at the box in my arms. It registers that tonight is not one of those happy endings we like to celebrate. Mugs, tattered diaries, pictures and old Cup-a-Soup boxes are the office worker's walk of shame.

'What the hell have you done?' She gawps as she reaches across the table to fill my glass while I busy myself with hanging my bag and coat over the back of my chair.

'This is what happens when you have a day off,' I titter with a wave of the finger. 'I might have quit.'

She gasps, recoiling slightly. 'You did not.'

'Oh, but I did.'

'What the fu …' she says waspishly. 'What happened? Are you okay?'

15

'I'm okay,' I lie with a huff as I collapse into my seat. Having confessed to someone makes things seem suddenly more real. I just quit my fucking job.

'As it turns out, the meeting with Roland this afternoon was to tell me that, although I'm amazing and our investors love me, someone else was getting his job. I might have had a brain snap and decided enough was enough. I'm sick of being passed over in favour of less skilled men.'

'Oh, what?' She bashes down on the table. A symphony of stainless-steel clatter joins her outrage. I love how passionate she is about anything involving her friends and family, even if it occasionally draws the ire of surrounding diners. Where I'd spent the last thirty minutes trying to tamp down an 'it's not fair' tantrum, her outrage bubbles forth freely and it reminds me of why I love her so in the first place. 'Who got it?'

I rub my face and flip the menu over as if I'm ever going to order anything other than fish and chips, mushy peas and curry sauce. 'Bloody Foot Fetish Steve.'

Now, I'm not one to spill secrets, but he got that nickname after an especially rowdy office party that involved him walking off into the night with a woman who charged by the hour. Not that there's any shame in that, but let's just say the stories that filtered back in the 'Don't tell anyone, but …' game of telephone were a riot. Hence, an office nickname was born.

'Penis.' Lainey tips her glass in my direction. 'That's what it is. It's the sausage factory churning them out again. You're perfectly capable. I mean, sure, you don't have the sailboat for weekends with the boys, and you have to sit down to wee, but does it matter?'

'I know how to do this job. I have *lived* art for years,' I press, hands jazzed out by the side of my head. When I raise my eyes to meet Lainey's, hers crinkle and laughter bubbles up between us. 'And I *do* sit down to wee.'

A waiter appears beside us, a cautious bounce in his step and an unsure smile. I order my regular fish and chip dinner and the longest Long Island Iced Tea they'll legally pour me.

'You know what, I should be on the Vimtos.' Lainey pokes the air. 'But I'll have what she's having.'

'Why the Vimtos?' I ask as our waiter departs.

'Wedding tosh tomorrow.' She waves a hand. 'Tell me more about this meeting.'

'Somewhere in the mix I'm sure he said they were moving in a more contemporary direction,' I continue. 'Can't quite remember.'

'What has that got to do with anything?' Lainey asks. 'You studied *art*, not just classical art. You fucking photograph it too, in case they forgot. If I sliced you with this knife you'd probably bleed out like a Jackson Pollock.'

'Maybe, but I haven't taken a decent photo in years,' I grumble. 'Yours today notwithstanding, the most I can manage is a Polaroid that reads like a Bond movie … for my eyes only.'

Life has been too busy for me to even consider photography. All right, I could if I forced myself but, after working long hours, finding time to socialise, and life in general, I must admit that it's one of my life's failings.

'Plenty of time for that now,' she jokes.

'What I don't understand is that Roland made sure to tell me how much the investors loved my knowledge of *classic* art.' I look at her. 'Do you think that might be it?'

'That sounds like a rubbish excuse.' She refocuses her attention on me and folds her arms across the table. 'They're not just going to dump the Italian bloody Renaissance in favour of an exclusive run of modern art. They know what brings visitors in and doing a complete switch into a new direction will only be a bad thing. Katharine, you were the best of all of us, you know that. Let's not even get into the workaholic tendencies.'

I roll my eyes. 'For what that was worth.'

Her mouth flatlines. 'What are you going to do now?'

'I have zero idea.' I draw my fingers through my dark hair,

tugging it out of the French knot I always style it in. An instant tingling relief crawls across my scalp. 'Anyway, going on about it won't fix it, will it? Talk to me about you. What's happening on Planet Lainey and Frank? How did your job interview this morning go?'

'I think I'm in with a shot.' She does a hair toss. 'Soho tech start-up, another ten thousand a year, don't mind if I do. Can start immediately post honeymoon.'

'Great,' I enthuse. 'That's brilliant. I'll keep everything crossed. What about wedding plans?'

She lights up immediately, the whimsical, breezy look of a bride in love floats across her face and softens her features. Reaching into a handbag the size of her torso, she produces a glossy ream of magazine. It lands on the table with such a thud the tealight candle flickers and cutlery clatters again. I push the candle aside to get a better look. I'm not keen on setting fire to the table; an arson charge never looks good on a résumé.

As we eat, we pore over pages of shimmering gowns, sharp suits, perfectly styled place settings, car hire companies, and every other painstaking detail a bride and her groom could possibly need to think about on their way to the altar. It's an exciting time, and I couldn't be happier for my friends. Lainey and Frank are two halves of a walnut, perfectly snug in their world, cocoon-like in the way they protect, love, and look out for each other. In my softest moments, it made me a teensy bit jealous.

They'd been engaged for eighteen months now, the sparkling black-tie party held at Sky Garden. Now, it was a matter of planning things at the pointy end. Wedding invites were recently posted, and the RSVPs had begun trickling in. It was now down to picking suits, final dress fittings, and searching out the perfect pair of shoes.

'You know, I have to ask, because I'm a qualified panic merchant.' Lainey downs the last of her drink and fixes me with a nervous look.

'Shoot.'

'Are you sure you're okay with not being maid of honour?' she asks, her face cinched as if waiting for the fallout.

'Are you kidding?' Glass held to my mouth, I let out an amused snort. 'I think it's great. I love you, but hell if I want to traipse around under layers of warpaint and three-inch heels all day.'

She breathes a sigh of relief. 'Gosh, I love you. It's just, my sister would go spare if she weren't involved. My mother would book the seventh circle of hell as a honeymoon destination, and Frank and I already agreed on having a maid of honour and best man only. Did I tell you they tag-teamed me into giving her the role? I got puppy dog eyes and "your sister is desperate to be a part of your big day" at ten paces. The little shit is making life difficult though.'

'Honestly, it's fine.' I shake my head and peel apart a flaky piece of fish. I'm not sure if it's the most amazing meal I've had, or if the alcohol's helping, but the fish is smooth and buttery, and I could easily eat a tonne of these chips. 'I will be there with bells on. Helping with the invites and place cards is more than enough involvement for me.'

In the last few years, I'd found calligraphy a great way to unwind and put my failing skills to the test. I think it has something to do with the fact I was better at writing than producing anything photographic. Smooth strokes of a pen always seemed more finite, more foolproof than selecting just the right f-stop or lens. I also didn't need a darkroom to see the final results. Working on wedding stationery had been a fun way to stretch my artistic muscle while still being part of something magical.

'Speaking of, what are you doing Sunday? Frank's heading for a round of golf with the boys if you want to come over. We can drown your work sorrows and my wedding woes and watch cheesy rom-coms with biscuits and coffee and maybe work on place cards?'

'Sounds great,' I say around a mouthful. 'I have all the time in the world right now.'

'You know, you still haven't told me who you're bringing as your plus one,' Lainey says in a way that tells me she's casting a long line and fishing for information. 'John, maybe?'

'I'll ask, though last time he said no.'

'You mean to tell me he hasn't realised yet that you are the most amazing woman he's ever clapped eyes on, and that he needs to wife you immediately?' Lainey watches me with her huge green eyes, mozzarella dangling towards her mouth from a height that implied I might have been looking at Michelangelo's Creation of Lainey. Well, pizza is life, isn't it?

'No.' I shake my head with embarrassed laughter. 'Probably not.'

My other New Year's revolution was to sort out my love life. As it turns out, that's not going entirely to plan, either. My not-quite boyfriend, John Harrison, started as a one-night stand that has spiralled out of control. It's lasted way longer than I expected and now feels like I've been living on the precipice of something more for months.

I wasn't asking for a gigantic rock that caught my sweater like a doorknob, although I was sure he could probably afford one on his lawyer's salary. All I wanted to know was where I stood. Girlfriend? Fly-by-night shag? Was it too much to ask him to help define what we were? Contrary to what Pink Floyd wants you to believe, suspended animation is not a state of bliss. We were allegedly exclusive, though had never really talked about it. Are we dating? Are we *not* dating? Maybe we should do the whole family introductions thing. After all, it had been nine months.

Not knowing where I stand makes me feel like I'm somebody's dirty little secret. Lately, that's begun chipping away and exposing my soft fleshy underbelly for what it was: tragically romantic.

'When are you going to nip that in the bud?' Lainey asks. 'Hey?'

'Not tonight.' I drain the last of my glass and look at her, locking that romantic daydream away. 'If anything, he'll be a nice distraction.'

She tuts and sighs, though I'm not entirely sure she disagrees with me.

'I know.' I hold my hands up defensively and her eyes widen with laughter. 'Let me have my small mercies. Please. All I'm asking for tonight is an orgasm. At least then something good will have happened today.'

'I know you say you're not dating—'

'We aren't *officially* dating.' I wipe a napkin across the smile on my face. 'We are simply exploring each other's naked forms. It's art.'

'It's all art, darling.' Lainey laughs. 'Speaking of dating though, this Friday night dinner is becoming a regular date for us. One that I enthusiastically support.'

Had life become so routine that the biggest night of my social calendar is a cheeky feed in the back corner of a 600-year-old pub? While it's nice to have close friends and regular catch-ups, it was obvious this pub had more of a life than I did. Outside of Lainey, the friend who keeps me grounded, there's John, the man I call after a few too many drinks or, on a night like tonight, when I need to lose myself in someone else.

And that's exactly what I do at the end of the night, not more than two minutes after my bus deposits me near my Camberwell block of flats. The dial tone and the sound of background traffic is my company as I start walking. When I think it's going to ring out, he answers.

'Katharine,' he says matter-of-factly.

'Hello.' I try but can't help the silly grin that threatens to light up the darkened street.

'Hello, you.' His voice dips and is now warm, familiar, and exactly what I want to hear. 'What are you up to at this time of night?'

'I'm almost home,' I say, listening to him mutter about how late it is. 'Late dinner with Lainey.'

'Late nights with Lainey sounds like a local radio show.'

'I know, I know.' I spin on the spot, randomly checking over my shoulder. A couple with their arms linked and heads dipped towards each other disappear into the shadows of a side street. When my box slips, I hoist it higher under my arm. 'What are you doing right now?'

'I have just walked through my front door after a *fascinating* phone call about a breach of contract case. In a few moments, I may pour myself a cheap whisky, and sit myself down on my sofa and watch the Thames pass by. Now, I think I'll tug seductively on my silk tie.'

I smile, worrying my bottom lip. 'Why don't you bring yourself, and that tie, around to mine? You can poke holes in my deposition?'

He snorts, and I can hear him untwisting a bottle cap. 'Poke holes in your deposition?'

'You like it? It's the only lawyer joke I know.'

'I am … yep, never going to hear that word the same way again.' He tries and fails at sounding disgusted.

'So, are you coming around to interrogate me, or what?' I try.

'Katharine, it's just gone ten thirty,' he whines. 'You can't come here?'

As much as I love the plush fittings and oversized shower at John's Pimlico flat, I tap my access card against the door lock and shuffle into my building. The box of belongings I've been lugging around all night gets dribbled along the floor and into the lift. 'It's been a long day. I've just got home. I'm going to head inside, then into my shower where I will endeavour to prepare more bad law puns for you. You've got twenty minutes.'

'It'll take me at least thirty on the bus.'

'I can clean my place up in thirty minutes, sure.'

John groans. 'You're gonna make me get up, aren't you?'

'I will get you up, yes.' I giggle, then thank the late night I'm the only one in the lift. 'Come on. I'm offering you no strings sex.'

'Let's clarify something,' he says through a chuckle. 'All of your sex is no strings, so this is just Malibu Stacy with a new hat.'

'Have you got a problem with that?' Though I say that, it pinches at something uncomfortable, a tight reminder of what I'm not getting out of this.

'On the contrary,' he mumbles. 'It's my favourite kind.'

'See you in thirty?' The elevator arrives on my floor and my reflection disappears as the doors slide open.

'Make it twenty.' He hangs up and dead air fills my ear.

Chapter 3

I roll over and reach for my bedside table, fumbling about for my phone and coming up with a pile of photos wedged beneath an instant camera. The first one is of John, taken only a few hours earlier in the grey and dusty morning light.

Across the hall, I can hear the shower running. It's odd in that it means he's stayed the night and hasn't left me a 'Dear Katharine' text like he often does. I wonder if I should pounce and ask what it means, whether these increased overnight stays signal something bigger about to happen, but I'm quite enjoying being snuggled in bed, listening to the sound of his humming occasionally floating above the water.

I twiddle the white-rimmed photo between my fingers. He's smiling out at me, face half obscured by a pillow that still smells of aftershave, black hair dangling in his eyes where his fringe is getting too long. I joke about him not getting his hair cut, when the truth is, I adore it this length. His left eye is open only enough to show me that immutable spark that hides behind his eyes for everyone but me and his mouth is perfectly carved into a tired smile.

Barely moments after taking the photo, the flash still casting shadows on the wall, he threw a languid arm around my waist.

Our limbs were still heavy and warm with sleep as he pulled me underneath him as we greeted the morning the best way we knew how.

Evidence of his stay is spread across the room, slacks crumpled beside the bed, shirt somehow hanging from the doorknob, and his tie is knotted around the bedhead for reasons I'd never speak aloud.

A crash in the kitchen steals my attention. It's not the cymbal-like clash of pots and pans of someone making breakfast, but the muted *clunk* of ceramic that doesn't quite bounce on tiles. My skin prickles because, unless John has grown tentacles in the last few hours, it means that there are now two people other than myself in my flat. Realisation hits me in a cold sweat.

Only one other person has a key to my flat: my brother. I sit up straighter and chew on a hangnail while I consider exactly how I'm going to get out of this. Hint: I won't.

Adam is thirty-eight, three years older than me, and lives with his wife Sophie in a bigger, brighter, and far more expensive flat in Gladstone House, where I'm certain the minimum dress code for some of the cafés is suit and tie. Bonus points for a horsehair wig.

I pull on the first pair of jeans I see, sniff test a loose T-shirt and take a deep breath. Sweat tickles down my spine as I step out of the bedroom.

When people ask me to describe my flat, I find it easier asking them to imagine a small but cosy hotel room. In fact, I've often wondered if this building wasn't a hotel built and discarded by some huge conglomerate. I have a bedroom, small living room, bathroom, laundry in a cupboard, and a kitchen-ette, which is where I find Adam. His mousy brown hair protrudes from the horizon of my kitchen counter like a shark fin in the ocean.

'And a very good morning to you.' I slip my hands into my pockets and rock on the balls of my feet.

He grumbles, still hunched over the floor, still mopping up his accident.

'You okay?' I lean over the counter to see more of him. He barely registers a glance over his shoulder.

'Dropped a bloody mug, didn't I?' He stands, tossing a limp brown bundle of kitchen towel into the sink. 'Anyway, I thought you were in the shower.'

'Ah, no,' I say. 'That's not me.'

He nods in the direction of a bouquet of flowers on the white stone bench; dusty pink peonies and roses, sweet peas and ivy wrapped in brown paper and held together with twine. 'Got anything to do with these?'

What is it about older brothers that makes younger sisters feel like they've done something to be embarrassed about? The moment a brother meets a boyfriend is always destined to be a little awkward, but this feels like it's about to get a whole lot worse.

I dig about my messenger bag for my phone and slip it on charge, surprised to find a barrage of messages from colleagues. Correction: *past* colleagues. Shaking that from my mind, because I do not want to talk about it, I busy myself searching for a vase. Digging the card out from between the foliage, I smile and feel heat bloom in my cheeks.

Here's to stolen moments – J x

As much as John and I couldn't decide what we were, I loved that he bought me the occasional bouquet. Especially when it involved opening my front door last night to find him in his suit and tie looking like he'd just stepped out of the courtroom. I'd already stripped down to my pyjamas and drunk the first glass from a bottle of wine, which is enough to tell you how different we are as people. As he tried hiding behind the oversized bloom of foliage, I'd clutched a fistful of waistcoat and pulled him through the door.

Adam plucks the card from my hand.

26

'Who's J?' His head bobs about in an impression of the chicken from *Moana* as he tries desperately to make eye contact with me.

'Somebody.' I snatch it back. 'What are you doing here, anyway?'

'Well, if you had opened the email I sent yesterday, you would know Dad has asked us to come home for lunch today.' He looks at me, wide-eyed. 'Complete with a robust "Are you two workaholics still alive? Or do I need to have a stroke before either of you make it up for a visit?" message attached.'

'No,' I say slowly. 'I noticed your email there, it just kind of slipped my mind.'

'Slipped your mind in the middle of the night.' Adam tips his head towards the bathroom. 'So, come on. Who is he?'

My brain does an Olympic level of gymnastics trying to work out how I'm going to get around *this* situation.

I could sneak into the bathroom and leave a spare key while bundling my brother out the door, using the excuse of needing breakfast to get him moving. Adam is always up for a full English and a pot of coffee at a greasy spoon. God, he'd been banging on about his favourite café for months before I first moved to London. When I did finally get there, let's just say he was more in love with the congealed bacon than I was.

Naively, I hope he'll drop the subject altogether, but there's currently another man in my flat and my brother *is* a lawyer which means that, as far as this was concerned, there's blood in the water and he's circling. Never mind the box of belongings sitting by the phone, the same box I dragged home from work last night; these flowers are much more exciting.

'Come on, you can tell me.' He crosses a finger over his chest. 'Pinkie swear.'

'Really?' I narrow my eyes and cock my head. 'Because that's not a pinkie swear.'

'It's not exactly a state secret though, is it?' He finally pours himself a coffee. 'Jeremey, Jason, Jarrod, Jared, Jarryd, Julian, Julius?'

27

I shake my head quickly, my eyes set towards my bathroom door. Yes, I can leave John the spare key, send him a text. He did it once for me at his flat. That's exactly what I'll do. 'Come on, let's go. We should go get breakfast.'

'Oh, no, no you don't.' He stops. 'Is it a she? Jennifer? Julie? Jessica?'

'Stop,' I grumble.

'Because it's okay if it is.'

'I know it's perfectly okay,' I say with a sigh. 'I'd just—'

'Can I buy a vowel?'

'No, you cannot buy a vowel,' I snap and stamp my foot.

'Katharine?' John's voice curls itself into a question as he appears from the bathroom. 'Do you think my penis ascribes to the golden ratio?'

Adam's eyes grow wide and his face lights up like the Blackpool Illuminations. Right now, I want to remind him of how much he looks like our father, with his brown hair full of salt and pepper fleck and dark eyes crinkling in horror at the edges, but I don't.

I clear my throat beneath a mortified chortle. 'That's not … no, that's not quite how that works.'

'What about my arse, then?' He stands in the small passageway, seemingly bracketed between the bathroom and my bedroom. Right as he's about to pivot like a runway model and show me his backside, he spots my brother in the kitchen. The towel drops slowly from his ruffled hair to his crotch. For the first time ever, I'm sure I see John blush. 'Adam. Hello.'

Adam turns to me, slack-jawed, full of brotherly repulsion. 'That is officially the second worst way he could have used the word "golden" in this flat.'

'Adam,' I scowl, feeling my cheeks douse in embarrassment. Strike a match of inappropriate brotherly comments, and I may well light up like a grassfire.

Silence stretches out between the three of us and my attention swings in a pendulum, back and forth between the two of them, waiting for something, anything. Eventually, John steps forward, fire-engine red Egyptian cotton the only thing protecting his modesty, and he extends his hand.

'Good morning,' he says.

Hesitantly, my brother accepts and shakes his hand. 'Ah, yep. Hello.'

'Much on today?' John asks casually.

Listening to him talk, anyone would think he was in a regular office environment, not standing in my flat dripping wet and under the increasingly heavy scrutiny of my brother, who's dumbfounded. But John's just so damn nonchalant about it all; cool and calm and confident, as if this were so ordinary and everyday.

'More than you, by the looks of things,' Adam says slowly, wiping a not entirely inconspicuous hand on the back of his trousers as he mumbles about hand sanitiser.

'Yeah, about that. I'm going to go get dressed.' John presses a kiss into my hair and the bedroom door closes behind him.

If the foot of God were to appear from the sky and squash me in some *Monty Python*-esque skit right now, I would not be upset. In fact, I'd welcome the sweet victory of death. Beneath the silence that stretches through my kitchen, we listen to John yawn as he dresses.

Though Adam is silent, I can almost see his thoughts playing out above him in comic book speech bubbles. He's shocked but, when John announces that he's leaving, that gives way to concern.

I follow John and pull the door closed behind us as far as I can without wedging my neck between the frame and the door and cutting off my own air supply. He blows his cheeks out and offers up a silent, anxious laugh.

'That's one way to make a man disappear up into himself,' he says with a smirk.

'I'm so sorry,' I mouth, cringing, before I whisper, 'I didn't realise he was going to be here this morning.'

'It's okay.' He takes a step closer and draws a finger down my cheek, sliding a lock of wayward hair behind my ear. It's slow and it burns, and it takes me right back to last night. 'Cat's out of the bag now, isn't it?'

That may be, if he would finally agree that we were something halfway serious. Hope sinks with the reminder that we *still* have not sorted things out. Again.

Pressing a hand to his chest, I can feel the heat of his body through his expensive shirt and smell my cheap and cheerful apple-scented body wash against his skin. Would it be wrong to kick my brother out and drag John back to the bedroom? I want to. A brief flicker of sanity stops me.

'About that. Can I see you during the week?' I venture tentatively. It's not our normal thing. We're strictly weekends and Friday nights only, but a girl can try. 'In light of today, I think there are a few things we need to talk about.'

His eyes search my face, and, for a moment, he wears the look of a man who's finally been beaten into submission. It lasts only a second, giving way to a soft smile.

'Please.' I'm almost begging. 'Don't you think I deserve to know where I stand? This has been going on for months and I still don't know what I am to you. I mean, what do I tell him when he asks? Do I say you're a boyfriend?'

John scoffs incredulously. 'He's not going to ask.'

'He's my brother. He'll ask.' I huff. 'And he will keep asking until he has an answer.'

John rubs at his mouth and lifts his shoulders though he won't make eye contact. 'Let me handle it?'

'That's not going to help me right now though, is it?'

'Tell him what you want, then,' he says, patience wearing thin.

I raise a brow. 'One night this week?'

'Wednesday or Thursday.' He sighs, though it's more a question. 'One of those should be quiet enough to sneak out early. Either way, call me. We'll sort something out.'

'Okay.' I cup his face in my hands and kiss him. 'See you then.'

Selfishly, I wish he would stay and own up to this, because I am not looking forward to what's about to happen.

Chapter 4

'Are you kidding me right now?'

Finally emerging from stunned silence, Adam waits while I dash about my flat getting ready for the day. A quick splash under the shower, a dash of deodorant, my hair piled up onto my head in a loose and lazy bun, and I'm almost ready to go. I bemoan the bags under my tired blue eyes and the first emerging grey hairs I spot in the mirror while Adam jangles keys impatiently.

Soon enough, I find myself tumbling out of the lift and into the echoing concrete grey car park beneath my building.

'Not last time I checked, no.' I scuttle alongside Adam, his shock and my defensiveness echoing from pylons around us. 'Are you sure you want to drive? It'll be midday before we get there. Would you rather not get the train?'

'Katharine, it's not *that* far.' Adam looks at me from the corners of his eyes. 'We used to do this trip all the time, remember? Anyway, you'd be better prepared if you opened your bloody emails.'

'You could call, too, you know. Or text. Like a regular human being,' I say. 'Like you could have called this morning. Or, you know, knocked before helping yourself.'

'I never knock.'

'I know!' I shriek.

He's walking so quickly I can feel my chest squeezing and heaving as I try to keep up with him. Even though my building has its own gym, I'm sure the last thing I ran for was a food truck.

'You and Harrison?' he continues.

I nod, my eyes wide. I'm not so secretly enjoying his shock. 'Yes. Me and John.'

'Katharine, I have to work with the guy.' His arm swings dramatically towards the lift we'd just tumbled out of, as if John might just reanimate at the mention of his name.

'Yes,' I repeat slowly. 'I know you do.'

'We share an office!'

'I'm also aware of that.' I try and fail not to laugh as we reach my car. I pop the boot and toss some front seat rubbish in there beside my weekend bag. 'Honestly, what's the problem? We're all adults.'

'He's not even the least bit attractive.' Adam snatches the car keys from me and mutters about driving. He is also notoriously tight with money; hence, driving *my* car.

My blue Mini Countryman is filthy, covered in the detritus of a rainy weekend spent in Bath with John about a fortnight ago. I shove those memories, along with my handbag and a half-drunk bottle of water, to the back seat and watch the sour look of disgust settle into my brother's features.

'Oh, but he is.' I smile and bite the inside of my lip. Not gonna lie, I'm a little bit enjoying this.

'No, he's not, Katharine. He's a cardboard cut-out of a man, a shopfront mannequin that you dress up and he dances for you, and he tells you exactly what you want to hear because that's what he's trained to do,' he argues. 'Thinks he's so bloody refined like he's Pierce Brosnan or some shit, not that Pierce Brosnan is anything to write home about.'

33

'Excuse me.' I feign my disgust, hand pressed to my chest. 'I did *not* watch *GoldenEye* for the plot.'

'Do you know they call him Remington when he's not around?'

I swallow down laughter. 'That's not nice. He's a lovely man. As is John. Very attentive.'

'Did you know—' Adam looks over his shoulder as he reverses from the parking space '—just last week he was telling me about this amazing girl he's seeing. "My blue-eyed girl" he called her. This is how bloody stupid I am; he all but told me it was you. "She's a brilliant artist, Adam, you should see her photos."'

'Who's telling fibs for five hundred pounds, Adam?' I laugh. 'I haven't had my camera out properly in years.'

'Then I don't want to know what kind of photos he's talking about.'

While I'd been preoccupied with worrying about my place in John's life, I'd never considered whether he'd told anybody about me. His blue-eyed girl? That's lovely and all, but he's never acted like I'm his girlfriend. It scratches at something warm, giving me a glimmer of hope that this isn't all in vain and that I'm more than a late-night stop for him.

'You *are* good, you just don't trust yourself enough,' he says. 'Then he goes on about how he's finally met someone who isn't after him for his money.'

'I pay him to say those things.' I plug my phone into the console charger. 'Also, I have my own money, thanks.'

'Please don't tell me it was *you* he took on a weekend away recently?'

'He told you about that?'

Now I'm completely confused. There are mixed signals and then there's full-fledged Wimbledon levels of back and forth. Why is John behaving like I'm a girlfriend if he can't bring himself to utter the awful word himself?

'Some country-club-cum-golf-course out by Bath? Oh, we heard about it all right. Wasted half a Monday morning meeting with it. Thankfully, he spared us the graphic details.' He sniffs as his mouth sours at the corners. 'And is that his aftershave I can smell? "I wear Tom Ford." Yeah, well I wear Lynx, get over it.'

'Might be.' I do a quick head check to find one of John's polo shirts crumpled in the back seat. 'And Lynx? You must drive the ladies wild. No wonder you smell like a high school changing room.'

'Wait, how did you even meet him?' Adam barely glances at me as he pulls out into traffic.

I shift to face my brother. 'Do you remember that get-together at your place late last year?'

It was a bitterly cold evening, fit for roast dinners and mulled wine. After spending the day scrubbing my flat from top-to-toe, an invite for impromptu drinks at Adam and Sophie's came through. I'd pulled on my favourite pair of comfortable black jeans, torn at the knees, a loose-fitting Springsteen T-shirt, and an old faithful pair of pants. My look was topped with an old peacoat and gloves. Nothing about me said I was there to meet anyone.

After a quick stop at the gallery to check for a delivery, I'd passed by the off-licence and purchased a bottle of both red and white wine, just to hedge my bets and have something to offer Sophie. From there, I walked up to Adam's inner-city duplex. It dwarfed mine, and came complete with a balcony, bespoke kitchen, marble fittings, outdoor entertaining area, and a refrigerator that talked to the internet. It was the perfect place to entertain, which coincidentally happened to be one of Adam's favourite things.

And there he was.

Standing by the heater with a wine in his hand, John drew his fingers through his dark hair. What first struck me was his chalky-blue shirt. It pulled at his shoulders and stretched across his chest so tightly I thought the buttons might pop. His black jeans were ripped at the knee like mine, his boots were unlaced, and beneath that businessman bravado there was something completely magnetic about him.

'Hello there,' he said as I clambered next to him for some warmth.

'Mind if I steal your warmth?' I asked.

'Only if you tell me your name.' He took a sip of his wine.

'Katharine,' I said, holding out my hand.

'Are you the Katharine I've been warned to steer clear of?' The corner of his mouth rose in a mischievous smirk as he shook my hand.

I frowned and pushed my lips out though I was on the verge of laughter. 'I don't remember telling you that, no.'

It didn't matter what direction I travelled in that night, whether I'd moved to talk to mutual friends or introduce myself to strangers, we continued orbiting each other. A shared joke turned into a flirt and, before I knew it, we'd spent a chunk of the evening buried in conversation by an oversized planter box.

He'd get a drink and offer to refill mine, we'd talk about my job and favourite pieces of art, and I'd laughed when he told me the last time he'd seen the inside of a museum was when he'd gone to visit his grandparents an age ago. Throughout it all, he made me feel like I was the only one in the room.

When he offered to walk me to the tube station later that night, we made a quick detour for his flat and were in bed not an hour later. Oh, and one of the buttons *did* pop.

'It's been going on that long?'

The car lurches to a stop while we wait for the lights to change. Adam turns to me, and I feel myself bristle. It irks me that he seems so het up about this. He has his own marriage to worry about, and it *is* my life. Surely, he could dial back the brotherly protection a notch or two.

'Surprised?' I try.

'So, what,' he stammers, 'are you telling me this was love at first sight?'

'I wouldn't call it love,' I say, fiddling with the audio controls until I find a radio station that isn't classifying my favourite school hits as 'classics'. I'm not that old. Yet. A cyclist whizzes by, precariously close to my side mirror. 'It started as a bit of fun.'

'A bit of fun?' The light changes green. 'Are you serious? Katharine, he's so dull. Let alone the fact that you deserve so much better than that.'

Dull wasn't a word I'd have readily used to describe John. He's always seemed so exciting, refined, gentlemanly, accessorised with fast cars and country club weekends. Sure, he works long hours. But I do, too, and when we see each other, we do often talk. Oh God, we talk work. Does that make me dull, too? I'm not sure I want Adam to continue. Not because it's not his business, but because I'm scared he might be right.

'Well, when we both have a free moment—' I explain.

Adam's silent, too busy concentrating as we scoot towards the M1. Part of me hopes he'll drop the topic.

'A free moment?' he blurts over the radio. 'A free … *Katharine*?!'

'You really do enjoy repetition, don't you?' I ask. 'No wonder you're a lawyer.'

'And you say I work too much?' Adam sighs. 'That guy is worse than me. Hell, he's even worse than *you*. I'm surprised he hasn't got a Cyberdyne Systems stamp at the back of his neck like a Ken doll.'

'He hasn't,' I quip back. 'I checked.'

He retches dramatically as we merge onto the motorway. I hope he's planning to wind the window down if he's going to be sick. I've had to clean vomit from the footwell of my car before (mine after a bad batch of rhubarb) and it is no fun at all. Sun starts to peek through the clouds, so I let the sunroof open enough to feel the breeze through my hair. It's the perfect day for a drive.

'And where's Sophie, then?' I ask, desperate to change the subject. 'Why isn't she coming with us?'

Something flickers in Adam's eyes and I know from years of

sibling arguments that I've touched a nerve. He gives his head a quick shake and turns his attention back to the traffic. 'She's away with friends this weekend.'

Let me say this upfront: I love Sophie. She is bubbly and welcoming, warm and an absolute joy to speak to. Adam moved to London a few years before I did and, when he first arrived, lived in a Clapham share house he found through friends. Sophie's parents owned the building, and she let rooms to pay the bills and get ahead financially. London wasn't somewhere we'd ever visited a lot as kids, so Sophie soon became his tour guide, local directory and social circle.

Twelve months after moving in, he asked her to dinner as a thank you for looking after him that first year. The rest is now sandwiched between untold numbers of shared social media posts and a wedding album that's always been proudly displayed in their living room.

'Away with friends?' I prod. If he's going to put me up on the witness stand then it's only fair I do the same.

'Yes,' he says with a sigh. 'They planned it ages ago. Girls' weekend at a hot spa.'

'Oh.'

'Oh,' he echoes.

'Not at some country club in Bath, then?'

'Shut up.'

We fall into an uncomfortable silence, one where his knuckles go white around the steering wheel and his bottom lip becomes a chew toy. I stare out my window and wait for the moment to pass.

It doesn't last long. By the time we hit the first services, where he fills the tank and I hide in the loos for five minutes of peace, he's already talked me through his client list for the month. I love hearing about his cases and courtroom victories; it's great to see him get so excited about what he does, but, boy, does he go on. And he calls John dull.

By the time we hit the last roundabout in Nottingham, he's swung back to the topic of John again.

He wants to know the ins and outs and, of course, he knows exactly how to phrase a question so I can't wriggle my way out of an answer. Handy for his job, not so handy for me, because all this interrogation is making me feel uneasy.

I deflect as much as I can. I don't want to field questions I'm not sure of the answer to. Yes, it's been going on a while. Yes, I really do fancy him. Yes, I hope it will become more and, no, I can't explain why he won't come to dinner. By the time we reach Sheffield, Adam's so wound up he completely ignores my request for a café stop. I'm convinced he didn't even hear me.

As we slice through the centre of town towards Greystones, there's a strange feeling sitting in my chest. We both try counting back to the last time we were here. For me, it's been a few months. Adam refuses to trust his memory, otherwise it's been almost a year.

We've seen Dad in between, of course. He's taken the train to visit us both and stayed a few nights in Adam's spare room, and Christmas lunch was hosted by my brother. But coming home today, the city almost feels brand-new, like she's trying to tell me something about how beautiful she is. Even our old detached stone-fronted home looks like somewhere I know but am not entirely familiar with.

'So, is it serious?' Adam asks, breaking me out of my hometown haze.

'You have nothing to worry about.' I pat him on the shoulder. 'At the rate I'm going, he'll probably never be your brother-in-law. Take a deep breath and count to ten.'

'Katharine.' He sighs heavily and gives the steering wheel a soft slap as we pull into Dad's driveway, which is decorated with an old Defender. 'I don't mean it like that.'

'Is this a party?' I switch subjects and narrow my eyes at Adam. 'Whose car is that?'

'As long as it's not an orgy,' he mumbles, tugging at the seat belt. 'Anyway, that's not what I'm saying. I can't stop you doing that, getting married. In fact, I think it would be wonderful if you did. A life partner is so much fun. I just worry about you, that's all. I've known him longer, so I've seen him go through one or two women, and I don't want you to become another casualty.'

'And I'm thirty-five and quite capable of looking after this myself.' I fix him with a look, and he turns a light shade of pink.

'I know,' he says quietly. 'That's what I'm worried about.'

'And who would you rather I date?' I ask. 'Hmm? Come on, Mr Perfect Match.'

'Why can't you just find yourself a nice artistic boy?' he asks, slamming the car door so hard I'm certain it'll fall off if we take a corner too tightly on the way home. 'Someone who can keep up with your wild conversations and that small art gallery you've got happening in your flat.'

'Sure.' I shrug. 'That way there'll be two equally neurotic people in my house. That would be *great*.'

'At least you'd have something in common,' he says. 'I'm only trying to look out for you, you know. I do love you.'

I want to pretend like I'm angry at his intrusion, but he cares so much that I can't be. So maybe I am a little miffed that the only thing he's focusing on is my love life. And maybe he has planted a few seeds I'm not sure I want sowing. He hasn't asked me about anything else on the way here, not my job or my friends or my otherwise inactive social life.

I decide that's okay, because I don't feel like talking about the rest of my life right now. In fact, it's been nice to not feel that bile-ish rise of unemployed panic in my throat for a few hours. I blow him a raspberry and walk along the stone path, through a Monet's garden of flowers, towards the front door.

I'm home.

Chapter 5

Adam holds the front door open and straightens a family photo on the sideboard as he follows me inside. Our footsteps echo along a hallway decorated in a collage of memories and we say a quick hello to a photo of Mum that takes pride of place atop a display cabinet in the dining room, which is full of her favourite china.

A jasmine-scented breeze carries laughter with it up the middle of the house, which appears empty except for Dad. As we enter the kitchen, he reaches into the windowsill and fiddles with the radio dial until the crackling sounds of Tchaikovsky register. One look at him, and the first thing that comes to mind is Picasso. His sunflower yellow T-shirt is accentuated with royal blue stripes and splotches that would be right at home in an Eighties music video. Mark Knopfler, eat your heart out.

'Well, shit.' Dad throws us a quick look over his shoulder, his dark eyes suddenly bright at our intrusion. 'You're both still alive.'

'I told you I'd get her here.' Adam slips his coat over the back of a chair, claiming his place at the dinner table. As if he were ever allowed to sit somewhere other than the side of the table facing the window; childhood habits die hard around here. I kiss

41

my father's bristly cheek and steal a slice of Brie from the cheese-board he's piecing together.

'As if you can talk,' I demur. 'What are you doing home on a Saturday morning? Hey? Come on, you're the one who instilled our work ethic.'

Adam reaches into the refrigerator and grabs for a Capri-Sun Dad insists on keeping in the refrigerator for him. A holiday snap from Italy feathers its way to the floor before he curses and picks it up again.

Dad runs an art supplies store in the middle of town, so his Saturday mornings were usually spent working there. Given it was his busiest day of the week, it was rare to see him home, let alone putting on a spread.

'Things have been on the up at the shop, so I've hired a few people to cover the occasional shift.' He hands me the cheeseboard. 'I thought a catch up might be on the cards.'

'Time to break out the sparkling.' Adam pops a cocktail onion in his mouth and disappears with his drink. From the sunroom, Dad's girlfriend, Fiona squeaks her excitement at the sight of him.

'So.' Dad looks at me. 'How's the museum? Running the place yet?'

I huff, my fringe doing a Mexican wave against my forehead. I really want to tell him what's happened, but now isn't the time to pour out my feelings on the parental chaise longue. At least not with an audience. 'You know, the usual. It's frustrating. Office politics, men, promotions that seem like a fantasy. But, yay art, right?'

'Big city life, huh?' He sounds as thrilled as I feel.

'You can say that again,' I mumble.

'Are you okay?' The bridge of his nose furrows. 'You look spooked.'

'Me?' I stuff a cube of cheese in my mouth. '*La vita è bella.*'

'You do know how that movie ends, don't you?' he asks.

42

'Dad, come on.' I grin, nodding in the direction of the hall. 'I'm fine.'

'I don't believe you.' He waggles an accusatory finger. 'Anyway, come out and say hello, see who I've managed to rustle up today. I've got someone I want you to meet.'

'Me?'

'Yes, you. You've got a lot in common.'

I grimace. 'Sounds ominous.'

He shepherds me into the sunroom, where I find Adam and Fiona, who is the sunshine of the place, her greying hair swept together in a chignon and her apron-smock smattered in a rainbow of paints. She's just as eccentric as Mum was, with a touch more bite, which means she's slotted into our family perfectly.

She's already drawn Adam into an animated discussion about a new piece hanging on the wall. It's as wide as I am tall, I'm sure of it, and it's a magnificent landscape of the Ribblehead Viaduct and surrounding Dales, full of oranges and greens and spurts of light. I love that, from a distance, anyone would be forgiven for thinking it was a photo. Looking around the room, at the empty seats and half-drunk teas, I spot another guest outside.

'Oh.' Dad pushes past me, drawing me into the backyard. A wayward arm reaches out to the man walking towards us, a confused look on his face. 'Katharine, this is Kit. He's an artist, like you, and he runs an art school out at Loxley.'

Help me. My own father thinks I'm so hard up for a shag he's setting me up with one of his *friends*. Kill me now. It all makes sense, the desperate need for us to visit today and, strangely, Adam's displeasure at John. Never mind the fact Dad's friendship circle is more eclectic than a Pokémon deck, so you can guarantee he's caught them all at some point. There's no guaranteeing what I'll get.

As Kit steps forward, I get a better chance to focus on him.

43

He. Is. Tall. I'm five foot seven and, even though it's only the difference of a few inches (some would argue that matters), I feel like he's teetering over me.

And he's solid. Not in that need-to-lose-ten-kilos way, but solid in a broad-shouldered, rips wood apart in the rain and plucks kittens from trees like low hanging fruit kind of way. Dressed down in faded blue jeans, scuffed boots and a white T-shirt under red-check flannel, I would not be shocked if he opened with: 'Actually, I'm a lumberjack.'

Blond hair waves over the crest of his head to a soft widow's peak, his eyes are the deep blue of an ocean that hasn't seen the tinkle of sunlight in a while, and there's a steely determination to his face. He steps forward and offers a reserved smile, one that considers me carefully.

'Lovely to meet you,' Kit says quietly. It's almost a mumble but, still, he reaches out to shake my hand. Now that he's closer, I can see his fingers are long and paint stained.

'Likewise.'

'I thought you two should meet,' Dad adds. Slowly, Kit's eyes leave mine and wander across to my father. I can see he's not entirely convinced of this, either. 'Katharine is a gallery curator at Webster Fine Art Gallery in London.'

A flash of recognition passes over Kit's face as he turns to walk away. 'Is that so?'

'That is so, and she's amazing at what she does.' Dad scuttles after him. 'I went to one of her opening nights about eighteen months ago. It was incredible. A weekend in London, black-tie, expensive champagne and fantastic finger food!'

'Well, if it was in London that makes all the difference,' Kit says.

'Oh, no, but the art was fine.'

'I'm sure it was popular.' He glances at me briefly before disappearing inside.

As I step back through the door after him, my elbow catches

on an orchid to my left. Its pink flowers wobble as the terracotta pot rounds and finally falls back into place, along with my nerves. Fiona and Adam turn to greet us and Dad ducks into the kitchen, reappearing with arms laden with more food.

'Oh!' Fiona pips her excitement. She'd been too busy in conversation with Adam to realise I'd disappeared. 'Katharine, have you—'

'We've met, yes,' Kit says haltingly. 'Peter was generous enough to do the introductions.'

Something about the way he speaks sits uncomfortably with me. Thankfully, I can't see his face, and I throw a confused frown my father's way. Who does this guy think he is? If first impressions count, this isn't a good one.

'Master of Curating and Collections,' Dad adds proudly.

'Well, then,' Kit says in a slow, slow grumble as I wait for the sting in his tail. 'Sounds like you might teach me a thing or two.'

And there it is. I'm suddenly flustered. I begin to speak, but words come out in a lopsided mess. Both Adam and Dad jump in to tell me off about downplaying my education. My own personal cheer team.

Everyone my father meets gets the same story, usually after he brags about Adam's first-class honours. As embarrassing as it can be, I'm also so thankful he gets excited over our achievements. Chalk that up to another reason why I haven't told him about yesterday yet. I find myself a seat on the opposite side of the room in the furthest corner, away from Kit. I'd rather deal with his grumpiness from afar.

Being on the other side of the room, however, doesn't spare me his presence.

'What's your favourite style of art, then, Katharine?' Kit asks, crossing his legs over in a mirror of mine. I immediately uncross mine. 'I mean, you must see plenty in your work, but what about, say, a favourite period?'

'Definitely the Romantic period.'

'Really?' Kit says, mouth downturned. 'Why?'

'Well, I mean, you've got Turner and Grimshaw, who both have the most stunning—'

'Grimshaw was Victorian era, but go on.'

I freeze, as does the rest of the room. From the kitchen, I hear Fiona drop some cutlery.

'He was, wasn't he?' As much as I want to appreciate his correction, it itches and sticks somewhere under my ribs, and not simply because I should know better. 'And I always thought Runge looked like he'd be a bit of fun.'

'Nobody recent then?' he asks.

'I don't really know a lot of recent work,' I say, scrunching my nose. 'Sorry.'

'Really?' Kit says. 'Why's that?'

'Oh, I don't know.' I lift my gaze to the ceiling as if the answer might fall from above. 'I guess, by the time I get home from work, the last thing I want to do is run out to another gallery. I spend most of my time around classics, so perhaps I'm just more predisposed to them.'

His brows kick up momentarily as he thanks Fiona for a coffee. 'We all have our foibles.'

A glob of sandwich lodges in my throat. Did he just imply I'm faulty because I enjoy the classics? God, he's only affirming my worst fears after yesterday, that there's something lacking in my life's repertoire. Is it that obvious that I'm a hack?

To save embarrassing my father, I stay deathly silent. I glance across at Adam, who hides his smile behind a hand. Dad doesn't know which way to turn, and Fiona is wearing a look that says she's surprised I haven't reacted. I wonder how Dad feels now, thinking that *this* was the guy I should date.

'Adam, how's work?' Fiona makes a show of turning to my brother.

I'm relieved when the room settles into casual conversation, giving me the opportunity to become an observer. Adam gives

46

the *Reader's Digest* version of what I've just spent hours listening to. Fiona talks about her latest adventures selling art at the market, while Kit does his best to convince my father he's wrong and that the latest artwork he bought is terrible. I'm not sure how I feel about being witness to all this.

I want to see this piece just so I can agree with my father. They seem like such an odd pairing, more so because I can't work out if the conversation is spiteful or sarcastic, and whether Kit is genuinely smiling or sneering. Perhaps it's all a game of one-upmanship? But that begs the question: why does he need to compete with *me*?

'Have you ever heard of her?' Kit directs his question to me.

I straighten my back. 'Sorry, who?'

'Marnie Buller.'

I shake my head. 'Sorry, no.'

He rattles off a series of names, none of them familiar. If I shake my head any more, I'll transform into a dashboard doggie. When he gets to the end of his list, he leans forward and rests an elbow on his knee, propping his chin up in the palm of his hand.

'Do you practise your own art?' he asks.

Suddenly, I'm made of glass. 'Well, it's been a while, but—'

'She's an incredible photographer.' Dad stuffs a cracker laden with baba ghanoush into his mouth. 'Landscapes mostly, a bit of portraiture. You did a lovely series of shots of the Town Hall once, I remember.'

My gaze slides towards Dad. Normally, I'd speak up at being talked over but, right now, I don't mind so much.

'He's right,' I say. 'Photos are my thing, but it's been an age since I've had the time.'

'You know, if it's been a while since you've made any art, you should take a class at Kit's to help rebuild your skills,' Dad adds. 'Hell, he's even sucked me into going. And it's great, you should see some of the stuff we're doing.'

'But she has a master's degree. Surely, she doesn't need me,' Kit chimes in as he slouches back into his chair. 'Right?'

'He's right,' I agree, begrudgingly. 'I think I'm okay, thank you. Just need a bit of time to myself, but I'll keep it in mind.'

I can't remember the last time I felt so out of the loop in a conversation of this kind. So, when Fiona leaps from her chair and announces she's going to organise dessert, I take the opportunity to follow her to the kitchen and away from the discomfort.

Chapter 6

'She wrote her thesis on Grimshaw.' Dad's voice floats through the walls and into the kitchen. 'I proofread it about a dozen times. Bloody brilliant if you ask me.'

'I didn't understand a word of it,' Adam chimes in.

All I can do is bury my face in my hands and laugh. Fiona gives me a light slap with the dish cloth despite the fact she's tittering too. Neither of us hear Kit's response. Perhaps it was too low and mumbled, perfect volume for a roast, or maybe there wasn't one at all. I make the decision there and then that, despite how amazing his art might be, or how wonderful his school for the gifted is, I don't like him. I've had my fill of art snobs lately.

In this moment, I'm glad for the sanctuary of the kitchen. It's comfortable and non-judgemental. Once upon a time, I'd spend nights and weekends helping Mum whip up all manner of gastronomic creations. Despite what Dad likes to think, she really was the cook of the two of them. I laugh sometimes, thinking about how frustrated she'd be if she ever saw my microwave gourmet paired with the first bottle of wine Sainsbury's has on offer.

Not a lot has changed here since she died. Besides Fiona, that is. We've still got the same beige laminate worktops that have almost worn through in Mum's favourite spot where she'd sit and lean into the counter while having a conversation and a brew. Knife wounds slice the surface in spots where Adam and I self-ishly made sandwiches without chopping boards. Even the mixing bowls are in the same cupboard by the oven.

'I thought you were just cutting up cake?' I ask. 'Do you want me to do that? I can make one if you like?'

Because of course I've made mountains of cakes lately. Not.

'Oh, you don't have to do that.' She fluffs and flutters and tries to steer me out of the way.

'Please, let me.' I reach above the refrigerator for a cookbook. 'It'll be nice to be out of the spotlight for five minutes.'

'Go easy on the old boy.' Fiona relents and lifts her mug to her mouth, eyes already crinkled conspiratorially. 'He thought Kit would be right up your alley.'

'Let me be very clear,' I whisper and pinch my fingers together as I lean into her. 'He's not going anywhere near my alley.'

'Oh.' She breaks into a scandalised laugh that lights up her face. 'No strike then?'

'Not even a gutter ball.'

'Oh, balls.' She giggles.

'No, no balls.' I laugh with her. 'None at all.'

We corpse all over again.

Before I have a chance to gather ingredients, Fiona is pulling packet mixes from the pantry and whispering about how Dad thinks she makes caramel mud cakes from scratch. She leaves me to bake if I swear never to reveal her secret. I cross my heart and, soon enough, am alone and listening for whatever conversation wafts into the kitchen.

I've barely managed to crack the last of the eggs into the bowl when I hear footsteps thudding along the hallway towards the bathroom. I pay no attention to them until they start up again. This time, they're getting closer. They're not the one-two shuffle of my father or the slightly shorter version preferred by my brother and I can still hear Fiona laughing in the sunroom.

It can only be Kit, and he's now standing in the dining room, staring up at Dad's makeshift gallery wall. It's covered in prints and postcards of Dad's and Fiona's favourite pieces and it's where I got the idea to do the same thing in my flat.

'Hello.' I spare a look over my shoulder and try to be as upbeat as possible, though I'm sure I sound desperate, panicky even. 'Lovely day today.'

I bristle and brace myself for whatever's bound to come out of his mouth but his only response is to offer me a disinterested grin before turning back to the art. He's so bad at faking a smile he can barely manage to crinkle his eyes.

It doesn't take long to realise, as he moves around the space, he's watching me. That's okay, because I'm watching him too. We just aren't doing it at the same time. I catch him in the corner of my eye and, when I turn away to melt butter, he's watching me do that. It's a silent tug-of-war.

'Can I help you with anything?' The room is so still I'm sure it's not the clock I can hear ticking, but the cogs in both our brains. He doesn't move or flinch. Even the conversation in the sunroom seems to have ground to a halt. Instead, he leans in closer to the piece he's in front of for a few more minutes. I rub the back of my neck. 'They're some of my parents' favourite art pieces.'

'It's an interesting collection, isn't it?' he asks, finally making eye contact.

I smile. 'It's certainly eclectic.'

'He loves his Picasso.' His head tilts and turns as he takes the work in from all angles. 'So, you're a photographer?'

'Pretend to be,' I say.

'Any favourites?' he asks, offering another cursory glance.

'I quite like Adams.'

'Ansel?' he asks. 'I don't mind the landscapes.'

'No, Bryan.'

He rolls his eyes and clucks his tongue. 'Figures.'

51

'Why does it figure?' I ask.

'Well, he's famous, isn't he? Mainstream.'

'Of course.' I feel my brow furrow. 'I wouldn't have heard of him otherwise.'

'My point exactly,' he says in a soft grumble as he waves a languid finger towards the wall. 'This one here seems out of place with the rest of them.'

I take a deep breath and fumble with the mixing bowl; I can't discard it quickly enough. There's just something about him that sets my nerves on edge. 'Ah … you want to know about that piece in particular?'

'What I don't understand is: your father has all this great art on his wall. There's Klimt and Monet, Picasso and Matisse and then this. It's got me beat why anyone would pay good money for it.' A long finger flicks at the frame. 'It's not a particularly skilled piece.'

If that statement is designed to capture my attention, consider me bound and gagged. I blink slowly and draw a deep, steadying breath.

'Go on then, Neil Buchanan, what's wrong with it?' I fold my arms over in challenge. I'm ready.

'It's just so clichéd.' He points to the offending parts of the small photo. 'I mean, the framing is all wrong. There's part of a tree in the foreground and the small fence keeps guiding my eye towards the bloody foliage. At least I think it's foliage. It's hard to tell because it's so out of focus, and I'm sure the selective black and white disappeared with the early Noughties. It's just such a postcard, isn't it?'

'Well, shit, I'd really love to read your master's thesis on the use of focal points and acceptability to modern art.' I look at him. 'Have you brought it with you? It's a long drive home, so reading it would give me something to do.'

The house is silent. Around his shoulder and down the hall, I can see my dad give me a thumbs-up. I turn my attention back to Kit, who's still staring at my photograph, the briefest hint of pink crosses the tips of his ears.

'Anyway, what if that's all it's meant to be?' I ask. 'Personally, I love receiving postcards. It means someone's thinking enough about me to want to share something with me. Above that, it says they're willing to put those words out in public by sending them through a postal service where everyone gets to read them on their journey. They're intensely personal.'

He turns his gaze to me, and something in his eyes trips my tongue over itself.

'Some would even say they're romantic,' I continue, trying to keep the lightness in my voice.

'If that's all it's meant to be, then it's wasting space on what is otherwise an incredible wall of art.' He cranes his neck to look at something closer to the ceiling.

I snort.

'Who's the artist?' he asks.

He's standing so close I can feel his breath tickling the tip of my nose and see the tint of paint he hasn't been able to scrub from around his cuticles. I pull the frame from the wall and turn it over, making a show of looking for the name.

'Oh!' I clap a hand to my cheek and feign surprise. 'Would you look at that? "Katharine Patterson, Scarborough Beach, April 1999". I think that means me. Yes. Definitely me.'

It's a photo I submitted for a school assessment. Dad decided it needed to go on his wall because it scored top marks, and he was proud enough of that.

'Maybe,' I say, turning to find his face slightly ashen, 'I can start selling postcards of it. Great business idea, thanks.'

He stumbles around for the right words but comes up blank. The look on his face is a little gawping fish, a little 'man put in place'. For the record, it's already a firm favourite in my limited experience of his facial expressions.

'I'm aware that it's not the most artistic piece.' I'm only

prepared to give him a minor concession, God knows why. He doesn't deserve it. 'But it seemed to resonate with my parents which, forgive me if I'm wrong, might be what art is all about.'

'Ah.' The corner of his mouth rises just so as he looks away with something like a nod. 'That explains that.'

There's no logical reason for wanting to impress him, it's nothing more than my competitive streak. After yesterday, I feel a desperate need to prove people wrong, so I offer up the camera roll on my phone. Among the selfies, food photos and the inappropriate photos of John I hide the screen for, are other photos I'd taken, ones I'd wanted to show Dad or Adam without having to lug prints around.

'I've taken plenty more photos since.' I shove my phone under his nose.

Though his eyes move around the screen as I swish left and right, pinching the pictures in and out, he stays resolutely, frustratingly silent. He's Shania Twain and I'm Brad Pitt, because nothing I show him impresses him much. Would it be right to say I'd love to strangle him right now? Instead, I bite my lip to stop me swearing and count backwards from ten in the echo chamber of my mind.

'What about you?' I try. 'Where's your artwork? Are any of *your* masterpieces hanging on the wall today? Oh, that's right, I don't recall seeing any.'

'I dabble.' He offers a bashful smile, and his entire face changes. It softens as light spills forth and changes the tension of the room almost immediately. I can only imagine what laughter would do to him. He'd likely combust. He returns to where he was only moments ago looking at a life drawing.

'Oh, you run an art school and you *dabble*, do you?' I ask. 'Well, I'm going to look you up, Mr Kit.'

'Why? You're going to exhibit my work in your museum?' he says. 'Sorry, *gallery*.'

'Now, that's a very clever way of asking. Five points for that.'

I waggle a finger at him as I retreat to the kitchen and pick up the whisk. 'But isn't the old saying "Those who can't do, teach"?'

He follows close behind. 'Oh, I didn't say I was asking.'

'Aren't you?' I crack another egg into the mixing bowl and toss the shell into the sink. I wonder if Fiona would mind so much if I threw one at him? 'Certainly sounds like you are.'

'And what if I was?' He leans against the counter and folds his arm over. If I want to leave the kitchen right now, I'd have to crash tackle him on my way through. For what it's worth, that's not beneath me.

I grin at him. 'I would tell you no.'

'Without even listening to a proposal? Or seeing my portfolio?' he asks with a disbelieving laugh.

I check him over my shoulder. 'Correct.'

'You know, that's hardly fair.'

'Is it?' I ask. 'Because I don't decide the exhibits we run. I simply curate them.'

'You make it sound so fancy, Miss Patterson.'

I smile and shake my head and hope he can't see my face in a reflection.

'Is that seriously what you want?' I turn to him. 'Gallery space?'

'Is that what you're offering?'

Against everything running through my mind right now, the shock and irritation and, hell, the sheer audacity of him, I smile. 'I'm not offering anything.'

'No?' he asks, head tipped. 'Why are we talking about it, then?'

'You're very tenacious, aren't you?' I ask. Frustration sifts through me and I take it out on the mixing bowl.

'Hardly.' He shifts and presses his palms against the bench. 'It's a no, then?'

'It's a no,' I say as sweetly as I can. 'I can't authorise anything, especially in my father's kitchen on a Saturday afternoon. Mr Webster would have a coronary, which wouldn't be the best look for me, given he already had one last year.'

'I'll bet if I were hugely popular and mainstream attractive, you'd sign me right up.' He snaps his fingers.

'That's not true.' Annoyance starts to climb my ribs again. It settles on my shoulders and pulls them tight.

'What's your next exhibition?' he asks. 'Huh?'

The unemployment queue, I think.

'Van Gogh,' I say, noticing how tired he looks under the skylight.

'Before that?'

I sigh and tip my head back. 'DaVinci.'

'Oh.' He smiles, tongue rolling around in his cheek pocket. 'So, basically all the famous dead guys.'

'All right.' I fling my hands up in the air, little particles of cake mixture rising alongside them. 'Pitch me.'

'Oh, so *now* you want me to pitch you?' He laughs as he crosses his arms.

'Yes, pitch to me.' I wave a hand. 'Come on, Mr Underground.'

'Mr Underground?' He bows his head and pinches his bottom lip. When he lifts his eyes to meet mine, I feel something in the room tip. Instinctively, I reach for the edge of the counter and clutch it so hard my knuckles lose colour. 'Let's see. Pitch, pitch, pitch.'

Kit begins pacing across the kitchen, both of us completely ignorant of the world around us, of the conversations happening outside, or that we might be missing out on them. I watch as he hugs himself and fills the space between the refrigerator and the kitchen counter.

'A retrospective on the nature of learning in the realm of art?' he tries. 'A progressive snapshot of art coming together. The journey from beginner to exhibited artist.'

I frown. 'You want to sell that to the board of directors? Half-finished paintings?'

'I want to sell it to someone.' He nods vehemently.

'Keep in mind, you just insulted my art,' I said. 'As a beginner artist. So, you know. You've gotta be better than that.'

'It's a legitimately terrible piece.' He chuckles, as if to lighten the mood. 'Amateur.'

'I was fifteen!' I argue. 'It's lovely. And I *was* amateur. What? Are you seriously going to tell me you have nothing of sentiment on your walls?'

His smile falters.

'And I'm going to sell prints now because of you. I hope you feel good about that.' I point at him. 'Watch out for my Etsy store.'

'Do I get commission?'

'You wish.'

'I wouldn't mind it, honestly.' He claps his hands together. 'It's because you're only in it for the fame, right? That's why you don't want me.'

'What?' I shriek. 'No, it's nothing to do with that. I cannot just walk into my boss's office on Monday morning, slap my papers down and announce I've found the next big thing. I don't even know who the artist is or what they're known for and, in fact, half the paintings aren't even finished, but never mind that. I'm sure it'll sell. The directors will want to know how many visitors I can attract, who are the big names on show, and whether it's going to be financially viable. It's got nothing to do with popular versus underground. It's really not.'

'But popular brings all the punters to the yard, doesn't it?'

'Of course it does.'

'Then it *does* have to something to do with that.'

'For the love of God,' I mutter into the mixing bowl. 'Will you give up already?'

When I finish mixing the cake and turn to look at him, he's gone, spirited away out of the room without a whisper of a footstep. In his place, my father, who looks highly bemused at best.

'That sounded interesting.'

'Where'd he go?' I peer around him towards the dining room. 'He was just here.'

'He's outside. He just sat down.'

'He is awful,' I whisper loudly. 'Walked right in here, insulted my photograph and then asked me for space in the gallery like I should be grateful for his time.'

'He did?'

'Yes.' I nod so hard I could put my neck out.

Dad laughs. 'Make it happen.'

'What?'

'Do it. Talk to whoever you need to at Webster and make it happen.'

'What?' I complain. 'No.'

'Yes, here, let me show you.' Dad's madly swiping and unlocking his phone, ready to show me the Gallery de Christopher. 'His work is so vibrant.'

I place a hand over the screen without looking and give him a stern look. 'Dad, no.'

'Katharine, he hasn't exhibited anything in two years. Please?'

I clench my jaw, pour the batter into a tin, and take out my mild rage by belting the tin against the counter under the guise of removing air bubbles. 'I can't.'

'Don't be silly. It's too good an opportunity to pass up. Do you have any idea the people who've tried to get him to show recently? He's turned away every single one.'

'Dad, I can't,' I say, this time a little more forcefully.

'Why not?'

'Because I don't have a gallery to show his work in.'

He snorts. 'Don't be silly. Yes, you do. Carlton Webster would love it.'

'Yes, but he wouldn't love me very much right now because I quit last night,' I say quietly, unable to meet his eyes.

'You what?'

'I said, I quit my job.' I groan and rub floury hands across my face. 'Marched myself right out the door.'

Dad holds a finger in the air. 'You wait right there.'

58

'No, don't.' I grab at his arm. 'Please don't make a big deal about this. You've got a friend here, and I went to the effort of making you cake. At least let everyone eat it.'

'Since when can you make cake?'

'I can bake.' Surprisingly well with the help of a packet mix, as it turns out.

Though he looks pained, he agrees, but it doesn't stop him dragging Adam and Fiona into an impromptu family meeting while I try and clean my mess. The four of us huddle around a tiny butcher trolley, each taking turns to wipe the left-over cake batter from the mixing bowl with our fingers.

'You know, I kind of already knew.' Adam slurps at his finger.

'You what? How could you possibly know?'

'Well.' His shoulders make for his ears. 'When you didn't answer your email, I called your desk. Whoever answered told me you'd just upped stumps and marched out.'

'Oh.'

'Why would you walk out?' Dad asks. 'Did you do something wrong?'

'What? No. I didn't do something wrong,' I say angrily. Why has he automatically gone for me as the blame? 'I got passed over for the senior curator role. Again. It's the third time I've applied and, honestly, I'd had enough.'

'And never mind the box of belongings on your kitchen counter this morning,' Adam adds.

'You saw that?'

'Focusing on that proved a valuable distraction,' he teases, making me blush at the thought of a naked John squaring off with my brother.

'There's nothing to be ashamed about, Katharine.' Dad plucks a half-eaten packet of biscuits from the top of the cupboard behind the teacups no one ever uses. We figured that was where he hid all his favourite biscuits not long after Mum died, and we walked in to find him mainlining a packet of custard creams.

Adam's got his lawyer hat on, trying to weasel his way into any side argument or point of law he can think of. Not that it matters, I tell him. What's done is done. That's life. I'll find another job and move on, and it will be okay. *I'll* be okay.

'Find another job?' Fiona asks. 'Where?'

'There are plenty of jobs.' Dad hands me the newspaper. 'If you're willing to change things up. You know, I could retire while you run the shop?'

'Oh.' My shoulders slip. 'No, don't do that. I'm sure I'll be fine.'

'Have you got enough money? Did they pay you out?' Fiona asks.

'Yes, and yes, probably,' I say with a sigh. 'I'll get paid out what I'm owed. Not much, but it's something. Honestly, it's not the end of the world. Let's just enjoy this afternoon. In case you've forgotten, we have a guest waiting. I'm sure he's absolutely thrilled about not being centre of attention right now. Let's just entertain. I'll sort this.'

And that's exactly what we do. I keep one eye on the oven timer and the other on the newspaper classifieds. Conversations go on around me, Dad's busy reading the arts pages and trying not to answer emails that are coming through to the shop. He's got staff for that, Fiona reminds him. Kit discusses a mutual friend, and Fiona is the floater who brings us all back into singular conversation occasionally.

One thing that strikes me, huddled in my chair in the back corner of the room, is that the more I browse the newspaper and online sites, it's abundantly clear my job prospects are limited. I peer over the top of the newspaper at Kit, who seems to have a radar and offers me a cursory glance before resuming his conversation. I flip him the bird behind the paper before continuing my search.

Sure, I could throw my hat in the ring for anything. I'd happily stack shelves or flip burgers if that's all that was on offer. Someone has to do those jobs, right? There's no shame in them, but they're not long-term plans for me. Also, they won't my cover rent, which is already in the upper quadrant of what I could afford to begin with. I need cashflow quickly and, with my limited job prospects, I have to think outside the box.

Kit leaves, and there are hugs and handshakes and requests to catch up again. I smile and nod and say all the right words, even promising I'll think about coming up for one of his classes. He's barely down the hall before I retreat to the living room and throw myself into my favourite recliner, legs tucked up under me and T-shirt pulled tight over my knees.

I am *never* going to one of his classes.

He throws one last look at me. 'Lovely to have met you, Katharine. You let me know how you go with that gallery space.'

Both Adam's and Dad's heads spin to me so quickly anyone would think Holy Water had been tossed about. I keep quiet, instead choosing to watch through the window as he climbs into a beat-up old enamel-green Defender. When he lurches down the street, Dad reappears in the front room.

'Did you like him? He's great, isn't he?' he asked. 'Did he show you his art in the end?'

'He's rude.' I shake my head slowly. 'So rude. And, no, I didn't see his art, and I don't really want to.'

'No,' he soothes. 'He's just a little blunt, that's all.'

'Blunt?' I almost yell. 'Talking to him is like being hit in the face with a frying pan.'

'One that's cold, or still on the hob?' Adam pops a crisp in his mouth.

'On the hob,' I deadpan. 'Highest setting. Molten.'

Though he's gone and well down the street, his words echo in my ears. Something about his interest in gallery space sticks. Not that he hadn't already been otherwise swilling about my mind like a heady wine, but it's possible he's planted an idea.

I couldn't offer exhibitions to just anyone while working at Webster. There were rules and procedures put in place that meant

61

Kit would likely never get past the gatekeepers. But, if I owned my own gallery, I could show whoever I wanted.

Including him.

If I wanted to, which I don't.

With a fizz in my feet and a tingle in my fingers, I retrieve the newspaper and a coffee from the kitchen. I tear the pages open, pass the 'Office junior wanted' ads, taste the bitter blend of ink that jumps from thumb to tongue, and land with a thud in the real estate section, specifically industrial sites that are up for offer.

My brain leapfrogs ahead, playing a holiday slideshow of moments I could only hope to experience. Opening nights, signing new artists, sold-out shows, hosting huge international names. Handshakes, hugs and takeaway dinners eaten by a sales counter as I worked late into the night. They'd be shows I could choose and curate. It's appealing but, in this moment, it feels like a mirage.

It doesn't take long for one listing to stand out.

'Oooh, look. This old place in West Bar up for sale.' I turn the paper to show everyone. 'Is it a fire station? It looks like an old bank, maybe.'

'You getting into the supernatural?' Adam hauls himself over the arm of the chair to look at the paper. 'Park the ECTO-1 out the front?'

'Piss off,' I say with a laugh.

'You'd be Egon.'

'Stop it.' Dad lashes out and gives him a shove. 'What are you thinking?'

'What if I opened my own gallery?' I look up.

It's like someone has hit the pause button on the room. Dad's got his coffee cup to his mouth and Adam stops mid-bite of a biscuit. An excited smile lands on Fiona's face as she claps her hands together. Only their eyes move as they catch each other for one concerned moment.

'It's the perfect space,' I continue against their silence. 'Corner

62

position, bright and airy, beautifully classic architecture. Stone building. The colours inside are a bit shite, but that's nothing a lick of paint can't fix.'

'You'd move home?' Adam asks. 'That's a huge decision to make in the space of twenty-four hours.'

'This is all hypothetical, but I could. Maybe I'd find a place in London. The foot traffic would be great, but it's bound to be hideously expensive.' I grab my phone and load up the same ad online and look at the listing complete with technicolour aubergine purple and burnt orange walls, and carpet with more stains than I want to ask about. 'But it works, right? Or is it silly?'

'It's not silly as such,' Dad says carefully. 'It's a great idea. It's just … finances?'

'Yeah,' I say, absent-mindedly. 'I do have a little cash stashed away. I've been wheedling money away for a deposit on a flat of my own, but it might see me through.'

'But you love your flat,' Fiona offers. 'I thought you enjoyed living in London?'

'Absolutely I do. I love the vibe.' I glance around the room. 'But maintaining the status quo hasn't worked out so well, has it? I've been there for, what, ten years now and what have I got to show for it? Bosses who give jobs to their friends, in an already competitive market. By rights, I should have been further along in life than this. I don't own my own home; I barely even own my car. Something has to change.'

What have I got to lose?

Chapter 7

As I sit on the bus the next day, feeling it bump and roll through streets, I twiddle my phone between my fingers. I'm still studying the estate agent's advertisement for the old bank in Sheffield. It hasn't been updated with a sold tag, so a glimmer of hope still dances on the horizon. When a voiceover announces the next stop as Elephant and Castle, I change buses.

A man who boards reminds me of Kit. As he searches for a seat, he makes eye contact with me and my chest loosens with a freshly expelled breath. Not him. I bristle again at the memory of his words and am glad when the stranger finally opts for the top floor of the bus.

With everything else on my mind, I try not to think about his blond hair or insults. Regardless of what he thinks of my photo, art has always been subjective. Just because he doesn't rate it doesn't mean it's terrible. Showing my work has always felt like the artistic equivalent of walking naked down the street and asking people to point out my flaws. If Kit is an artist worth his salt, he already knows this. I pop a mint in my mouth and peer out the window to the inner-city landscape.

The high-rise buildings full of shimmering glass are a world away from the suburban landscape of yesterday, the rows of semi-detached houses, charming front yards, and supermarket superstores. Today, after so many years, the city feels foreign to me, as if I know my time here is winding down, whether I've made a final decision or not.

On our way out the door this morning (because Fiona insisted we stay the night), Dad handed me bundles of newspapers he'd rooted out of the recycling. They were full of job ads and opportunities, he reminded me, if I wanted to look at something else before throwing myself into the world of owning a business. He knows from experience it's not easy. Tacked on the end was that it was fine if I wanted to move home, too. My old bedroom was always there for me. I promised I'd at least think about his offer.

As much as I love my dad, I'm thirty-five. I don't want to be sneaking men down the hallway in the middle of the night, especially considering that squeaky floorboard everybody manages to find in the dark has never been fixed.

The early morning drive home with Adam was a complete contrast to the questioning I received on the journey up yesterday. Unlike his usual bull in a china shop approach, he prodded with gentle questions as he tried to measure my direction, to help me piece together all my alternatives. No matter what I wanted to say, or the ideas I spitballed, I couldn't find the words to sum up exactly where my brain was at.

Opening my own art gallery is such a tantalising idea. It would mean skipping all those years of hard slog and diving straight into a role I've created for myself. I would truly be the captain of my own ship, displaying the art I wanted to, when I wanted to, and without worrying about losing out on work to someone who's both less experienced and happy to compromise their principles and play games. My work would finally stand for something.

On the downside, it would be a massive leap of faith. I can't pretend it would be anything less than the biggest gamble of my life, and the idea of risking all the money I've saved sets my brain to spin cycle. Anyone undertaking a venture of this scale would feel the same.

It would also mean shuttering the life I've known in London and leaving it all behind. Friends, acquaintances, gallery contacts and, most importantly, my brother. It's dialling back the years even further and starting completely from scratch. Fair to say, I feel like a bit of a failure right now.

Heading back into employment and proving myself through promotions is appealing if I decide I'm keen on coasting through life with the nine to five crowd. It's the accepted norm, isn't it? Lose one job, sidestep immediately into another one. That, and no one would be able to say I'd skived on the hard yards later on, could they? But even as I searched job advertisements at two o'clock this morning, moonlight illuminating my childhood bedroom, there was a niggling voice in the back of my head that shouted, 'Well, you did walk out for a reason, and it had better be good.' That was before realising the number of roles for thirty-somethings with a master's degree are, not surprisingly, few and far between.

I decide the best course of action is to investigate both options equally: make plans as well as continuing to apply for jobs. A foot in both camps makes sense. At least if I spread my net wide and score a job, it'll bring some money in if the gallery plan goes pear-shaped. I hope it doesn't; I already have my heart set on it.

I glance up from my phone in time to see my stop. I shuffle along with pedestrian traffic and head towards Lainey's new flat.

She lives with Frank in a two-bedroom Bermondsey duplex. After scouring the internet for months and dragging me along to more open days than I care to remember, they collected the keys less than a month ago. It's rundown, needing a serious coat of paint and the front yard is muddy rubble, but they wouldn't have it any other way. It's affordable on their wages while still being close enough to the city. For me, I love that it's a nice change of scenery from my fifth-floor flat with views of a laneway coffee shop and what I'm certain have been more than a few drug deals.

Lainey's brow creases as she opens her front door. She's wearing a crown of sawdust. 'Did you sleep last night?'

'I'll bet John stayed over,' Frank sings out from the kitchen.

My brain trips. If only that were the height of my problems. Surprisingly, he's been firmly planted at the back of my mind in all this; barely rated a mention, which tells me more than I'd care to admit.

'No, nothing like that.' I step past Lainey into their cramped but comfortable lounge room. It's the first room they renovated upon moving in. This morning's coffee cups are still sitting on a perfectly reflective glass table, and a chunky aqua throw that would look right at home in a John Lewis catalogue is a new addition to the grey fabric sofa. I drop my handbag on one of the recliners and follow her through to the kitchen, where Frank makes me one of his perfectly poured coffees. Today, a frothy little cat greets me.

'You okay?' he asks, angling himself into my line of sight. 'You know, considering. Lainey told me. Sounds shit.'

'Me? Yeah, I'm fine.' I cradle my mug and focus on its contents in an attempt to avoid conversation. 'Thank you.'

I watch as my friends go about their carefully crafted morning routine. Coffees are drunk, looks are shared, and words I can't begin to understand are exchanged. Couples always seem to have their own secret language, don't they? Only when I see these two am I reminded I don't share this with anyone.

I suspect it's what I'm missing, too. That warm ease of comfort. John and I don't have shared words or codes for anything. We don't even have a favourite restaurant we can meet at. We simply exist in each other's orbit for one of Maslow's extremely basic human needs. At some point, it's not enough, is it?

When Frank leaves for the day, carting a set of golf clubs

behind him and mumbling about the needs of the bank manager outweighing the need to visit the hardware store (arm swinging towards the hallway wall covered in splotches of sanded-down plaster), he takes Lainey in an embrace. Arms wrapped around her, he dips her into a Pepé Le Pew pose and peppers her face with kisses. She laughs so loudly, I'm sure the people in the next street can hear her.

'Sorry,' she offers a sheepish apology as she reappears, cheeks flushed. She busies herself with rinsing dishes before setting her sights on a pile of wedding paraphernalia on the dining table.

'Don't apologise,' I scoff. 'Anyone offended by that needs their head examined.'

'How was yesterday?' she asked. 'Someone snapped you up yet?'

'Actually, I ended up in Sheff yesterday. Dad harangued Adam about us visiting, so we drove up for lunch. Got home about ten this morning.'

'That sounds lovely.' She smiles serenely. If only she knew.

'Yeah, it was good to get away,' I say. 'It made me realise I need to go home more often, actually.'

'You and me both.' She looks momentarily reflective. 'Are you still okay to work on place cards today? You've done a bit of travel, so if you're too tired, we can hold off.'

'Absolutely,' I enthuse. 'Let's get these done. I've been looking forward to this.'

As we unfurl an A3 piece of paper across the table, I push placemats and a vase aside to make room for it. It's a haphazardly drawn blueprint of their reception venue, including tables, a dance floor and stage where the band will play. Scrawled across each table are the names of everyone lucky enough to be seated together.

'The singles, the married four hundred years, random relatives we have to invite because parents will be parents, work colleagues, and friends we've had forever,' Lainey explains as she piles a bunch of eggshell blue and white cards on the table. 'Not all mutually exclusive, funnily enough.'

'Do you have a list of names?' I look at the sheet doubtfully. 'I wouldn't want to, you know, spill ink and destroy this.'

'Yes, yes of course.' Her face lights up and she digs through her things again.

Sitting together at the table while I cut and fold place cards, even writing on them with slow and deliberate strokes of a fountain pen, is a relaxing way to spend the day. With the radio playing in the background and a bowl of peanut M&Ms between us, we spend our time chatting about everything but my last two days.

It's nice to push it all aside and feel normal again, as if I'm not constantly thinking about the rest of my life hurling itself into the sun. When we stop for a break, I flop onto the sofa as if I'd just got off night shift.

'Can I ask you a question?' Lainey ventures, crossing her ankles on the edge of the coffee table.

Already sprawled out on the corner chaise, I roll my head to look at her, pop another chocolate in my mouth and wait for her to continue.

'Are you okay? I mean, for real okay.' She winces like she's waiting for me to blow up. When I remain silent, she continues, 'It's just that you haven't really talked about what's been going on. You've talked about the weather, your flat and a piece of art you want to buy. We've compared shopping bargains and the price of milk, but there's an elephant in the room and I don't think his name is Dumbo.'

'But that's okay.' I draw my knees up to my chest. 'Today's all about your wedding, your cake tasting and your duck breasts.'

'Yes, but a lot has happened in your life the last few days, I'm just worried you might not be dealing with it properly,' she says. 'You're normally far chattier than this. You've not even mentioned John.'

'It's certainly been busy.' I turn to look at the television. 'And John still has a lovely penis.'

'You can talk to me, you know,' she says. 'It won't go anywhere.'

For a moment, I contemplate exactly what it is I want to tell her, who I want to tell her about but, in place of words, laughter bursts forth at her solemn declaration. I know she means well, there's not a moment she doesn't, but she does look a little like she's about to tell me I'm terminal.

'What?' she asks, confused.

'So, ah, yesterday was interesting.'

'Tell me, tell me.' She bounces in her seat. 'Was it John?'

'Sort of.' I narrow my eyes. 'But not entirely.'

I start from the top and we roar with laughter at the idea of Adam finding John, naked as the day he was born, asking about golden ratios. We dissect the brotherly interrogation on the drive up, and both wonder if there's not a little bit of jealousy at play. Not in some weird incestuous way, but in a way that now says Adam has to fight for my attention, and with a work colleague no less. After all, I tend to drop everything whenever he asks for my help. Conceivably, he thinks that won't happen now.

Lainey makes all the right noises, and nods along as I speak. I follow her back to the kitchen where I watch her put together a grazing plate full of cold cuts, cheeses, and cornichons which absolutely don't warrant a joke or ten about their size. I quickly brush over Kit and how Dad introduced us. When I get to the part about opening my own gallery, she frowns and her jaw drops. Not in a bad way, more in an *I Can't Believe It's Not Butter!* way.

'I'm just not sure,' I say with a sigh. 'I love the idea of working in London, but I'm such a small fish in a very big bowl. Sheffield would give me more of a chance to be a bigger fish, wouldn't it?'

'Your own gallery? That is out of this world.' She holds a finger up. 'Why are you not there right now hanging pieces on the wall? Churning up that fishbowl? The Katie Patterson Gallery, new and exclusive and next level.'

'Firstly, because it's Sunday.' I stuff an olive in my mouth. 'Also, because it's hugely risky. And because Katie makes it sound like I'm five years old.'

'Isn't everything risky?' She spins her finger like a roulette wheel and invites me back over to the sofa. 'Every single thing we do is a risk. It just depends on how much we want it. First dates, getting engaged, marriage, family, new jobs. Like it or not, this is our life now.'

'Do you think it's a good idea though?' I ask, pressing my phone into her hand. 'I mean, just look at this place. It's stunning, classic architecture, built when things were made to last, and there's space to live upstairs. I mean, the inside of it looks like a carnival ride, but at least I won't have to resort to my childhood bedroom.'

'Oh, Katharine.' She gasps as she scrolls through the photos of the old building. 'You know I'll miss you dearly, but you need to do this. This is exactly what we were talking about the other day. You said yourself you wanted your own gallery. And you always had potential to do so much better than Webster. And I'm sure, if you thought about it, you'd agree with that, too. Also, I know a good accountant who could set you up.'

'I'm going back up to look at it tomorrow,' I say, feeling her excitement settle in a flutter. 'And Frank's on speed dial, you know that.'

'He'll be so thrilled when I tell him.' She claps her hands together.

'Wherever I land, I'm still helping you with this wedding stuff though.' I point to the mess spread about the table. It looks like a primary school art project, scissors and glue, pens and pencils tumbled over.

'I know you will. Also, rewind for a second,' she says. 'I need to know about Kit the *artiste*. You dodged him quickly, but he sounds cute.'

'Cute? Hardly. He's about ten foot tall, dirty blond hair, and

71

he's got this constant wrinkle of a frown between his eyes like he's thinking of a million things at once.'

'So, basically you with a penis.' She pops a cherry tomato in her mouth.

'No. Please.' I laugh. 'I'm not permanently angry.'

'Only semi.' She turns into me. 'Where is he on the snuggle scale?'

'Snuggle scale? I'm not snuggling him.' I pull a face. Gross. He probably smells of thinners and angst.

'Come on. Where would you fit?' she asks as she begins miming poses. 'Are you head on the shoulder or head under the chin?'

'Are you serious?'

'Look, I don't know how I'm going to get an accurate mental image of him if you don't tell me these things,' she says with a teasing laugh.

'Under the chin.' I stick my tongue out and stuff a cheese cube into my mouth. 'Happy?'

Lainey is silent but, from the pinched look on her face, I can tell something's brewing.

'What?' I ask.

'Are you going to show his work?' she says with a look and a smile that implies she's two seconds away from naming our first-born.

'What?' I ask, scrunching up my face. 'No.'

'Why not?'

'Because I don't like him.' I speak around the cracker in my mouth. 'Also, I tried searching for him this morning on my way over and came up blank.'

'What do you mean blank?' she says with a laugh. She knows when I say 'tried searching' it means I've been Googling for hours. 'I mean, of course I know what blank means, but …'

'Blank as in what have I got to go on but a first name and occupation? I skipped out on asking his surname so, now, it's like a needle in a haystack. In fact, if you type in Kit slash art slash Sheffield, all that comes up are those squeaky black plastic art kits that you buy ten-year-olds at Christmas time.'

'So?' she begins. 'Message your dad, he'll tell you. Actually, I'm going to message him.'

'Ah, no thank you very much.' I snatch her phone from her hand and toss it gently onto the sofa. 'I don't want Kit knowing I'm searching for him. Heaven forbid he thinks he's right.'

'Who are you going to show then, if not the first artist who throws themselves at your feet?'

I shrug.

'Let's see what I've got here, then,' she says, eyes wide.

Lainey disappears to the kitchen again, and I listen as she riffles through her handbag, muttering to herself about 'It must be here somewhere'. She returns, brandishing her iPad and a small red leather notebook above her head like an athletics trophy, and she's grinning from ear to ear.

'What is that?'

'My little red book of artists,' she says. 'Everyone who's ever emailed Webster and asked for gallery space or done the old "asking for a friend" type message on socials.'

I'm curious and terrified all at once. I watch as she flops down in the space next to me and folds her legs up under herself. She hands me the notebook and I begin thumbing through the pages. Surely, she doesn't think this is the answer to Kit's secret spy identity.

'Are you serious?' I ask. Some of the names I recognise as the big stars of London's art scene, others could be just random names from the phone book. 'There aren't as many names in here as I thought there'd be.'

'Artists are funny creatures,' she says, grabbing the book and holding it open at 'A'. 'Some of them are way too backward at coming forward. Others are trying to climb through the windows like the zombie apocalypse.'

Starting on the first page, we type each name into Google and start scrolling through pages of art. From the weird and the wonderful, classic to experimental, we wade through Instagram showcases and Twitter rage-fests as we compile a list of potential artists for my gallery that didn't yet exist.

'Who's next?' Lainey asks.

'Christopher Dunbar,' I read from the book. 'Very professional-sounding name, innit?'

'I think I remember him for that exact reason,' she says, fingers flying across the keyboard. 'Very measured and polite and—'

'Oh, shit.' I gasp as his website and his face loads on the screen.

'What?' she asks.

'That's him.' I point. 'That's Kit.'

'It is?' she cries.

'Yes!' I say, tapping on the unsmiling face peering back at me from the screen. The photo is black and white, and I'm not sure if he's trying to be edgy or arty, or if he's just in pain. It's hard to tell.

'That's *him*?'

'Yes,' I shriek. 'He approached Webster?'

'He certainly did.'

I reach across and tap the 'About' tab. A brief biography loads quickly.

'Christopher "Kit" Dunbar runs an art school on his sprawling Loxley property. Fifty acres of roaming paddocks and views of the reservoir, with bird-watching huts and random shelters dotted around for when inspiration strikes,' I read the website aloud, wondering why I didn't think to search for the art school this morning. 'Not that he's boasting about size or anything.'

'Oooh, and he has an online gallery.' Lainey's finger hovers over the screen.

'Click it, click it.' I bat my hand towards the tablet and wait for the images to load. 'Let's see if he's as good as he likes to make out.'

Part of me wants his art to be so bad it looks like a kindergarten reject, covered in pasta shapes, gold paint and glitter, not even fit for the family refrigerator. What's left of the calm curator part of me wants it to be so good it makes me question why we weren't already friends; let alone the fact we'd never crossed paths before. So, when the page loads and I'm presented with several different images, my axis tips.

One at a time, lively, colourful portraiture loads on screen, daubed in large brush strokes with bright squiggly colours, and far too full of emotion for a man who seemed pained at the idea of something as simple as smiling at me. There's a landscape in a similar style and a few other random still life pieces, but it's the portraits that truly showcase his talent. I'm both curious and moved.

Immediately, I want to see his works up close, to touch them and see the layers of texture, the hardened globs of paint. I want to ask him how and where they're created. I want to breathe in the smell of his studio and relish the view from the window. If there even is a window. Above all, I do a complete reversal. I must exhibit his work. I detest him and, yet, my stomach puckers and my breath catches.

'Are you seeing what I'm seeing?' Lainey points to a sold price beside one of his pieces.

'I'm trying not to,' I admit, but the undeniable truth is commission on those pieces would have any gallery owner salivating.

Inwardly, I kick myself for turning him down so quickly yesterday. Hindsight is a wonderful thing, isn't it?

The rest of the site is clean and minimalist; a sign-up page for his art school and contact form tells me not much more than I learned by spending time with him.

'Loves discovering new and emerging artists, provides support and advice to those at the start of their careers,' Lainey reads.

'Saint Christopher of the Thinners,' I grumble. 'For all the support he offered yesterday.'

75

She pivots in her seat and looks at me as I pace the room. 'I feel like this has just answered some of life's big questions for you.'

'I mean … maybe? Dad says he hasn't shown his work publicly for years. But, then, he just about jumped on me for space at Webster yesterday. He was like a dog with a bone. And he's emailed you in the past, so what gives?'

'Maybe he was just querying everywhere, or maybe he doesn't want to do local.' Lainey flicks back to his photo and mutters something about him being attractive. 'But you'll never know if you don't ask. And, if you don't ask, the answer is always no.'

I nod and shrug and mumble around the hangnail I'm trying to destroy. 'It's just such a curveball, let alone the massive risk. I was on this trajectory. I had everything mapped out. I was going to get this job as senior curator, work at it a few years, head overseas for a few more then come back with my knowledge and magical contacts and make it explode. All while maintaining a work–life balance, finding a supportive husband, and popping out a few kids.'

She scrunches her face. 'I think you need to look at this a different way.'

'How so?' I take a pause.

'Have you considered asking the vendor to rent the property to you for a set period?' she asks. 'You can open your gallery and have a go at it without quite as much commitment as a mortgage. You've been saving for your own place, so you can probably cover the cost of rent, but it mitigates your risk a little. I mean, what's a few months' rent in the scheme of things? At least if it goes tits up, you don't get repossessed.'

I scratch my fingers through my hair. While I'm reluctant to touch my savings, I don't have a lot of options at this point, and this isn't the worst idea I've ever heard. 'True.'

'As you said, if you go north, you could set yourself up as *the* person, the woman to speak to about art in the area. You'll be responsible for holding the best shows in the city, all while doing it under your own brand. Not for some crotchety old man, not while begging for corporate donations. You. Your words. Your soul.'

'It would be a great opportunity to reset, wouldn't it? Clean slate and all,' I say, blooming on the buoyancy of her words. After my last few days, she was exactly who I needed to talk to. I am so glad I didn't cancel on her this morning when I thought I might be running late.

'I think it might be. Why not give it a go? Hold an exhibition, have a killer opening night and, if it works, then you can scoop up the property. And frankly, if John *still* won't come to the party after he sees what an amazing businesswoman you are, leave him behind in your trailblazing dust. It's time you took the leap and put yourself first instead of playing second fiddle to everyone else's wants and needs.'

'How did John become part of this discussion?' I ask.

'He's *always* been part of the discussion.' Her eyes flutter at my apparent stupidity. 'You need to do something about him. Whether you both come to a decision to move forward and make things official or if you, you know.'

I sigh. 'I know.'

'I mean, what do you want from him?' she asks.

'Well, you know …' My voice trails off. 'Everything?'

Lainey scrunches her face like I've just pinched her in a tender spot. 'You know what? Sit down. As your best friend, it's my job to tell you the truth.'

I look at her, a glass of water poised at my mouth. Slowly, I lower myself back into my seat.

'This has been going on for how long now?' she asks.

'Almost nine months,' I say. 'Off and on.'

'Right, well, if he can't give you a shred of commitment, if he can't even decide what you are to him in that amount of time, he's the last person you need to be keeping around.' She stops only long enough to draw a deep breath. 'You need to ask yourself if every day with him is getting you closer to what you want in life. Don't bend to suit him, and don't ask him to bend for you, because it will not work. Find someone who clicks into place like a jigsaw puzzle. If he doesn't do any of that, then ride like the wind, Bullseye, because it's not worth it.'

Her words floor me. Where Adam took the softly, softly (for him) approach yesterday, Lainey is straight out the gate with a raw truth that only she can muster. There's a niggling awareness in me that she's absolutely, nail on the head right. Still, the sad irrefutable truth is that I adore John and, as much as he likes to tell me that he's happy with the way things are, there are moments in the dead of night that tell me otherwise.

Huddled beneath blankets, we talk about his family, his parents and their acrimonious divorce, summers spent in opposite cities, and growing up fast. I can tell you the name of his favourite childhood pet (Rusty, a longhaired whippet), and that he lives for the *Back to The Future* trilogy.

He speaks highly of Adam, even if they don't always see eye to eye, even though listening to him talk about contract law is guaranteed to put me to sleep in under ten minutes. I love how he looks at me in the morning light. I love how he smells, a heady mixture of soap and man and warm bed. I love how he feels in my bed, at how well we match both in and out of it.

Still, she's right. We accept the standard we walk past, and I've been letting this issue slide for far too long. The only person winning from this is him because, no matter what happens and how many times we avoid the topic, I stupidly let it slide and then nothing changes.

Not to say I hadn't thought all these things and more, but hearing Lainey speak her opinions aloud makes me realise I have so many more options in life than my own limitations, but there's really only one solid achievable plan that appeals to me at the end of it.

I don't want to work for someone else, slogging away for the benefit of others. It *is* time to put me first, to put my name up in lights and show everyone what I am made of. All I need to do is convince Christopher to run an exhibition after I turned him down. The thought of having to deal with him again is already spiking my blood pressure, but I've convinced countless suited men to donate millions to a gallery before, so surely this wouldn't be too epic a battle.

The big problem would be snaffling the old bank on a limited lease. And, like Lainey said, if I don't ask, the answer is always going to be no.

Chapter 8

Some of my favourite childhood memories centre around Christmas Eve and that giddy feeling of something amazing about to happen. As I grew older, that was replaced with the fizzy excitement of a driving test or university placement, knowing that each corner could change my life. It was the anticipation of everything not quite in my grasp, but waiting right around the corner, which is how I feel about life right now.

My night was spent switching between job rejection emails and trawling RightMove. Competitive me got riled up each time my inbox pinged, hoping for that change of direction I was desperately after. But each job I lost out on only spurred me on to want to find the perfect building for my gallery.

I picked through listing after listing of similar sized buildings, in both London and Sheffield, comparing features, locations and costs. That way, no one could accuse me of jumping the gun and racing for the first option that popped out. But of all the places I found, modern or classic, none of them felt right. I couldn't see my dreams reflected in their windows the way I could the old bank building.

Speaking to Lainey only solidified my feelings. I could use the money I had saved for a deposit to pay the rent. I wasn't flush by any stretch, but I had enough to get the business up and running. After all the calculations and what-ifs, I worked out I had six months to prove myself.

In that time, I could host an amazing opening night – because parties – and be in business long enough to know whether my experiment worked. At the end of that time, if it hadn't worked out, I could pull the pin knowing I'd at least tried. Wasn't that the least I could ask of myself? Losing money was a risk I was going to have to take, no matter how scary it was.

I scribble the number of the estate agent down in the front of my diary, but waiting for the morning to roll around so I could call was like waiting for my lotto numbers to come up.

Phone pressed to my ear, I pace my kitchenette as the dial tone rings out a handful of times. It's almost midday before I do get hold of someone and, when we get to talking schedules, the earliest I can see the building is Wednesday. I flop back on the sofa and stare at the ceiling. A spider scurries away.

This isn't the worst thing in the world. While I'm in London, I'm a few hours away anyway, but knowing that isn't stopping the bird in my ribcage from dive-bombing into every window it can find in the great comedown.

Still, it's an opportunity. Before I get onto the big-ticket item of a venue, I can't walk into this venture without knowing my competition or my game plan. With nothing else to do, I toss an overnight bag in my car and shoot back up to Sheffield to study some of the galleries in the area.

Dad dances on the spot at the sight of me strolling into his store mid-afternoon, takeaway cup in hand, muffin in my mouth and looking for a place to sleep. There'd never be any problem staying with him, but it's always polite to ask. The store is empty aside from him.

'I can't say this is a massive surprise.' He smiles as he downs a box of brushes and crosses the store to hug me.

'Okay if I camp with you a few nights?' I say. 'Until Wednesday?'

'What surprises me is you went home in the first place,' he says. 'You can't shake it, can you? That building, I mean.'

I wrinkle my nose and jiggle my head a bit. 'I think I'm going to do it.'

'Good.' He grins as he begins unwinding a key from his keychain. 'Well, you have my support.'

'You don't have to do that.' I dangle my old keys from my finger, brimming with all the touristy charms and keyrings a university student would pick up in her first year in London. 'If it's okay, I'll be home for dinner. I've got some things to do first.'

'Haven't developed any allergies, have you?' he calls after me. 'All that fancy London food?'

'I'll bring the wine,' I answer as I shoulder my way out the door and walk to the first gallery on my list.

I can't pretend I'm going to be the first person to own a business. It would be stupid to do so. There are always going to be others. But if I'm going to survive past the first few months, I need to find my point of difference. What are others doing, and what was I going to bring to the table that would be so completely unique that I'll be overrun with artists jostling to show their wares?

Talking to gallery owners as I wander the city gives me an opportunity to start piecing together what's happening in the area, how they source their art and who they work with. One has a revolving roster of the same artists. Another that's in an old house and smells of mothballs and old carpet showcases landscapes from only locals, and another that's strictly modern art has a dedicated student space. Still, it's not quite right for me.

I want an openness and inclusivity, and an ever-changing schedule will bring fresh, exciting voices that capture attention. Whether they're modern art or classic doesn't bother me. I know from my work at Webster that I can straddle both worlds. And, as much as I'd love to be able to headline with massive artists, I need to be realistic. Until I make a name for myself, the big names will be elusive. I hate to admit that he's right, but Christopher Dunbar may very well be exactly who I need right now.

I return to Dad's that first night with my mind brimming with ideas. Scribbled notes become mind maps, directives, exhibition ideas and sketches of an imagined floor layout. An unexpected bonus of all this brainstorming is that it unlocks something I'd long thought buried. I was now desperate to get my old camera out.

Late Tuesday afternoon finds me in Loxley Common with Fiona's digital camera dangling from my neck. It's not quite my old film camera – I'd left that one back in London – but it scratched an itch. The urge to create art had been nudging at the base of my mind for months, but I'd ignored it in favour of corporate life and ladder climbing.

Now, I hungrily snap images of the world around me. Because it's been so long, self-doubt rears her shouty head as I try to get an old gate in focus, but I do my best to ignore the noise in favour of capturing something, anything. It works, and I'm soon zooming and framing trees and playing with dappled light and a spare lens I'd packed.

By the time I arrive home to the smell of what would be an amazing dinner, it's starting to feel natural again, like those university summers spent with fingers imprinted with the ridges of a shutter button. With shots of trees and textures, benches and neighbourhood fences loaded from the memory card, my laptop begins to resemble a small studio. Photos are loaded and cleaned up as I dabbled with editing software I was sure I'd long forgotten how to use. It makes me miss having the school darkroom to use at a whim. Film cameras are so much more fun than this.

A darkroom. I scrawl that quickly on my notepad, too.

I go to bed satisfied with my lot for the day. I'm okay. Today has helped me remember that I'm good at this. *Take that*, Kit,

Christopher, whatever your bloody name is. As I drift off to sleep, I cross my fingers and hope the building I'm about to inspect is everything I've dreamt it to be.

I'm out the front door hours before I need to be on Wednesday, telling myself I can grab breakfast and jot down questions while I wait. Sitting in a café on the high street proves near impossible, my leg trampolining around the place, so I get up and walk off my anxious energy on the way to West Bar. It feels like the slowest thirty minutes on record, and I catch every red pedestrian crossing known to man.

When I turn in from the main street, I skip out onto the kerb and look up to see the building hovering above me. From the outside, it's just as incredible as the photos. Built during the Victorian era, there's plenty of beige stone and tall, arched windows. There's a small car park off the side street, which is overgrown and very green, but cleaning it will be the easiest part of the whole project, I'm sure of it.

One of the appeals of the building is the corner location: twice as visible to the passing traffic. Even though there's old mail stuffed through the door, lying faded and curled on the ground, and the windows are a bit murky, I can see it will be bright and airy when opened to its potential. I just hope it's structurally sound.

Though I first saw it in the newspaper on the weekend, I didn't stop for a look on the way home. With my ideas still in their infancy, it hadn't even crossed my mind. But, before I've even shuffled through the front door, I can tell the building is absolutely breathtaking. I know my decision already, for better or worse.

'Katharine?'

I pull away from where I've got a hand cupped on the window. 'That's me, hello.'

'Ava. We spoke on the phone earlier?' The bangles on her wrist jingle in time with the building keys and, before we can finish our introductions, I'm breathing in the dusty scent of a room that's been locked for months.

'What do you think?' Ava hands me a glossy brochure to accompany the tour.

'I think I'm in love.' I peer up at the original parts of the ceiling, moulded plaster that's shaped into long rectangles. It's a Gatsby touch, something that makes the place feel a little more homely and will add weight to the notion that this is a serious business. Because it is, duh.

'Excellent. I'm glad to hear. Now, as you can see the bottom floor is quite bare, which is great.' Ava reaches out to the wall and a bank of grey pendant lights flicker to life. 'It's a blank canvas for you to do whatever you want, right?'

Even if some of the walls look like they've been painted after a game of pin the tail on the colour wheel, I can see what she means. One of the rooms tucked away in the ground floor warren is screaming out for a small gift shop where visitors can purchase prints of all the beautiful art they see and exclusives from local makers, and I'm already inspired by the idea of the flow of traffic around the space and through all the rooms.

'Polished floorboards for the most part, though they're a bit scuffed.' She flashes her hand about her feet. 'If you come upstairs, I'll show you the living quarters.'

As I climb the stairs behind her, I spy the carpeted room that formed the 'most' clause of her previous sentence. It's grotty and stained, but I'm blinded by love. The upstairs area isn't exactly the height of sophistication either. Floorboards are worn back to bare wood in spots, laminate is peeling from the cupboards above the sink, and the oven looks about forty years old and is covered in scratches. But it works. Right now, that's all I need. I can build up from here. Plus, there's a certain charm about the old dame that makes up for the lack of aesthetic.

'The last tenant operated a clothing store from the ground floor,' Ava explains.

There's enough storage space, and an en suite bathroom, so living here would be a piece of cake. In fact, it looks like it would be amazing fun. There's space for an office and maybe even a darkroom. It's the perfect plan. There aren't nearly enough film developers anymore and hiring the room out to photographers could bring some extra income. I'm so buoyed by the idea I might float off down the nearest drain and into the River Don.

'Any thoughts?' Ava closes the door on a bathroom that has surprisingly modern fixtures. This whole building is an eclectic mix of the last 150 years.

'I absolutely love it.' As I say this, a thrill chases itself around the back of my mind. 'It's everything I need.'

'Glad to hear it.' She smiles. 'Would you like to make an offer?'

'This has been on the market for a while, hasn't it?' I begin. My stomach begins to roll like foam on an ocean.

'It has,' she says. 'We have had a lot of interest though. In fact, we've got another party coming to view it this afternoon.'

'And, if I'm honest, it's way out of my price range right now.'

Her face falls. Actually, it doesn't so much fall as a mid-winter storm passes over it. 'Right.'

I try and still the air with a hand. 'Would the vendor be interested in, say, a six-month lease? I can pay equivalent rent with an option to purchase at the end of the agreement. If they find a buyer in the meantime, we can renegotiate.'

She considers me for a moment, the corners of her mouth pinching. I need to work harder to convince her.

'And these walls really need painting,' I continue. 'In fact, you might find a lot of buyers aren't in love with the array of colours. What I was thinking was a solid single colour. I'm happy to do the painting – and any other work – at my own expense, if that'll help sweeten the deal?'

'I'm going to have to talk to the vendor,' she says slowly, eyes darting about as she starts pointing to the stairs. 'Let me just make the call.'

She disappears and I'm left on tenterhooks, thinking about how my dreams could vanish in the space of two little letters. I can hear passing traffic outside, the pneumatic hiss of another bus doing the rounds, and it sounds completely different to the echoes of the city. Without anything other than Lainey's not-quite-sound financial advice, this might be the dumbest thing I've ever done, even sillier than skydiving in New Zealand or bungee jumping at a festival or that time Lainey and I thought drunk rollerblading through the middle of Sheffield at 3 a.m. downhill and against traffic was a great idea.

Who am I kidding? At least this won't kill me. Bankruptcy, yes. Death, no.

As a distraction, I check my inbox. Again. In a moment of weakness late last night, after a few too many glasses of cava and some textual prodding from Fiona, I sent a query through to Christopher's website. She said he'd called her on Monday and asked after me, wanting to know more about my role at Webster. Maybe it was a sign he wanted to show his work after all. Who knows? As Lainey said, I wouldn't know if I didn't ask.

I did my best to play it cool and casual and give off more of an 'it was great to meet you' vibe than anything else. Slipped into the end matter, I mentioned I was thinking about opening my own gallery and would like to talk to him about the possibility of a collaboration. If he was still interested.

It's been crickets ever since. Some business he's trying to run if he's not prepared to answer enquiries. I scroll his website again. There are new photos – a piece by him with a hefty sale price attached. He must have seen my email. He can't not have, when you think of all the steps we take when we get online, all the little procrastinating tools we use before getting to the big stuff of doing actual work. I keep flicking through until I find his phone number and hit the dial button.

Then, I wait.

My heart thuds in time with the *whop, whop, whop* of a helicopter flying closely overhead. I have no idea why he evokes this feeling in me; I've made these types of calls dozens, possibly even hundreds of times before. He's an artist, I'm an—

'Christopher Dunbar.'

My breath catches in a pinch at my side as he cuts off my thoughts. 'Christopher, hello. It's Katharine Patterson, how are—'

The dial tone sounds in my ear. I don't want to think he's hung up on me deliberately but, when I try his number again, it's otherwise engaged. I blow him a raspberry, if only to make myself feel better, and stare at my phone in disbelief.

'Are you okay?' Ava's managed to sneak upstairs and is standing in the kitchenette with me now.

'Me? Yeah, just—' I pull my tongue back in my mouth and drop my phone into my handbag '—just a client.'

'It's like that, isn't it?' she says in a show of solidarity. 'And I've just spoken to *my* client, who is happy to run with a short-term lease.'

'They are?' I squeak.

She smiles like this is a relief for her, too. 'Better to make some money than have it sit here empty, he tells me. Actually, I told him that but, you know, men. He was also very keen on the idea of someone other than him painting the place, strangely enough. So, if you'd like to come back to the office, I'll get some paperwork sorted.'

'Absolutely yes.'

My brain is furry at the sides, a horse with blinkers on as I follow her downstairs and out the door. I don't even register that she's locking the place up because all I can think is: *I did it*. I bloody well did it, and I want to shake and scream and jump up and down, but that might not come off as one hundred per cent professional businesswoman, so I smile demurely and tell her I'll meet her at her office in twenty minutes.

'You've got a lawyer, haven't you?' she asks, holding her car door open. 'Just to get them to look through the paperwork?'

'I might know one or two,' I say.

'Excellent. See you soon.' She slips into her Vauxhall, and I wait for her car melt into the traffic before I scream with delight and dance around on the spot.

An elderly lady gives me a look and scuttles across the street to avoid me.

Chapter 9

I race back to London, calling Dad from the motorway, my brain already a New Year's Eve of firing synapses and bursts of ideas. There's so much to do I can scarcely sit still, and my bladder has me stopping at more services than I'd like. I'm strangely appreciative of finding myself in the gridlock of Wednesday afternoon London traffic, relying on tooting horns and emergency sirens to sweep the noise inside my head away.

'Dad said to keep my eyes peeled.' Adam smiles. I've bypassed home in favour of his office. His and John's secretary, Natalie, lets me straight through without the charade of checking if he has time. 'So, what's the deal?'

'Are you alone?' I take a cautious step into the office, craning my neck towards John's desk. I'd rather talk to him about this in private, not through some third-wheel discussion I might be having with my brother.

'For now.' Adam waves me in. 'Come in, come in. Tell me what's going on.'

Their office is starkly neutral and modern and not at all what I think of when I imagine a lawyer's office. My mind automatically goes to rich green leather and mahogany furniture, Don Draper and aged whisky, but this is all bright beech

and monochrome that looks like it belongs in an IKEA catalogue.

Even the building looks like a Lloyd's of London afterbirth.
Adam's on the third floor, civil law. It's vastly quieter than crim-
inal on the ground floor or family on the second floor.

'Well?'

I bounce on the spot. 'I'm going to do it. I'm doing it. It's
mine. They agreed I can rent; I can paint the walls. I can open
my gallery.'

Adam rests back in his oversized leather chair, forearms hoisted
up on the armrests. He looks relieved at my news. 'That's so great!
You sounded set on it even at the weekend. Congratulations.'

Managing to trip over my step, I take a seat on the other side
of his desk and toss my contract down in front of him. My leg
jiggles again. 'Can you check this?'

He leans forward and presses his glasses up his nose. 'You
know I won't represent you, right? If anything goes wrong, I don't
want to get caught in the middle. I can read it, give you my
opinion and then get someone else to read through it. Might take
a day or two.'

'That's fine.' I flail out into the seat. 'Oh, but I want to do it
now!'

'And not your boyfriend, either.' Adam looks at me, brows
raised. 'But, do me a favour?'

'Sure.'

He nods his head in the direction of the other side of the
room. 'Tell him before you sign anything.'

I scowl. 'My career isn't dependent on him.'

'I know that,' he says, exasperated. 'And I know I'm not his
biggest fan, but I think you should at least tell him what you're
doing before you pack up and move away.'

'It's not *that* far,' I say. Now I've stopped moving, I can feel
exhaustion seeping into my limbs. I need a nap. 'But I was definitely planning on telling him.'

'It will be too far for a relationship,' Adam says. 'Especially where he's concerned. You know the hours he keeps. I know we used to fly up the motorway on weekends, but do you think he's going to do that on the regular while you're busy getting established, or vice versa?'

As much as I hate to admit it, he has a point. Still not changing my mind about the gallery though. I pull my phone out and dial John's number. Adam pokes his tongue out at me.

'Hello, you,' John answers. 'Just letting you know I have to be quick. I'm about to walk into a meeting.'

'Where are you?' I ask.

'Heading into a coffee shop,' he says. 'I'm talking a client through a contract.'

I hear the cry of a door hinge in the background. 'Right. Listen, are you still free tonight? Remember we talked about catching up? I need to talk to you about something.'

'Tonight?' he asks. 'How important is it?'

'It's fairly important,' I drawl. Adam shakes his head. 'I have news. Big news.'

Silence stretches out long enough for me to make out the chatter of a queue and the shout of a coffee order. My heart freezes and, immediately, I wish I hadn't rung.

'John?' I ask. 'Are you there?'

'You're not pregnant, are you?' he asks.

'What? No.' I draw back and pull at face at the receiver.

'What is it, then? Is it something we can talk about over the phone?' he tries. 'I can give you a ring when I get in tonight.'

'I'd rather not,' I say, watching my brother leave the office. 'Can we meet for supper?'

'Not really, no,' he says. 'I'll probably be here for another hour, then back to the office until about nine or ten.'

My shoulders slip. 'Okay. All right.'

'I'm sorry, I'm flat out this week,' he scrambles. 'I know I said midweek would be good, but it's just not.'

'We're all busy,' I grumble.

'Listen, we've got a work dinner Friday night. Why don't you come to that?'

'You mean those things I've not otherwise been invited to?' I ask, surprised at the sudden turn of conversation. 'This is a new one.'

'Yeah, well, everyone knows now. So, may as well.'

'My, don't dial up the romance too much,' I say.

'I'll text you through the details,' he says, greeting people in the background. 'Maybe we can skip out early and grab supper then.'

'Sure.' I huff.

'You okay?' he asks, already focused on something other than me.

'Perfectly good,' I lie.

My balloon bursts. Not that it was unexpected, but his dismissal and distance feel like a rollercoaster that has slid to a halt at the top of an incline. I finish the call quickly and let him get back to his meeting.

Adam returns with two mugs and a packet of biscuits dangling from his mouth, which results in a crinkly, muffled, 'You o'right?'

Leaning on the armrest, I place my chin in the palm of my hand. 'He is who he is.'

We split some Jammie Dodgers, dunking them into coffee that's far too fancy for an office as we chat about the weekend. Though I sense Adam is avoiding the heavy topics, especially with his carefully chosen words, I let him ramble about how he wishes we'd stayed in Sheffield the whole weekend and not done the Sunday dawn flee.

We both admit we've been far too caught up in our own bubbles lately. He's missing the simple things, beers with friends, relaxing with a football match and not being in the office maybe a little more than I was, and I make him promise he'll visit once I move.

93

'Visit? I'll be helping you move, don't worry about that.' He pokes his tongue out. 'Get you out of here.'

I laugh. 'You would.'

When he drops a hint about his own meeting, I gather my things and tuck a copy of the contract in my bag. Before I can say thank you, Adam stops me with a sharp shake of his head. No thanks needed; it's what we do.

'How are things in here?' Honestly, I'm scared of the answer, but also oddly curious. 'Not awkward at all?'

Adam smirks. 'Besides being unfairly traumatised by the sight of your boyfriend's penis?'

'Besides that.'

'It's like a daily virtual turkey slap,' he says with a chuckle. 'Every time he walks past, all I can think of is a backyard hammock.'

I nearly choke on the final crumbs in my mouth. 'Stop it.'

'Did you tell him to sod off?' Lainey slips from the stool by my kitchen counter and follows me to the sofa. We land with a huff and I pull my legs up under me.

'What? No.' I frown. 'He said he was busy, so, you know. I should be taking that on face value because, well, he is busy.'

'God, what is it with men right now?' she blurts. 'Actually, what is it with men all the bloody time?'

As I left my brother's office, I realised how grumpy I was about John's response. This is important to me. Opening a gallery may be the biggest thing I end up doing but, somehow, his job always comes first, even if I need to talk about something crucial. What if I was pregnant? Chances are he'd have made me wait until Friday to tell him anyway.

I called Lainey and she showed up on my doorstep with a bottle of wine in one hand, Chinese takeaway in the other, ready to rage through John's shortcomings, which were becoming more obvious by the day. Oh, and my big news. We both screech with excitement at the rental agreement, and she helps brainstorm as I blather about designs and ideas. We segue into wedding demands which turns into more seething at John before we get back on to the gallery.

'Are you going to?' Lainey asks, spreading the sweating plastic containers across my coffee table. 'Tell him to take a hike, that is.'

'As much as I want to say that's a difficult decision right now, I think he's going to make it for me.' I offer her a glass of wine and we toast this new chapter of our lives. 'I mean, I get it. He's busy. Adam's forever busy, but at least he makes time if I tell him it's important. He always has. I remember I'd barely been in London six months when my car broke down on the motorway. He skipped right out of work, bought a battery, and sorted me out before heading back to an afternoon of court. I can't even get a coffee out of John.'

'Yes, but that's because he's your brother and he loves you.' Wine sloshes about in Lainey's glass as she leans forward and gives me a look that says, *And John doesn't*.

'You were right, you know.' I swap my glass out for a bowl full of rice and Szechuan chicken.

'About what?' she asks. 'Also, yes, of course I was right but, please, continue.'

'I'm just going to tell him,' I say. 'I'm going to tell him he can be part of this if he wants to. But, if it's all too hard then thanks for the memories.'

'It's a fair approach,' she says, one shoulder grazing the bottom of her ear. 'It's not, not true.'

'It sucks though because I really did think he might be it.' I sigh. 'Only I could tangle myself up in knots like this.'

'The One is out there.'

'If I don't go to seed first,' I say with an empty laugh.

'Speaking of knots, did you catch up with your new bestie while you were up north?' Lainey asks.

'My what now?' I ask. 'If you're referring to the magnificent Mr Dunbar, that's a big fat no. And he's definitely not my bestie.'

She wrinkles her nose. 'Not even for a brew?'

'He's so weird.' I frown, batting some paperwork from the coffee table. 'I called him because I did actually want to talk to him about the gallery while I was up there.'

'And?'

'He hung up on me.'

Lainey roots around in her bag, phone appearing quickly while muttering about what his problem might be. Google doesn't reveal much more about him. There are articles about the opening of small shows, photos of his anxious smile staring out from the screen, records of what his work has sold for, but nothing else comes up.

Dad said he stopped showing two years ago, but that doesn't explain him touching base with Webster, or his dogged questioning of me. There's no big bang, no scandal to indicate the end of a career. He simply disappeared. In the end, we toss the phone aside in favour of finishing dinner. I already know that's going to be much more satisfying than trying to work out the riddle of Christopher Dunbar.

'He's certainly a bit of a mystery, isn't he?' Lainey asks, moving to refill my glass.

I beat her to the punch and cover it with my hand. No more wine tonight.

'It's more than that though. I'm just so sick of coming up against people in this business who discount me because I'm female or don't have the right connections or I've never held a show of my own work. It's like a rite of passage. It feels like: no show, no skill.' I look up from my meal. 'Hell, Christopher thinks I'm terrible because I like classic art. You cannot honestly tell me I wasn't qualified for the job at the gallery.'

'You absolutely were qualified,' Lainey says, chopsticks paused mid-air. 'And you do have the connections. All anybody has been able to talk about this week is "Why did Katharine walk out?", "How did she *not* get that job?" Sally says hello, by the way, wants to catch up when the dust settles. Frankly, I think Steve is feeling the pinch. Mind you, that little germ has been running around with that shit-eating grin he always wore after corporate meetings.'

'Probably because that's exactly what he was doing in those meetings,' I bite. 'He always did have terrible halitosis.'

'Do you know what he did today?' She's already smiling as she leans forward. 'He came over to ask me how to change his email signature. His bloody signature. And they want him running the place? It's absurd. And Frank wonders why I want out.'

'Have you heard about your interview yet?' I ask.

She shakes her head.

My shoulders fall. If they gave Steve the job and he's completely incapable of the basics, what does it say about what they thought of me? Am I worse than that? I won't lie when I say my confidence has taken a hit. For all my tiny victories this week, doubt seeps in, in the middle of the night and keeps me awake. And, given I haven't the faintest idea where I'm going to begin when it comes to the gallery, I'm wondering if they weren't on to something.

'And they picked him over me?' I ask.

'They'll work him out soon enough,' she says gaily. 'Just kick back, relax and wait for the shit show to begin.'

'That's the thing though. I can't relax. I don't have the time to relax.' I scratch at my forehead and try to think of all the things I need to get done. 'On the way home today, I was just thinking that there's social media, business contracts, marketing, finding artists who'll answer their phones, and that's just the stuff visible from space.'

I feel a little peaky at the idea. It's the kind of panic that leads to procrastination and watching telly all night but doing that would only stoke the anxiety fire so badly I'd end up with first degree guilt over doing nothing.

'Katie, you have had a whirlwind of a week. Why don't you stop, just for tonight? Run a bath and mainline some Epsom salts. It'll do you good.' She waggles the wine bottle as I walk over to the kitchen. 'Get drunk.'

'I wish I could.' I stand staring into an empty refrigerator. 'But if I sign this contract, I get the keys on Saturday because they're desperate for rent and, really, how much time do I have to waste? I'm on a six-month lease. Less, if they get a buyer, so I need to make this happen. Like, yesterday.'

'When are you planning on opening?' she asks.

'Ideally, in a fortnight.'

'Is that realistic? You've got to do your financials and register a business and all that paperwork, which Frank can help you with, by the way.' She waves a hello from the sofa. 'That's me, your friendly neighbourhood accountant pimp.'

'All right.' I grab for my diary and flip through to a yearly planner. 'Let's say four to six weeks, then. Is that long enough?'

She nods and shrugs and begrudgingly agrees. 'Think about it, by the time you get the artists, insurance, and advertising, let alone cleaning the place up. It's not going to be easy, and it's all you.'

'It is,' I answer. 'All me.'

'So, what do you need to do to make that happen? Let's put together a list.'

I glance up at the wall clock. The time is nudging 9 p.m.

'Oh, no, you don't have to. You've probably ... won't Frank be waiting for you to get home? You guys are weeks away from getting married. There must be a million things you'd rather be doing for that. Never mind the fact it's a weeknight.'

'That's *exactly* why I'm here.' She offers me a sarcastic look. 'Honestly, I'm sick of dealing with it right now. Plus, you've helped me a lot lately, so let me do this for you.'

'Is everything okay there?' I ask. 'All the plans are coming along?'

'Oh, hell yeah,' she says. 'It's the little things now. Stationery, order of service, that kind of thing. After they're done, I just have to turn up on the day.'

'And you probably should turn up.'

'Right, so what do you need?' she asks. 'Think back to your Webster days. Hopefully, you haven't completely dumped us already. What has to happen to get this up and running?'

'A million dollars would be a great start,' I joke. 'A few sugar daddies.'

Lainey cringes. 'Ideal but can't quite help you on that one. I could crowdfund you a Happy Meal though.'

I laugh and rest against the counter. 'I need artists. I need an opening exhibition. And, for all my moaning, I do want to ask Christopher. He's local, he's seemingly well connected, so he'll draw a crowd, but he's not answering my calls. Or messages.'

'Forget about him,' she says. 'He's rude. We don't have time for people like him. Plus, you already know plenty of other artists. You *do* have connections, despite your sad, sad woe-is-me face. And we have my little red book. You don't need him.'

We find the list of names we wrote down the other day and highlight a few of the best with big red asterisks. I know I want new and local artists, but a stable of popular favourites will help get the gallery off to a positive start. They can bring the attention before I swoop in with local artists.

In the end, my list contains old friends from university, or people I've met in my day-to-day life at the museum. This gives me a solid pool of over fifty contacts to begin with. Seeing so many names before me gives a bit of life to the plan. It doesn't feel quite so monumental for these five minutes.

'Now I need something to email them about, right? Social media, website, that kind of thing,' I say. 'We used to have this pro forma at the museum. Mail merge or something similar. Hello, insert name here, thought you'd be keen to know about the new gallery.'

'Now you're cooking.' Lainey stuffs her fork in her mouth. 'Start by getting them interested in the place first. Have you set up your socials at least? Invited everyone to like them yet?'

'No, no.' I shake my head, heading back to the sink for a glass of water. 'I didn't want to do anything until I was certain this was a thing. You know, jumping the gun and all.'

'Well, now that you are.' She smiles broadly and cracks her knuckles. 'This is where I use my superpowers.'

With a laptop nestled on the coffee table between us, we upload photos and think up page names. I keep it simple, deciding to name my gallery the Katharine Patterson Gallery. Simple. While I pace the living room talking about fresh talent, positive space, innovative gallery, Lainey shapes it into something that sounds snappy, sophisticated, and completely bloody brilliant. I don't have a logo yet, nor do I have any branding, but that's not something I can solve on a Wednesday evening.

'Actually, it is,' Lainey says as she swipes at her phone. 'I know this amazing guy who does a bit of work for Webster. He's got me out of a pickle at short notice before. His business has really kicked on after getting some big-name brands on board. When he started, he was only doing websites, but now he does socials, branding, everything. Actually, I think Frank's company might've used him as well.'

I reach for my phone. 'Let's call him.'

Even though it's late, he answers and is more than happy to accommodate. In fact, he's chomping at the bit for a quick bit of cash. Ninety minutes later, my bank balance is a touch lighter, but I'm sitting on my sofa looking at a placeholder website with an introduction, location details, a biography and contact form, all in elegant black and white with a classic font that will be easy enough to turn into signage. I've got header images for social media, suitable profile pictures, and I'm feeling like I've hit the jackpot. Sure, it's simple, and perhaps I could have done it myself if I had time to waste, but if I'm going to do this on my own, I'm going to have to learn to delegate tasks.

As we work our way through one final coffee, we invite friends, family, anyone who's (un)fortunate enough to be a social media contact, to view my new gallery page. Watching the likes, shares, and comments trickle in is a funny thing. I don't expect a sudden influx of interest, but I know from university that artists have a brilliant whisper network. We can sniff out oil paints and dark-room chemicals at fifty per cent off, local arts trails, and empty galleries that are calling out for talent.

Still, I'm surprised when half a dozen friends become twenty, then forty and, within the hour, my inbox starts pinging with people keen to get into the gallery. *My* gallery. There's no point pretending to be blasé about it; I'm absolutely thrilled. Things are heading in the right direction. Already.

'This is such a great response,' Lainey says, clapping her hands against her thighs. 'Now, you know you've forgotten the most important thing, right?'

'I have?' I ask, scrolling through my inbox for the umpteenth time. 'Everything looks in order. We've got everything, right?'

'Hello.' Lainey smiles. 'The party on opening night.'

Chapter 10

'I have a question for you.' With the phone wedged between my ear and shoulder, I run a towel over my head and cast a glance around my bedroom.

It looks like a tornado has blown through. There's a suitcase flung open against the wall like I'm in holiday mode, ticket stubs and receipts dug out of drawers sit by the alarm clock, and a small shelving unit that once lived in my wardrobe is now upturned by the window.

In less than twenty-four hours, I'm moving halfway across the country and I am not prepared.

'Shoot,' John says. I can hear him flipping mindlessly through paper.

'What's the dress code tonight?' I ask.

'Oh,' he pips, realising we've not yet discussed this. 'Ah, semi-formal. It's not tops and tails, thankfully but, you know, *nice*.'

'Fancy wedding?' I spy the perfect red cocktail dress in my wardrobe. It shimmers in a way that gives off a whiff of expense, but the only silky part is the lining. I scoop the rest of my clothing out onto my bed. All that's left hanging are tonight's dress and tomorrow's jeans.

'Exactly,' he says. 'Great analogy.'

Silence fills the line as I wait for him to maybe initiate a deeper discussion.

'Katharine?' he asks. 'Are you there?'

'Yes,' I say. 'Are you?'

'Anything else?' he says.

'It might help if you told me a bit more about this dinner. Where is it? What time? Should I meet you there, or would you like me to come straight to your place?'

'Shit,' he hisses. I can picture him pinching the bridge of his nose. 'Sorry. My brain is all over the place this week, just trying to get everything done before tonight. I'm leaving straight from here. Can I text you the address?'

'Sure, okay, fine.' I rub at my temple as I shake my head. 'I'll see you there.'

I was hoping we'd leave from his flat, that we'd share a glass or two of wine while we got ready. It would limber me up enough to tell him my news. Naturally, he'd be devastated that I'm moving home but swear to give his enthusiastic support and we'd dash off into the night ready to take on the world knowing things were moving in a positive direction. Instead, the phone rings off and there's no invite; it's just me and my jumble sale flat. Nerves settle in the back of my throat.

I've spent the last two days packing and cleaning, raiding my local café for hot pies and cardboard boxes. My letting agent wasn't thrilled I was leaving, insisting I pay out the final twelve weeks of rent as per the agreement. More money I can't afford down the gurgler. And I've enlisted Adam's help to drive the moving truck. He really wasn't joking when he said he'd see me out of town.

At first, my packing was an enthused loop of neatly folding clothes, making sure the rest were washed and ready to tuck into a suitcase that's seen me around the world and back again. Crockery and cutlery were swaddled in newspaper, with only requisite stranglers left on show, and my rubbish bin began overflowing with food packets that appear to have expired eighteen months ago. Clearly cooking is not my forte.

Sorry, Mum.

I excavated old items from the back of my wardrobe, becoming distracted by photos and shoes I hadn't seen in years, and the odd dog-eared paperback that had fallen behind the bed. There were stacks of things for keeping and for throwing away, and carefully balancing items atop of boxes that were too full to close.

Later, a text message arrives from John. There's an address and a 'can't wait to see you' tacked on the end. I slip the important things – ID, bank card and lipstick – into the pocket of my dress and make my way out the door. The last thing I see as I leave is my new rental contract stuck to the refrigerator door.

When I arrive at the sleek concrete and glass function centre near Blackfriars, I expect to find John waiting for me. It seems like the polite thing to do, something you might do for the woman you're apparently seeing. Twenty minutes later, when it becomes clear that's not going to happen, my previous excitement at what tonight could mean flits out the door as I walk in.

My name is on the guest list which, for some reason, surprises me. I'm guided inside and towards the lift lobby.

Moments later, I step out onto a balcony that looks like it's been dropped from a Hollywood movie. Views of the London Eye, OXO Tower and the Monument shimmer in the gloaming. There are tall potted plants dotted around herringbone parquetry floors, stools with spaghetti strap legs and small bar benches to place drinks upon. John spots me, an almost surprised look dancing across his face as he breaks away from a group in the corner.

How he manages to make a plain black suit look so suave at the end of a full day of work is beyond me, but he does. My irritation ebbs momentarily.

'You look good enough to skip the party for.' He beams as he leans in to kiss me, his blue eyes sparkling under the lights. 'Shall we?'

'Skip the party?' I ask, the scent of his aftershave drifting between us. 'Please. You smell fantastic.'

'You're not so bad yourself.' With a hand on the small of my back, he guides me towards the bar where I order a cocktail and a dose of courage.

We're surrounded by suits and ties, tuxedos even, that tell me this is a little more than 'fancy wedding' formal, and it feels like such a world away to what I'm used to. My job or, should I say, my old job paid well enough and our corporate nights were always a treasure trove of fun, but there's something next level about tonight.

I feel eyes settling on me. People who'd always associated me with my brother, who's not here yet, are now realising there's something else happening. Something they didn't know about. I can see the surprise in their eyes and hear it in the whispered questions as we flash past people on our way to a quiet corner. Rupert, his boss, reaches out to shake my hand as I pass.

'Are you not going to introduce me to your boss?' I ask.

'Don't you already know him?' John places his drink on the ledge and slips his hands in his pockets. 'Anyway, you wanted to talk about something.'

I did. But now, knowing he doesn't want to introduce me, I wonder if he truly deserves to know anything at all? I look at him, his features set somewhere between interrogation and concern.

'Maybe later.' I chase the straw in my cocktail around and take a large sip.

'Oh,' he says, surprised. 'It seemed rather important, is all.'

'Yes, that's why I wanted to tell you during the week,' I simper.

His brow folds into a valley. Even I'm surprised at my response. I hadn't meant to bite. Well, not so hard, but it's been one hell of a week and, really, is a few hours of his time too much to ask?

As it turns out, I can answer that question: yes, it is. Everything I wanted to say slips back down into a quiet place and I say nothing. We're called into dinner, which is when I catch Adam slipping into the function. Solo.

I wish Sophie were here. She would be a friendly face and someone to talk to over the chorus of shoptalk that settles onto our table. Adam explains that she's working late in Hampstead but said to say hello. Conversation quickly turns to rulings and precedent, difficult clients, and ones they wanted to laugh out the door. While I don't mind listening to Adam occasionally, a whole table of people starts to be too much. I'm grateful for the sight of dinner.

Food steals away conversation and stops me having to answer awkward questions from someone to my right. Because, for all my excitement about being invited tonight, I'm painfully aware I have no answers to those questions couples are asked.

How we met is harmless enough, but what about the rest? Do we have plans? I suspect not, and I'm not keen on lying to people, either. But I must, because if I start telling everyone about my new venture, then everyone finds out before the man sitting beside me. Being here tonight is not high up on my list of good ideas. I breathe a sigh of relief when John directs my attention away from a question and towards the front of the room.

'I don't think this next award will come as a surprise to anyone in the room tonight.' Rupert March looks down his nose, past the podium and towards me. He winks as John, who gives my thigh a gentle squeeze as his eyes crinkle up in the type of blissful happiness that should only be reserved for post-coital moments.

'The In House Counsel of the Year award. Or as I like to call it, most billed hours,' Rupert continues over the sound of friendly ribbing at our table. 'I could go on about how everyone's contributions are equally valued, and I can assure you they are. However, I've seen the notes from the cleaners after having kicked this one out the front door in the last dying hours of the evening. John

106

Harrison, you have by far outstripped anyone in this room with your ridiculous eighty-hour weeks. I'm not sure if I should congratulate you or quietly weep at my own ineptitude. And I'm the one who owns the place!'

Derisive laughter combines with enthusiastic clapping to propel John towards the front of the room, not entirely as embarrassed as he should be. For every overworked week, I could guarantee there was an apology in my inbox; a missed date, a cold dinner, or a restaurant I'd been sitting in on my own waiting for a man who'd never arrive.

John takes hold of the heavy glass statue and reads the etching on the base before peering out at the rest of the room. 'Next partner, right here,' he mumbles into the microphone as he waits for the noise to die down.

Still, no matter my annoyance at all those cancelled plans and late nights, I could never begrudge him his ambition. We're all entitled to work towards our own ideal and, watching him stand before everyone in his crisp suit and perfectly coiffed hair, I *am* oddly proud of him. It's in total conflict with every other emotion fighting for space inside me right now, but he is brilliant at his job and he deserves this.

'I fear I must admit though, it's not solely *my* work that has resulted in my being up here tonight. It's a combination of all of you.' He pauses. 'The last-minute emails, thanks, Sarah. The random queries from Michael, you're a champion, and the memes that come from our bastion of good taste, Nicholas. It's Adam sending me to the photocopier because I'm standing by the door and I've somehow looked like I've had nothing to do for thirty seconds. And, by some means, in between that, I get to hang out in court and do my thing for the people.'

He stops talking long enough to take in the adulating laughter that rises above the sound of chinking cutlery and mummering of waiters delivering more wine.

'Now, there is someone I desperately need to thank, someone

I'm forever indebted to and who will put salt in my coffee instead of sugar if I don't mention her.'

Adam reaches across and gives my shoulder a brotherly punch. Pride puffs me out like a seagull, and, for once, all those cancelled dates and cold dinners begin to feel worth it.

'The most important woman in the room. Natalie, my secretary.'

I hear mumbles at the edge of our table. I can't look away from the stage, though I catch Adam cupping a hand over his eyes. I blink a few times and feel the tide recede in my mouth. I'm drier than a sandpit in summer and the taste it leaves behind tells me a cat's been using that sandpit as a litter tray.

'You are the reason the boat is upright when it could have run aground so many times already this year. From organising, chopping and changing meetings, taking all those little calls I don't have time for, suggestions on case notes, and for your first-class attention to detail. I could not have achieved any of this without your knowledge and support. You will always be more than just a secretary.'

My stomach decamps and claws its way across the function room floor, leaving entrails in its wake. Every single set of eyes at our table are fixed on me, waiting for my reaction. The worst part is, I can't do a thing except applaud along with everyone else and give Natalie a watery 'I swear I'm not about to pop' grin. She's offering profuse apologies, but I'm not about to make a scene and ruin everyone's night, as much as I would love that.

Because it's in this moment I realise that, even though I may get my discussion later tonight, we will never amount to a thing. Despite promising me repeatedly that he was open to the idea of a full and proper relationship, against everything I had hoped, he is never going to change.

There'll never be family dinners, engagements, weddings, or a family of our own. I suspect, for John, it was never going to be that in the first place. While the room calms and everyone finishes congratulating both him and Natalie, I sit at the precipice of the table counting a laundry list of ways the last nine months have been a waste of my time. This is why we've never introduced family, why he wanted to keep it 'exclusive, but casual', why he does everything he can to avoid all those hard discussions I want to have.

Now, as I watch him traverse the room, I wonder how I'd never seen this for what it was, how I'd been so epically blind to it all. I am an idiot. While Natalie, bless her, gives off a glassy-eyed beam, everyone else at the table wears a look of awkward expectation. John enters my line of sight, looks at me and freezes.

Finally, he realises his error. His mouth bobs about, a fish in its last gasping breaths. It's not as if he's going to take those words back either. There's no way he'll say, 'Actually, sorry, Natalie, what I meant to say was Katharine', because imagine being the man who tells a woman she's not actually *that* important after all.

I stare right back at him, and I continue to do so, because there is no way I'm giving anyone the slightest reaction. I can hear the shattering crystal in my chest, tinkling down the staircase of my ribs and slicing painful holes in my diaphragm. But I don't move because I can't bear the thought of making a fool of myself in front of these people, my brother's colleagues and bosses.

Don't cry. Don't cry, I tell myself repeatedly, drawing my bottom lip through my teeth and biting down so hard I fear I'll dig a hole through my chin. Around the rushing of blood through my ears, or maybe it's the leaking of my brain, I hear murmurs of 'Oh God', 'Someone pass the popcorn', and 'Can you believe what he just did?'

'Well done.' I smile, my voice mangled. 'Congratulations.'

'Katharine.' He sinks into the seat beside me. 'I am—'

His next few words stumble out like he's auditioning for a mid-Nineties Hugh Grant romcom. So, I'm relieved when someone else takes the initiative to charge their glass, because I am having none of his apology, even when he moves in for an over-the-top kiss. How can he not see this? How is he so utterly blind to the awkward looks being exchanged and my brother mouthing words at me I can't understand?

Like every quality faux pas, the room quickly returns to its normal state, and we're joined by wait staff who are doling out a drab dessert of Belgian chocolate mousse or *tarte au citron*, as if calling it anything other than lemon tart will make it any less bitter. And, God, I know this is not the end of the world, but when he wants to emphasise the most important woman in his room, a woman who happened to not be me, well, my heart crumbles like the biscuit base of the tart in front of me.

'Can I get you a drink?' John asks. 'Would you like to nip outside for that chat?'

Because of course he desperately wants to talk when it involves him making penance.

I draw back and look at him, something like a smile fixed on my face. 'Whisky sour.'

'Since when do you drink whisky?' he asks, amused, narrowing his eyes and drawing his hands across his mouth.

'One for me, too,' Adam speaks up.

It's then I decide that I can't stay in this situation any longer. Sitting here after what's just happened is nothing short of humiliating and, the moment John's back is turned, I stand, say my quiet goodnights and head for the door.

It's not the bus stop I'm racing for. That would mean standing at the corner for twenty minutes so I can wait for the fallout. Instead, I head for the tube. Wind whips around my face and blows my hair into my eyes as I scamper across Blackfriars Bridge and away from him.

Except it doesn't, because he's soon out the door and chasing me down.

'Katharine!' John calls. After all, it's not hard to spot a girl in a red dress late at night. 'Kate!'

A woman with a pushchair, helium balloon bouncing above

her wrist, tries to get my attention, but I push through the crowd pretending like I can't hear either her or John. An overhead announcement is staticky and barely audible, much like the traffic in my brain. Walking towards the blustery end of the platform, I wish I'd remembered to bring my coat tonight.

'Katharine?' John appears. 'What … Where are you going? I went to get a drink and you'd vanished.'

'And thank you *so much* to my girlfriend Katharine.' I glare at him. 'Not the most important person in the room though, just so you know. Probably not even my girlfriend if I'm being honest with her.'

He presses a palm to his forehead and paces. 'Katie.'

'Sure, she can't make coffee like Natalie, but she does have a biblical number of apologetic messages in her inbox, cancelled dates and "Sorry, love, running late" texts. Probably because her boyfriend is too busy filling someone else's inbox.'

He holds a finger up to still me. 'No, no, don't even think about going there.'

'Why not? After all, that was a lovely impassioned speech you gave up there.' I begin. 'About another woman.'

'You know I would never do that to you,' he says helplessly, shoulders dipping.

'Do I?' I raise a brow, crossing my arms over my chest.

John rolls his eyes and my blood boils.

'Nine months.' I point as I stalk towards him. 'Nine thankless months, and tonight is what it amounts to? The first event you've deigned to invite me to, and I get to listen to *that*? I mean, for God's sake, I don't expect a medal, but you thanked everyone in the room but your own bloody girlfriend, then came looking to me for validation as if you'd done the right thing while I had to sit there and pretend like it was nothing.'

'I am so, gah, I am so sorry.' He clasps his hands together. 'Please, you have to believe me. I was up there, and the lights and I was all flustered and … Katharine, I am sorry. You know

111

I value you above every single person in the room.'

'You value me?' I shout. 'What am I? A fucking car?'

John shakes his hands wildly, head swinging to and fro. 'No, no, no, not like that.'

'You know, it certainly explains the late nights.'

'Really? And what about all the times I've called you only to be told you're working late writing some bullshit notes about a finger painting. "Sorry, but unless you want to watch telly on my sofa?"' he ends, mocking me.

Another train blusters in, drops a load of passengers, and zips off down the line again. The force of wind from the train causes his fringe to flap, just a little.

'Are you seriously throwing this back on me now?' I ask. There are commuters at the other end of the platform trying to inconspicuously move closer to the commotion. 'What's wrong with spending a night together at home?'

'Please, just come back to the party,' he pleads. 'Please. There's nobody else. I promise you. It's only ever been you. Only you.'

'Do you love me?' I ask. Even if it were only me, I'd been playing second fiddle to his job for far too long.

'What?'

'It's not difficult,' I say. 'I want to know if you love me.'

'Don't make it about that,' he says.

'Well, you either do or you don't. It's not a difficult question.'

He can't say it because he doesn't. It's the ultimate kick in the guts. I stand in silence and hope for the next train already. He reaches out for my hand. I snatch it away. Now is as good a time as any.

'That thing I wanted to talk to you about?' I say, my voice quavering. 'I'm leaving.'

'You're what?' His head tilts like he hasn't quite heard me correctly. 'What do you mean you're leaving?'

'I'm moving home. To Sheffield.' I swallow down a lump in my throat. 'I quit my job last week. Not that you know because work precedes whatever this was. I wanted to tell you, of course, but you needed to stay and work late with Natalie, so here we are.'

His mouth moves, but nothing comes out. I stop myself from blurting out the reason *why* I'm leaving. It's not his business anymore, and maybe it never was. It makes me wonder if I should have told him any of this at all.

'I can't keep going like this.' I look up at the station monitor. Two minutes and it'll be done. I glance down at my feet momentarily and see the flutter of my heart in the fabric of my dress.

'What do you want from me?' he asks. 'What is it? Is it marriage?'

'I'd like some sort of commitment, yes.' My chin draws back into my neck. 'Is that too much to ask? Or, you know, maybe putting *us* first sometimes would be lovely.'

'And what if I don't want to get married?' he says. 'Then what?'

'And what about having a family? Or have you changed your mind on that, too?'

Eyes cast to the floor, he rakes his fingers through his hair as he shakes his head.

'What was all that garbage about future planning?' I ask. 'Were you just telling me what I wanted to hear? You know what? Don't answer that. You're a lawyer. Adam was right, it's what you're trained to do. I should have known.'

'It wouldn't be fair to leave you to do all the heavy lifting.'

'Don't be so bloody sanctimonious,' I scoff. 'As a woman, it's what I'm stuck with anyway. I'd have to birth them, remember?'

He tips his head back and makes a guttural noise. 'And let's say we do? What happens in ten years' time when I've got my own firm and I'm at work all hours of the day and night? That wouldn't be fair on you or our children.'

Our children. The idea prickles at the back of my eyes.

'So, come home at …' I stop and take a deep breath. 'No. No more. This is circle work. I'm done.'

'You're what? You're done? What do you mean you're done? You can't just walk away.' His gaze follows me as I move towards the approaching train. 'Katharine?'

'Oh, but I can.' I smile as he blurs in my vision. It makes him look like a penguin. 'I really can.'

'Katharine, please, let's just go home and talk this all out. We can work out what we both want and sort something out moving forward.'

Shit, if corporate jargon isn't the original anti-aphrodisiac, I don't know what is.

'No,' I say, my voice breaking.

His porcelain façade cracks. Not much, but enough for me to know I've finally broken through. The corners of his mouth turn downward and, for a brief pause, I'm sure I see his lip tremble. 'Kate, please. I am so … God, I'm so sorry I made you feel like this.'

'What happened in that room, what's been happening all this time, tells me I'm not a priority for you.' I rub my eyes with the heel of my hand and blow out a calming breath as the next train approaches. 'And what the hell is the point of any of this if we aren't each other's priority?'

I step into the carriage and watch as John stands dumbfounded on the platform. He doesn't reach out, step forward or otherwise make a move. He's anchored to the spot and, as the doors sound their alarm and close, he slides quickly into the distance. My final view of him is with his head bowed, shoulders slumped, and hands stuffed in his pockets.

When my front door finally closes behind me that night, I collapse against it and sob for the first time since I walked out of Webster. I cry for my past, for my future, and for everything that has just vanished.

Chapter 11

'You made a grown man cry last night.'

Adam stands at my front door with a greasy bag of breakfast, a wry smile, and what seems suspiciously like a hangover. With a disapproving look, I snatch the bag away and let him into my apartment. It's not quite 7 a.m. on a Saturday, which is no time for anyone to be awake. I'm still in my pyjamas though I've barely slept a wink and, today, I'm moving halfway up the country.

No, it hasn't sunk in yet.

What is striking, however, is the notion that my life has amounted to not much more than a few piles of boxes pushed up against windows and leaning against walls. At least that's how it feels.

'Don't tell me you're here to defend him.' I reach over the kitchen counter and switch on the kettle. 'There'll definitely be salt in someone's coffee today if that's the case.'

'On the contrary.' He meanders through my things. 'I'm proud of you.'

I offer an amused sniff and pilfer the first of three hash browns. As I make coffee, I watch his face change from confused to mildly disgusted when he happens upon underwear that wouldn't fit into my suitcase. He turns his attention to an old coffee mug, which he waggles in the air.

'Do you remember this holiday?' he asks. 'When driving a few hours to Scarborough, and not some ski village in the Alps, was the height of sophistication?'

'I do.' I smile. 'I loved the puffins.'

'You were *obsessed* with those things,' he says, placing the mug back. 'All they did was attack me, the little bastards.'

The memories are a sweet distraction from the dull ache in my chest. As much as last night needed to happen, I'd be silly to try and convince anyone I'm happy about it. Nobody ever wants to feel the way I do right now. Asking Adam to expand on his comment would be nothing more than self-flagellation, but I'm also oddly curious as to the finer details. I tap my nails against the kitchen counter and flip the coin of decision.

'How'd you know he cried?' The question springs forth as I hand Adam his coffee.

'Well, he didn't come back to the party.' He clatters a spoon around in his mug. Gosh, I love my brother, but if he keeps belting the spoon about, I'm going to get him an apprenticeship in the bell tower of a French cathedral. 'But he did call me about an hour after he left. I was already on my way home, so, I thought I'd do the right thing and stop at his place and just ... What the *hell* did you say to him?'

'The truth?' I say, lifting my mug to my mouth.

Adam shakes the last few drops of milk from the carton. 'Anyway, he says he was trying to call you, but you weren't answering. For once, he didn't know what to do with himself and was pacing around the place like his head was on fire.'

I reach for my phone. It's flat, so I toss it back into my handbag. 'And you said?'

'I told him he should probably leave you alone.'

'You're still my brother.' I snap my fingers and offer him a high-five.

'Anyway, he was dumbfounded that you actually pulled the pin. I used the old "the woman is a tea bag" and, when he was calm, left.'

'Tea bag,' I deadpan. 'You equated me to a tea bag?'

'What? Tea bags get stronger in hot water, what are you … oh, no, don't be … why are you the one who makes it grubby? I didn't mean it like *that*.'

Though I laugh, I'm sure Adam knows more than he's telling me. His giveaway is his face. For a lawyer, he's got the worst poker face I've ever seen, at least when he's around family. If there are holes in the dyke, his eyes flit about excitedly and he draws his bottom lip through his teeth, as if chewing half his face off will avert his attention. When it all gets too much, a tiny dimple will form in his left cheek, which it's doing right now.

'Anyway, how are you?' he asks. 'Are you okay? Be honest.'

My cheeks fill with air. 'Not entirely happy about it all.'

'How so?' He leans against the counter and puts his mug down.

'Oh, it's just everything, isn't it?' I scratch at my forehead. 'You go into these things thinking something will come of it. It's all very lovely and sweet, and now I feel like I've wasted my time. And not just with him, but with the job, too. Everything I've spent time building, and now I'm going back in time ten years and moving home.'

'Now, see, Mum would have called this experience to add to life's résumé.' He offers me an understanding smile. 'It'll all come in handy, I promise.'

'Maybe.' I clap my hands together. 'Anyway, let's get this show on the road. I only want to do one trip. I'm sure you feel the same.'

'Funnily enough, I had to stop Dad driving down last night,' he says with a soft chuckle. 'He called and was adamant he was coming to help. Adam, don't worry, he said, I'll be there by ten. I talked him out of it. Anyway, I'm meant to be dropping the truck back in Sheff tonight so, yes, let's get you moved.'

Getting all my boxes into the truck is the easy part. It's big furniture that seems to take forever. My dining table goes downstairs on its back, like a turtle, and my mattress gets jammed in the lift door. Instead of being worried about the door repeatedly opening and closing, gnawing on my bed like a dog with a chew toy, Adam starts shouting, 'Pivot! Pivot! Pivot!' and we fall about laughing.

Today marks the only day I'm officially pleased I don't do weekly grocery shops. It means my refrigerator is next to empty. While Adam wheels it away with a trolley we manage to borrow from a neighbour, I stick around to do one final clean.

'Look what I found.' I wander out of my bedroom when I hear Adam return.

When I'd come to the realisation I wasn't destined to be a successful photographer, I'd folded up my tripod, buried my studio lights at the back of the wardrobe and hidden my vintage Rolleiflex camera away. It had been so long since I'd seen it, I honestly thought it was back in Sheffield. I don't recall ever using it in London.

'Christ, that's a throwback,' Adam says. 'You used to take that everywhere with you, but I never see it anymore. Where'd you find it?'

'In the back of my underwear drawer.'

'Gross.' With a grimace, he tosses the hot potato back into my hand. 'Not what you normally find in the back of an underwear drawer.'

Though I'm laughing, I offer him a playful slap. 'Stop it.'

'You ready to go?' he asks.

'Is anyone ever?'

Fiona appears at the top of the stairs, hair swept up in a bun and wearing her usual paint-splattered smock. Adam, Dad, and I have been unloading the truck for an hour already, and she's just arrived brandishing a brand-new mop and what looks like a washing basket full of handy items for the new renter. Through the clear cellophane tied with white ribbon, I spy bleach, spray cleaner and cloths, mouse traps, disinfectant and those little stars that stick to the inside of the toilet.

One of my favourite moments of the past ten years was hearing Fiona's take on how she met my father for the first time. After a divorce that can only be described as Mt St Helen's on a bad day level of catastrophic, she moved to the area and came into Dad's store looking for a specific brand of oil paint.

All she wanted was to pick up where she left off on an old hobby, but Dad tried telling her she was using the wrong paint, that it didn't mix as well as the brand he sold, and it escalated into what Dad likes to call a 'spirited debate'. She threatened to shop elsewhere and he relented, agreeing to order in a bunch of paints for her, and a few extra should she need them later. He took her number and promised to call when they arrived, and the rest is history. Peas in pods and all that.

Turning the basket at angles, I can also see sourdough bread laced with apricots, sultanas, and figs. A sweet cinnamon scent wafts up with each squeeze of the basket. There's also a block of butter from a local dairy and my favourite brand of local milk with cream on top. Breakfast tomorrow will be nothing like my regular grab-and-go from Pret.

'This looks amazing.' I place the basket on my dining table and wrap her in a hug. 'And you're incredible. Thank you.'

'It's really, really lovely to have you back,' she whispers. 'Your father is especially thrilled.'

'Don't.' I retreat and point at her, my bottom lip trembling. 'Give him a week and he'll be sick of the sight of me.'

'I doubt that very much.' She gives me a motherly look as she moves across the apartment. *My* apartment.

Adam crosses the threshold with my last box of junk. He looks as exhausted as I am, shaking his arms out as he thumbs towards the bottom of the stairs. 'Looks like someone's already planning the grand opening.'

Dad is pacing about the place, checking over each room and calling up his suggestions for what he thinks should go in each room. 'Oh, and caterers. Lots of caterers!'

Fiona raises a finger to her lips. 'He hasn't shut up about it.'

Right now, opening night is the last thing on my mind. Furniture is strewn across the place, I'm exhausted, my head aches and the last twenty-four hours have been an emotional spinning wheel. On the upside, the move was painless, with only one stop at services for a lark before continuing up the M1. I had met Ava, the estate agent, at her office, where I signed all the final paperwork and took possession of the keys and the building.

The flat above the gallery is thrice the size of my London apartment. I've gone from a cosy budget hotel room to an open-plan penthouse suite, not that I'd dare complain. I like to think of it as my reward for dealing with a tsunami of trash this week. With what little I own, it's more than enough room for me without having to spread out into the other rooms. If I break the space up into thirds, I've got all my needs sorted.

It had all felt surreal at the time, inspecting the building and asking for permission to do things that generally make a landlord's eyes twitch. Now I'm here and my belongings are filling up the place, it feels oddly familiar and comfortable, nourishing even.

At the far end, closest to the fire escape, there's a kitchenette, and we waddle my refrigerator into the corner beside the door. The en suite off to the side looks like a recent addition. My extendable dining table finally gets the chance to shine, and I let it fold right out and drag it into the middle of the dining area. I move it again to accommodate my sofa and television.

The front end of the flat becomes my bedroom. My bed, bedside tables and lamp are all shoved beneath the space by an open window that overlooks the street. When everything's in place, I stand back and take it all in.

I don't think I've ever had this much room to myself. It's

freeing, if not a little overwhelming, and I'm already so much more in love with it than I thought possible. When everything's tidy and in place, it'll be so homely. Even the Tupperware orange wall doesn't bother me so much anymore. In fact, I might keep it. My low-rise shelf full of art books almost suits it. I quickly decide my art is going on the wall above it.

'Now what?' Dad sidles up beside me.

I scratch my fingers through my hair. 'I think I'll worry about the rest of it tomorrow.'

'Correct answer,' he says.

Without a thorough clean, it was a little useless unpacking everything. Instead, I do the bare minimum, running the vacuum across the floor, wiping down benchtops and making sure my television didn't die en route. Oh, and crack open the brand-new bed sheets Fiona has gifted me, because I am sleeping like a queen tonight.

When Adam suggests a takeaway dinner, we huddle around his phone and shout the names of dishes at him like we're in a bingo hall. An hour later, a delivery driver unloads his loot at the front door. Before he leaves, he quips that he thought the place was abandoned. Where have we been all this time, in the basement?

We're weird, I'll give him that, but we're not quite the family from *The Burbs* just yet. Simply moved back to the area, I explain as he does an embarrassed shuffle back to his scooter. And despite his first impression, when the four of us are together we do work in a lovely synchronisation.

Fiona wipes down the table, which has suffered a light scratch on its journey today. Dad lays out placemats and all the plastic cutlery that had been stuffed in the takeaway bag. I find candles at the bottom of a box, and they serve as makeshift centrepieces while Adam pours out wine. For a moment, we sit in stunned silence, taking each other in, my brother and father wearing identical smirks, Fiona with her face hidden behind an oversized

121

glass of wine and me, dumbfounded that I actually took the leap to get here.

'Well, shit.' I take a deep breath. 'I'm back.'

'Only took you ten years,' Dad says. 'Oh, I'm just going to try my luck in London for the summer. I'll be right back.'

Adam sniggers, which starts everyone else laughing. As we eat from each other's plates and fight over the mix of Indian, Chinese and Thai cuisines, we take turns replaying our own version of London's Greatest Hits. All the old stories I thought were long buried come churning up to the surface again. It's the second week in a row we've done this as a family and, I must admit, I'm enjoying it way more than I thought I would.

'So, Adam, where's Soph?' Dad asks. 'She okay?'

Until now, he's looked more relaxed than I've seen him in months. That tired grey glint in his eye had disappeared long enough for him to look under forty again. Now, he shifts like he's been winded. 'Yeah, she's fine. She's good, just a lot of work going on right now. Plus, she felt like she'd kind of get in the way today.'

'Rubbish.' Dad places his glass down a little too hard. 'She could've helped with something. We would've found her something to lug about.'

'That's what I said.' He looks away quickly. That was a lie. 'Next time, hey?'

'Not to worry.' Fiona looks at my brother. 'How's your week been otherwise?'

'It's been busy.' He nods, twisting noodles around his fork as he nods in my direction. 'But this one here is giving me something else to think about.'

I groan. 'Sorry.'

'No, it's fine,' he insists. 'It's been a nice break actually. I think I'm getting too caught up in the Monday to Friday of things, so I'm appreciating being dragged out of it. Fresh air and different faces and all that.'

'What have you got coming up? Any big cases?' Dad asks.

'I'm hoping for a quiet one this week. I'm meeting the estate agent at Katharine's flat on Monday morning. Easier than her coming back and forth,' Adam explains as he casts a glance my way. 'Can you make sure you keep your phone on you this week?'

Shit, my phone. In the hullaballoo of moving, I'd forgot all about it.

'Thank you for reminding me.' I leap from my seat, dig around for my phone and its charger and plug it into a socket by my bed.

The room is quiet as I wait for that spark of life, the little battery icon to disappear before I find out who, if anyone has been trying to get hold of me. It's barely awake before a quick succession of notifications start popping up.

'Someone clearly wants to get hold of you,' Dad quips. 'Not someone you've got squirrelled away, is it?'

'What?' My head snaps back at him. 'No.'

That's not entirely a lie. They haven't met John because, as it turns out, they were never going to. Though, judging by the half-dozen missed calls and increasingly desperate text messages, he might have had a quick change of heart after I left him on the station platform last night. I swallow down nerves and grapple for a change of subject.

'You know who isn't particularly good at answering his phone?' I ask, flopping back down in my chair and point at my father. 'Your friend Christopher.'

'Hey? Kit? No, I was just talking to him at the craft market this morning. We caught up for breakfast before looking at art stalls.' Dad reaches across the table for the bottle of wine. 'Do you want me to call him for you?'

I shake my head. 'It's fine. I was hoping to talk to him about holding an exhibition here, but he's not answering emails or his phone.'

'That's easy fixed.' He grips the edge of the table and leans into the conversation. 'Come to class tomorrow morning.'

I snort. 'No. Thanks, but no.'

'Why not? He'll be there. You want to talk to him, it's the best place to find him.'

'I'm sure he'd much rather I didn't.' I look away nervously. 'Plus, I'm sure his class is already full.'

Whatever comes out of my mouth in the next five minutes doesn't register. My father has it in his head that I'm going tomorrow morning, no matter what. It'll be good to polish my skills, he reminds me. I can be as flash and business-y as I like during the week, but I need to take the time to relax and meet new people, he says with a wink and a smile.

Urgh. Clearly the love boat is still docked and awaiting passengers.

Chapter 12

That's exactly how I find myself outside Christopher's home just before nine o'clock on a Sunday morning. After cursing and muttering and trying to explain to Dad that I didn't want to go and that Christopher certainly wouldn't want me there, I relent and find myself taking the short drive out of town towards Loxley, along the river and up into the small gravel car park.

All with the sound turned down so I can see where I'm going.

As my car rolls to a stop, I catch sight of the property in front of me. Like his website says, it's a sizeable lot set against rolling acreage. The old-world charm of the stone homestead is offset by lush hedges and the more draconian concept of security cameras on high.

I remember this place from my childhood. Not because I've ever been here, but because it was always the grand old home seen on drives out of town, to picnic by the reservoir, or to the cemetery to visit Mum. I'd always wondered who lived behind the crotchety wooden farm gate.

Now I know and, sometimes, I think not knowing is more fun.

Considering class is due to begin in twenty minutes, I'm surprised to find I'm the sole occupant of the car park. The only other sign of life is an A-frame, complete with hand-drawn chalk lettering, pointing us towards an old barn-cum-classroom. Even birds are sitting prone on the hedge like they're checking names and numbers.

Not for the first time today, I wonder aloud why the hell I've decided to come all the way out here. While my father was adamant I join the class this morning all I really want is an answer. Christopher was the one who so desperately broached the topic of gallery space, who'd emailed my old workplace, so why was he being so evasive now? Why couldn't he simply answer an email, or hold a phone conversation?

That idea alone makes me laugh and, yes, I'm aware I probably look a little insane sitting here on my own.

Did I really need an answer from him this badly? By his own admission, and my own knowledge, Sheffield is a creative community. There are plenty of other local artists I could work with, let alone the sheer volume of contacts I already have. They would probably also do it without insulting me.

It's this thought that convinces me I should start my car and leave, forget the exhibition and Christopher, and get on out of there with my dignity still intact. That is, until I look up from my phone and see him walking up an incline towards the classroom with a wheelbarrow bouncing under the weight of its load.

He looks up, directly at me, and my breath catches. His expression is blank, though I'm sure I look like a deer in the headlights. I can't duck and leaving would only make me look a bigger fool than I already am, so I do the only thing I logically can and get out of my car and start walking towards him.

'Good morning.' Nerves vault through me as I try concentrating on the crunch of gravel underfoot.

'Let me guess, you're the extra person your father was talking about bringing today?' Christopher keeps walking. 'Christ, I've won the lottery.'

126

'Can I speak to you?' I pick up the pace, scuttling alongside him, grabbing and pulling windswept hair out of my face. 'Please?'

'Aren't you doing that already?'

I take a deep breath and resist the urge to trip him. 'I want you.'

He lowers the wheelbarrow and takes a slow deep breath.

'Well, I must say, that's the most forward a woman has been with me in years.' He glances at his wrist. 'We don't have long, but I'm sure I could—'

'I didn't mean like *that*.' My face is on fire. His response is gifting me wildly inappropriate mental images and I'm having trouble separating them from the here and now. Unfortunate. 'I saw your art.'

'So, you've got an internet connection.' He gives me a healthy dose of side-eye as he picks up the wheelbarrow again. 'Good for you.'

'I like it,' I try, hoping I sound upbeat. I race after him. 'In fact, it's amazing.'

'Great,' he grumbles.

'I'm not lying.'

I don't know how he's still pushing such a heavy load uphill. I'm barely keeping up with the walking part. My nerves have now settled into a jelly mould wobble in my legs. This is not the hill I want to die on today, but I'm not sure Christopher is going to give me a lot of choice in that matter.

'The thing is, I moved back to the area this week to open my own gallery.' I huff and puff as I try to keep up. 'And I want to hold an exhibition of your work.'

'Now.' He stands taller, pigeon proud and hands on his hips. 'This is certainly a turn of events, isn't it?'

'A little, yes.' I nod. How is it, of all the men I've ever come up against in my job, he makes me feel the smallest? I'm suddenly unsure of everything I've ever felt confident in.

'However, by your estimation, you shouldn't want my art,' he says. There are secrets hiding behind his smirk, I'm one hundred per cent certain of it.

'Why not?' I counter.

Silence. God, this is just like a fencing match. *En garde, pret, allez, bout*, without the *corps-à-corps*. Stab, stab, stabby. Unless you're counting my terribly uncomfortable mental images from moments ago, that is. Well, that's a different type of stabby at least. I try and gather moisture in my mouth.

'Why wouldn't I?' I press. 'You're an incredible artist.'

'Go on, then,' he starts. 'Pitch me.'

'Pitch you?'

'Yes, *you* pitch *your* idea to *me*.' He gestures back and forth in the space between us. 'Think of it as a role reversal of the other weekend.'

I take a steadying breath and waft a hand above my head. Hopefully an idea catches on the tips of my fingers. 'I think it'll be a brilliant display of local art. You'd get final say on what pieces are shown, of course. I'd like you to be the first artist I showcase at Patterson Gallery.'

Christopher lets go of the handles and the wheelbarrow crashes to a stop by the sliding door of his studio. 'No.'

'What?' I sputter. 'Why not?'

His eyes widen. 'Because I don't want to?'

'Why couldn't you have just said so by replying to my email?' My voice rises. 'How hard would it have been?'

'Was I supposed to answer that?' He lets his eyes meet mine, but barely. With a single brow arched and the tiniest hint of dimple, I'm convinced he's enjoying being difficult. 'It read more like a rambling essay into the abyss. Were you drunk? Please tell me you were because there's no other explanation that makes earthly sense.'

'I'd like to think a reply would have been the polite thing to do,' I continue, flustered as my heel sinks into a soft patch. The air is suddenly warmer, the scent of fresh grass carried on its wings. 'Or, you know, you could have called back when our call dropped out the other night.'

'It didn't drop out,' he says as he inspects a spot on the palm of his hand. 'What's your vision, Ms Patterson? What's the concept you're running with? And make it snappy, class starts in a few minutes.'

'Why are you asking *me*?' I shriek. 'You were the one who came to *me* looking for space.'

He's too busy trying to dig a splinter out to even look at me. 'Did I say that?'

'You did.' I fold my arms across my chest.

'I think you'll find you only assumed that.' He lifts his head enough to greet the handful of students who are now filing into the studio. 'Now, are we done here?'

'No, no we aren't done here.' I follow him up the step and into the studio while somehow managing to toss my dirty boots aside.

Everything feels very primary school, from the rows of coat hooks to the samples of classwork tacked up against the side wall. The only difference is, there's a room full of adults drifting in and finding their seats.

'Hello … Hi, everyone. Sorry I'm late.' I race for the last of the musical chairs. I figure if Christopher won't hold a decent conversation with me, then I'll sit here and wait until he does. I can play this game.

Before I have a chance to warm the seat, Christopher approaches.

'Get up.'

'What?'

'You're not sitting there. Get up.' He waves a hand, enticing me across the room, through a sliding door and into a storeroom that's as brightly lit with bulbs as it is filled with art I can only assume he's collected on his life's travels.

It's all quite cat with a laser pointer for me because I don't know what to look at first. These pieces are stunning. On further inspection, I recognise his style in some of them. He taps my elbow.

'What do you want?' He stuffs his hands in his pockets and peers down at me. Once again, I feel very seen and unsure of myself. 'You've traipsed all the way out here this morning. It can't just be for an exhibition.'

'What do I want?' I ask. 'What did *you* want?'

'I want to be left alone to do my work and concentrate on my school,' he says. 'I'm done with shows.'

'So, why all the hubbub about gallery space then?' I ask.

His eyes widen. 'Because I was curious about how one would go about obtaining gallery space.'

'So why not just say that?' I baulk. 'Or have you changed your mind and don't want to deal with me because I'm a woman? Is that it?'

He sniffs. 'Don't be so arbitrary, Katharine. You're better than that.'

A compliment? He's going to try and throw me off the scent with a compliment?

'Let me run an exhibition then.' I shove my hands on my hips so hard I'm sure I'll wake up with a displacement tomorrow. 'Let's work on this. Together. You and me. You paint, I'll curate, and together we'll decide which pieces to show, have a bit of back and forth about notes. I can print brochures, get wall plaques made, even get some advertising in the newspapers, social media. I've got plenty of contacts from London who'd be keen to come to the party.'

With a sharp shake of his head and a roll of his eyes, Christopher lets out an annoyed breath and slides the door open. 'Miss Patterson here says she's going to organise an exhibition of everyone's work in the coming weeks.'

Ecstatic gasps float through from the next room as the chatter raises a few decibels. I flinch and force the door closed, not before spotting an excited Fiona giving me the thumbs up and 'Well done.' A cool breeze whips through from the window at the end of the room. Horror clutches at me. That is not what I said at all.

'Not for them,' I hiss, hoping like hell I don't sound rude or ungrateful, though I suspect that's exactly how I sound.

'Well, you aren't showing *my* art.'

I nod vehemently. 'That's exactly what I'm doing.'

'And how do you suppose you're going to do that once I toss you out?'

'You can't toss me out,' I sputter.

'I assure you, I can.'

'You invited me in.'

'What are you, a vampire?' he asks.

I wince and shake my head. 'What?'

'Never mind.' He waves a hand. 'That's the deal. They get a show. I was never asking for me.'

'Why?'

'Why not?' he asks. 'What's the matter? They aren't popular enough for you?'

I snort ruefully. 'It's not that.'

'That's exactly what it is.' Christopher points at me. 'You are one of those highfalutin wannabe art snobs who pisses on anything that's either not within a five-mile radius of big magical London or not going to get their name in lights.'

'That's not true,' I retort. 'I just … I can't show those pieces to the public.'

'Why not? They've put pencil or paint or charcoal or any other medium to canvas. It's art, isn't it?' he says. 'Weren't you the one who said to me art was in the eye of the beholder?'

Oh, he is good. If I wasn't so riled up, I might just tell him how much I admire his game face right now.

'That's stretching the definition of art *very* thin,' I say in a frustrated whisper. 'I can't be showing half-finished drawings and expect people to buy them.'

'I'll bet if it was a half-finished Degas, you'd be all over it.' He tinkles his fingers in my face. 'Ants at a picnic.'

'No.' I shake my head and purse my lips. 'That's not true.'

'"Specialising in photography, Katharine Patterson graduated first in her class and went on to write her thesis on the cultural influence of Annie Leibovitz. She cites her inspirations as Dorothea Lange and Leibovitz." You're *exceedingly* original.' He levels me with a knowing look that cuts right through me and leaves me feeling like a windsock at Heathrow on a stagnant day. '"Though her love remains with still images, her favourite painted piece is Self *Portrait in Uniform* by Richard Carline." Did I get it right? Am I missing anything?'

I swallow. 'No. No, you didn't.'

With a slight nod, he pushes the door open again, drawing us back into a room now full of people. Their attention is set firmly on us, on me and, as I follow him towards the door, I realise I am the rice paper roll of photographers: translucent and with my insides exposed. I'm not ready to leave, yet he's not about to give me another option.

Stepping outside at his invitation, I turn back to him. 'How the hell did you even *know* any of that?'

'It seems your old employer hasn't completely wiped you from memory yet,' he says. 'I want my students to experience what it's like to be part of a show. They deserve it. That's why I asked you about gallery space. Not for me. I don't need your help. I don't need anybody's help. These people need a lift into the art world. Those are my terms, take them or leave them.'

Before I can get another word out, he slides the door shut, leaving me standing in the breeze.

I glower and lift my middle finger to his retreating back.

Jerk.

Click, click, click.

Oh shit, shit, shit, bugger, no!

My car groans, heaves and waves its wipers at me, eventually slipping into a silent death. An angry sob escapes my throat. This cannot be happening.

'You cannot be serious,' I mutter at my Christmas tree dashboard, every warning light seemingly flashing at me.

All I want to do is scream, shout and stomp right back into his classroom and demand he help me because, if it wasn't for his rubbish attitude and quick dismissal, I'd probably be sitting in his class as a paying student at least pretending I was interested in painting. But I'm not. Instead, I'm stranded here with little other option but to ask him for help, and I know exactly how that will go.

After everything I just went through in front of a group of strangers, I cannot bear the thought of him coming out here and lording it over me. Just imagine it, the sight of him, head under my hood and that mocking smirk that sits so comfortably on his lips as he announces to the class that I'm out of fuel or the battery terminal is corroded enough to break the circuit. The only way it could get worse is if it were something as simple as that.

I take one, two, three deep breaths as I loll my head about and listen to the unhappy grinding and clunking of stressed bones. I pull the key from the ignition and wait.

Drumming my fingers on the steering wheel, I consider my other options. There's still a quarter of a tank of fuel, so that's not the problem. And I'm sure the gauge isn't faulty; Adam would have said something had he noticed recently. I could call him to come and help, but one look at my watch tells me he's already on the train home.

It's got to be the battery, not that I can afford a new one, but what am I supposed to do? Dad isn't here, but if I call him, I can guarantee Christopher will only end up involved anyway. Fiona is inside, but getting her to help involves me going back inside and brings me back to square one.

What a colossal mess.

'One last try,' I whisper. 'Pretty please.'

I jam the key in and turn, listening as the whine gets quicker and the engine finally, thankfully, kicks over. Before my car has a chance to so much as think about conking again, I throw it into gear and tear off down the road. I do not pass Tesco and do not collect two hundred things I don't need.

Adrenaline carries me all the way home and upstairs to my sofa where I collapse into a heap and curse the utter stupidity that made me think going out to Loxley this morning was a good idea. I close my eyes, rub my face and hope that when I open them, this was all a bad dream.

I wake near dinnertime. The apartment is stuffy in the summer sun, my head is thick with sleep and I'm sure I've drooled on the cushion I've curled myself into. On the upside, I feel better. Refreshed, even. After everything that's happened the last few days, I was bound to crash at some point. I sit up, run my fingers through tangled hair and wonder: what do I do now?

While I munch on a Marmite toast dinner, I raid what's left of Fiona's gift basket for spray cleaner and kitchen towel. All I mean to do is wipe down kitchen counters and windowsills, but it morphs into something bigger. Before I've so much as considered switching the television on for the night, I've cleaned bellies of cupboards and unpacked all my utensils into the whirring dishwasher.

When I do get a chance to look at the television, something doesn't feel right. It's the angle of the screen playing with the reflection from the windows, and I shift it just a smidgen, knowing the best part about living here is that there are no neighbours to complain about noise from the pesky new neighbour upstairs.

The thought alone is enough to spark something, a reminder, a gentle nudge from the universe. *This is why you're here*, it's saying and, while I want to sit on the sofa all evening and bliss out in peace and quiet with that packet of biscuits I'm sure is hidden somewhere, I know I've got hundreds of things I should be doing.

As exhausted as I am, I fire up my laptop and park myself at the dining table. A game of cat and mouse plays itself out on the television in the background, and I pour out the dregs of a pinot noir and settle in for the night. This may have been the norm for me in London but, now that I'm doing this for me, it feels fresh and exciting. I can't wait to get to the other end of the process.

I'm in the heart of the city, but it's not nearly as loud as London, at least not in the same white noise echo that seemed to follow me everywhere. Sure, there are car horns and rattling buses, but it's nowhere near the volume I'm used to. A feeling of peace settles somewhere in the back of my mind and, oh, how I've missed this.

When my screen blinkers to life and my inbox finally loads, I double-check that I'm in the right account because, unless there's an error, I have no fewer than 120 emails waiting for me. It's not been quite a week since the website went live and here I am with an influx of artists keen to show their work.

Some are from friends who've caught the news I've moved north. Colleagues from Webster have sent their numbers, offering whatever help they can. Considering the circumstances under which I left my job, I'm exceedingly grateful, and I tell them so. I add them to my phone and promise I'll call if I need help. Then I knuckle down and get to the artists.

Each email is a variant on the next, not that it bothers me in the slightest. There are only so many ways you can say please and ask for help, but there's one question that sticks its neck out over and over: when are you opening?

It's the most important question of all, really, and one that I'm not even one hundred per cent sure of. For, as much as I talked through my business ideas with Lainey and scribbled others on napkins and in the back of notebooks, I never had a firm opening date. Securing this building was the big hurdle that all the rest balanced on so, tonight, I'm finally going to make that decision.

With my diary spread across the dining table, it soon becomes obvious that setting a date won't be a matter of simply throwing a dart at a board. Before any of this happened, I promised Lainey I'd help her with her wedding, so I mark out nights for the hen do and the big event itself. Let's face it, I'm not rolling back from London first thing on a Sunday morning with a hangover to launch a gallery. No chance.

Lainey's wedding is five weeks away, which negates the weekend before it as well. That leads me to ask: Do I want to rush through opening a gallery in four weeks' time? I have no idea exactly how much work is going to be involved in getting the ground floor up to scratch.

There may be hidden problems as yet uncovered, and I want to make sure my idea isn't slapped together and thrown out into the world like a cheap and cheerful pizza. I want to do things properly, take my time, get the walls painted, the floors cleaned and, importantly, secure that elusive opening exhibition. So, it's a solid no on opening in four weeks' time.

Still, six weeks feels too long. By that point, I'll just be wasting time waiting to open the doors. However, the wedding *is* a midday affair on a Friday in the middle of London with a reception to follow immediately after. If I can get everything ready before I leave for London and return home later that night, there's no reason why I can't open the day after the wedding.

I circle the last Saturday in August, not quite five weeks from today, and send an updated message across social media. We have a date, and I've committed by telling everyone about it. Now, I just need to make it happen.

So, where do I begin?

Chapter 13

Urgh. Bills.

They've begun already. I snatch up the envelopes from where they've just been stuffed through the brass slot in the enormous green front door. There's one from Adam's firm, a bon voyage card from Lainey and Frank, and something from the letting agent. Money, money, money. Let me tell you, it's less funny on the way out of your pocket than on the way in.

Though I grit my teeth and keep one eye on my account balance the entire time, I pay the invoices immediately and file them away with the rest of my paperwork upstairs. The last thing I need is a collection agency knocking on the door before I've even opened for trade.

I pop Lainey's card next to the television, with the cheap and cheerful pink peonies I picked up on this morning's grocery run. They add a spray of colour to the room, as has the bargain basement melamine vase they're sitting in. I don't care that it cost me less than a pound on the clearance trolley. I care that, with a few cute touches, my flat is beginning to feel like home.

With last night's hastily scrawled business plan in hand and a fresh cup of coffee, I wander downstairs ready to put things into action. I'm excited for the start of the journey, though I feel like all the cleaning and painting is going to be the least engaging thing to post about on social media. That is, until I scroll through my phone and spot an American gallery documenting their renovations through side-by-side comparisons, videos and live action shots.

I check in with Lainey, who almost reaches through the phone to shake me by my shirt collar. Yes! Good idea, she confirms. It'll give me something to talk about while building brand and buzz.

'Hurry up and post a picture!' she cries as I Facetime her around the ground floor. 'It's totally relatable, too. We've all been there with a paint roller. Who'd have thought we'd both be renovating at the same time? So exciting!'

'Don't remind me,' I say, scratching at a dint in the wall. 'I feel like I've bitten off way more than I can chew.'

'Yeah, it feels like that, but small steps. Just think of it as one wall panel at a time. We're just about ready to paint the entry. I'm so pumped. Oh! And I'll have to come up and see this place now you've settled in. How are you placed for Saturday?'

'Saturday—'

'Oh! And wedding stuff. I need to show you some things.'

After reassuring her I'll likely be stuck with a roller in hand, but that she's welcome to help, we ring off and I'm left to my thoughts again, though there is the optimism of Lainey's words carrying me around. This won't be so hard. I hope.

There are nicks and divots in walls and paint chipped from corners. The lighting sits at an odd height, something I'm not sure I noticed in the milk-drunk baby love I had for the building. I'm not sure I can do a lot about it without growing about four feet taller, and the higher I look, the more it looks like Charlotte has escaped the farm and moved in with all her offspring. Some gallery. Oh, and I know why one room is aubergine purple, because with ten-foot ceilings, it's going to be an absolute dick to paint over.

Not that I have a deep well of experience when it comes to

painting walls, and don't get me started on polishing floorboards. Even my attempts at canvas look like the local zoo threw a brush at Emily the Elephant and told her to go wild. My role at Webster had me cataloguing and studying art, liaising with artists and keeping records. Exhibition design and decorating was left to a separate team, where my involvement lasted only long enough to know they were hitting targets.

I'm certain I never even painted my London flat when I moved in. It's not that I don't know how to, it's just that I'm wildly out of my depth, let alone the fact I have absolutely none of the tools I need to do it. But I know who does.

I snatch up my car keys and exponentially growing to-do list and head to Dad's. Thankfully, my car starts first go. I was not looking forward to forking out for a new battery.

'Hello, gorgeous girl.' Fiona floats down the hall towards the front door. 'Was wondering when I might see you again.'

'You were?' I pull the door open and step inside.

'Sure.' She spins on her heel and beckons me to the sunroom. 'You know, after Sunday and all.'

"Urgh.' I groan. 'Don't even go there.'

'It's just not gelling for you two, is it?' she asks.

'Nope,' I pip quickly. 'Can't win 'em all though, can you?'

'Certainly not,' she says.

Silence filters in long enough for me to hope she doesn't mention Christopher any further. I'm not sure I could stand someone else defending him, telling me he'd be so lovely if only I'd just give him five more minutes of my time. *He really is very talented, a wonderful painter and generous friend.* But she stays silent, her eyes twinkling like a naughty child. From experience, that means she's bursting at the seams to say something, but she won't.

'Go on.' I heave a sigh, giving her a look that says please make this as painless as possible.

'Your father just wants you to see you settled and happy.' The words explode into the room like a burst balloon. 'And he thought you two would really hit it off. He *is* lovely, but I'm going to stop right now.'

'But I *am* happy,' I say with a small bewildered smile. 'Slightly stressed, but otherwise decent. My career is at Cape Canaveral awaiting launch. Sure, my love life is a little bit London canal boat, but you know.'

'Don't knock those canal boats.' Fiona waves a paintbrush. 'Tried living on one of them for a while. Could never quite get the mechanics of painting, shagging and living in the same ten square foot of area.'

I laugh. 'And all three at once would be a stretch.'

'Ain't that the truth.' She turns her attention back to a piece of flatpack on the dining room floor. 'Did try. Unsuccessfully, I might add. The shagging is quite okay if you get them under you, but the rest? Forget it.'

It's not as if I've had the best luck with men to begin with. John notwithstanding, there was Jamie in my second year of university. Everything was jogging along nicely until I learned he'd found himself a new girlfriend at life drawing class – the model. Then there was Bret. If the odd spelling wasn't enough to give him away, perhaps the recycled catchphrases and manbun should have been. He disappeared in a haze of beer and Ping-Pong balls while attending someone else's Freshers' week. That someone was Janett. She read classics and over-pronounced every syllable. They're married now, with a minibus full of strawberry blonde cherubs.

I also wasn't keen on adding to my small list of one-night stands. They were never as fulfilling as you imagine they'll be in the downlights of a sweaty club with a gut full of gin. I'm getting older. If I went in for anything now, it would be something I knew was going to be solid and long lasting, and I was entirely sure Christopher *didn't* fit that bill. Despite the built-in cheer squad.

140

'All right. I'll drop it,' she says. 'Anyway, what brings you out here today? I'm about to have lunch if you'd like to join me?'

'No, thank you though.' I wave a hand. 'I've just finished breakfast. What I'd really love to do is raid the garden shed if that's okay.'

'Always.' She unhooks the key from near the kitchen door. 'Do you need a weed trimmer?'

'No, actually. Well, not yet. I'm going to start painting, I think.'

'Ah, the exciting parts.' Her face crinkles into a serene smile. 'Let's go see what we've got.'

As we dig through dusty boxes looking for cobweb brushes, paint rollers and extension poles, I talk through my plans. It's nice to have a sounding board who isn't Lainey, my father or my brother because, while they're 187 per cent supportive, I know Fiona is also practical.

'I mean logic tells us to start at the top and work down,' she says as she reaches into an old cupboard and thrusts a paint tray at me. 'Fix up the ceiling and lights, then the walls. God knows you don't want to do the floors and then get paint all over them.'

'You know, even though I know that, I still feel like someone's going to tap me on the shoulder and say, "Not like that, you fool."'

'It's not inadequacy you're feeling,' she says. 'I think it's more an issue of expectation. You've got all these ideas of what you want to achieve and now all the movement has stopped, it's going to feel like a bit of a crawl waiting for the end result.'

In the corner of my eye, a spider moves, sending my nerves through the roof and my body darting for the door. Fiona howls with laughter, even if she does follow me outside just as quickly.

'You may be right.' I brush myself down and check myself over for any rogue passengers. 'I've got this idea in my head of how I want it to look. I can see it. If I concentrate hard enough, I'm sure I can touch it. Hell, I dreamt it last night. It just seems so out of reach.'

'Have you written down what you see in your mind's eye?' she asks, pulling a cobweb from my hair.

'I have a business plan,' I try.

'No, no. Like a mood board. Pinterest the shit out of it, girl.'

I shake my head.

'You know what?' she begins. 'Give me a few minutes. I'm coming shopping with you. Let's see if we can't do this on the fly.'

There's nothing like the paint counter at B&Q to bring it home that you're finally a card-carrying adult. Cards as in paint chips, as in I have a Dover cliff wall of options in front of me. It's big and tall and my ideas all feel a little chalky.

The thing is, selecting the right shade of paint is important. Can you imagine what Mona Lisa would look like with purple hair? If she had anything other than that rich brown hue, it just wouldn't work. It's the same with the gallery; I choose the wrong wall colour and I know it won't sit right. I toggle between frosted white, orchid white, almond white, cornflour white, and a dozen other shades of white that just don't match the image I have in my head.

'I want something warm.' I turn to Fiona, who's got a royal flush of yellow chips. 'You know that kind of colour that makes people feel like they've stepped into a friend's kitchen with a bottle of red and the promise of a warm meal.'

'For the record, I like the sound of your kitchen.' Fiona titters. 'Shame you can't cook.'

'Oh, stop it.' I cluck my tongue. 'I do a wicked Uber Eats.'

I traverse the aisle again, trying to make sure I've not missed anything. The clunking indecision of my brain is soundtracked by the *tap, tap, tap* of a rubber mallet at the mixing station. I fiddle with a packet of drop sheets that hang from an end shelf. My trolley is already full, but I will need to make sure I don't destroy the floorboards.

142

'What do you think about this?' Fiona has her phone angled at me. A carousel of highly curated Instagram DIY images swipes across the screen.

'Hmmm, that beige is nice.' I move back to the previous picture. 'Webster was beige though.'

'Beige is boring, darling girl. You're individual, amazing, inspiring! You certainly don't need to be copying them.' She winks as she pulls up a picture of a lemony wall offset with daffodils and a vintage bicycle. 'How about something like this?'

I make a face. 'I never really envisaged yellow. I was more leaning towards a blue or grey. Rich. Warmth. Opulent. Fancy.'

'In that case, pick something like a British Racing Green or a Dark Grey. Think Mr Darcy, Chatsworth House, brandy and smoking jackets.' She hands me the most magnificent dark grey chip and I am instantly sold. 'What do you think? Shall we try some sample pots in a few colours?'

We pick the dark grey and the orchid white.

An hour later, I'm staring in disbelief at the pile of things by the back door while Fiona tries shuffling a six-foot palm and its brand-new glazed pot towards my staircase. As it turns out, painting is a grand idea until you have to pay for twenty litres of ceiling white, ladders, rollers, extension poles, trays, drop sheets, edging tools and everything else we tossed in the trolley on our way around the aisles. It's like anything, isn't it? You get the product cheap, but it's the accessories that send you broke. I put the receipt away before I can think too much about how much this is going to cost me by the time the place opens.

'Your flat looks super comfortable. You've done a great job.' Fiona treads carefully down the stairs, handing me a coffee as she approaches. 'Right. Where do you want to start?'

'Amazing, thank you.' I wrap my hands around the mug and take a sip of coffee. My brain un-ratchets just a smidgen. 'I was thinking the back room might be the best place. Something small.'

'I like your thinking.' Fiona turns on her heel and walks away.

The first room we tackle is, as my father would say, the first child. It's easy, carefree and it sucks you into a false sense of security. Taking it in turns, we sugar soap walls and climb ladders to clear away spiderwebs and dust. By the time we start painting the ceiling, we've got ourselves into a workable routine.

The room is small enough that, by late afternoon, we've slapped two coats of paint on the ceiling and have peeled back the lids of the sample pots.

It occurs to me that I've never done anything like this with Fiona. When she started seeing Dad, Adam and I were both already firmly entrenched in London life so, while we've interacted in the regular scope of family dinners and birthday outings, weddings and funerals, neither of us have ever really spent huge swathes of time with her. That only makes this moment more special.

I'm not her child and she doesn't have to help me, yet here she is guiding and explaining with all the patience of a saint. Realising this makes me want to leap from the top of the ladder and squish her in a hug.

'Should we paint these samples next to each other?' I ask.

She nods slowly. 'If they're next to each other, you're looking at the different colours in identical light. It'll give you a better feel for them.'

With one pot each, we mark out rough squares on the wall. Of all the stuff we've done today, this is my favourite part. Ceiling white is great for freshening the place up, but colour is character. With each stroke of the paintbrush, it feels like the room is coming to life, my project is becoming more real.

'What's the winner, do you think?' I ask.

Fiona places her brush in a jar of water and moves up beside me. 'You know, in the store I would have said the off-white, but I love the dark grey. It looks so grown up. Sophisticated. Canapés and class.'

'Doesn't it just?' I splash another swathe across the wall. It's

144

so gorgeous that my excitement tempers my tiredness. 'How lovely.'

'I tell you what, let's call it a day. Come home for dinner,' she says. 'It's been a long day, the last thing you want to do is cook.'

'Oh, no, I can just microwave something. Don't go to any trouble.'

'It's not trouble and you're not microwaving, either. That's a terrible idea,' she says with a laugh and a shake of her head. 'Let me cook you a meal.'

Water splashes and races down the sink, drowning out Dad's tinkling radio as we peel potatoes. While Fiona and I natter about what we need to do to get the place painted this week, Dad makes noises about needing a solid plan and not jumping in headfirst as if that wasn't exactly what I've been doing up to this point.

'It's just the paint, Dad,' I say through light laughter. 'I've already done the scary stuff.'

'Yes, but you're full speed ahead. Even the brightest lights burn out if they're working too long, you know.'

It's true that it's not essential everything is finished immediately but getting the paintwork out of the way will be one less hurdle to worry about. Knowing it's done and the building is as physically ready as it can be will free up my brain for other, more pressing matters like setting up the darkroom, meeting artists, working out schedules, advertising, and opening night. Dad chimes in and says he'll get someone to cover the shop so he can help paint on Wednesday and Thursday.

'And you can come home for dinner each night, too.' He watches me as I place clean glasses on the table.

'Oh, what?' I laugh. 'I can cook.'

He stops me with a look.

'All right, all right.' I wave my hands about. 'I'll come for dinner. Sheesh.'

And I do.

The three of us huddle in the back room on Tuesday morning to take a quick vote on which paint colour looks the best. I'd been so convinced until I woke up with cold feet, but the dark grey wins and I head back to B&Q with my credit card and crossed fingers.

Soon enough, the gallery becomes a rotating roster of friends and art shop employees that Dad has worded up to come and pull a shift on the paint roller. It's the last thing I expected and I was more than happy to put in the hard slog myself, but I can't talk him out of doing anything else.

All this help turns what felt like an insurmountable job into something a bit more manageable. While I'm in the front room trying to cover the hideous aubergine walls, Fiona takes charge of a small team in other rooms, and Dad provides trays of sandwiches for lunch each day. Every time I wander the rooms to check on progress, there's something new happening and, at the end of each day, I retire to the sofa at Dad's and eat whatever's put in front of me.

No doubt there's been a discussion I haven't been part of that's rendered Christopher null and void in this week of painting and cleaning. I haven't heard him mentioned as an option for help, which I'm somewhat relieved about.

Each time I think about this though, I imagine a discussion springing up at his school this weekend. The idea of people talking about being out here together while he was left out leaves a dull burn in the pit of my heart. I know only too well what it's like to be excluded and I'm immediately angry at myself for passing that on to someone else, even someone as frustrating as him.

Of course, the week is not without its incidents. By Wednesday afternoon, I'm standing over a plumber's crack, while he does his best to unblock the men's loos. My first thought is this is the last thing I need, but a stiff coffee and a mouthful of biscuits results in a more philosophical me that decides this is the best time for everything to go wrong. The last thing I need is a backed-up toilet on opening night, of all things.

By Friday morning, I'm almost done, even if I can't quite believe it myself. Every surface has been gifted two coats of paint and, for the most part, it looks good. Actually, it looks bloody fantastic. When I send her a photo, Lainey quips that it looks so good she wants to have her wedding reception in there. As it turns out, she's not the only one.

All the photos I've put on social media, the short video and little written pieces are gaining traction, likes and comments coming in from around the globe, each of them cheering me on. I won't even pretend I haven't been burning the candle at both ends keeping up with all the interaction and emails.

As I wander the place just before 8 a.m. in my pyjamas, arms, legs and every other muscle I never knew I owned aching, I'm still answering questions when I stop in the front room. A mild panic sets in because the aubergine room is being difficult and, after two coats of paint and a night's sleep, I can still see an awful mottling colour beginning to show through. It's not much, but it's enough that I know it's there.

I grumble, shaking my head and filtering through a handful of receipts. I have no other choice, I have to buy more paint, and I have to do it today.

If someone had told me that the paint alone was going to cost so much, I might not have made it this far through the process. With no weekly income and a fast dwindling savings account, handing over more cash on something I'd failed to factor in is starting to pinch. I know it's only a temporary thing, that this will all be over soon, and I'll once again have an income (hopefully), but it's hard to ration out money to unknown causes.

Thankfully, the final coat takes. It's an all-day, labour-of-love type of job, but it's incredible to stand back and look at the finished product. No older colour seeping through, the grey matches the rest of the rooms and, after a few more photos for the memory bank, I'm officially done. As I finish washing my paintbrushes and retreat to my flat for the night, there's a knock on the front door.

The knocking gets louder, but this time it's moved to the back door. I turn on the spot, feeling my socks catch on a rough patch of floorboard, and race towards the back of the building, before whoever it is has a chance to disappear.

'Who's there?' I ask, realising I need to get a peephole fitted to the door. Or a camera. Something.

'It's me, your favourite boy from London.'

Chapter 14

I pull the door open, breath seized as I prepare for the worst. When I spot my brother, dressed in jeans and a crumpled linen shirt, duffle bag at his side, I let out a bagpipe wheeze and feel the pinch of a heart valve returning to life. Poking my head out the door, I check for a car I didn't hear arrive. There is none. I turn back to Adam.

He flings his arms out wide. 'Surprise!'

'You shit, you had me going there for a second.' I wave him inside. 'I didn't recognise your voice.'

'Please, these dulcet tones?' He reaches down for his bag, and kisses me on the cheek as he bounces inside. I follow him upstairs, watching on awestruck as he drops his bag by the coffee table and helps himself to the dregs of last night's bottle of wine. He fluffs a cushion and flops down on my sofa, legs akimbo in a Sharon Stone swish.

'Should I ask what brings you all the way here this afternoon?' I ask. 'Again. Hashtag blessed.'

He smiles in a way that reminds me of his baby photos, chin tucked in and giraffe eyelashes on display. This is exactly why all my friends in school were after him. 'The power of Adam compels you.'

'Oh, please.'

'All right, so the train brings me here.' He leans forward. 'Little sister, how do you feel about getting drunk tonight?'

My eyes widen. 'I suspect you've already started down that path.'

'Warm. I had one or two on the way up.' He tips my wine glass to his mouth and grimaces. Yeah, it was a cheap bottle. 'Can I crash here tonight?'

'I'll make you a deal.'

He claps and throws himself backwards. 'Done.'

'You don't even know what it is,' I say with a laugh. 'Come on. Pay attention.'

'Shoot.' He leans forward, suddenly serious, invisible pencil at the ready. 'What is your counter-offer on the claim this afternoon?'

'Moot court?' I say with a chortle. 'Really?'

He shrugs.

'I'll get drunk with you tonight if you tell me what's going on with you.'

'Bzzzt. Wrong answer.' His head flops about as he laughs. 'Try again.'

'Adam,' I warn.

'Look, can we not?' he asks, hands out wide. 'I just don't want to talk about it. Make me another offer.'

'All right, then Mr High-rise.' I make a show of scratching at my chin. 'Do you know anything about floorboards? I was planning on giving the ones downstairs a bit of a scuff and polish this weekend.'

'I'll have you know I helped Dad with the ones in the kitchen a few years ago.' He waggles a hand. 'Wouldn't call myself an ex-*pert* as such, but I could probably feel my way around in the dark.'

'Could you help me?'

'Absolutely I can,' he says with all the conviction of a game show host about to turn the cards on a winner.

150

I nod. 'Good. All right. In that case, just promise me you'll eat something before you have another drink?'

'Are you saying you'd like to buy me dinner?' He presses a hand to his chest and discards my wine glass like a child that's been shown a shiny new toy. 'Why, you shouldn't.'

'Come on.' I grab at his hand and drag him off the sofa.

On our way out the door, Adam insists on having a quick look around. The scent of paint and cleaners linger, but his face lights up at the change. It looks like an entirely new building compared to the day I moved in. I hop about and tug at a threadbare sock as I follow him, explaining all the issues that sprang up along the way. While I'm concerned about a patch I can see I missed on the ceiling, he gives his opinion on everything from the light fittings to the choice of paint colour and the state of the floor-boards.

'Isn't it amazing how much can change in one little week?' he asks, thumb and forefinger pinched together.

'It's getting there,' I concede. 'We'll see how it all looks after the weekend.'

'So, what's the deal?' he asks. 'Are you just polishing them, or are you stripping them right back?'

My top lip curls. 'That's the thing. I don't want to spend too much money. It's a rental. Also, my bank account is currently haemorrhaging. If I end up owning the place, then I'll strip them and start afresh. For now, presentable works.'

'Eh, that's easy.' He sniffs. 'Good thing I'm free all weekend, then, isn't it? Oh, I'm catching up with the lads for dinner tomorrow night, but otherwise, I'm yours.'

I reach out and clap a hand on Adam's forehead. 'Who are you and what have you done with my brother?'

'Buy me a drink, and you'll find out.'

Despite his request, it's Adam who buys the first drinks while I stalk the bistro of the nearest pub for somewhere to sit. Families, couples, a pool table, work functions and bingo. A booth by the window is free and all ours. It's sticky and someone's left the last of their dinner behind, but I push the plate aside and shuffle across the seat before someone else pinches it.

'Do you still drink cosmos?' Adam pushes a sloshing glass across the table. 'Or are you on the whisky sours now?'

I snigger at the reference. 'While I'm still breathing, a cosmo is fine.'

'Good, good,' he says, bouncing about as he wrangles himself out of his coat. 'I was worried about you when you said that. I was like "wait, she's never drunk that before".'

'Just me being salty.' I smile and try to find the straw with my mouth. 'So, what's this then? Two weeks in a row. Anyone would think you like me.'

'I wanted to see you, is that okay?' he says enthusiastically. 'And you're my little sister, so I do like you. In fact, I happen to like you a lot.'

I set my drink aside and lean into the table. 'You could have called if you wanted a chat.'

'Yes, but I said I wanted to *see* you.' He pulls a face. 'Bit different to picking up the old Bakelite.'

'How was the trip up? You staying all weekend?'

'Sure am.' He plucks a few menus from behind the condiment box and hands me one. 'And the train was great. I skipped out of work early and beat the crowd.'

I study his face for a moment. He's wearing the disbelieving 'what's with all the questions?' expression that comes with raised brows and averted eyes. Even his shoulders are folded like origami swans. This is just like him though, clowning around pretending like he got on the train and travelled three hours simply because he missed me. As flattering as that notion is, I'm certain it can't be all.

'You skipped out of work?' I ask. 'Adam, this isn't like you. What's going on?'

'Well, I switched a few meetings to Monday and didn't have court this afternoon, so here I am.' His eyes widen. 'Am I not allowed to miss you?'

My lips turn down into a sad pout and something presses my throat closed. 'You miss me?'

'Don't sound so shocked, of course I do. You know, we used to spend quite a bit of time together in the big city. Lunch on Wednesdays, daily phone calls and questionable emails. My inbox is verging on starvation this week, by the way, very boring. Crawling across the technological desert in search of water.'

'I promise I'll start emailing you just as soon as I get this under control.' I reach for my drink. 'What have you been filling your week with instead?'

'Let me see.' He peers up at the ceiling and takes a deep breath. 'Basically, being an amazing kickass lawyer.'

I watch him for a moment, the corners of his mouth faltering.

'You know you can talk to me, don't you?' I ask. I don't mean to blurt it out but watching him pretend like there's nothing going on is breaking my heart. When you go through the things our family has, you become acutely aware of each other's plays and I can see exactly what he's doing right now. 'I promise it goes no further.'

'Oh, you mean like that time you told Dad about my getting nicked for shoplifting?' He eyes me over the top of his pint, a quick eyebrow lift as if to prove a point.

'I was twelve.'

'And I'll have the roast of the day.' He smiles weakly and tucks the menu back in place. 'Don't skimp on the Yorkshire pudding, either. We are in Yorkshire after all.'

'You're a shit.' I scowl as I get up from the table.

While I wait my turn at the bar, I watch the crowd as they hand over notes and small change, the pull of beers and glug of wine bottles. A cool breeze catches the nape of my neck and I turn to the offending door to see Christopher step inside. He pulls a flat cap from his head and stuffs it in his back pocket.

Four more people walk in with him. I'm too exhausted and preoccupied to consider who they might be.

'Hello, Kit.' The barmaid perks up. I duck my head away and hide, pretending to look at the drinks card in the hope he hasn't seen me.

'Hello, Caroline,' he coos back. 'How are you this evening?'

'All the better for seeing you.' She folds her arms across her chest and leans into the counter in that way that says: hello, yes, I'm here for you. 'What's up today?'

'Just out for a family dinner,' he says, grappling for a handful of menus. 'The usual. Have you been working on anything lately?'

My ears prick up at the mention of his family because that would be one hell of a conversation to hear over a plate of bangers and mash. I try not to make it too obvious that I'm craning for a look. I can see someone I suspect is his brother, the same prominent brow and bright eyes, though his hair is browner than it is blond. There's a dark-haired girl next to him who's wearing the pained expression of someone trying to be polite. Oh, and the backs of two greying heads.

'Nah,' she says. 'Too busy at this place. Some nights I get home and just want to uncork a bottle and go to sleep. How about you?'

'Creatively constipated today,' he says with an annoyed sigh. 'Figured getting out of the house for a bit might be a good idea.'

'Well, I'm glad you decided to visit.'

Hearing him flirt is such an unusual thing to witness. The man I'm looking at, oversized grin on offer, seems such a world away from that one who's so far been presented to me. While I want to be irritated by him, he's joyous and carefree and it feels infectious.

And what on earth is that feeling chasing around my ribcage

and crawling up the back of my throat? Surely, it's acid reflux and not something like jealousy? It cannot possibly be that, not after the way every possible interaction I've had with him has gone. Though, I can't deny that this is the positive, carefree experience I'd desperately craved from him.

No. Surely not?

It's definitely the bacon butty I had for breakfast coming up to say hello. Anything else right now is just way too much of a complication I don't have time for. I can't, and don't want to, go through anything like John again, so I bury those thoughts away in the biscuit barrel of my mind and hope he goes away.

Except he doesn't. There's a moment where he turns around but does a double-take and steps back towards the bar, and me. I shy away from his gaze and hope he takes the hint. Don't look at him. If you can't see him, he's not there. I chance a momentary glance, and he spots me. Damn it.

'Hello, Katharine,' he says, a hint of smile tugging at his mouth. Surely, he's not happy to see me.

'Hello.' I tap a coaster against the counter.

'How are you?' he asks.

'If you're about to talk to me, I'm going to assume it's because you've changed your mind.' I angle my gaze towards him. Go. Away. My reflux is getting worse with every step he takes, every move he makes. That's it, I'm buying shares in Gaviscon.

'What *is* that in your hair?' He reaches out and begins tugging on clumps of my hair. 'Is that … have you got lice?'

My heart slams against my chest as I push his hand away. 'I do *not* have lice. It's paint. I've been painting.'

'It looks like lice.'

'It is *not* lice,' I stress. 'Leave me alone.'

'What are you painting?' he asks. 'And have you been using a sprinkler to do it?'

'The Sistine Chapel,' I snap. 'Thought I'd paint a bunch of dicks all over a ceiling.'

Christopher smiles and leans on the bar and pokes his tongue into his cheek.

'I'm painting that gallery you don't want to be involved in. Though, feel free to help instead of being so critical,' I continue.

'Now, I never said I didn't want to be involved. Don't put words in my mouth.'

I tap my foot and check the time on my phone. Finally, the barmaid takes my order. Christopher waits patiently until she moves away with a wink and a smile. For him.

'I told you I wanted to show my students' work. I'm more than happy to help you with that.'

'Yes, some help twenty different interpretations of your backyard would be. Can't wait for people to stand in a room full of wide-open fields and sky.' Finally, I look at him. 'You do realise you're treating me like I'm a joke, don't you?'

'Wasn't it Mick Jagger who said you can't always get what you want?' he says, waving to someone across the bistro.

I huff. 'He's not exactly a guide to life.'

'I don't know, he *is* still alive.'

'And so is Keith Richards, so that's not the world's greatest analogy.' I smirk. 'Look, what do you want? Really? What is it? You frogmarch me out of your studio and now you want to talk like we're old friends?'

Just as he's poised to answer, the barmaid returns with my change. She counts it into my palm and clucks her tongue. 'Listen to you two, anyone would think you're about to swap kids in the car park at Maccies.'

With that, I raise my brows at Christopher, smirk and walk away, though the idea of a smaller version of him is enough to guarantee me a coronary. Imagine it, small and blond with fluffy hair and dark critical eyes. Adam's seen the whole exchange and is already perched halfway out of the booth when I get back. He takes one look at me, one look back to where I came from, and considers his options.

'Sit down,' I grumble. 'Don't worry about him.'

'Isn't that the guy from Dad's the other week?'

'One and the same,' I say. 'Brilliant artist. Massive cock.'

'Really? You're a quick mover.'

'Adam.' I glower. 'Not like that.'

'You know, if I didn't know better, I'd say he likes you.'

I retch, fidgeting with my napkin. 'He bloody well does not.'

'Ehh.' He scrunches his face. 'I saw the way he looked at you.'

'Oh, you did, did you?' I say with a laugh. 'And how was that?'

'He was all kind of soft and open, a little smiley.' He rounds a finger in my face. 'Blushing like you are right now.'

'Don't you start.' I push my change down into the pocket of my jeans. 'You do realise the only reason he was at Dad's the other week was because Dad was playing matchmaker.'

'Clearly it worked.' Adam sniggers. 'You were getting on like a house on fire. If that fire was lit with petrol and a match and was burning off toxic plastics.'

He's quiet for second as my attention follows Christopher back to his booth at the other end of the bistro. I return to find Adam watching me, a knowing smile on his face.

'Not a Van Gogh's chance in a Sunglass Hut,' I say and Adam wheezes with laughter. 'Anyway, everything with John is all still a bit, you know. And, if he does like me, then why is he so combative?'

'Oh, and you aren't?' he says. 'But I'd hazard a guess that you frighten the life out of him, which is fair. It's a natural response to you.'

'Stop it.' I laugh softly. 'Right now, it's enough for me to be working on the gallery. Once that's up and running, then I'll worry about ruining myself over another man.'

'Ruining yourself,' Adam says with barely concealed disappointment. 'You make it sound like a death sentence.'

I pull a face. ''Til death do us part.'

I glance around my brother and out into the other end of the bistro. There he is, laughing and smiling, not a care in the world. He must feel my eyes on him because he looks my way. I turn away immediately, grabbing at my phone as it starts to ring.

'What's with the face?' Adam asks. 'Who is it?'

'John keeps calling,' I say dismissively. 'Anyone would think he hasn't got the break-up memo.'

'Are you going to answer him?'

I switch the ringer to silent and tuck my phone away where I can't see or feel it. 'I'm sorry if this has made work awkward for you.'

Adam shakes his head. 'Honestly, it's fine.'

'Yes, but it's not though, is it?' I ask. 'You know, he reminds me of that Gerry Rafferty song, where he sings about thinking you have everything, but realising you were wrong.'

Adam starts humming 'Baker Street'. 'I only wish you had given me the heads up so I could be prepared.'

A tap at the window from one of Adam's old school friends interrupts our conversation. There are excited faces and finger phones and phone numbers scribbled on a napkin and held up to the window.

'Ah, that's great.' Leaning into the window, he grins and waves as they disappear down the street.

'Remember that thing Mum used to do?' I ask. 'Tell me your favourite thing that happened to you this week.'

Mum would do this if she knew we were upset or worried. Concentrate on the good and the rest falls away, she'd say. Adam rubs at his temples and considers his options. Flirting with a random woman in the queue at a café yesterday, he says.

'It was nice to just feel that flutter?' He jiggles a hand by his chest as if to illustrate the point. 'You know what I mean? She was incredibly sweet, but totally unaware of it. Good banter, too.'

I smile and thank the waiter who brings our food. 'I do love a good bit of bants.'

Adam is grateful for the change of pace. Childhood muscle

memory kicks in, passing condiments back and forth. As if we notice it at the same time, we both freeze, him with pepper suspended in the air between us and me handing out more napkins. I laugh and snatch the pepper away.

'Hey, so, can I ask you something?' Adam asks, seemingly more sober than he was earlier.

I tip my head as if I don't understand. 'You know you can.'

He concentrates on his meal, tearing his pudding apart. 'How did you know it was over? With John, I mean.'

Ah, there it is. The admission I'd known was coming for months. What strikes me is that the question comes in such a casual manner, as if this isn't the most important conversation we've had in years. Instead of being relieved that he's finally said something, I feel a terrible sadness wash over me. This sucks.

'You mean aside from that rubbish at the fancy corporate dinner?' I pop a lump of potato in my mouth.

Annoyed, he narrows his eyes like that's not quite how he meant it. 'But what about before that?'

I place my cutlery aside and fold my hands in my lap. 'Right, so there were a few things that had been bubbling away, things we'd talked about, things I'd wanted to talk about, but that had never been resolved.'

'I think he's realised his mistake, by the way. All I've heard this week is "She was the best thing that ever happened, and I let her go."'

'Well, if he had made a bit of an effort to define what we were.' I glare knowingly at Adam. 'Or, you know, let me introduce him to family.'

'He really didn't go in for any of that?'

'Didn't want to do family, friends, social functions, any of it.' I slice the air with a hand. 'Which is ridiculous when you think about it. Guy's prepared to sit through a law degree but can't sit through a Sunday roast. Even dumber is the fact I went along with it for so long.'

'Well, exactly.' Adam digs about his plate. 'Sticking out a degree doesn't exactly scream commitment-phobe.'

'Adam, he refused to go to Lainey's wedding with me. Point blank.' I place my fork down. 'And every time I thought we might finally sit down and, you know, define things, he made some excuse about having to work.'

His lips curl. 'But he's just so dogged about everything else in his life.'

I raise my brows. 'You're telling me.'

'But, I mean, how do you even have a relationship with someone who works that much anyway?' he asks. 'I refuse to believe the guy even sleeps.'

'Well, it wasn't much of a relationship, was it?'

'I suppose not.'

Satisfied that our conversation has taken something of a confessional turn, I shift in my seat before I ask, 'So, is it over? Has Sophie moved out? We haven't seen her around for a while.'

Adam shakes his head. 'No. I think it'll be me doing the moving out.'

'I hear there's a flat in Camberwell going cheap.' Even though I'm trying desperately to keep things optimistic, something heavy has settled in my chest and I feel that weight in a shuddering breath. 'Does Dad know?'

'No. I'm not sure how to tell him.'

'I won't say anything,' I say. 'It's your business to tell.'

'Having said that, I'm not even sure it's over. We had this massive row a few months back. I'm talking full on screaming match and it's been one thing after the other since.' He dithers about. 'So, it's like when you know something's wrong, but no one's saying anything? It's the bogeyman who'll go away if only you don't acknowledge him.'

'Have you talked about it at all?'

'Ah, tried that.' He nods. 'More arguing. So, I actually don't know where I stand.'

'Right.'

'I guess the reason I mention that, in a roundabout way—' he taps his coaster on the table and looks over at the bar '—is because I think you should call John and make sure he knows that it's over.'

'I thought I made it clear enough.' I frown, confused. 'But I'll throw your offer back at you. Buy me a drink and I'll call him.'

'You're on.' Adam shuffles off his seat and disappears.

As he disappears, I pull my phone from my pocket and look at another text message that's come through. It rankles me, but if I do this quickly, get it over and done with, I can get on with my night. Fifteen minutes, tops, and I'll be on my way. I stare at John's number tapped out on the screen for an uncounted moment before I hit dial.

'Kate.' Relief washes through his voice, so much so I think twice about correcting him. 'Hello.'

'Just returning your call,' I say. 'Calls.'

'Thank you,' he says. 'How are you?'

'Fine, thank you. You?' I stuff a finger in my ear to hear him better over the din of the pub. A DJ is setting up for the night in the front corner and a rowdy group of guys have just shoved their way through the door and to the bar.

'I'm not so bad.' He clears his throat. 'I'm glad you called, actually.'

'You are?'

'Katharine, I am so ashamed of how I behaved,' he blurts like he's been holding his breath all week. 'I was completely awful, and I put you in a terrible position and I want you to know that if I had my time again, I would do so many things differently. Not just that night, but everything.'

'I appreciate that, thank you.' I bow my head into silence, unsure of what I'm supposed to say next.

'Katharine?'

'Yes?' I try.

'I would do things differently.'

'I heard you,' I say.

More silence.

'So, your big move.' I hear his office chair creak. He's *still* in the office. 'You're all done? How'd that go?'

'All done,' I say. 'I've been here a week now.'

'How is it?' he says. 'Is everything okay? Do you need anything? Where are you living? Obviously, I'm not asking for details if you don't want to tell me, I just want to know that you're okay.'

'It's really lovely. I'm close to the middle of town and thoroughly enjoying being back in the fold.' I pull at a loose thread in my jeans. 'Just spending time with family and settling in. Hoping to get around to old friends in the next few weeks.'

'Oh,' he says. He tries to sound excited for me, but I can hear the disappointment lingering. 'Good. Good. I'm glad.'

'Anyway. I'm just having dinner with Adam and he's told me I should call you, so here I am.'

'Katharine, I'd really like to see you,' he blurts. 'I have a lot I'd like to say. In person, that is. It doesn't feel quite right over the phone. Will you be in London anytime soon?'

I roll my eyes. Travelling to London negates the idea of him having to do any legwork, which was the root of all this to begin with. The words are there, sitting right at the back of my throat, tickling at my tonsils to get out, but I swallow them down. I'm too exhausted to fight with him.

I glance up and my eyes lock with Christopher's. I'm sure I see him frown in concern.

'Not anytime soon. I'll be down for Lainey's wedding, and to tidy up a few loose ends, but I won't be in town for long.'

'Was I supposed to be going to that?' he asks.

'I asked you at the time and you said no,' I say. 'Remember your whole thing about not wanting to get too involved?'

'That backfired, didn't it?' he grumbles.

'Yes, it did.'

'I'm sorry,' he says. 'I truly am. I can do better.'

I don't know what to say to that, so I clear my throat instead.

'Can you call me when you're next in town? We'll grab lunch and talk through this.'

'No. I don't think that's a good idea,' I say. I'm not going to lie, this hasn't been the easiest option, moving across the country. The best, yes, but not the easiest. I'm not even sure I want to see him; there's every chance I'd end up in bed with him because it's oh so easy. 'I have to go. Be well, John. Goodbye.'

'But, Kate—'

'John,' I plead.

'What if we could just—'

'Stop.'

'I'm happy to come up and see you.'

'John, listen to me,' I say. 'Let me go.'

He gives a rattly sigh. 'If that's what you want.'

'It's what I need.' I fiddle with anything that might distract me.

'Goodnight, Kate.'

Discarding my phone like it's about to burn me, I look up to find Adam watching me from the bar. Knowing the call is over, he returns with two half-finished drinks.

'All right,' he says, handing me a glass as he sits down. 'Do I need to punch him in the face? Please say yes.'

163

Chapter 15

'Katharine, this is amazing!'

Lainey looks up and around as she twirls across the ground floor, delighting in the sound of her heels clacking against the floorboards. I won't lie, the echo does have a solidly fancy note to it. Having made good on her promise to visit this weekend (even if I'd written it off as excited ramblings), she'd called from the car park just before ten o'clock.

Bleary-eyed and having slept through my alarm, I peer down at her from the upstairs window. She looks like she's stepped out of a country club magazine shoot, with knee-high boots and billowing hair. I race downstairs in my pyjamas and wrap her up in a hug. Until the moment I see her on the back step, clutching coffee cups and beaming a smile up at me, I hadn't realised just how much I'd missed her company.

In the time since I moved, we've chatted on the phone and have been burning up the messages more than usual as I learn how to update my website, but it's never quite the same as a tight hug or the total belly laugh that face-to-face physicality can bring.

'Thank you,' I say, hiding a yawn behind my hand. 'It's finally starting to feel like a real thing. I still need to get the darkroom set up, but that'll be next week, I think. Or the week after.'

'You're going in for a darkroom?' she asks. 'I know you were thinking about it.'

I shrug. 'Yeah. There's a room upstairs across from the flat. It'll be another tool, whether I develop film for other people or hire the room out to photographers. Income streams and all that.'

'Impressive.' She retraces her steps back through the room I have earmarked as a gift shop. 'Everything on track?'

'So far.' I follow her. 'Just waiting on paperwork. Permits and stuff. Oh, and I need to sort through all the artists who've contacted me. And one hundred other things I've probably forgot about.'

'I'm so excited. It's looks amazing when you see the photos online, but it's *so* much better in person. You must be thrilled?'

'I really am.' I cross my fingers as I point in the direction of the stairs. 'Come and check out my new flat.'

'Oh my gosh, yes.' She darts past and takes the steps two at a time. 'How are you finding living here? It must be strange to be back.'

'Just be quiet,' I caution, as if bouncing my hands will tamper the noise. 'Adam's—'

Not here.

What?

In his place, a note on the dining table telling me he'll be back soon. He's good, I'll give him that much. I hadn't heard him slip out, but I also hadn't noticed he was missing when I woke up. There's every chance he's been gone for hours already. Not bad, considering we're supposed to be polishing floorboards today.

I dial his number, but he doesn't answer. I can't help but feel a prickle of irritation start to rise.

'So, what has it been? One week? Two? It all happened so fast.' Lainey pokes around the room like a cat getting used to a new home. She peers out the window above the kitchen sink. 'It's only been one, hasn't it?'

'It has been one exceptionally long week,' I say, firing off an exasperated text to my brother.

She takes one look at the empty wine bottles on the side and the dirty mugs in the sink and claps her hands. 'How do you feel about heading out for breakfast while you fill me in?'

We take a quick stroll to Kelham Island. Once an industrial mecca, it's now full of fashionable apartment blocks and gastro pubs that have risen from disused factories in streets that are now lined with expensive bicycles and polished cars.

'I forgot how lovely this area is.' Lainey peers up at a residential complex that fits perfectly with the red-brick grimy windowed aesthetic of the area. 'Could you imagine opening a gallery around here?'

'I can.' I step into a café with squeaky-clean windows, chalkboard signs and dangling Edison globes. 'Prices aren't too bad either, but I couldn't find anything suitable. There was one place that came close, but it would have meant moving in with Dad and Fiona, and I'm sure they'd quite like to keep their privacy.'

'Imagine sneaking boys back down that hallway now.' She grimaces despite the giggles. 'Remember that party at the end of first year, where we both brought boys back to your Dad's? I think I slept in the sunroom, didn't I?'

I clutch my face at a memory I'd almost forgotten. 'That squeaky floorboard right by the kitchen entry.'

'Do you know, I don't think I ever told you this, I was in the kitchen the next morning. I'd bailed my guy out the front door, I can't even remember his name now, and your dad comes walking into the kitchen in his pyjamas—'

'Gah, him and his pyjamas.' I cringe. 'At least he wasn't naked, I suppose.'

'And he just stops on the spot and bounces on that squeaky floorboard.'

We collapse with laughter. Slipping back into our old routine is chicken soup for an overworked soul. While I'm anxious to get things done, I remind myself to stop worrying about where my brother has disappeared to and remind myself that I have more than a weekend to deal with the floors. He'll call me when he's free.

'All right.' Lainey splays her hands out on the table as she returns from ordering breakfast. 'Talk to me. Where were we last? You were going to John's work do the night before you moved. How'd that go?'

I shake my head. 'We broke up.'

'Wait, what? You did?' she shrieks. 'When?'

Previously, on … I rewind back to the afternoon on Lainey's sofa, the same day we'd searched out Christopher online. So much happened in the week following that I rattled items off like dot points: estate agents, contracts, cancelled plans with John, who'd panicked at the idea of me being pregnant, and the high-end embarrassment of not being the most important person in his room.

We turn over conversations and dissect looks, words and catch-phrases in the hope that something, somewhere makes sense. But, like all broken records, replaying it constantly won't fix the problem. And it doesn't help.

'Oh, sweetheart,' Lainey coos as breakfast is placed before us. 'I'm so sorry. You should have called; I would have come to collect you.'

'Honestly, it's fine.' I still her with a hand to the wrist. 'I was right near Blackfriars anyway, and it wasn't as if I didn't know it was coming. It was simply a matter of semantics by the time the alarm sounded.'

'Have you spoken to him since?' She frowns as she leans into the table. 'Or has it been clean cut? It's been that long I can't remember what protocol is with this stuff anymore.'

'The funny thing is.' I swallow hard. 'He's been calling incessantly all week and I've just kind of been hoping he'd go away.

167

According to Adam, he's had a change of heart. Anyway, we spoke last night, and he was desperately trying to talk me around. I'm talking Mufasa clinging to the rock kind of urgency, pulling out every trick in the book, throwing out every option he could, which is just—'

'It's absolute tosh is what it is.' Lainey holds her hands up by the side of her head. 'Katharine, I am so sorry you're in pain, but please tell me you aren't considering going back to him.'

'Oh, no. God, no,' I say with a bemused smirk. 'No, that's done. And I'm not in pain, not at all. If anything, this past week has been great for reflection. I mean, what else are you going to do when you spend twelve hours a day with the up and down of a paint roller?'

'Better than twelve hours of in and out.' She snorts and sips her orange juice. 'And what did your painting wisdom tell you? Did Bob Ross appear and tell you he was just a happy accident?'

I snigger. 'Hardly.'

It was Wednesday afternoon, right after Fiona and I had sat on the back doorstep with dainty china cups and cucumber sandwiches to have in the sun, when things started falling into place. My brain was a bingo hall and, one by one, the revelations dropped from the basket. The thing with John is, our entire relationship was never ever about what was mutually beneficial – even though the beginning pretext was certainly that. It was always about him.

Here I was, thinking I was a sharp, sophisticated woman, and yet I'd found myself being emotionally swindled by, as Adam phrased it, a trained liar. I'd been drawn into the self-deprecating jokes about art, the suave sophistication of everything that came with sharp suits, a shimmering Pimlico pad, and the sweet words that usually signalled that he was about to ask for a night together.

The more I turned this over in my head, the more I realised my needs were often casually brushed aside under the rug of working late, being terribly busy, or wanting an early night, though I accommodated him freely. While the realisation left me with a hollow feeling, I suspect it had more to do with the shame and embarrassment of being taken for a fool and not out of some romantic notion that my true love and happily ever after had been scotched.

'Yeah, but penis,' Lainey whispers behind her hand. 'We all go a little cuckoo for cock-o from time to time.'

Even though I feel my face burn as I bury it in my hands, I laugh. I laugh at the silliness and the accuracy and the fact that I can see the lighter side of it all. Because of that, I don't feel like I need to spend the rest of the day analysing. What's done is done, and there are so many other things happening in my world that I should be concentrating on.

'Anyway, that's that.' I pour out the last of a pot of Earl Grey. 'Talk to me about wedding prep. How's Frank? What's he doing today? How's Webster? Sally popped up online for a chat the other night. She needed some help with stuff and didn't want to ask Roland or Steve.'

'Well, Frank is at my parents'. Mum wanted help with something, so I dropped him early this morning. Webster's a mess, but you already know that because it's never been any different. But you'll love this, because I'm living for it at the moment.'

'Go on,' I say with a barely concealed laugh.

'So, Steve stuffed up and promised an artist an exhibition and then forgot all about it, so we had a high noon duel in the foyer. There were a lot of closed-door meetings on Friday about how we're going to handle it.'

I cover my mouth and laugh. She's right, there's a teensy bit of smug satisfaction that comes from knowing he's stuffed up so badly. Who am I kidding? The schadenfreude is a strawberry milkshake, and I'm so very thirsty.

'As for wedding prep,' Lainey says, wiping the tears of laughter away, 'the groomsman and bridesmaid are sorted, our parents are still completely insane, and I'm just about finished with everything except for ...'

I watch on as she pulls some coloured card from her handbag, pressed carefully inside a hardback book. It's the same shades of blue and white we used for her place cards. She passes it carefully across the table to me. I know what it means before she even opens her mouth and I hope I don't break out into a cold sweat.

'Menu cards,' she says with a smile.

'Oh,' I blurt.

'Now, I know it took ages to do the place cards, but do you think you'd have time to make these?' she asks, producing a printed mock-up of a menu. 'I know you're busy right now, and I know it wasn't something we originally planned, so I completely understand if you say no.'

'No, absolutely. I have time.' Honestly, I have no idea if I *do* have the time, but I promised I'd help, so I'll make the time. Anyway, what kind of friend would I be if I sent her down the aisle with mismatched stationery? 'How many do you need?'

'There's ten tables, so maybe thirty?' She wrinkles her nose, a sure sign she knows this isn't going to be the quickest job on earth. 'All written out in the same style as the invites and place cards.'

Thirty copies of the same wording, each of them needing to be perfectly presented. It suddenly makes painting walls seem like a walk in the park. I suppose at least it will be a nice change from holding a roller above my head.

'Do you have thirty sheets?' I ask. 'Maybe a few extras if I screw some up? Forty is a good number.'

'That's the thing.' She points. 'I tried the paper shop on my way home last night, but they were out. I thought maybe your dad would have some in stock.'

'Okay, sure.' I sit back. 'Actually, you know what? Let's go to there now.'

We settle the bill and skirt back through the city centre, along West Street and towards Patterson Arts. It's the well-worn route

170

borne of school afternoons and carefree weekends, setting up in the office at the rear of the shop while waiting for Dad to close for the day.

A tram rattles along as we scuttle past shoppers and across the road, nattering about a student bookstore and games parlour that are now things of the past. As I dodge a lorry and step up onto the kerb, I stop still at the sight of someone approaching from the opposite direction.

'Christopher.' I still, my hand on the door, sure that I can feel my pulse throb in my fingertips.

'Katharine.'

Of all the things I needed today, this wasn't it. I have to introduce them. I can't not do it; Lainey already knows who he is from our afternoon of internet sleuthing and, well, if I don't, he's going to throw my failure back at me under some pretext of my own rudeness.

'Lainey, this is Christopher.' I flourish a hand towards him. 'Christopher, my best friend Lainey.'

Lainey holds her hand out, peering up at him with something akin to reverence. Here he is, I want to say, that guy we were virtually stalking, which sounds creepy, but it's the only way she knows him so far. As he was when he met me, he's standoffish and quiet, a sharp nod and a hello just about all he can muster for her. He doesn't take her proffered hand, and I watch as it falls back to her side and she hitches her handbag up onto her shoulder.

'Are you coming in?' I ask, leaning into the shop door.

'Thank you. Just stocking up on supplies for class tomorrow.' He steps past me after Lainey, who zings off towards the paper section. 'You?'

'Looking for cardstock.' I tuck dark wisps of hair behind my ear and turn my attention back to my friend. 'I volunteered to make wedding stationery.'

'Right, well,' his voice drifts off as he moves away. 'Have fun with that.'

I'm unsure of what that's supposed to mean, but I don't have room in my head to decipher him right now. Picking up another gallery's flier from the front counter, I turn and head towards the back of the store.

As I bound through the aisles, my world suddenly smells of mothballs, dusty canvas, and the summer of 1993, the first time I worked school holidays in the shop. A framed newspaper article by the door tells everyone who passes that my parents opened the shop in the Eighties, both smiling out from the photo.

Whenever I've visited Sheffield, it's been to home and back again. There's a gnawing realisation that, now that I'm back and settled in, now that my life has changed so drastically, I regret ever leaving. There's a warmth and familiarity to the shop that can only come from happy memories.

Today, Dad's not working. There's someone I've never met behind the counter. With her red hair up in Princess Leia buns and a pencil behind her ear, she's got a sketch pad and a stick of charcoal for company. All I remember from behind that counter was the thrill of serving my first customer, thinking I'd changed the world somehow, while Mum sat in the office out back. She was always busy working on accounts while Dad ran about with a hot pink feather duster and outlandish apron. I let that memory push me further into the store.

The shelves are overflowing with every conceivable product an artist might need, from pencils, paints, charcoals, canvas, thinners and brushes, darkroom chemicals, and everything in between. Oh – the darkroom! I take a quick photo to remind me to make a shopping list for developers, lights and supplies.

'You okay?' Lainey peers at me from the end of the aisle, concern etched on her features.

'Me?' I straighten my back and wave her towards the cardstock. 'Yeah, I'm good.'

She leans in conspiratorially, checking for life behind me. 'He looks like he has a stick up his bum.'

'Stop,' I whisper. 'Don't be horrible.'

After every run-in I've had with him, I don't know why I'm defending him other than I'd hate to hear someone talk about me like that. Lainey gives me a questioning look as she returns to her mission. I turn my gaze across the store and there he is, chin tucked into his chest, brow furrowed as he scratches at the back of his head. Whatever he's looking at has his utmost attention. I hope he's so focused that he didn't hear her.

We keep digging through the pigeonholes of colour, comparing and contrasting exactly the right shade of blue – and would it matter considerably if there was the tiniest bit of difference between the menu cards and the invites? The understandable answer is yes, absolutely.

'Bingo.' I pull a handful of eggshell blue card from the back of the pile. 'This looks like it.'

'That's exactly it.' Lainey grapples for it like an overexcited child and makes a noise like a startled bird.

She counts through the pile and, the further she gets, the more her face falls. I continue searching to see whether, if by some miracle, there's not more sheets hiding behind one of the other colours. There aren't, and there's not enough in her pile for what we need. She says nothing, but I can see her nostrils flare as her breathing quickens.

'What are we going to do?' she asks. 'We're fifteen short.'

'That's okay. We can order more.' I turn to look at the girl behind the counter. She looks up and smiles.

'What if the paper doesn't come in time?' she almost cries 'I need my menu cards!'

'You'll have them in plenty of time,' I stress. 'You don't need them done immediately, and I'm not going to be able to do all of these this afternoon. Place an order. I can pick it up during the week and *voila*: menu cards.'

'Can't we try other stores?' she asks. 'Isn't there another shop in Devonshire Street?'

'You want me to buy from a shop that's not my father's?'

'What are you? On commission?' she snaps.

I'd like to think I understand the pressure she's under, but I don't appreciate the attitude. Hairs rise across my arms and up the back of my neck. 'What?'

Despite my irritation at her fresh case of Bridal Brain, her words give me a lightbulb moment. I'm not sure if it's a fizzling bulb swinging in a dank dripping room, or the beginnings of a golden goose idea, but I turn and weave my way back through the store, slipping through the aisles until I find Christopher.

'Back for more?' he asks as I approach.

'You know me,' I quip, picking up a masking fluid and pretending to read the label. 'Can't keep away.'

'Cheap shit brand,' he says quietly.

'No commission,' I blurt.

Slowly, he places a paintbrush back on the shelf and turns to me. 'Excuse me?'

'Also, you're better off with this brand of paintbrush. The fibre is finer, and it glides through paint better.' I grab for another brush and wave it in his face. Wait. Where did that come from? It feels like an old script trying to upsell products to students on rainy afternoons. 'What if I did a show with no commission? Would you agree to that?'

My stomach clenches as I wait for his answer. He's considering my proposal, I'm sure he is by the way he meets my eyes and looks away just as quickly a number of times. Then again, he always seems as if he's thinking about everything all at once. Hugging myself, I shuffle about on my feet and wait for an answer. Behind me, Lainey has thought better of hunting down every shop in town, and slinks over to the counter to place an order.

'You want to open your business on a no commission show?' Christopher breaks the silence.

'That's correct.' Even I can hear the tremor in my voice. 'None at all.'

'Are you seriously that desperate?' he says through a rueful laugh.

'I am not desperate.'

He sniffs. 'It's either that, or Daddy's topping up the current account.'

'Are you shitting me?' I say firmly. 'Nobody is financing this but me. I can walk out this door right now and call any number of artists in London. I have a Rolodex full of them. They'd be right there in your place, but I'm asking you because I like your work and want to show it.'

'By all means, call them,' he says. 'Pick someone who's already firmly entrenched in the set instead of looking for someone new and undiscovered locally. Yes, let's praise the same banal, black and white world where you look at the same art all the time.'

'What the hell is your problem with me?' I say, raising my voice.

'What the hell is your problem with local artists?' he counters. 'I don't understand this reluctance, Katharine. Just pick someone already. Or are we not good enough? The old north–south divide dies on its sword.'

'Are you not a local artist?'

He stares at me.

'You know, I don't understand you,' I continue, hands slapping against my thighs. 'You want to sell your art, but you don't want to show it. Instead, you're happy to offer up your students. People no one has ever heard of, by the way. And then you tell me I don't support local art even though, last time I checked, *you* are local. I don't get it.'

'So you keep saying,' he snaps.

'What have I done wrong? Have I come in and upset your balance of power?' I continue. 'Have I eaten into the attention sprinkled on you by the adoring public? What is it? Because, right now, I can't work you out.'

'Katharine, I—'

'Katharine, I nothing.' I'm so enraged I'm scared of what's about to come out of my mouth. 'I have tried and tried and tried with you. I want to work with *you*. You. Not your class, but you. And every single time I come near you, you belittle and criticise, and you slice that wound open further. Well, I'll tell you what, I'll crack open the thinners, shall I? You can just splash it on like Hendo's.'

He dips his head in something I hope might be contrition. His mouth moves and eyes glisten as they dart about in a silent call for help, but nothing comes out. Everything is perfectly, terrifyingly silent.

'You think you're special because you've got your school for the gifted and all I did is, what, quit my day job? Like that makes me less worthy of anything than you? Give me a break. You've got so many walls up around you it's like running a fucking gauntlet just to get you to hold conversation.' My voice scratches and breaks. 'You don't want to work with me? Fine. I don't care anymore, go find someone else to insult and leave me alone.'

I turn to find both Lainey and the girl behind the counter staring in shock. The way we're positioned in the shop, it's like the unholy trinity of ridiculousness. Lainey does the Ramsay Bolton sausage wave with the cardstock she's collected. I'd laugh if I weren't so furious.

'Are you done?' she ventures carefully.

Chapter 16

'He is bloody awful.' Lainey makes a face like she's caught the tail end of a foul smell as she scurries along beside me. 'Even the girl behind the counter was gobsmacked. She called him a twonk. Her name is Lolly, by the way. She's lovely. She says the paper will be in this week.'

I stop still and look at her, narrowly avoiding a collision with a bicycle courier who skirts around me, bell ringing in frustration. At least their passing gives me a tickle of breeze. Between my frustration at both Christopher and her today, my mind goes blank.

'And you've been chasing him?' Lainey continues.

I give her a curt look. 'Not anymore. Obviously.'

Somewhere in this adventure, the lines have blurred between my competitive streak (getting him to agree with me) and the desperate desire to open with a bang (having him show his art again would attract attention, I was sure of it). Then again, I'm not so sure they were all that mutually exclusive to begin with. The result? I am livid, and not through some sense of loss, but because there's a niggling feeling poking me in the chest that's telling me Christopher was right in his initial assessment of me.

I am a snobbish, spotlight-chasing idiot.

'But what about the list we made?' Lainey says as we start walking again.

That, and I already have an inbox full of desperate artists looking for a show.

We're barely at the end of the street when my phone rings. Finally, it's Adam returning my calls. I find that, instead of being relieved to hear from him, my annoyance only heightens. None of this would have happened, I wouldn't be feeling like this, had I been at home, breathing through a dust mask and swimming about in floor varnish. And I certainly wouldn't be tearing back down West Street, plucking at my blouse to try and fan myself while entertaining an epiphany about just how shallow I truly am.

'Where are you?' Adam asks before I've had a chance to say hello.

'Where am I?' I hiss into the phone as I round the corner. 'Where are *you*? We're supposed to be doing the floors today. You promised me, Adam, and you've David Copperfield-ed into the ether.'

'We are doing the floors!' he cries. 'You were still asleep, so I left you a note. Even I know better than to wake you.'

'Yes, but you didn't tell me where you were going, did you?'

'I went down to B&Q with Dad. We're back here now, you slacker.' He laughs. 'Also, if I'm David Copperfield, does that mean—?'

'For the love of God, give me twenty minutes.'

When I do arrive home, I find Dad's old work van, which is more mystery than machine, sprawled out in the car park. In a previous life, it moonlighted as a campervan, back when he could still convince Adam and I that a weekend in the Peak District would be more fun than we'd know what to do with. The rear hatch is wide open, and the side door has been slid right back, a proper automotive centrefold.

From inside the gallery, I can hear metallic screeching, heaving

178

and the type of laughter that tells me something more serious is happening than running a polishing mop over the floor or sanding down splinters. We kick off our shoes by the back door and step inside, Lainey close behind, talking about all the renovations Frank finished in the last week. It sounds so much easier than all of this.

The smell of sawn wood fills my nose. It's strangely calming in a way I hadn't expected. As I reach for the stairwell bannister, I spy a toolbag by the entrance to the back room, that small space behind the main gallery area. It's big enough for half a dozen pieces at a pinch, but the intimate vibe is part of its charm.

I've put a lot of thought into that room, and I want to offer it to Fiona as a permanent exhibition space. While one of her favourite things to do is to head to markets and sell her work, I'd love to see her recognised as she should be, and certainly only if she agrees to it. After today, I feel like that needs to be a caveat for everything: only if they agree.

The one drawback to the room was always the carpet. Red and stained, it looks like it's been rolled up and used to dispose of bodies. But, as the room comes into proper view, the first thing I notice is that that carpet is now curled and sagged over itself in the corner like a discarded stuffed animal. Tack strips that once kept it attached to the floor are broken at angles like metal in a wreck. In the middle of it all, Adam and Dad are hunched over with crowbars in hands.

'Please, please tell me I'm imagining this,' I say with a groan. The calm feeling I had only seconds ago vaporises like deodorant on a summer day.

They both stand slowly, hands clutching at hips and eyes crinkling in identical spots. The father and his mini-me. Dad looks at Adam, Adam looks at Dad, and they both turn to me.

'It had to go,' Dad says, gesturing to the space by his feet. 'Anonymous decision.'

Adam clears his throat. 'Unanimous.'

'Anyway, it matches the rest of the place now.' Dad skirts past me. 'Have you inspected this morning's handiwork? You're going to love it.'

'No.' I swallow down my argument. 'I haven't.'

'Right, well, this is what we did while you were being ladies who lunch.' Adam follows at the rear. 'Hello, Lainey.'

She smiles coquettishly. 'Hi, Adam.'

Here's one thing you need to know about Lainey and Adam: they're both ridiculous flirts. She knows it, he knows it, and though they've had some raging arguments in the years we've all been friends, they skirt around and play with each other like it's a game. It's always, always been harmless fun to see who can outdo the other.

Dad steps out the morning's work. Loose nails have been hammered down, they've hired a sander and run it over the floorboards, vacuumed their mess and still had enough time to rip up carpet and start on that room. Guilt isn't the word for it. While I've been out sucking down iced coffee, drooling over pastry, and complaining about men, my two favourites have been here toiling away. They make me all kinds of squishy.

Adam hands Lainey a mop. 'Here you go, you two can get to work with the varnish.'

'Oh.' Her cheeks redden. 'No, no, I have to go. Frank's waiting at my parents.'

'Not even one room?' he asks.

'You don't want me doing this.' She bumbles about and hands the mop back to him. 'I'll ruin it. I dropped a sample pot of paint all over the kitchen floor this week. Wasn't sure it'd clean up for a while there. Frank's still salty about it.'

Adam gives her a gentle, disbelieving look. 'Come on, Lainey, don't be so hard on yourself.'

Even with his attempted wheedling, Lainey slips out quickly and sheepishly, and before any of us can persuade her otherwise. That leaves the three of us to finish the job while I have an imagined conversation about fessing up to the landlord that resembles something close to question-time in the Commons.

Dad thrusts the mop, varnish and thick brush at me. 'It's all yours.'

'Hang on! What am I supposed to do?' I hold the mop out before me. 'Just back and forth like I'm cleaning a floor? And what about the brush?'

'Do the edges with the brush, fill in with the mop. Like a colouring book. There's not much more to it than that,' he says. 'Keep a light hand, otherwise you'll be waiting all week for it to dry.'

'What's a light hand in the context of this? 'How do you know all this?'

'Because here in the north, we have to do these things ourselves,' Dad says.

I guess that's settled then; even my father thinks I'm a big city wanker. My shoulders sag as he walks away.

Starting in the far corner of the front room, I brush varnish into corners, careful not to coat the fresh gloss white of the skirting boards. Being this close to the ground, it feels like a mammoth task, and I slip, trip, and slide more than once. And, when I knock the varnish over and swear loudly, Dad comes out to find me on my hands and knees, in the middle of a salt circle of varnish on the verge of tears.

'No need to cry over it,' he says quietly as he helps me up. 'We'll just smooth it out. If it takes a while to dry, at least you aren't opening tomorrow.'

I'm a mess. My palms and fingernails are crusting over with varnish and I'm sure I've managed to get some in my hair. I stand on the spot as I watch him move about the room like a natural. It's in this moment I realise I feel completely inadequate about this whole adult who owns a business, business. More front than Liberty, as Mum would say. All style, no substance.

In the back room, it sounds like Adam's on the phone.

'Was that you in the shop today with Kit?' Dad dips the mop slowly into the polish.

I say nothing but wipe my eyes. *Don't remind me.*

'Lainey made that order in your name, by the way,' he says. 'You might want to ask her to pay for it next time you see her.'

'Oh.' No chance of lying about being in the shop, then. 'Sorry, I hadn't realised.'

'Do you want to tell me what happened?' he asks.

Any chance of me getting out of this conversation all but evaporates when I remember I've mopped myself into a corner. It's going to take jungle gym manoeuvres to get out, and I don't feel like pulling a hamstring over it.

'He doesn't like me.'

'That's not true.' Dad's not looking at me, but I know he's serious.

'I took your advice and asked him to show his work at the gallery.'

He looks up. 'And?'

'It was a very adamant no, absolutely not, don't even look at me like that because it's not going to happen,' I say. 'I even offered him zero commission.'

'Katharine, you know you can't operate a business like that.' He stops what he's doing and looks at me. 'You need to make money.'

'I *know* that,' I say, hands bouncing at my sides. 'It's just … why does he have to be so rude about it all? First, he complains I won't show anyone local, so I offer him a show and he says no, then he tells me I'm some wannabe art snob when I suggest calling in an old friend in London.'

'And there we have it,' Dad says gently.

'Am I a snob?'

He winces as he pinches his thumb and forefinger together.

'Really?' I plead. 'Don't say that.'

'Sweetheart, you're not a bad person, you just need to understand. You can't come here and set up shop and then bring all your big-name friends up from London when there are plenty of artists right here. You're going to rub people up the wrong way. London has plenty of places. We need more spaces to nurture local art, and I think you'd be great at that.'

'Big names attract people though,' I argue.

'Maybe at Webster, but you aren't there anymore, are you?' he says. I step aside, into a tacky spot and up onto the bottom stair as he sweeps the mop across the final patch of floor. 'And I know people have been coming to you with their portfolios because I hear about it when they come into the shop.'

'It's just for the opening. After that, I was going to run locals.' I scratch at the back of my head. 'I need to kick off with a bang. Which is why I wanted Kit. I thought he might be it, but he's just so stubborn, isn't he?'

'He can be,' he says. 'But the big lump has been through a bit, so, you know. Maybe you're approaching him the wrong way? You can be a little pig-headed yourself.'

Everyone has things happen in life that don't go to plan, but it doesn't excuse bad manners, does it? People can still be polite and hold regular conversation without being in such a hurry to bait others into an argument. I don't remember Dad being awful after Mum died. But I bite my tongue, because I haven't done enough of that lately and I also don't want to get too involved in someone else's business if they're not the person telling me. His story is his own; the rest is just gossip.

Still, you can always count on family to tell you the hard truths, and while I don't agree with Dad's dismissal of Christopher's attitude, I keep quiet. Instead, I ponder how I'm going to work my way through this mess. Realistically, I don't have to look too far for an answer. I have an entire inbox full of talent, so maybe I just need to look at things from a different perspective.

Adam interrupts, tearing past at a rate of knots, heading out the door to catch up with some friends and asking if it's okay to stay at Dad's tonight. We follow, cleaning up after the afternoon's work. As we chat, Dad is keen to offer advice on who to look for in my inbox and who he's seen pass through the shop.

'What are you doing tonight?' he asks, shaking water out of the brush.

'I don't know.' I muck in and rinse a mop head. 'Are you offering dinner?'

'Unfortunately for you, Fi and I already have plans, so you're out of luck.' He winks. 'You might have to learn to cook.'

After he leaves, I fire up my laptop and decide it's finally time to tackle the inbox. Among the back and forth ping-pong of previously answered emails, I wonder how I'm going to start sifting through all these prospective exhibitions.

There are so many people here, too. The influx has slowed to a trickle, but it's still artists who are keen to work and be seen, and I'm responsible for that. Many of the emails contain hi-res scans of their work and links to websites, but sometimes photos just don't do art justice. I want to see the pieces in real life and meet these people.

I call Lainey and wonder aloud how difficult it would be to set up a booking system on my website. It's not hard at all, she explains, but with wedding stuff, work, and renovations, she can't help me with it for the next week at least.

After dropping everything for her paper today, and the fallout from all that, I can't help but feel a bit put out. She's got what she wanted and that's what matters.

My web design skills are only as developed as mashing the 'Buy Now' button after too many drinks, which leaves me to do things the old-fashioned way; I get on the phone, calling every single person from the bottom of my inbox to the top.

I slip back into a routine that's so well worn it's like riding a pushbike. With my diary sprawled out in front of me, I take notes, upload some pictures from today's work to social media, and fill in appointment slots. I don't get through everyone, but

I do work until the odour of varnish in my flat becomes head-achy, which is when I snatch up my car keys and head for the supermarket.

This evening, I head to one of the superstores instead of my usual shop in the middle of town. I figure, with the need for fresh air, it'll keep me out of the house longer and walking the aisles might be a good way to clear my mind.

The shopping list on my phone competes with the occasional call back from an artist. It's not a mad rush, but it's enough to distract me as I walk through the fruit and veg aisles. When my phone sounds for the third time, I hoist my shopping basket up on the edge of a fruit bin and yank my diary out of my handbag.

One slip, and a pyramid of oranges scatters across the linoleum floor like balls down a bowling lane. I'm on my knees, the human equivalent of a Hungry Hungry Hippo, collecting as much fruit as I can when a mud-encrusted boot appears. It stops one last orange being juiced by passing shopping trolleys.

'Thank you.' I reach for the wayward citrus and look up to see who's helped me. 'For the love of … you know, you're exactly like Beetlejuice.'

'What? The brightest star in the sky?' Christopher asks.

'It's not the brightest, smartarse,' I deadpan as I stand and brush myself off.

He smirks. 'It's one of them.'

'What I actually meant was, instead of repeating your name, all I have to do is think about you and you appear.'

Shit. I did not just say that.

But I did, and his face lights up, brows that touch the sky and a mouth that forms a delighted 'O' as he chirps a laugh. 'My, Katharine, that's quite the revelatory statement.'

My cheeks flush watermelon red and I cannot believe I let that slip. After watching each other for a brief, intense moment, I worry my lip and turn away. Lemons, I need lemons. Do I need lemons? I don't know. I don't even care, but they're as good a distraction as I can get right now.

'You're a long way from home,' he says as he follows me.

'So?' I say. 'I like this Tesco.'

'Why this one?' he asks. 'Why not one closer to home?'

'Because this one's bigger.'

'Oh, so it's a size thing.' He nods and purses his lips. 'Got it.'

'What?' I squint in disbelief. 'Where did that come from?'

I glance across to a man who's trying desperately to pretend he can't hear us as he sorts through the Granny Smiths. Shaking my head, I try and scuttle away from the fruit and veg, grabbing for a premix salad on my way.

'What?' Christopher chortles. 'All I'm saying is that it's bigger, so it's a more satisfying experience for you.'

Dumbfounded, I stare at him.

'You can get everything you need,' he continues. 'What? It's logic, isn't it?'

'That's *not* what you meant.'

'Yes, it is,' he says, with all the seriousness he can muster. 'Katharine, you aren't being crass, are you?'

'And why are you here?' I turn his question back on him. 'It's even further from home for you. Don't *you* have alternatives?'

'I do, but I like this one.'

'All right.' I offer a sideways glance and hitch my shopping basket higher on my arm as I move into the next aisle.

'Actually, I'm glad you're here.' Christopher says, still hot on my tail.

'Are you though?' I ask, reaching for a packet of Hobnobs. 'Really?'

He reaches for butter shortbread. How vanilla. 'Absolutely. You see, I came to realise this afternoon that I have not been as professional as I could have been when speaking with you.'

'No, no, don't. I don't want to do this here.' I'm not even sure I've heard him right, and I look around nervously. I wonder if everyone here knows what I know, or if our conversation is somehow being broadcast on loudspeaker, because I'm feeling so exposed right now.

'I really think we should,' he says gently.

'Nope.' I shake my head and start to move away. 'Nuh-uh.'

He grabs at my hand like he's desperate to stop me leaping from a plane. Again. 'Katharine, please.'

Stepping back slowly, I take in the sight of my hand encapsulated in his, warm, smooth and oversized. An involuntary thrill chases up my spine and catches in my throat. 'Okay.'

'I have been rude,' he continues. 'In fact, it would be fair to say I have been more than that.'

I swallow. Hard. He looks utterly distraught. I feel my bottom lip retreat because, as uncomfortable as he looks, he is giving me the most genuine apology I've ever heard in my life. It pains him. And it pains me, too, especially considering the conversations and realisations I've had today. While I keep my eyes fixed on him, because maybe this is all an apparition and he'll vanish like a candle in the breeze, he cannot look at me.

I open my mouth, words scrambling my mind, but he stills me with a hand. That weird tinkly supermarket music scratches in the background. Though it's at volume, there's no chance of it matching the winter squall of blood tearing through my ears.

'No, don't interrupt me.' His head dips. 'I'm on a roll here.'

'Sorry,' I squeak.

'I was incredibly blunt with you when we first met.' He stares at a point on the ground as he scratches his forehead. 'You obviously know I'd been chasing space at Webster and, when your father mentioned you worked there, I may have got a bit excited.'

'Excited?' I give up a snivelly laugh. '*That* was what you call excited? Christ.'

'Well, no one's ever shortened my name to Christ before, but if you like.' He lifts his gaze to meet mine and, as it does, a dimple burrows its way into his cheek.

'Oh, stop it, you.' Laughter springs forth and crushes the iceberg that's been sitting between us for weeks. 'Your work wasn't the arena I was in anyway, so it would never have been me knocking you back.'

'And this afternoon.' He draws a deep breath. 'I was so out of line. I had no right to say the things I did, and I regret them immensely. It's not my job to tell you how to run your business and I also don't believe in wrapping apologies in excuses as it only serves to lessen the intent of said apology. So, I'm sorry.'

Before he's even finished, I can feel my mouth and chin tighten in defiance of the blur in my eyes. I thumb away some tears and take a deep breath.

'On the back of that, I've spent a lot of this afternoon thinking and, for what it's worth, I would like to work with you,' he says. 'If you'll still have me.'

I shake my head and laugh. 'The catch?'

'I'll give you five or six pieces for a show,' he says, stilling my obvious excitement with a finger. 'If you take the rest of the class, too. There are some immensely talented people in that group who just need a leg up.'

'You're not budging on that, are you?'

'A rising tide lifts all boats, and all that.' He drops his chin into his neck and peers up at me from under dark eyelashes. 'You'll love them. And you will take commission.'

'Look at you,' I say with an amused scoff. 'Give you an inch—'

'Oh.' He barks a laugh. 'It's much more than an inch.'

'—and you take a mile.' I feel my cheeks blossom under the weight of his words.

'You of all people should know how hard it is to get paid in the arts, and I refuse to let you work for free.'

'The gallantry,' I say with a gasp, stepping further down the aisle. 'Anyway, it may surprise you to know you weren't the only one doing a bit of thinking today.'

'No?' With a small hand gesture, he offers to take my shopping basket. I let him, and the physical load it relieves almost feels like a metaphoric one, too.

'Actually, it was more a chat with Dad.' I stuff my hands in my pockets and trail along beside him.

'I really like your father, for what it's worth. Very insightful man.'

'Well, as it turns out, insight was the order of the day.'

'How so?' Christopher asks.

'I suspect I may also owe you an apology.'

'You do, do you?' He looks up at the ceiling and smiles brightly. 'Today *is* a good day.'

I swallow my laughter. 'Stop it.'

'All right, okay, what was his insight?'

'It was basically that I'm as awful as you say I am, and you're right about me being a snob and, yes, local artists.'

'Now, I never said you were awful.' He waggles a finger at me. 'Snob, yes. But definitely not awful.'

'Either way, the first show belongs to you.'

'And my class.'

'And your class,' I confirm.

'I like this. This is good,' he says. 'Do you have much left to buy? Want to workshop this while I grab some groceries?'

For the next forty minutes, we follow each other around the supermarket and natter about what the exhibition might look like. While I start on the proviso that I need to see the type of work his class is churning out, it's a warm, gentle discussion, better than anything we've managed until this point and, while we settle on the theme of Local Icons, we also talk delivery time-lines, release forms and using Christopher as the central contact for his class.

The business owner in me wants to buck that idea. After all, it's *my* gallery, but I begrudgingly concede this role to him when he suggests that it might be easier for him to field questions from a dozen other people, instead referring only the difficult stuff to me. With everything else competing for space in my brain, this feels like the better option.

'Does this mean we'll see you at class tomorrow morning?' he asks as we stand under the walkway in the car park, ready to go our separate ways.

'Me?' I scoff. 'No, you don't want me to try to paint.'

'Don't be like that,' he says. 'Everyone can paint.'

'Oh, what,' I say. 'With my postcard photography?'

'I knew that was going to come back to bite me.' He scratches the back of his neck.

'I'll come if you paint me a picture of the gallery.'

'I'm not painting you a picture of that heap,' he baulks.

'That heap?' I bite. 'You love my heap. You're desperate to get inside my heap.'

I narrow my eyes at him and he mimics me. I could easily get used to this newer, more playful version of him. Dare I say it, my last hour has even been enjoyable.

'Come on, you'll love it,' he says. 'Plus, it'll give you a chance to meet everyone, see their work and talk them through our project.'

'"Our",' I repeat. 'Love how you've slipped that one in there.'

'Slipped it right in.' He winks as he starts walking away. 'See you tomorrow, ten on the dot.'

'Wait!' I call to his retreating back. 'Do I need to bring anything?'

'Just your portfolio.' His tongue rolls about his cheek pocket as he backs away. 'Need to know if you're up to scratch.'

Chapter 17

'Here she is,' Christopher says with a slight smile as I slide the classroom door shut behind me.

I breathe a sigh of relief that he appears relaxed. For as much as I was looking forward to being here this morning, to talk to him and his class about our exhibition, I'm still painfully aware that not all our meetings have been as productive as yesterday evening. And I'm late, so I was expecting a grumpy Christopher.

'Sorry.' I grimace, holding up my portfolio as if that's my get out of jail free card. 'Busy morning.'

It's the tiniest white lie. The truth is, the first hour of my morning was spent booking more artist interviews, apologising for calling so early, but explaining I wanted to get things rolling quickly. After yesterday, I've got coal in the engine and I'm barrelling forward at a million miles an hour. That was how I lost track of time, ending my last call as I bounded down my stairs, marmalade toast between my teeth and blouse buttoned in the wrong holes; something I only noticed five minutes ago in the car park.

'I guess we can finally get started.' Christopher flashes a knowing smile to his class. 'For those of you who haven't met her yet, I'd like to introduce Katharine Patterson, artist, photographer and, now, gallery owner.'

My skin tingles. It's the first time anyone has introduced me like that and it sounds bloody amazing.

A murmur rises like a wave from the back of the room. Unlike last week, I'm allowed to finish greeting everyone, traipsing around handbags and easels to take the only seat left at the front of the room. The art that I pass along the way is out of this world. Had I known I'd be contending with this level of quality, Christopher and I may have spent less time locking horns and more time planning.

'Now that she's here, I'm sure she's bursting to tell you about a project that we'll be working on with her.'

Five minutes to regroup, that's all I want. I'm still breathless from scuttling up the hill towards the classroom. But everyone's looking at me as if I'm about to make all their hopes and dreams come true. And, because they're all seemingly inexperienced, I feel much more pressure than dealing with the seasoned artists at Webster.

You've done this before, I remind myself. I've talked to rooms full of multinationals and millionaires. I can manage a Sunday morning art class. All I have to do is manage expectations.

'Katharine?' Christopher prompts.

'You're right. I *am* bursting to tell you,' I enthuse, stepping to the front of the room. 'But before I get onto talking about our exhibition, I should tell you a bit about who I am, how I blew into town, and why you should trust me with your work.'

I give a brief tour of my history: education through to employment, how I ended up home in Sheffield and the journey of bringing a gallery to life. Anticipation ripples through the room when I start talking about my visions and ideas for the space, and there's a moment where I get so lost in the joy of talking about what we're doing that I forget I've got someone in the wings watching me like a hawk. Everything flows perfectly. That's how I know I'm doing something good.

'So, when I first approached Kit about who he thought should be involved in the opening exhibition, he told me he knew the perfect group of people.' I stop. 'All of you.'

I wait for the chatter of excitement to die down before I continue.

'The theme of the exhibition is Local Icons. That could be anything that holds a special place for you. Maybe it's Brammall Lane, the Steelers, Hendo's, or a factory your family has connections to. If any of you are like me, you've probably had generations go through one of the coalmines or steel mills around here. There are no restrictions on method or medium, size or design, but keep in mind that these pieces will be for sale. All I ask is that you create something that makes you feel.'

'May I climb over the top of you?' Christopher only steps back in when I nod. 'As of today, we only have four weeks until opening night, so I'm giving you all the PIN to the door lock here. You're free to come and go as you please over the next few weeks to complete your piece. If I'm not in this room and you need help, please knock on my front door, or call me.'

'What about you, Kit, are you going to be part of the exhibition?' someone at the back of the room pipes up. 'You can't just hang us all out to dry, figuratively speaking, without showing your own art.'

When his only response is to smile sheepishly, the goading begins. I pull my blouse up over my mouth as I listen to the entire class pile on him. Cries of, 'Come on', 'Why not?' and 'You have to' echo through the room. When someone throws in an 'I'll only do it if you do', that's when the room really comes to life. Christopher looks at me and smiles.

'You're enjoying this, aren't you?' he asks.

'I am *loving* it.' I reach around and rub his back.

It was worth coming here this morning if for no other reason than to watch him try and dodge this barrage. In moments, he goes from confident and assured to bashful and pink-cheeked, and I'm so here for it.

When everyone settles, he says, 'You know this class is not about me. You lot are the talented ones, but Katharine drives a hard bargain, so you will see some of my work at the show, too.'

The badgering is quickly replaced by cheers and whistles. I love how much this group seem to love and respect him, and how they all bounce off each other, because it's showing me a completely different side to him this morning.

'I want you all to spend this morning thinking, brainstorming, coming up with an idea for a piece or two?' He looks at me for clarification.

'We can probably fit two pieces per person,' I agree, doing a quick head count. 'That works.'

'Take a walk around the property to clear your head and think about what you consider to be a local icon. Katharine and I will be around if you have any questions. Or, if you like, feel free to begin, all your tools are where they've always been.'

For a moment, we're drowned out by the scuffle of chairs and chatter. I'm waved back into the storeroom at the back of the classroom. It's the same room he marched me into last weekend, so it's a little strange that, this time, he wants me here.

'Are you okay?' he asks.

I tear my attention away from the art that fills the walls and look at him. 'Me?'

'Yeah, you said you had stuff going on this morning. Is everything okay?'

'Oh,' I pip. 'That. Yeah, just returning phone calls. You'll be pleased to know I'm meeting with artists this week.'

'Are you meaning to tell me you listened to my advice?'

'Listen to you?' I mock. 'Pffft.'

I'm afforded a better look at my surroundings today. Many of the paintings look like his own hand, full of large brush strokes and colourful squiggles. Oh, and the emotion. Lifelike eyes glisten and appear to be looking directly at me, their expressions a knowing compact between the subject and the artist. I'm a moment away from asking him to paint me, because I'm so, so curious to know what he sees, when I spot a small canvas near the sink.

It's a woman with smiling eyes and a messy blonde bob tucked casually behind an ear. Christopher freezes when he notices me staring.

'What are you looking at?' he asks, though he can't not know.

'She's gorgeous.' I step closer. 'And so happy.'

'She was, thank you.' He grabs at paper and pencils. 'Let's go.'

'Who is she?' I ask. 'I mean, she must be important. You've got her next to the sink, so you look at her often.'

He stares at me like he's not quite sure he wants to answer. His chin dimples as he purses his lips and clears his throat. 'That's Claire. My wife. Or, at least, she was.'

'Wife?' I mouth. Something uncomfortable sweeps through the room.

'That's what I said,' he says.

'Where has she been while you've been whizzing about the supermarket with me?'

'She's been dead.'

He's so po-faced that they weren't the words I was expecting to hear. My heart clenches. 'Oh, Christopher.'

He shakes his head. 'Don't.'

'I am so, so sorry.'

'And you did anyway.' He sighs.

Now I truly want the ground to open up and swallow me.

'Are you … do you …?'

'I'm fine,' he says, gesturing for me to leave the room. I don't want to. I want to keep looking at the painting. I want to hear the secrets she wants to tell me. 'Come on.'

'Don't say that. It's not fine.'

'It's been two years now, so it is.' He kicks a cupboard door shut. 'In the grand scheme of things, at least.'

I slide the door shut, determined not to cut this conversation short. 'Is that why you won't show your work?'

'Yes.'

'Do you want to talk about it?'

'There's not a lot to talk about,' he says. 'The abridged version? Car accident.'

'The long version?'

He pauses, rubs a hand over his mouth and stares at a spot on the ground by my feet. It's his nervous tell, I know that now. 'I was having a meeting for what was meant to be my first major show and she was on her way to meet me for dinner afterwards. You know how you spend years trying to break into the crowd and then everything begins to line up and a buzz starts? We were both busy that day and I was desperate to be there early so I left her to find her own way there.'

I don't know what to say. He's just laid bare every single reason he's had to dislike me and what I'm doing. I am a constant reminder of how he lost his wife. Another layer of understanding settles around me, and I make a note to tread more carefully in the future. We linger in silence a little longer.

'Anyway,' he says. 'Like I said, it was two years ago. It sucks, I'm not going to pretend it doesn't. But it's not a gushing wound anymore. It's more like a raised scar now. Ninety per cent of the time it doesn't bother you, but occasionally you'll bump it on something or someone sharp and realise it's still a bit tender.'

I want to scold him for sounding like he's trying to brush it aside, so bloody insouciant about it all, but I can't. Losing Mum upended our lives for what felt like years. Eventually, though, you realise the world doesn't stop turning and you need to try and fit back into your place as best you can, even if the shape doesn't quite hold right anymore. It is what it is and there's isn't a thing you can do to change it.

'I understand,' I say finally. 'Sort of, I guess.'

'I know you do.'

'It's not your fault,' I blurt.

Christopher turns away and opens the door. 'If I hadn't been chasing the spotlight and the fame and all the adoration, maybe it wouldn't have happened. Or maybe it still would have. Who knows?'

'Thank you for sharing that with me.'

'It's fine. It was bound to come out sooner or later,' he says, reaching for sketchpads and a tin of pencils. 'It's not some grand secret. I'm only surprised your father hasn't already told you.'

'He's not much of a gossip,' I say. 'Not sure if you'd noticed.'

'You get that from your mother, then?' he says with a smirk.

'Oh, piss off.' I reach for some of the things in his arms. 'Here, let me help you.'

We trundle down the hill towards a small wooden hut in the first paddock. The sound of summer grass swishes about my calves, seeds clinging to my jeans. A group of people dithers about in the field, phones in hands, deep in debate.

'They like my class because it's so lax and you can't fail,' he says. 'Not really.'

'What do you do? Is there, say, a set curriculum, or do you work on something different each week?'

He shakes his head. 'This is the first year, so I'm still feeling my way, but I like classes to be more student driven, which is code for I have no idea what I'm doing. If they want to paint or draw or whatever, then I'm happy to offer advice as they go. I know it's not structured, but I don't think one size fits all when you're dealing with people of different skill and interest levels.'

'That makes perfect sense.' Everything in my arms tumbles onto the bench. I clear a space so I can sit.

'Am I allowed to see your portfolio now?' The bench seat moves under his weight as he gets comfortable beside me.

I slap the black folder into his hand and watch nervously as he flips through the pages. There are the early university architectural photos, moody dark buildings against sharp bright skies, Peak District sunsets, mock advertising campaigns I had to submit for grading, and the occasional portrait.

I find myself apologising for the quality of some of the older stuff, telling him what I'd do differently now. It's the defensive position of someone desperately hoping to impress, especially after his first assessment of my work. If I explain it, he'll understand. I recognise it from phone calls I've had in the last few days. Now, here I am falling into the same validation trap. It's true, I want him to be impressed.

'Stop apologising,' he says, turning the page. 'Oh, I love this shot.'

I look across at the photo. It's mossy grass and an icy reservoir surrounded by an orange and grey sunset at Bamford Edge.

'That was an end of year camping trip with some other arts students,' I explain. 'A heap of us packed up cameras and oils, canvas and pencils, and took off for some inspiration and motivation. Not too long before I started at Webster.'

'Did you enjoy it there?' he asks. 'At Webster, that is.'

'I thought I did,' I say quietly. 'Now, I'm not so sure.'

'You're better off out of the machine.'

'It was worlds away from what I'm trying to do now,' I consider, though his words floor me. They're supportive in a place I didn't expect to find them. 'There are things I loved about being there. Access to the big names, surrounding myself with beautiful art, and all under the bright lights of the big city.'

'On the other hand?' he asks.

'It was quite a boys' club in the end. No matter how much I worked, it never seemed to be enough.' I sigh. 'As busy as I am now, I'm enjoying being my own boss. There are days where I've been pottering all day, painting or whatnot, I look at the clock and realise it's evening, but it hasn't felt like work at all. I care so much about it, about getting it right and doing it for me, that I keep going until I'm satisfied.'

'That's how I feel about this place.' He waves at the world beyond the hut. 'I get to paint and sell my work and maybe pass on what I know to other people without trying to impress people or chase fame or any of that.'

I frown at him.

He leans across and whispers, 'No offence.'

'Except that it was me pursuing you.'

'Don't worry, I noticed,' he says with a laugh as he places my portfolio on the bench and shuffles closer.

'Can you give me some advice on an idea?' I fold myself over and lean into his line of sight, batting my eyelids like a flickering candle.

He swats at me with his pad of paper. 'Considering I've spent the last few weeks trying my best to chase you away, my advice is probably the last thing you need.'

Another compliment. Today has been a tiny victory, but one I'm grabbing with both hands. I'll save the gloating for next time I see Lainey; it'll make one hell of a story. For now, I take a photo of Christopher as he sketches out something beside me.

'What are you doing?' he asks, peering up at me.

Looking at him from behind the safety of my phone, I feel as if it's him who's seeing me for the first time. The hardness in his face is barely registering, replaced by something gentle in his eyes. He's really quite lovely when he's not trying to push people away.

'We have an exhibition to announce,' I say. 'And I need a slightly more cheerful photo than the one on your website.'

He rolls his eyes but says nothing.

Over the next few minutes, sketches and histories are forgotten as we scribble down and refine the small, seemingly insignificant announcement post. Sure, it feels like a huge thing for me, but I don't want to assume I'm going to move mountains just yet. Frustrated sighs give way to revisions and, eventually, we come up with something we both agree on.

'This may sound like a silly question,' I begin, slipping my phone and our new announcement back into my pocket.

'You'd be surprised what counts as silly around here,' he says.

'How did you end up here?'

I watch as he looks off into the distance. His mouth shifts and he sighs once or twice. I suspect he's trying to work out exactly how much to tell me.

'Originally, Claire and I were living in this tiny flat in the middle of town. I'm talking the living room doubled as the dining room, the studio, and entertaining area. What we really wanted was somewhere with sprawling views, room for a family and a studio, all that fluffy stuff. So, when this place popped up, we slapped down the deposit and popped the champagne. About a week after that, she died.'

I cringe. 'I'm so sorry she didn't get to move in.'

'Me too. Anyway, in the aftermath of that, I didn't want to do the art thing anymore. I blamed her for anything that went wrong in my life for the next twelve months. Forgot to pay a bill? Claire, art, boo. Car broke down? Claire normally booked it in for a service. Go to make dinner but find I'm out of ingredients? Claire was the list-maker and shopper. So, when I moved out here about two months after the funeral, I boxed everything away and forgot about it.'

'How'd you feel after that?' I ask.

'Strange. For a while it was nice to walk inside and see nothing but a regular house. It's that old adage out of sight, out of mind, right?'

'Absolutely.'

'But time does its thing, you get past the big milestones; one month becomes six and friends pull you aside to remind you that life goes on. It was around that time, I found I wasn't so much sad, but I was angry and frustrated. Actually, your father has talked about this with me before, along with the dumbing down of conversations. People start talking to you a little differently, slower. "Are you okay, Kit?", "How are things going with you today, Kit?", "Is today a good day or a bad day, Kit?", "We're all here for you."'

'I remember those days,' I say. '"How's your heart today, Katie, would you like to talk to me about anything? It's okay if you don't, but just know that we're all here for you." Which, of course, they're not because at some point people lose patience and disappear back into the bushes and figure you'll eventually work it out yourself.'

He chuckles. 'See, and you know they mean well, they just don't know how to deal with it properly. Nobody does, even if you're the one in the eye of the storm.'

'Correct.'

'Anyway, I left my job as an accounts manager.'

'You were an accounts manager?' I chortle. 'I didn't see that one coming.'

'I had a suit and tie job and sat at a desk and counted beans.'

I try to imagine him walking around corporate land in business attire, and I'm surprised to find I quite like the idea.

'Anyway, twelve months goes by and I met your father at a local craft market one weekend when I was looking at Fiona's work. We got to chatting and he offered me some shifts at the shop.' He brushes eraser shavings from his paper and holds it out to inspect. 'And, I don't know, one night I was just moping about feeling like something was missing, so I got a canvas out and started painting again. I didn't want to go back into the whole cycle of exhibiting because that was still raw, so I decided to start this up and see where it went.'

'And now you just sell online?'

'See, that is such a weird experience. I didn't expect anything to happen, but one piece sold, then another, and it's continued. I generally move one or two a week. It's daylight robbery, really.' Christopher stands and peers around the corner of the hut. 'Once people saw I was online, they were on at me to exhibit again, but it didn't feel right. The school is what feels right.'

'Can I say something?' I ask.

'Always.'

'I'm thrilled you're going to show. Your school is fabulous, and I can see these people enjoy being here with you. They hang off your every word, but your work should be seen by people too. Forget what I think of modern art or renaissance or Lady Jane, or any of that. When I see your work, I'm moved. I feel, and I feel deeply. You should show that.'

'It feels like a huge thing,' he says.

'It is, absolutely it is. But don't you think, maybe, if you don't take that step you'll be stuck in the past forever? At some point, it's time to step out and be you again, isn't it?'

He looks at me. Understanding washes fear from his face and replaces it with soft, sad regret.

'Is that why you haven't got any recent photos?'

I reach out absentmindedly and pat his thigh. His hand shifts and curls around mine and that's how we stay for the next half-hour, watching birds flit and shake about in the rain, trying and failing to sketch with only one hand each. Still, neither of us lets go. We don't need to say anything else because, for the first time, we understand each other perfectly.

Chapter 18

I'm so proud of you.

Congratulations!

This is amazing – I've never heard of this gallery before. They're on my visit list NOW.

I can't wait for opening night.

Digging into a bowl of cereal, I scroll through comments on my newsfeed. The announcement we made yesterday, the one I thought might not be more than a blip on the radar? Well, it's exploded.

Because here I am, not quite at sunrise on Monday morning, streets are still, and the city isn't quite awake yet, but the rest of the world clearly is. Not only are there the usual comments from students, friends and family, but there are collectors from across the world who've picked up on this. They're already asking how they can buy paintings that, to my knowledge, aren't even finished yet.

This kind of response is exactly what we both needed.

Naively not expecting too much from our announcement, I spent last night organising my week's appointments. One hundred and sixty-five people had contacted me about gallery space. So far. When I removed internationals, Londoners, anyone outside the greater city area, and those I'd already made appointments with, I was left with eighty-five more artists to meet this week. It seems like an impossible task.

I made spreadsheets and wrote notes, cue cards to use as a post-university cramming exercise for everyone lined up for this morning. I had decided to hold the interviews upstairs in the flat so, unless I wanted people thinking my unmade bed was an invitation, all I had left to do was clean.

After running the mop over the floor once last time, I load up the percolator and switch my phone to silent. I'm ready. At least I think I am. I've got five minutes until my first meeting, I'm dressed in my best casual, cool I-swear-I-know-what-I'm-doing look of expensive jeans and blouse, my hair no longer looks like I've climbed out of Chewbacca's fur and I've pulled out the make-up for the first time since I moved here.

'You absolutely know what you're doing.' I still myself for one final moment before there's a knock at the door. I bounce down-stairs excitedly to find a dreadlocked man standing on my doorstep, oversized portfolio in hand and a nervous smile on his face.

'Hello, I'm Derry.'

'Derry!' I shake his hand and wave him inside, and my week begins.

The gallery is a revolving door of curious faces and excited artists. My head swirls with all the possibilities, and I can't quite help but leap a dozen steps into the future and imagine what life might be like in six months when this all works and business is booming. I am strikingly grateful that so many people are already willing to take a chance on me and my vision.

And the art I see is incredible. It makes me want to be front and centre at one of Christopher's classes, get myself all good and covered in oil paints just so I can learn to be half as good as them. There's so much variety, both medium and style, and I find myself getting excited all over again. I've seen a lot of it already in my inbox, but to see it all in person tells me I'm going to have a lot more trouble picking a roster of exhibitions than I thought.

When Fiona rings on Friday afternoon to tell me Lainey's paper order has finally come through, it's the perfect opportunity to get out of the house and process my thoughts on everyone and everything I've seen this week. I grab my keys, a small shopping list and head out the door.

As I walk the streets, I realise I haven't had much time to think about Lainey or her menu cards recently, never mind work on them. I managed one as a practice run but, by the time my appointments have finished up each evening, I've been ready for dinner and bed.

The realisation that I also haven't heard from her throws me off kilter. When I lived in London, we saw each other daily in the office, talked incessantly and *always* made time for dinner together. Not having that friendship within reach leaves a painful hole in my chest. I fire off a text message to her as I step inside the shop and look up at the sales counter, expecting to see Dad.

But Christopher is standing there, apron knotted around his waist and pricing gun in hand. He looks happy if a little caught off-guard, and I find myself pleased to see him. We have the shared excitement of the exhibit to riff off now.

'What on earth are you doing here, Beetlejuice?' I ask, hoping my humour lands its intended target. 'Are you determined to be everywhere I am?'

'Now, hang on just a second.' He places the pricing gun down, splays his hands across the counter and leans in. 'You know I work here sometimes so maybe you're the one stalking me. Have you thought about that?'

'I am *not* stalking you.' I smile as I walk towards the back of the shop.

'No, but you are,' he calls. 'You pop up in my inbox, on my

phone, you come barging into my class and upend it and, now, you're in here. Like a Magic 8-Ball, all signs point to yes, Katharine.'

I narrow my eyes at him as I slink away, which he readily copies. I hate that he's right, though I'll never admit it. Fiona is laughing as I walk through the office door.

'He's very jovial today,' I whisper.

'Oddly, he's been like this all week.' She winks at me. 'Absolutely no idea why.'

'Oh, no, don't you do that. No.' I wave a flustered hand by my face, peering out the door towards where he was just stood. It's odd to consider that, after everything, I'd be the one responsible for his good mood. Surely not. Maybe he just got laid. I'll bet that's it.

'He's incredibly excited about the exhibition,' she continues. 'As in broken record.'

'He is?' I close the office door. 'We haven't spoken since Sunday, I think. I don't know, it's been a long week.'

In fact, I *know* it's been that long since we spoke. Despite all the online traffic and fielding enquiries, it seems we've both been so busy we haven't had time to talk.

'How'd you go this week?' Fiona drags my attention kicking and screaming out of cyberspace.

'Amazingly, thank you,' I say, taking a paper bag from her. I check to ensure all the sheets are in there. 'How much do I owe you for this?'

'It's only a few quid,' she says. 'Just pay up the front with Kit.'

Kit. It's such an odd nickname. When we first met, he always seemed so gruff and blunt and not at all playful in the way his nickname suggests. Even with what I know now, I can't wrap my brain around any name other than Christopher. I lean into the door, spying him in one of the aisles. He's not eavesdropping *at all*.

'I'm just going to grab some other stuff on my way out,' I say.

'Sure thing.' Fiona offers me what's left of a limp tomato sandwich. 'Come for lunch this weekend?'

'I'd love to.' I hug her and step back onto the shop floor.

Now that I've met with artists, my focus for next week is setting up the darkroom. If I can offer film processing, not only will it prop up cashflow, but it will be the perfect excuse to indulge in my own photography.

The last time I developed film may have been university, or just afterwards in the darkness of my bedroom. I'm sure I'll be able to pick it up again quickly. With a little help from Google and the furthest corners of my memory, I'd spent the week compiling a list of everything I needed to buy.

I'm so busy stuffing my basket with safelights, trays, developer, stop bath and fixer, that I momentarily lose Christopher in the store. It's not until I'm headfirst in an aisle of photography paper that he rounds the corner and stops on the spot.

'Hello,' I say.

His mouth twitches as he peers into my basket. 'Chemicals? Sinister.'

'It's for the darkroom,' I say. 'And boiling random bodies.'

'A darkroom?' he says. 'That's one thing I've yet to master.'

'You mean there's something you don't know?' I clutch at my chest.

'You'd be surprised.' He follows me to the sales counter, where I start unpacking everything from my basket.

'You know, you should be nicer to me. I'm your boss.'

He snorts. 'You really aren't.'

'Technically, I am,' I try, though I'm having a hard time not laughing. 'Line of succession and all that. Works for the Queen.'

He snorts long and loud. 'You idiot.'

I lean over the counter to check the total as he rings up the last item. 'Yikes.'

'You okay? If it's a problem, I can put some of this aside and you can come back for it later?'

There he goes again on the toss of a coin, from raging innuendos to compassion in no time flat. I probably should put some of it back, but I'm too far gone now. I don't want to look like a retreating idiot. I'm committed to the cause.

'No.' I scowl, quickly remembering the problem I *do* have. 'Actually, what are you doing tonight?'

'Well, hello there,' he says, surprised. 'Are you going to cook me dinner?'

'She can't cook!' Fiona calls.

My jaw drops as I hand over my credit card. 'I can cook.'

'She exploded eggs last time she boiled them.' She pops her head out of the office.

Christopher sniggers as he packs my bags and says, 'Please tell me that's not true.'

I stare at him.

'It *is* true.'

He laughs again. 'Katharine, that's terrible.'

'I forgot they were on the hob. I'd much rather have eaten them than clean them off my ceiling, I promise you.'

'So, you're not offering to cook?' he continues.

'What? No.' I shake my head. 'I was going to ask for your help though.'

'Sorry, what?' He leans further in. 'You may have to repeat that.'

'I need help.'

'Sorry, I still can't hear you.' He leans in, hand cupped over his ear. 'You'll have to speak up.'

'I said I need your help.' This time, I'm louder. 'Happy?'

'A little,' he murmurs. 'What do you need help with?'

'So, I spent this week meeting heaps of local artists and now I have all these submissions to go through. While I can sit there and calculate social media followings and tick a box that says I like their art, I've realised I'm not up to speed with the local scene yet. I thought you might have a better idea. I'd be keen to hear your opinions.'

'Oh,' he pips.

'Don't tell me you're surprised.'

'A little, yes. If you like, I can swing past after we lock up here today,' he begins. 'I'll probably be about an hour or so?'

I nod. 'I can work with that.'

Chapter 19

An hour later, I'm pacing like an expectant father, running through a list of things that need doing before Christopher arrives. Surfaces have been wiped clean, piles of papers tapped into shape, filthy dishes stashed in the dishwasher and I've done an FBI level of checking and hiding anything that could be incriminating.

Even though we've had some lovely moments these past few days, and even though I know both the flat and the gallery are clean, I'm terrified he's going to take one look around and tell me it's too dark, too small, unacceptable and we'll be back to square one.

When I hear the rolling crunch of tyres on gravel in the car park, I bolt downstairs and swing the front door wide because here I am, I'm so excited, please don't let this be painful.

'Hello.' I bounce on the balls of my feet.

'Hey.' He winces as he slams the door shut.

'How was the last hour of your shift?'

'Fiona is nuttier than a cashew factory,' he says, reaching back into his car. 'But she told me I had to bring you some milk, so here you are.'

As he walks past, he thrusts a pint into my hands and wanders inside, leaving me staring at the bottle of milk. I'm on the verge of changing his nickname from Kit to Advent Calendar, because he comes with a new surprise every day. He's even bought my favourite brand. Unreal.

'Katharine?' he calls. 'Aren't you going to show me around?'

I jolt. 'Coming!'

I walk him through the gallery, talking about all the work we had to do, highlighting the especially tricky parts, and what I'd like to see happen in each room.

Listening for his responses, I soon realise I'm almost hanging off every word he says. He's supportive and suggestive in a way that doesn't override my original ideas but builds and works on them. It's an extra set of eyes I didn't know I needed right now, and I'm so grateful for his input.

'I adore this colour.' He runs a finger across the wall. 'It's going to be really effective. Cosy.'

'You know what would make it look even better?' I ask.

'Art?'

'Yes.' I clap my hands. 'Shall we?'

'Lead the way.' He gestures towards the staircase.

'Right, so I'm having a slight dilemma,' I explain over my shoulder as he clomps up the stairs behind me. 'Because I only have a set run of time, I'm not sure who to show and how long for.'

'What was the standard for exhibitions at Webster? When you weren't turning down your favourite Sheffield artists, that is.'

'Oh!' My mouth pops. 'That wasn't me.'

'No, I know.' He steps inside. 'Come to think of it though, I might frame that email as a reminder that they always do come crawling back.'

'Oh, stop it.' When I turn to scold him, he's already laughing. 'You're awful.'

While I dither about playing hostess, collecting drinks, and putting the milk away, we have a lovely bit of back and forth

211

about the optimum exhibition length. If time weren't an issue, I'd likely do month-long runs. At Webster, some of our exhibitions ran for three or four months each, but we could afford to do that on the back of the names we showed. Here, on limited time and with such a huge range of options, we decide three weeks is a good timeframe.

'See, that's what I was thinking, but it feels too short.' I look at him. 'Don't you think?'

'I've seen it done for some of the smaller places around here,' Christopher explains with a shrug and shake of the head. 'And you're not cutting people short. You aren't pushing them straight out the door. You're giving them a good span of time, but also cycling new faces through the door. Remember, each artist will bring their own social circles in, so … Why am I telling you this? You know this.'

'Never underestimate how much I don't know.' I waggle a finger at him. 'But this is great. Brilliant.'

While I divide my diary into three-week blocks, he reaches for one of the portfolios piled on the table. As he does, a half-written menu card slips out onto the table. Funny, I thought I'd put all that away. With a flash of surprise, he picks it up and turns it over.

'I didn't think Uber Eats was this fancy with its menus. Unless this is what you're plating up for dinner?'

'Ah.' I try and pluck it away from him, embarrassed, but he holds it out of reach. 'That's for Lainey's wedding.'

'Loud girl from the shop?' he says.

'That's her.'

'And that's your handwriting?' He looks at it again.

'It's my fancy handwriting.' I shoulder him gently. 'Don't expect any pretty notes anytime soon.'

'Katharine, this is stunning.' He holds the card at an angle as if looking for finer details.

'Thank you,' I say quietly. 'Though it doesn't feel particularly

212

stunning after umpteen invites, place cards, or whatever else she decides she needs.'

'You've done all that?'

I start rattling off points on my finger. 'Engagement invites, engagement thank you cards, wedding invites, place cards, menu cards, and wedding thank you cards to come.'

'That's a hell of a lot of work,' he muses. 'Was this a school taught thing, or something you picked up on your own?'

'Remember you were talking yesterday about not wanting to create your art after Claire died?'

'Yes, of course.'

'That was my version.'

'You're writing my Christmas cards this year, so you know.' He hands me the card, which I stash, along with the rest of them, in the drawer of the coffee table. 'I'll pay you, of course.'

'You're not paying me to write Christmas cards,' I say dismissively. 'Don't be silly.'

'I am if I say I am.' He fixes me with a look I can't quite put my finger on. 'And she should be paying you for your work, too.'

'No,' I say, maybe a little too defensively. 'We've been friends since university. That's a long time and we've been through a lot, so, you know. Plus, it seemed like a great way to be involved.'

Even though I make excuses for her, deep down I know he's at least halfway right.

'What?' He leans back in his chair. 'Why are you looking at me like that?'

'Did you want to stay for dinner then?' I ask.

My question hangs in the air for an unkept moment and, when he looks down at his lap, I wonder if I've overstepped the invisible line of friendship.

'Sure.' He shrugs. 'I was planning on takeout once I was done here anyway, so why not?'

'How do you feel about Thai?' I ask.

Evidently, he feels very good about it, because an hour later

213

we're hunched over plastic containers with an uncorked bottle of wine. An arc of favourite portfolios is spread out across the table and we can't come to an agreement about who to choose next.

'Now, I know you love your old-fashioned art.' Christopher holds up a folder for an artist who's a brilliant Renaissance mimic with a negligible social media following.

'This isn't about personal preference though, is it?' I ask. 'We did plenty of shows at the museum that I didn't love.'

'Really? Like what?'

I sit quietly for a moment and spin the roulette wheel of my memory. 'I don't love cubism. We did that about three years back. It was awful.'

'Good to see we agree on two things, then.'

'We do?' I feel myself turn into him. 'I mean, I get it. It's art and it's in the eye of the beholder and blah blah blah, but what the hell is going on? It looks like a game of KerPlunk on an acid trip.'

Christopher roars with laughter. Pure, loud, delighted laughter. In the short time I've known him, he's always given off this air of someone who takes the world far too seriously. He can be boorish and wickedly blunt but, right now, all I can think is *Oh God, I made him laugh, I made him laugh ... I. Made. Him. Laugh.*

'That is brilliant.' He wipes tears from his eyes. 'Ker-Plunk.'

'What else have we got?' I reach across him, steadying myself with a hand on his shoulder. I return to my seat, but my hand stays, shifting only slightly further down his back. I'm sure I don't imagine the fact he leans into my touch.

I say nothing, instead concentrating on picking and sorting and working our way through the rest of the folio. Christopher is mostly quiet with his opinions, though he talks through the common-sense stuff like having a balance between the very new and the established, huge follower numbers and small numbers but an effective presence.

214

When we finish, we've narrowed the list down to six artists, filled out my calendar, coloured and drawn up a Gantt chart. I feel terribly accomplished and blown away by his help.

'Now, all you need is contracts,' he says, cleaning one pile of paper while I sift through another. 'Send them off, then all you need to do is wait, really. Once you get into the cycle of it all, it's a waiting game.'

I offer him another drink to say thank you, but he chooses to pack up and go home. He's quiet as he gets ready, and I'm not entirely sure if I've said something to upset him or touched on a sore point, so I don't push it any further. After the way things have changed between us, I feel nauseous at the idea that I might have inadvertently undone that.

Downstairs, he turns to me as we reach the car park behind the gallery.

'Can I tell you a secret?' He leans in and fixes me with such a look I'm certain he's about to unload nuclear codes on me. 'Can I trust you with that?'

I avert my eyes for a moment and, when I look back, he smirks. 'I suppose so.'

With a hand on my elbow, he leans into my ear and whispers, 'All those portfolios we worked through tonight?'

'Yeah?'

'I have absolutely no idea who any of those people are.'

'You what?' I shriek, yanking him back as he attempts a quick getaway. 'What do you mean you have no idea who they are? We just sent invites out to the top six!'

'Which you picked,' he says. 'You didn't need me.'

My jaw drops.

'Katharine, you need to trust yourself more,' he says. 'You did all of this, I just sat back and nodded. You've done it before. This is just a different scale.'

'I didn't do that,' I sputter. 'You've been much more help than you realise. In fact, I may very well have been lost without you.'

215

My admission stills the air, and, for a moment, we do nothing but watch each other. I feel my limbs getting shaky. I can't believe I just said that aloud.

'Yes, you did.' His keys jingle in his hand. 'See you Sunday?'

'Art class?' My head tips. 'Yes, of course. Sunday.'

With that, he kisses me on the cheek and leaves me gawping after him. I'm a goldfish, my glass bowl has been smashed and I'm flopping about without water.

When I turn around and walk back inside, his coat is still slung over the sofa.

Chapter 20

'Did you know Christopher's wife died?' I ask.

Adam takes a piece of cardboard from me and steps up the ladder. I watch with bated breath as he tries wedging it into the tight space of the window frame. When he appeared on my doorstep this morning desperate for something to do, I'd already spread myself about one of the spare rooms upstairs, measuring and cutting cardboard. After spending the weekend working on the admin side of the business and Lainey's menu cards, I was desperate for something creative of my own. I wanted to set up my darkroom.

I chose a smaller upstairs room with a sink and running water. Despite the window, it's the perfect location for it. But, if there's one thing I've learned about darkrooms this morning, it's that they're not quite as easy to construct as the internet will have you believe.

'Dad mentioned something about him last night,' he says. 'You know, one of those whispered comments that give off a whiff of taboo even though it's not that big a deal.'

'It's quite a big deal, I think. You know how it was with us.' I rush in under him and drag foam tape across the bottom of the board, all my extremities crossed for a perfect seal. 'Two years ago. Still a bit fresh, isn't it? I don't think Dad would be hiding that conversation to save embarrassment, maybe just as a bit of respect.'

'It seems unfairly cruel to lose a spouse at such a young age.' I can hear the strain in his voice as he forces the top corners into place. 'It's not quite like divorce, is it? At least they can tell you they hate your guts and run off with the co-worker they swore wasn't the reason for the two a.m. text messages. Death doesn't really give you answers, does it?'

'I guess not.' I peer up at him as he takes the tape from me and works along the top of the window. Finally, the light begins to disappear from the room. 'He's a brilliant painter though.'

'Is that so?'

'And he's agreed to exhibit, so that's good.'

'Uh-huh.'

'I went out to his school last weekend to meet everyone. That was nice,' I say. 'And yesterday too. Took my camera this time; it was nice to potter around and take photos after spending all week in the office.'

'Katharine, do I detect a bit of crush?' he says.

'What? No!' I scoff. 'I mean, he's not as awful as I thought he was, but he's still a bit, you know.'

'Snobbish like you?'

I gasp, though it barely hides my laughter. 'How very dare you.'

Of all the things I've thought about, and I've done a whole lot of thinking since I left him by the side of his driveway yesterday afternoon, none of it has been in a romantic context. My brain has been running business at a million miles an hour for the last few weeks. There's no room there for romance, and I'm sure he feels the same way.

'He is you, but with a penis.' He looks down at me, brows raised. 'Seriously. He's dry and stubborn and nobody can tell him anything once he's set his mind to something. That's you, and that's exactly why you rubbed each other the wrong way.'

218

'I am not like him.' I baulk at the accusation. 'And I don't not like him. We've had chats. He's … he's okay. We get along well when he's not being rude.'

'Yeah, you are,' he insists, leaning back to inspect his handiwork. 'You might find his attitude is a coping mechanism. If he's acerbic enough that people aren't sure where they stand, then he doesn't have to get too close.'

'Really?' I ask. 'Dad was never like that.'

'Katie.' He glances down at me. 'He was. You were just too young to realise at the time. All those times I shepherded him off to the pub? They were because he was getting unbearable. He was fucking awful for the first year.'

Just when you think you have your teenage years sorted, along comes someone to tell you what you knew was wrong. It's amazing to think that, in our family, there are three histories that all tell the same events. It's another one of those adult realisations that stops you silent for a while.

Adam steps down from the ladder while I pull the door closed. We're in almost total darkness, just a few sneaky shards of light slipping through the top of the window and underneath the door. We add another layer of board to the window, overlapping what's already there and I push a draught stopper against the door. There, now we're in almost midnight darkness. It's as perfect as I'm going to get it without cutting off ventilation completely.

While Adam cleans, I set the room up as best I can with the supplies I picked up at Dad's shop yesterday. I set out designated wet and dry areas, mark spots for chemical baths and mixing jugs, and set aside a corner for retrieving film from cannisters. When he returns, we close the door and switch on the safelight, brothel red and just bright enough that we can see each other.

'Looks really good, Katie.' He turns slowly, taking it all in.

'Not so bad, hey?' I nudge him. 'Pretty clever.'

'You are brilliantly smart and horrendously tenacious. You simply need to trust yourself a bit more.' He gives my shoulder a squeeze. Before he can get away, I slip my arms around his middle and drag him in for a hug.

'You know, you're not the first person to say that recently,' I say.

'Whoever said that is obviously a smart person.'

As is his style, Adam tries to duck out with the minimum fuss, making excuses about heading out for dinner with old friends and wanting to check in on emails beforehand. The least I can do is persuade him to join me for afternoon tea. He won't accept so much as £10 for his help today, which I've negotiated down from a higher sum, but he's always found it impossible to pass up afternoon tea.

I pluck a new roll of film from the bottom of my handbag and stuff it into my camera as we walk out the door. We wander about looking for a bakery we both remember from childhood but settle for a booth in the café at the Millennium Gallery when neither of us can find it.

'Before you run off today,' I begin as I slide a tray of tea and scones onto the table.

Adam stops texting furiously and puts his phone in his coat. 'Yes.'

'Can you talk to me about you?' I ask. 'Your silence is bothering me.'

He frowns. 'Doesn't normally.'

'This is different.'

We play a quick game of rock, paper, scissors to determine who gets the blueberry jam and who gets the bramble. I gratefully take the blueberry.

'Please talk,' I say.

'About what?'

My brother hasn't said much about himself since he arrived this morning with a bagful of groceries. 'Just in case you need them', he reasoned. All I know is that he's taking some personal days from work. Oh, and the throwaway comment about 2 a.m.

text messages. I'm beyond grateful for his help, I just don't want it to be at the expense of him getting his own help if he needs it.

I flash him a sarcastic look. 'Sophie.'

'Do you want me to be honest?' he asks, sucking jam and clotted cream from his finger. 'Or do you want the easily palatable option?'

'You know we always do honesty.'

And we've done it to the point where sometimes we've been a little *too* honest. I remember one discussion we had when I was living with him and Sophie. It was my first year in London and word had filtered back to Adam that I was both lazy and leaving the house a mess. It was terse and at times his accusations seemed unfairly founded, but things needed to be said either way. I sulked for a few days before everything went back to normal.

'In that case, I feel like I've had the rug pulled out from under me,' he says. 'I know I said at the pub the other week that things weren't looking great, but it still doesn't prepare you for it. I'm furiously angry, but I've got nowhere to expend it. You spend so much time being lulled into a false sense of security by routines and alarm clocks, five-year plans and financial planners, and then it's just upended when she comes home and says she's decided over lunch with a girlfriend that it's over. I mean, how is it fair that they know my marital status before I do?'

I don't have a wealth of experience when it comes to relationships – at least if I'm talking long-term. The few boyfriends I've had lasted between six and twelve months, and my latest experience amounted to nine months of bad decisions and an empty bed, so I can't really give the 'If it were me, I would' speech. What I can do though is listen, and sometimes that's all that's needed.

And I suspect I'm right, because he talks all the way through afternoon tea, a walk up The Moor and back home again, where we sit on the back doorstep and natter about life some more. When he eventually leaves, I squeeze him so tight he might pop and wave as he steps up into the first bus that arrives outside the gallery. I work through a few quick emails about the gallery, then I have nothing but a full roll of film and a few hours until sunset to while away the afternoon.

I take the opportunity to wander around and think about nothing other than apertures and focus, framing and angles as I photograph trees and park benches, flowers and crumbling buildings, rogue cats and my beautiful gallery and its intricate details. I stop a few clicks short of the end of the roll; Christopher wants to learn how to develop film, so he can use the final shots when he's ready.

Except, I'm desperate to try the room myself. Standing by the back door, key in lock, I dial his number. I look up and see a hanging basket that's been left to turn to dust. A nice little flowing *something* would add more homeliness to the place. Just as I think my call is going to ring out, he picks up.

'Kit Dunbar.' He sounds distracted.

'Hey, it's me,' I say.

'Hello, you,' he answers. Something inside me quivers at the familiarity in his voice. 'How are you? I still haven't scared you off, have I?'

I lean against the back door and peer out into the empty gravel car park. 'No. You're going to have to try harder than that.'

I'm not sure, but I think I hear him mumble something that sounds like, 'Good.' Nerves xylophone across my ribs as I take a deep breath.

'What are you doing?' I ask.

'Right now?'

'Hmm.'

'Tonight, it's jam sandwiches for an early dinner,' he says. 'Rock 'n' roll, I know.'

'Now, see, I think you're looking at this entirely the wrong way.' I close the door behind me. 'Jam sandwiches are completely underrated.'

'Does it count that I made the bread?' he asks.

'Look at you, Earl of Sandwich.' I bite down on a knuckle to stop myself from laughing. 'Also, for future reference, I believe fresh bread is one of life's delicacies. When it's home-made, it's even better.'

'In that case, I'm hanging up on you so I can eat in peace.'

'After that?' I say. 'Do you have any plans tonight?'

'Why? I'd ask if you were planning on taking pity and cooking me a meal, but you can't boil eggs,' he says. 'But I must warn you, I don't do pity well. I'll hang up if you start rolling down that hill.'

'Definitely not. You'll get no such thing from me.' I pull the refrigerator door open. 'As for dinner, I can't offer you anything unless you have a thing for two-minute noodles or a microwave meal of chicken and cashew.'

'Gourmet,' he says with a laugh. 'Fiona would be appalled.'

'She'd be bloody terrified is what she'd be,' I say with a laugh. 'Anyway. Tonight. Plans?'

'Are you about to ask me on a date?'

'What?' My breath catches and something pops inside me. 'No. Absolutely not.'

'Thank God for that,' he grumbles. 'I've actually just sat down to draw something. Thought I'd use ink and watercolour. I envisage I'll add it to the collection of those paintings you can't have.'

'You're a horrible man.'

'Terrible,' he echoes. 'Though that word has two meanings.'

'That's terrific, actually. Terrible is simply that.' I smile, drawing my bottom lip through my teeth. When did talking to him become so much fun?

'Aren't you clever?'

'So. the darkroom is ready.'

'It is?' he asks. I can picture him on the other end of the line, his back a little straighter than thirty seconds ago.

'Want me to teach *you* something for a change?'

'I do seem to recall there being some line in there about those who can't do, teach.'

'Oh, stop it.' Now I'm unabashedly laughing. 'You know, you really are something.'

'You're just making life difficult now.' He groans. 'I'd really quite like to get this project finished. It's rather important. Can we pick another time? When else is good for you?'

'I'm quite free this week, actually.'

'How does tomorrow sound?' he asks.

Chapter 21

I check and double-check and make sure I've got everything set up properly. I am absolutely sweating that I'll stuff something up and look more of a fool than I'm convinced I already do. When I hear a knock on the door, I snatch my camera up from the bench and race down the stairs with a spring in my step and a beat in my chest.

Without so much as a single thought to what or who might be on the other side, I wrench the door open, thrust my camera out into the open, and take an unposed, unguarded photo of the first thing I see.

The result? Christopher standing there with a face full of doughnut and paper bag in hand while another parcel remains wedged under his other arm. I fall about laughing at the look of innocent surprise on his face. It's going to make an epically candid photo. I wonder if he'll put that on his website instead of the solemn looking one that's currently there. I giggle as I wind the film onto the next shot.

'What on earth are you doing?' he says through his final mouthful, powdered sugar floating into the air.

I offer him the camera. 'Last few shots. Want to take some before I lock you away in a dark space?'

'Please.' He hands me both bags. 'Hold these.'

'Just so you know, I'm going to hold these doughnuts in my mouth.' I dig about in the bag, drawing some of the sugar and cinnamon up with a damp finger. 'What else did you bring? Do you know how to use a manual SLR camera?'

'I made you a loaf of bread.' He fiddles with the lens. 'And yes, I do.'

'You made me bread?' Though it's a struggle, I manage to pull apart the end of the second parcel. It's yeasty and warm and makes me think of cosy cafés on rainy days where you can snuggle into another person with freshly roasted coffee and a yellowing dog-eared book. Paradise. 'You do realise, if you keep bringing me carbohydrates, I might keep you.'

Keep you? Where the hell did *that* come from?

'Fun fact: I got up at five o'clock this morning to make sure it was baked in time. So don't say I don't ever put you first.' He's terrible at hiding the pride that sparks in his eyes.

'Christopher.' I gasp. 'A proper gentleman knows the woman should always come first.'

He stands there in complete and utter silence, camera dangling from his hand. For a second, I wonder if I've overstepped the line, said too much too soon, again, and I watch him with wide eyes, doughnut poised at my mouth.

'Katharine,' he says, with all the seriousness of a funeral director.

'Christopher.'

'Do you honestly think I'm some sort of Neanderthal?' he says as he lifts the camera and clicks a shot of me hiding sheepishly behind a doughnut.

I'm laughing again when I wave him through the front door. 'I was aiming more for *Homo erectus*, myself.'

'Get inside.' He gives my shoulder a nudge. 'Before I lock *you* away in a dark space and throw away the key. Honestly.'

'I'm so excited,' I say as I follow him upstairs. 'You have no idea how disappointed I was that you were busy last night.'

'Really?' He sounds surprised.

I bury my nose in the loaf. 'I can't believe you made me bread. Thank you.'

'Do you have jam?' he asks, wandering around and making himself completely at home.

'Thick cut marmalade.'

'Bloody heretic.' His top lip curls as he reaches for his bag and retrieves a jar of strawberry jam. It lands on the bench with a solid *thunk*. Is it too early in the day to admit that he's making an amazing impression this morning?

I adore these types of moments, the ease of interaction, comments tinged with sarcasm and the laughter that follows. Not only can he give and take it in equal measure, but it rounds and softens him as a man, sloughing away my earlier image of him as a grumpy loner. He's not that at all, he's simply guarded. Like Adam said: at arm's length.

Even after spending last Friday evening with him as I sifted through artists, even with the laughter and kind words, I'm surprised at this morning's interaction. I'm also hesitant because this, whatever it's becoming, is still crystalline fragile and morning fresh, and I'd hate to overstep the mark and shatter everything. As I place the bread on the side and fill the kettle, I keep an eye on him as he peers into the darkroom.

'This is impressive,' he calls back to me. 'Well done.'

'And you've never used one before?' I ask.

He shakes his head. 'Never.'

I wedge myself in beside him and switch the light on. 'Do you want to learn it all, or do you just want to watch?'

'As much as I like to watch, I'd love to learn, please,' he says. 'I use a digital camera to photograph my work for archiving and online sales, but I've never had this opportunity. It's brilliant, thank you.'

After all the criticism and uncertainty, his turn of enthusiasm is lovely to see. That he believes I could teach someone of his

227

skill level is thrilling and fills me with a cup of courage. I'm chomping at the bit while also feeling strangely nervous.

I leave him to finish the last few shots left in the camera, racing downstairs to lock the door before checking again that I have everything I need laid out on the bench of the darkroom. As I measure and pour out chemicals, I can't help but feel I've forgotten something.

'Shall we begin?' I ask when I notice him in the doorway.

'Do I need to take notes?'

'No.' I smile. 'I'll put something together after if you'd like.'

'I can work with that.'

After a brief introduction to the tools on the bench, I pull Christopher further into the room, close the door and switch off the light. I'm pleased to see it's just as dark as it was yesterday.

'How are your eyes?' I ask. 'Are they adjusting?'

'Normally, my eyes are brown.'

I snort. 'Stop it.'

'They're fine. Can't see a bloody thing, but that's fine.'

'Good.' I reach out for his hand and pull him closer to the bench. 'You look better in the dark anyway.'

'I've always said it's my best angle,' he says, stifling a laugh.

As I guide his hand through the blind process of uncapping the film cannister and finding the leader, I'm painfully aware of how his hand is sitting around mine, how his fingers brush gently as they slip between mine and find their way in the dark. More than once, my mind stumbles, and I'm left standing there utterly lost for words.

'You okay?' he asks after a moment of silence.

'I'm just thinking.' I swallow. 'It's been a while.'

By now, I'm trying to help him wind film onto a spool, but I can't quite get our hands coordinated. Try as I might to guide him around the equipment, it's almost impossible from this angle. The frustration anchors my feet to the spot as I think how I could make this work. I've never taught anyone before and, despite our early laughter, I'm worried that getting this wrong would be far too humiliating. I slip under his left arm and stand in front of him.

'Right. This is going to be much easier if you're behind me,' I explain.

'That's not one I've heard for a while.'

'Stop it,' I hiss through barely concealed laughter.

And he does. Within minutes, the film is wound onto the spool and deposited safely into the cannister for processing. I switch the light back on and talk about chemicals and waiting times; a lot of repetition and avoiding eye contact, but we eventually have a long slip of film that's ready for the next step. After I hang the film up to dry, we split the loaf of bread and pour out strong fresh coffee for lunch.

There's no denying that the tenor of our earlier conversation has shifted the temperature of the room. Every word crackles with charge and yet, as we eat and offer each other shy smiles, we talk about everything but those words and what they might mean. If I'm honest, I'm not sure I want to open that can of worms because, even though I already know I don't want today to end, it still feels too soon after John.

I don't think I'd cope if I were to throw myself into a relationship so quickly and have it go wrong all over again. Then again, maybe I could if this didn't involve the gallery. But it does. Everything now is so intermingled and precious that, if I jumped at this and it did end badly, there's every chance it would bring the gallery down with it. And I can't risk that. So, I let it slide.

For now.

We return to the darkroom, where I switch on the safelight and deal out another round of chemicals. It takes some finessing but, with a bit of patience and crossed fingers, I work out the correct exposure for a print. Slowly, our first image appears – the gallery in the late afternoon light. I repeat the process a handful of times before I hoist myself up to sit on the bench and hand over to Christopher, who seems genuinely excited, if a little nervous, to try his hand at a new skill.

Compared to developing the film, the photo processing is the easy part. At least with the safety light on we can see our way around. Christopher is a brilliant student, quiet and attentive and, soon enough, he's doing everything on his own. While my legs dangle aimlessly from the bench, he zips back and forth from paper, chemical baths, the sink, and the string our prints are being hung from.

'It's you.' He turns to look at me from his spot by the sink, a photo of me held up against his chest.

'Eating, again,' I joke at the sight of my smile appearing in the shape of a half-eaten doughnut.

'What are you talking about?' His attention shifts from me, to the photo, and back again. 'You look lovely.'

Hello. I was *not* expecting that.

From where I am on the bench, I lean in for a closer inspection as he steps back towards me. He lifts his eyes to mine briefly, dropping them again as his hand slides across the top of mine. Then, silence as I realise I wasn't imagining this the other day. His skin against mine feels amazing. My insides light up like a fuse, zipping, crackling and sparking all the way, and I concentrate on the only sound in the room: breaths that are coming in short shaky spurts.

He moves carefully, as if he's thought this all out beforehand. It begins with a tiny tilt of the head, a pretence of getting a better look at the image. I shift back as he leans in and slips between my legs and, here we are, foreheads pressed together and my knees up by his hips. I am so very torn right now.

'Finally, you're the right height,' he jokes quietly.

My mouth dries because I'm in an absolute state about what I'm willing to let happen next. A thousand options, reasons, and clauses flash through my mind. Hours ago, I would have shouted 'No!' to the sky. Right now, though, this feels incredible. Yes, he

230

would be worth it. But what about the gallery opening? The distraction? No, a shuddering exhale, what if this goes wrong and upends not only the exhibition, but my livelihood, dreams and ambitions?

When I open my eyes, all I can see are his long lashes and boyish smile. He reaches out and cups my cheek with his hand, drawing my face towards his. I groan when he shifts and brings his other hand to my back. Right now, I can't be sure I'm breathing. His nose brushes the edge of mine, his lips sweep so gently I can barely feel the breeze they leave, and his hands slip under the hem of my shirt and curls around the softness of my hips.

I can't do this. Not now. So, it's no surprise a tidal wave of relief washes over me when my phone rings.

Just as carefully as he'd held me, he lets go. I don't have to ask him how he feels; I can see the disappointment and confusion etched in his face as we scramble around each other and out of the room.

We've been locked away so long that the sun has almost set, the area lit by orange streetlights and my rapidly blinking phone. I search for light switches I haven't yet memorised and grab for my phone. There are ten missed calls from Lainey. Seeing her name there reminds me I haven't seen or heard from her in almost a week now. I don't think it's anyone's fault, but our regular Friday night pizzas, and the closeness we seemingly shared in London, have already become a thing of the past, and I miss that.

'Lainey,' I answer, flicking a bar of lights on. Christopher has already busied himself with washing coffee cups and packing up. Does this mean he's getting ready to leave? I try waving at him to stop, but he pays me little heed. Eventually, I have to grab at a soapy hand to stop him.

'Katie, thank you *so much* for finally answering.' She sounds out of breath. 'I've been trying for hours now. Where have you been? Are you all right?'

'I am so sorry.' A panicked Lainey isn't one you want to mess with. 'What's up? Are you okay?'

'It's my final dress fitting tomorrow, and my sister has just told me she can't come.'

'That's awful. I'm sorry.'

'Will you come instead? I want someone other than the person looking for my money to tell me it looks okay.'

'Hold up.' I scuttle across to the dining table and deep-dive for my diary. It's covered in Post-it notes and is full of bookmarks and receipts and flinging it open only serves to cover the place in retail confetti. Circled in bright red letters, I've got a meeting with a printing company in the morning. 'What time is your appointment?'

'Midday. You can make midday, can't you?'

I sigh. With a surreptitious look thrown my way, Christopher is becoming less able to hide the fact he's listening. I shake my head and roll my eyes at him. I'm keenly aware of how uncomfortable he is right now. I'd give just about anything to bring the mood in the room back to normal. I also don't want to be negative where Lainey is concerned because I'm so thrilled that she's thought to ask me, even if it does put me between a rock and a hard place. Again.

'Katie? Please?' she begs.

'Isn't your mum going to be there?' I try.

'Naturally, but I need you there, too,' she says. 'I need you, I need you.'

'Look, If I make it, it probably won't be for midday,' I explain. 'I'll probably be there a little after one o'clock. As I said, I've got an appointment first thing—'

'Change it?'

Woah. Until now, I'd smiled and nodded along with the occasional pushy comment, but this feels like things are being taken to a whole new level. Surely, she doesn't expect people to drop everything so she can try on a dress? Especially considering it's the final fitting, which means it's a done deal already. The success of my business isn't quite as certain.

'I can't. This is important to me,' I say. 'Depending on when it winds up, I should leave here with just enough time.'

'Please can you just be there? I need you there.'

I pinch at my forehead and, knowing I can't do much else to appease her, I tell her I'll do my best and end the call. Christopher is already halfway out the door.

'Where are you going?' I ask. 'Don't you want to finish what we were doing?'

My voice drifts. I already know his answer by the look on his face. I've seen it on men more times than I'd care to admit.

'I'm sorry, I shouldn't have done that earlier.' He picks at his fingernails as he speaks. 'I hope I haven't made you uncomfortable.'

'What? No, of course not.' Immediately, I regret that he feels this way. 'But maybe right now isn't the best time? For both of us. Just with, you know, the gallery, the school, getting everything organised.'

It's only when I stop talking that I realise I'm breathless. I'm gasping like I've run a marathon.

'I really don't know,' he concedes. 'Maybe?'

'You know what?' I scramble. 'Why don't we just take a few days and we talk about it later?'

'Actually, I'm not even sure I'm ready anyway,' he says. 'Goodnight, Katharine. I'll see you around.'

Chapter 22

Everyone has those mornings where something simply doesn't feel right. It's not something that can be explained, like forgetting to charge a phone, or discovering an odd pair of socks. It's more a charge in the air. That's how I feel right now, life slipping off kilter as I step into the bridal shop. A bell above the door tingles to alert the God of mischief that it's time to suit up.

There's a tiny lie in that statement though. I'm certain I know what's wrong, and it began in the space between my darkroom, kitchen and car park last night. The thought of Christopher's face as he stood by the door making excuses for his behaviour makes me want to sob, the distracted eyes and downturned mouth. Even if I'd also decided I didn't want anything to happen, the memory is too much.

Add to that my phone call with Lainey, and I was in two minds about being here today. Weddings are stressful things to organise but, even though I love her like the stars, I started my meeting this morning feeling rankled and hurried. As I stood in the office of the printing company, going over the cost of didactic boards, fliers and business cards, I constantly had one eye on the consultant and another on the clock.

They could tell I was rushing too, I'm sure of it. I can't afford to make people feel like that, so I took a deep breath or ten, told myself I'll get to London when I get there, and did my best to concentrate on the issue in front of me.

As it was, I had to race up and over the platform at Sheaf Street as the last call for the train bellowed across the station. And, though I had no control over the speed of the trip, I never truly managed to calm down until I toppled out the other side of a bus ride to the Chelsea bridal boutique. I had nearly three hours to chew over the events of last night, and that didn't bode well for my emotions.

There's enough tulle in this shop to sink a container ship, and I can't quite put my finger on the smell. It's a little plastic polyester with a dab of lavender to calm the nervous bride, mixed with a dash of eucalyptus to perk up the mother-of. Not too much, mind you – one strike of the wrong match and the place would melt in a Vincent Price spectacular.

I will admit, just quietly and between the walls of my mind, that some of these dresses are stunning. When I dig past the sequins, beading, boning and ghastly veils (as if he doesn't know what you look like already), I find myself staring at a boatneck dress that is plain yet elegant, soft but heavy at the same time. It looks like a cloud I'd happily fall through. For now, all I can do is imagine what I might look like in it.

It would be a small wedding, a handful of people, and somewhere quiet. There's no sacred churches or noisy public gardens in sight. I've got more cake than I'll ever be able to eat, a dessert buffet, and it's not so serious that people feel like they're at a black-tie event. I peer up to my right to find Christopher standing in a tuxedo.

Wait. What?

How did he get here?

I stuff the dress back in the rack quicker than the Roadrunner on a freeway and give my head a quick shake in the hope Christopher might fall out of my made-up scenario. Nope, he's staying put, clinging to the edges of my mind. And because he is who he is, he rebels by climbing straight back up into my daydream and making himself comfortable, gluggy paintbrush between his teeth in lieu of a flower.

I take a deep breath and press a hand to my chest and feel my heart thudding heavily beneath my shirt. Welp. I am dead.

'Aaaaaand let me just take those before we have an international incident.' From out of nowhere, a staff member with tightly pulled hair and the world's best posture flits into view and back out again, absconding with the tray of coffee and bag of cupcakes I'd just paid way too much for at an overpriced food truck.

'No, but I won't spill them.' I make grabby hands while she Mario Andrettis around the corner and out of my life. 'That's breakfast and I'm hungry!'

'Dresses from all over the world!' she spruiks from somewhere in the distance. 'I'll be back to help you pick one in a moment.'

Now, that'd be a great trick if she could pull it off.

'Is that you, Katharine?' Lainey squeaks over the top of everything.

Trying to find my friend among the aisles of dresses is like trying to make it through the labyrinth to Jareth's castle. I follow her chorus of 'ouches', 'be carefuls' and 'I need my boobs' until I find her perched on a platform outside a fitting room. Immediately, I'm glad I made the decision to be here today because she looks stunning. There are no other words for it. Lainey is going to make the most incredible bride.

She's been cinched and fastened into her dress, which is classic A-line with lace sleeves and plunging neckline. She's got her hands up near her armpits while a seamstress drifts about her feet with a mouthful of dressmaking pins. I offer help, but there's nothing I can do except take a seat on a silver velvet sofa opposite Camille, her mother, who gives me a stressed hello.

'Is it okay?' Lainey asks, eyes downturned in worry.

'You look beautiful,' I say, and I mean it.

236

'Are you sure?' she tries as she fluffs the skirt. 'You don't have to say that just because you're my friend. You can tell me.'

'Honestly, Frank's not going to know what hit him.' My voice breaks.

'Did you bring food?' Lainey changes topic like the wind. 'I'm sure I heard you talk about food.'

'I had coffee and cupcakes, but they got confiscated.' I give an apologetic shrug. 'Hopefully, we can get them back at the end of the exam.'

'If I don't eat something soon, I'm going to be carb neutral,' she announces, sweeping back into the change room and pulling the curtain shut behind her.

'Lainey, sweetie, you want your dress to fit.' Camille offers a pinched face, 'no offence' grimace before turning her attention back to the demands she's giving her daughter and the dressmaker.

'And it will,' Lainey calls from the other side of the curtain. 'There is no *way* I'm dieting just so a bunch of your friends can turn up for a free feed.'

Camille tuts a sigh and gives her head a tight shake. I guess that tells me all I need to know about the state of the union this morning. I shrug. What more can I do?

'Are you bringing anyone to the wedding?' Lainey asks.

'I'm not sure,' I say, frowning. 'How much longer do I have to decide?'

'A week or two?' The curtain sweeps aside, leaving Lainey standing there in her underwear with a pool of dress at her feet. 'Is that okay?'

'Perfectly fine.'

She fixes me with a look that begs for further explanation. 'And are *you* okay?'

'I really am.' I give my best reassuring smile. 'Better than fine. Life is wonderful right now.'

In the corner of my mind, somewhere by my shoulder, I'm sure I hear Christopher whisper, 'That's right. It's because of me.'

237

I flick the metaphoric devil from my shoulder and train my attention back on my friend.

'So, who are you thinking of bringing?' she asks, strained. 'Have you met someone? Remember, whoever you bring will need a place card.'

For the first time in our friendship, I feel like I can't explain yesterday to Lainey. Not yet. It's not that she wouldn't understand. I'm sure she would. Maybe it's just because I don't even know what to label it yet. Does it even need a label? For all I know, yesterday could transpire to be nothing more than mixed signals and shared embarrassment. The last thing I want to do is put anything out in the universe and have it bite me on the arse at the first roundabout.

'I might bring Adam,' I offer. I probably wouldn't. 'He might like the night out.'

'You'd bring your brother?' she asks. 'Did you know your gallery was the first time I'd seen him in years? Maturity suits him.'

'Surely you've seen him before then?' I ask, trying to think back to events over the last few years. I can't picture them in the same space.

'You know what you could do? You could advertise for a plus one.' She steps out of the cubicle to the sound of her jeans zipper and shakes a finger at my scrunched face. 'Hear me out. I've known people who've hooked up like that. Happily ever after. A guy at Frank's work did it. Had been on Tinder for eighteen months, tried speed dating, blind dating, every other type of dating you could think of. I think he was just at that age where he was like, "Okay, I need someone." Ad in the newspaper? Boom. Married. Boom. Second baby due next month.'

'I'm okay as I am, thank you.' I cross my legs at the knees and watch her spin in the mirror to make sure she's dressed herself properly. I love her so much, but she's definitely got a dose of wedding brain.

While she gathers her things, my mind floats back to the

darkroom yesterday. I'm still trying to process what it means and whether I'm quite ready to take that leap of faith so soon after John. I know I told myself I didn't want to jeopardise the gallery, especially if something went wrong, but if I put work before a relationship, doesn't that make me just as bad as John?

'Are you okay?' Her eyes catch my reflection. 'You look upset.'

'Me?' I point to myself. 'I'm great, just a little exhausted, that's all.'

'You should have opened a gallery in London,' Lainey's mum offers.

I have no words.

Camille has barely slapped down the final payment for the dress and is racing down the street squawking about a tennis club meeting when we're tearing at the bag of cupcakes. Our coffee is now iced, but we swallow everything down like rabid animals as we laugh and talk like we've not seen each other in months.

Lainey's like a screaming pressure cooker, ready to pour out all her troubles this afternoon. From her too-involved mother to her barely-there father, playlists, first dances, and last-minute hiccups, she wonders aloud why anyone would be so desperate to get married.

'Anyone would think it's *her* getting married.' She looks behind her just to be sure her mother really has disappeared.

'Ah, she's just excited.' I bite my tongue and decide not to tell her how much I'd give for my own mother to be too involved in anything I'm doing. 'Or, you know, limit the stuff you invite her to?'

She groans. 'I couldn't not invite her today. She's paying for the damn dress.'

That doesn't sound like the worst trade in the world, when you consider the prices I spied scrawled on swing tags in that shop. As we walk, I learn the boys' suits have been ordered, the matron of honour is under control and there's a bonbonnieremaking weekend if I'd like to come along. I tell her I'll think about it, but I'm sure the gallery is going to keep me busy.

'You know, I was thinking of putting disposable cameras on each table.' Lainey takes me by the hand and drags me into an American diner full of skating girls and milkshakes in metal tumblers. 'Is that a bit unfashionable?'

'Actually, could you?' I ask as we slip into the first booth by the window. 'Aside from the fact it's not naff at all, I built a darkroom last weekend. While I'm learning, I'm also teaching someone to use it. We could do with the experience. And the only way we're going to get experience is to have film to develop.'

'Hang on, wait, you've employed someone? I didn't think you could afford that yet?' She looks concerned, and I can see her brain flipping over like an airport departures sign as she rearranges her cutlery.

'No, no, no,' I say. 'I haven't employed anyone. Christopher wants to learn.'

She snorts. 'The same Christopher you couldn't get far enough away from last week?'

I glance about nervously. 'That's him.'

'Well, then,' she says excitedly, shimmying on the spot. 'Now we're getting to the truth. What kind of help are we talking about? Are we knocking up doors and windows or are we knocking up to some Marvin Gaye?'

'No.' The flames of hell lick at my cheeks. 'Not that kind of help. No. We sat down and talked through our differences. So, that's that.'

'I really don't like him.'

Immediately, I regret saying anything. Not because something scandalous needs to be hidden, or because I'm doing something wrong, but because I need some time to myself to work out exactly what this is or could be without interference. And I feel like Lainey might bulldoze the conversation with her own feelings. Oh, and because thinking about Christopher and the look on his

240

face as he said, 'I'm not even sure I'm ready' on his way out last night touches on something sore.

But that's the thing about shedding first impressions and getting to know people, isn't it? Your entire mindset can change on the flip of a penny, the slip of a hand, or whispered words in the dark. It's confusing and beautiful all at once.

Katharine nine months ago would have leaped straight into bed with him without thought to consequence. This morning, the gallery would have been a mess of clothes, empty wine bottles, and notes on the bedside table. If this ever amounts to anything more than bumbled apologies, the person I am today wants to nurture this, whatever it may be. I want to keep it safe and build something solid, and the realisation takes me by short-breathed surprise.

'Katie? Earth to Katie.' Lainey is snapping her fingers in my face.

A waitress has managed to skate through the maze of tables and is ready to take our order. I feel a little dazed, a touch excited, and absolutely terrified of what this all means. I fumble about for a minute before I order the first thing I see, a cheeseburger and milkshake.

I clear my throat. 'In other news, I've got all my artists sorted for the first six months.'

'Also.' Her eyes light up. 'I can't believe I haven't told you.'

'Told me what?' I ask. Yep, I've just been brushed aside. Again.

'We're going to do a bit of a combined hens and bucks thing in Sheffield,' she says. 'You know, for everyone who can't make it to London. I thought that might be easier. You've been up and down so much lately.'

Does that mean I'm uninvited to the London event? I don't want to ask because I'm sure I know what the answer will be, and I don't want to hear it. Well, she wouldn't say it so much as imply it while dancing around how good a deal it is for me. It's dawning on me today that, perhaps, I'm not as important to her as she is to me. My insides curl up and hide behind the metaphoric sofa.

'That's a great idea,' I say, despite my feelings. 'Who's coming?'

'Mostly cousins and stuff, but probably some of the old gang, too.' Her gaze follows another waitress who's gliding behind the order counter. 'Why don't they have men in roller skates, do you think? I mean, equality, right?'

I chuckle as I dig through my bag and check my phone. It's silent. No messages, no missed calls, not a sausage. 'Who would you put in skates?'

'Let's see. Frank? No, no, scratch that. He's unbalanced on a bicycle, let alone roller skates.'

'All right, then. Someone famous?' I ask.

'I don't know, maybe Sam Claflin?' she tries.

'Good choice. Though I always thought he looked a little like Adam.' I zip up my bag and relax back into the booth.

'But, what about you? You haven't told me who you're putting in roller skates?' she asks. 'What's his name?'

I hem and haw and huff so hard I can feel my fringe tickling my forehead. Christopher zooms past. 'I don't know. How about Henry Golding?'

'Inspired choice.' She offers an approving look. 'Now, let me fill you in on more wedding stuff.'

We spend the rest of the afternoon tucked away in that diner, ordering hot chips and milkshakes, apple pie and vanilla ice cream. Mostly, we talk about Lainey's wedding. For the most part, I'm okay with that. It gives me time to work on the thoughts clouding the back of my mind. As I head home that evening, I don't have a definitive answer, but I do know I need to talk to Christopher because, if I haven't stopped thinking about him all day, I wonder what's going through his mind, too?

Chapter 23

Does guilt abate after a few days? Asking for a friend. Not a friend, actually, just me.

My finger has spent the last few days hovering over the call button, stuck in a state of shaky limbo as I try to work out exactly what I want to say to Christopher. There's a desperate need to apologise, to explain myself and blurt out everything that my past year has been. Seems simple, yet I've struggled to arrange the hodgepodge of words in my head, going so far as to grab a pen and paper to jot down my thoughts. The page is still blank.

At university, I could take notes until the sun came up, working and reworking facts into cohesive arguments and acing essays. Now, I've gone blank. I guess that's how I know this is more heart over head, and how this is so beautifully unique to anything I've ever known before.

I don't want to work today. It's Friday. On top of everything that's racing through my mind, the back and forth of Lainey's dress fitting and a day stuck on the computer yesterday, I just want one day to myself. I forgo my morning routine of checking and double-checking emails and social media and, instead, decide to enjoy breakfast at a café I've never been to as I watch the world go by.

Commuters whiz past on their daily journeys, cyclists and escargot vans vie for space while I sit happily on a milk crate chair with my coffee and fresh juice, attempting to frame the scene in a photograph. The camera on my phone is hardly a substitute, but I'm sure it'll make for a nice post later in the day.

When I'm done, I head to a back-alley gallery. This time, it's not about scoping out the competition or looking for business ideas. All I want is to absorb art with an open mind and enjoy not having to do any of the work. Who knows, maybe it'll inspire me to make more of my own. Now that I know the darkroom works, I've got one less roadblock in my way.

Standing in a marble-floored space looking at a piece that's been constructed with string and brightly coloured paint, I can't say I like it. Sure, there's a plaque next to it with notes about what the artist wants to convey, but I just can't gel with it.

'What do you think the artist is trying to say?' asks a voice beside me.

'Oh,' I say, and it comes out in a way that isn't just a sign of surprise, but one of relief and I'm-so-bloody-happy-to-see-you when I find Christopher standing beside me. He's got his hands stuffed in the pockets of his khaki slacks, linen shirtsleeves rolled up to his elbows, and I don't want to know why he still has bed hair in the afternoon.

'Hello, Kate.' He grins down at me.

For the love of all that's sacred, I love how my name sounds when he says it. Even if it's a nickname I don't love, I let it slide. My mind draws a complete blank and we fall silent. I watch as his eyes move about my face.

'Hi,' I pip.

'Hello,' he repeats.

'What brings you out here today?' I say.

'Can I—'

244

'—I'd really like it if we could talk,' I say.

'Can we please?' he urges. 'I've got so much I need to say but I feel like a fool and I don't know where to begin.'

I breathe a sigh of relief and almost laugh. 'Firstly, you are not a fool.'

'Let me start with the fact I owe you an apology,' he adds.

'You don't have to do that,' I say.

'B-but I have to because I obviously got the wrong—'

'Honestly, it's—'

'And I would hate to think—' he continues as if he's not heard me at all.

I kiss him. I reach up, hold his face in my hands and kiss him. It's not the stuff of romance movies where everything's perfect and rain tinkles down from the sky. For one, it's a little awkward. I spend the first terrifying moments thinking my calves are about to cramp on me because I'm stretched up to meet him and, when I'm not panicking about that, I'm worried I've just done the wrong thing. Then, something wonderful happens; he relaxes into me and kisses me back.

He leans down into me and my legs are more relieved than they've ever been. His mouth is warm against the air-conditioned gallery and his fingers slip and twist between mine, holding me tightly in place as if I'll blow away if he lets go. I revel in him for a quiet moment, enjoying how different this feels from John. Instead of thinking he's trying to take something from me, it almost seems as if he's still apologising. I'm sorry I walked out; I've changed my mind; yes, please keep doing this. The amazing thing is, I *want* to keep doing this.

When someone, somewhere in the back of the room clears their throat, he pulls away only enough to run the tip of his nose down the length of mine.

'You didn't get the wrong idea,' I whisper, my voice tittering with nervous laughter. Only when I loosen my grip do I realise I've been clutching a handful of his shirt.

He sucks in a deep breath. 'Shit. Yes. Okay.'

'How do you feel about getting out of here?'

Crossing the city centre, we grab some chips and head for the shade of a tree in the nearest park, all while trying to untangle hands and mouths. Or maybe we don't want to untangle ourselves. This feels huge and precious, and we both know it, and the whole time Christopher is bursting to finish his apology.

'You know, I've been meaning to call you, I just wasn't entirely sure what I wanted to say.' I keep my eyes fixed on the greasy parcel that sits between us on the wooden bench.

'I think I panicked. I mean, we both saw that I did. It's just that I've been on my own for a while now, so the idea of starting over and going through all that stuff again is scary,' he says, offering me first pick of our lunch.

'Absolutely it's scary. All those introductions and new names and fitting in.' I shudder. 'Has my father ever told you about the time he introduced us to Fiona?'

He shakes his head. 'No.'

'All right.' I pivot so as I'm facing him, pulling my ankle up under my knee. 'Dad rang Adam and me on a conference call, which we never do.'

'Really? Because you kind of give off that vibe of a family who would do weird shit like that.'

'Oh!' I laugh. 'Are you serious?'

'Well, yeah. I mean, you're all so in each other's pockets. Don't get me wrong, it's nice to see, but it's so alien to me. My parents more or less leave me alone ninety-eight per cent of the time. We have supper occasionally and it's all very "How are you, son?" and that's it.'

And, I suspect, that's exactly why he spends so much time with my father.

'I can't imagine that,' I say. 'Bizarre. Anyway, he invited us up

246

to dinner. He explained he wanted us to meet someone and didn't want to tell one of us before the other.'

'You do realise neither of you can do wrong in his eyes.'

'That's because we can't.' I pat his knee. 'So, on he goes, he's telling us about her and adds in that if we don't want to stay the night, he would pay for a hotel because he knows that this might be awkward for everyone. Immediately, we both jumped in and said of course we'll stay. It's Dad. If he's happy, what's the problem, right?'

'That's still a lovely gesture.'

'Honestly, I think it's a little sad he was worried we'd react like that, but nevertheless, we popped up and met her. She was dressed in a Minion outfit because she wanted to paint something fun and she said that got her in the mood. So, immediately we were like "She's perfect for him."'

Christopher laughs. 'Yeah, that's definitely her.'

'It gets to dinnertime and Dad needs something, so I volunteer to go up to the supermarket. Fiona says she's coming, too, and you just know something's coming, right? We pop into The Moor. I don't know why we ended up there, we just did. Conversation is all lovely and what about the weather and tell me about your job, that sort of thing.'

'And then?' Christopher hangs his elbow over the back of the bench and rests his head on his fist.

'I turn around and she's stopped walking and she's in tears and I ask her what's wrong because I think I've said something to upset her. I don't know this woman, maybe I've touched on something without knowing, I don't know. So, she dries her eyes and she says, "I just want you to know that I'm terrified of you and your brother."'

'Shit, that's heavy.'

'What do you say to that though? It's such a massive thing to be so open about.'

'And what did you say?'

'I just hugged her and told her it was okay.'

'Look, your first problem was shopping in The Moor,' he says. 'That'll make anyone cry.'

I laugh and wipe my eyes. 'Oh, and I suppose you're a Devonshire Street lad, are you?'

He winks and I fall about laughing.

'Anyway, moral of the story is it took Dad ten years to do anything and it was still terrifying, for everyone, so whatever you're feeling is okay and you don't owe anyone an explanation as to what you are or aren't doing.'

'You're amazing, you know that?'

'Eh.' I give a half-shrug and screw up my face though I can feel my insides turning to water. 'Took you long enough to realise.'

'How do you get along with her now?' he asks, popping a chip in his mouth.

'I love her. She's been amazing for Dad, and he adores her. As much as we all love Mum, we can't change any of that. He should be happy, right?'

'And what about you?' he asks.

'Here's my theory.' I pick at a loose thread on the knee of my jeans. 'If we do this, if you do still want to do this, then I want to do it properly. I don't want a quick fumble in a darkroom. I want to know you and, so far, I feel like I only know the big stuff.'

'The big stuff?'

'Let's see.' I stumble over the elephant in the park for a moment. 'Lovely Claire and the art school come to mind. I know some of your friends, only by default because they're my parents, but I want to know the little things, the everyday stuff that slips through the cracks.'

'Like what?'

'For instance, I was thinking about you while I was in Graves Gallery earlier.' I silence my ringing phone and slip it back into my pocket.

'You were?' he asks.

'It's just that, I don't even know what your favourite painting is,' I say, sounding more of a question than a statement.

The answer flashes across his face lightning fast. 'For pure enjoyment? *Almond Blossom* by Van Gogh.'

'Stunning,' I agree. 'Calming and soft and beautiful. Makes great wrapping paper.'

'Wrapping paper?' he almost shrieks. 'Katharine, sacrilege.'

I bite my lip and smile. 'What about technique then?'

'Technique? Believe it not, I'm a sucker for Turner.'

'Turner?' My mouth pops. 'Christopher, you are not secretly a fan of romanticism, are you?'

'I don't mind a bit of romance.'

'Why Turner?' I ask. 'Why the technique?'

'You know there's some Turner at Weston Park, don't you?' He pushes himself off the park bench. 'Come on, time for a field trip.'

I get up and follow him and, as we make our way towards the museum, we lose the rest of the world in a discussion about Turner and the romantics. Finally, as we step into the museum, he admits that he'd been to London to look at the modern classics exhibition I'd worked on almost twelve months ago.

And I'm left slack-jawed and surprised by him all over again.

Chapter 24

'Please tell me you haven't started the menu cards?' Lainey asks.

They're prophetic words. I mouth a silent 'thank you' to the postman and walk back to the flat. Tearing at the first envelope, I realise all my paperwork has finally come through. I've got a registered business and permits to sell and trade art, and now I'm rolling down the other side of the hill towards opening night. Ten days may feel like a long time, but it will no doubt disappear in the blink of an eye.

'I've done five of them,' I say. After the bluster of setting up a business these last few weeks, meeting artists and painting walls, sanding floorboards, and filling out rainforests of paperwork, writing out menu cards was one of the few things I'd had energy left for this week. It's slow work, but I've managed to finish one per night. 'Why?'

'Because we might need to make a slight change.'

I sigh and look up to the ceiling. I would channel my inner John McEnroe and tell her she can't possibly be serious, but she's Lainey; she is serious. I'm only glad I've not had a chance to do more.

'An entrée,' she explains. I can picture her 'treading carefully face', the pinched fingers at the sides of her face, followed quickly by her—

'Are you pouting?' I ask.

'What? No,' she says with a dismissive laugh. 'I might be?'

'These things happen,' I say, though I'm rubbing my forehead like a genie might appear and make this all okay. 'Who's allergic?'

'Urgh, so my mum was talking to my aunty, who has just rung me to say us she'll go into full shock if she's in the same room as oysters,' she says. 'Her words, not mine, "washed up puffer fish".'

'Probably don't want to do that, then,' I say, trying to keep my tone bright and airy. 'Can you email me through the new menu, make sure it's spell-checked and perfect and I'll get them done. But, listen, if we could just talk—'

'You are the best, thank you.' She hangs up without another word, leaving me staring at my phone and wondering where my friend has gone, both from my life and from my phone.

There's so much I want to share with her. I want to tell her about Christopher and how things have changed, how I had read him completely wrong, and about having a proper on-the-doorstep snog for the first time since I was a teenager. She'd likely revolt and tell me why he's such a bad idea, but I'm sure I could talk her around.

But she's too busy for me. I haven't had time to catch up with old school friends since being in town, and I've never kept a huge social circle because work has sucked all my time, so she's kind of it for my friendship group. Except she's not anymore, is she? Because she's zipping in and out of my life like a mosquito, and only when and if it suits her.

My phone has barely hit the charger when her email pings. With her wedding approaching faster than the Eurostar, I sit down at the dining table and pull out a fresh sheet of card.

The sooner I'm done and this wedding is over, the better.

And I don't stop working on invites until I'm summoned to my parents' for dinner later that afternoon.

The weather is decent, so I take the opportunity to walk, slipping past the old high school and turning into the driveway to find Adam's car already parked up. I laugh to myself at the idea that he's finally been forced to buy his own fuel. Joke's on me though, because he's sprawled out on the sofa, Jabba the Hutt-like, with an entire packet of Penguins and a pint of milk.

I wish I had that kind of time to myself. I poke my head through the door and say a brief hello, and he offers me the last biscuit, the white flag of the defeated. Down the hall and in the kitchen, Fiona's madly chopping what looks like a mint and watermelon salad while making up lyrics to classical music.

'Hello, you.' She leans in for a kiss as I slip my arm around her waist. 'Your father won't be too far away; he's just closing up. Can you help?'

She steps aside and I take over meal prep while she busies herself with Jenga stacking the dishwasher. With my skills, the dishes would've been the better option for me, but it's nice to help either way.

We hear Dad before we see him, the swing of the screen door and his animated nattering about something I can't quite grasp. I take the salad bowl and make for the dining table. I turn and walk—'Oh, *shit*!'

My first instinct is to cover the salad with a protective arm. I've done a good job, the last thing I want is to spill it all over the floor, even if mint's true calling is in a mojito and not a salad. I look up and oh, my knees, my poor weak knees. My cheeks flood with warmth and my breath catches because … his face. Why does he look so lovely today?

'Katharine.'

'Christopher, hello.'

Even with my mind buried in menu cards, I haven't stopped

thinking about him and how we spent yesterday afternoon talking.

Walking and talking and debating the finer points of art in Weston Park. I can hardly believe it myself. The same Katharine who flew straight into bed with her last boyfriend spent the afternoon just chatting. And it was perfect.

It wasn't that barely breaking surface tension stuff of first dates (wait, did yesterday count as a date?), but the real in-depth stuff that gets into the crevices, burrows into hearts and fills tissues with snotty tears. That's the difference between someone who looks at art and says 'finger paintings' and someone who can dissect layers, shadows and symbolism.

I like to think I'm switched on, that I can see things coming a mile off. But if that were true, it wouldn't explain me hanging on to John by my fingernails for months, and it certainly didn't explain how it was that Christopher had managed to sneak up and get through the keeper.

He's done a serious number on me and, right now, all I can think is that I desperately want to feel his mouth on mine and his fingers curled through my hair again.

'How are you?' He reaches for the bowl in my arms. 'May I?'

'If you touch that bowl, Kit, you're staying for dinner,' Fiona teases as she skirts past and winks at me. Urgh. Was it that obvious?

Immediately, he yanks the bowl from my hand and almost drops it on the dining table. 'I've been trying to call you.'

'You have?' I scramble for my phone. Yes, he has. 'Are you okay?'

'Yes, of course, I'm fine.' He says, angling his screen towards me. The question: *Do they know?* typed out in a message. 'I just wanted to show you some of the pieces that had arrived for the exhibition.'

I shake my head. No. Nobody knows. I haven't seen anyone to be able to tell them, though I'm hardly about to go and advertise my personal business when I'm not even sure what it is myself. Yet, I'm acutely aware we're being watched like we're behind plate glass and someone's charged an admission fee to the show.

I'm relieved when Adam appears from the living room. Not only does it take the spotlight from us but, with the handshakes and hellos, it gives me a little breathing space while everyone settles themselves into seats.

'We have some news.' Fiona places a plate of nibbles on the dinner table.

"We have some news". I reflect on those words for the brief second I'm allowed. It's one of those rare sentences that immediately captures a room's attention. Not surprisingly, it was Adam I was expecting this from, not our parents.

And it's the type of statement reserved for announcing births, deaths, marriages, or any otherwise serious business. I can't see Christopher's reaction, as he's seated beside me, but Adam and I exchange a concerned look because, unless one of them is dying (please, no), they're either getting married or procreating. I'm not sure which of those two options is scarier.

I wouldn't put it past them to have a baby. Not that the idea is offensive, it's beautiful, but that would make me thirty-five years older than whoever my sibling may be. I'd always thought I'd like a sister, but maybe not one who'd be young enough to push me around in a wheelchair before she hit forty.

'Look at your faces.' Dad laughs. 'Don't worry, we aren't toppling the empire.'

Adam scoffs as if this is not a big deal. Not at all. 'Don't be silly.'

'What have you done?' I ask. 'Don't keep us in suspense.'

But they do, and when the oven timer buzzes to announce dinner is almost ready, we almost jump out of skins.

'Okay, so, Fi and I have bought a summer house in Scotland,' Dad says, still laughing as he reaches for her hand. 'Well, it's more a yurt but, you know.'

'A what?' Adam blinks rapidly. 'What? A yurt? Katharine, do you know what a yurt is?'

Sometimes, just sometimes, my brother can be a little lost when dealing with things that don't come between the covers of an act of law.

'It's a bit of a …' Fiona waves her free hand '… a tent type of building, just near Loch Lomond. We're going to transition into off-grid living.'

'Basically, weed-smoking hippies growing vegetables?' Adam mumbles, a bit louder than I think he'd hoped. 'Eating roadkill.'

'All things being equal, yes.' Fiona grins. 'Maybe not the road-kill part, but a more sustainable life, sure.'

My insides unknot themselves and scurry back into position. Gosh, this is such a *them* thing to do. Adam and I have lived through the embarrassment of walking in on the experimental sex-on-paint-covered-canvas period, the Andy Warhol masquerade ball, and the Machu Picchu holiday that filled our phones with llama selfies and landed Dad with a concussion when Fiona got overexcited with the selfie stick. At this point, it's fair to admit that a baby would have been the most surprising option here.

'That's quite the move,' Adam continues. 'Who's going to run the shop?'

'Is there a problem with the shop?' I ask. 'Because if there is, and it's a foot traffic issues, I was planning on heavily promoting through the gallery.'

'There's no problem. It's performing well. In fact, the last twelve months have been brilliant. But I'm almost seventy now, so it's retirement time.' Dad looks directly at me. 'Time for someone else to run the show.'

'Oh, no, come on. I'm barely getting the gallery together,' I say with a laugh. 'What? You want me to buy it?'

'Nonsense, you're more than capable,' he says. 'Unless you'd be interested, Kit?'

Christopher's stops chewing. 'I hardly think it's appropriate to be asking me. Adam?'

'Shit, I can't even draw a potato. I'd be stuffed trying to sell crayons.'

'I mean, this is not an immediate thing, so we don't need to decide tonight.' Dad looks at us each individually. I sense that, as much as he wants to retire, he's going to have the worst time letting go of the shop.

'I think that's a better idea.' Fiona stands. 'Anyone for a drink?'

'Before you get drinks.' Adam holds up a stop sign hand and shifts nervously in his seat. 'While you lot are off playing yurts and entrepreneurs I've been hanging on to a bit of news of my own.'

Brothers. I sigh. Like that, my mood switches and tears prickle the back of my eyes as I wait for Adam to gather himself. Here comes the avalanche.

'Should I, would you like me to leave the room?' Christopher reaches around and clutches the back of his chair, poised for a getaway. Adam shakes his head.

'Should probably just come out and say it.' He takes a deep, steadying breath and clenches his fists against his thighs. 'I'm sure you've probably all guessed by now, but Sophie and I have separated.'

And that's it. Months of secrecy and excuses for a single sentence. Stunned silence replaces the hum of a cooling oven. A bird chirps by the back door. I hate that he's refusing to look anyone in the eye when he's got nothing to be ashamed of.

I reach across the table and give his hand a tight squeeze. Dad seems the most shocked of the lot, whereas Fiona's wearing the look of someone who's been there, done that. Somewhere deep down, I'm sure Dad had an inkling, but his big fault (if I were forced to pick one) is that he does like to see the best in people. Sometimes, that clouds his judgement a little.

'You okay?' I ask.

Adam gives his head a tight nod. His lips are so tightly pursed I worry he's about to bite them both off. 'You know what? I really am. I've been in a kind of limbo for months, so to have an answer now is good. Well, you know, not good, but better than not knowing.'

We sit in contemplative silence for what feels like forever. What exactly are you supposed to say to someone who's hurting like that? Chin up, it'll get better? Sure, it probably will, but that's not quite what he needs right now.

'Oh, Sophs.' Fiona claps her hands to her cheeks. 'I'm sorry, sweetheart.'

To say that we love Sophie is an understatement. Because we've known her so long, she became a pseudo sibling in the family. Her family often joined ours at Christmases and New Years. To think that all that shared history isn't enough makes me incredibly sad.

Everything has been relatively amicable, he assures us, at least for now. It's just a part of life. Except, it's not just life, is it? It's painful and awful and, if it's hard to watch as an outsider, I hate to imagine what it's like in the eye of the storm. They've split the furniture; they'll sell the apartment and move on. He doesn't go into further detail and I'm not sure anyone's game enough to ask the question.

'So there you have it. My news. Not nearly as fun as a yurt.' Adam says teasingly. 'Sorry.'

'Don't apologise,' I say.

'Actually, I should be thanking you.' He looks at me, eyes wet. 'You've been incredible through all this. With everything you've been dealing with, with moving and setting up your own business and everything that's been a part of that, you're still dropping everything to make sure I'm okay.'

Beneath the table, I feel a warm hand squeeze my leg.

Chapter 25

'A yurt,' Christopher blurts, breaking the silence as we wait at the traffic lights.

With my elbow nestled against the window and my hand over my mouth, a snigger becomes rolling laughter. As much as he tries not to, he does the same.

After dinner, conversation turned back to Scotland, the yurt, and how the idea even came about. For the record, it was a recent glamping weekend that stole my parents' hearts, and their minds. Wallets, too, evidently. As lively as the conversation was, when Christopher offered to drive me home, I leaped at the chance to spend time with him.

'What the hell does he want a yurt for?' He looks at me. 'I mean, I get it, he's eccentric, but this is taking it to a Howard Hughes level of extreme, isn't it?'

'I don't know.' I wipe away tears. 'I can't answer that.'

The rattling old car lurches forward as the light turns green. 'There's no reason why he can't grow vegetables in suburban Sheffield.'

'And I'm certain Fiona has been to t'ai chi classes here before, so going back there for them doesn't make sense,' I add.

'Maybe they just need a tree change,' Christopher says, hand held out in question. 'Right? You had a city change, maybe they need a tree change.'

'Anything is possible with the two of them.' I take his hand in both of mine. 'Though, I'm not sure I want to shoulder the blame for this.'

'What about the shop?' He shoots me a quick glance. 'I feel like you don't want it, which is strange, for me, when you consider family history. I suspect you're far more sentimental than you let on.'

'*Moi?* Sentimental?' I bat my eyelids. 'Absolutely.'

He pulls my hand up to his mouth and kisses it.

'I don't *not* want it,' I say. 'I just don't know that I'll have the time. What about you? You enjoy working there.'

He curls his lip. 'Look, I don't know. The thing I love about that shop is not that I'm earning money. I make enough with the art, so that's not the problem. It's getting out of the house that's good for me. If it weren't for the shop, I probably wouldn't venture anywhere other than to skulk around galleries or buy toilet paper. I just don't know that customer service is entirely my thing.'

'That's probably the one thing I'm still a bit worried about with the gallery, dealing with the public.' I shudder as we pull into the car park behind the gallery. 'Aside from that, what did you think of his suggestion?'

It probably couldn't have been clearer that things had changed between the two of us as the first thing we did after dinner was sit next to each other on the sofa. And, while Dad nattered away about plans and the shop, we scrolled through photos of Christopher's students' exhibition work like proud parents at a graduation ceremony. If it wasn't that, it was the slideshow of his own works in progress that had me gasping, cooing and pinch-zooming at the expense of the room around me.

It was around that time Dad suggested Christopher and I buy

into the shop together. There was an awkward silence when, I suspect, we both realised that SnogFest in the park yesterday did not a marriage make. Also, it's apparent my father thinks I don't have enough on my plate right now.

'We'd be making quite the commitment,' he says, shutting off the engine.

'Does that scare you?' I ask. 'Making a big commitment with me?'

He looks at me and shakes his head. 'Weirdly, not at all.'

I pivot so I'm facing him and sandwich my hands between my thighs. 'Not quite the conversation you expect to have so soon with somebody, is it?'

For a moment, we sit in the darkness and watch each other, faces changing with thoughts.

'No, I suppose not.' He rubs a hand over his mouth.

'Also, it's my dad. He may yet change his mind,' I say. 'I wouldn't read too much into it all.'

Christopher takes a deep steadying breath. 'In that case, there's something in the back seat for you.'

I close my eyes and bite my lip, laughter threatening its way up again. 'I have to say, that's the most creative way I've ever heard *that* put.'

'What?' he asks. 'No. For crying out loud, Katharine, you're a rotter.'

'I'm not the one who just tried getting me in the back seat.'

He reaches around and pulls a small box from the footwell behind my seat. 'I'll have you know this car is the literal worst for shagging in. Been there, done that, got the scar from the craft knife I forgot was uncapped.'

I suck a pained breath between my teeth as he shows me the 5p-sized cross on his elbow. 'Ouch.'

'Anyway.' He hands me the box. 'I was going to post this today. I thought you might appreciate the irony.'

No bigger than a paperback book, there's a severe red 'Do Not

Fold' sticker on the front of the package. I give it a shake but can't make out the contents. With a confused look, I slide my finger under the corner of the cardboard and peel it open.

A small board slips out with a tissue paper note wrapped around it that reads: *Postcard-y enough for you?* I flip it over to find the most magnificent ink and watercolour drawing of the gallery. *My* gallery. The windows reflect the sun, a black A-frame on a grey footpath advertises *amazing art* and, if you squint past the beige stone with green doors and white-rimmed windows, you can see a dark-haired girl behind a counter.

Underneath it is a small pile of printed, identical, ready for sale postcards.

Slumping over my own lap, I gasp as the image blurs in my eyes and the lump in my throat threatens to choke me. I don't mean to cry, truly I don't. I like to think I'm not much of a crier but after everything that's happened the last few weeks, creating my own whole new world without a prince or a magic carpet has not been easy.

I swallow it down. Hell, who am I kidding? I didn't need a prince. I am enough as I am, although the man sitting next to me right now is coming close to being just that.

'Do you like it?' he asks.

'Do I?'

'Yes, do you like it?'

'Oh, Christopher.' I scramble across the front seat in one deft movement and kiss him like I've been waiting to do all night. With mouths and bodies pressed against each other, caught in the barely there space of a driver's seat, I cup his face in my hands, while his explore, grappling with the back of my jeans before he reaches beneath my shirt.

I've had enough front seat experiences to know that I have never been kissed like this. The immense give and take of his mouth, his breath on my neck, his fingers wound through the crown of my hair. When I reach for the button on his jeans, he claps his hand over mine and pulls back just enough to bring me into focus.

'Maybe not tonight,' he says, breathless.

I let go. 'No?'

He shakes his head. 'I have to be out early tomorrow, and I know that if I walk through your door tonight, I'm never going to want to leave.'

'No rush,' I whisper. If I'm honest, I feel like an empty piñata at a party, but I understand. We did say properly and slowly. I slip back onto the seat of his thighs and catch my breath, the toot of the horn enough to startle me and send my nerves through the roof. 'When can I see you again?'

'Are you upset?' he asks.

I shake my head.

'What are you doing tomorrow?' he asks. 'I'll likely be free from mid-morning onwards.'

'I was going to come and see you, to see where you paint, but now I need to redo these wedding menus, so I'm going to be stuck here.' I tip my chin in the direction of the upper floor.

'Why don't I bring the art to you then?' he says. 'We'll spend the day simply being creative with each other.'

'Creative with each other?' I smile.

He chuckles and drops his head back on the headrest. 'Oh, you.'

'Yes, please do that.' I nod and kiss him one last time as I slide off him and out the driver's door. My box of postcards is held securely under my arm. 'Can I buy you breakfast first?'

'Make it brunch, and I'm yours.'

262

Chapter 26

Christopher is an hour late.

We'd decided on a brunch venue through a volley of bleary-eyed messages this morning. I've checked and double-checked that I'm in the right spot, Google-mapped and even asked the waiter if there's maybe another similarly named place in the area I might have missed. There's not.

He's not here, and I'm starting to wonder if this isn't London all over again; the 'I can't stop thinking about you' sweet talk, followed by a disappearing act.

Until thirty minutes ago, he was in constant contact with photos and assurances that it would be 'completely understandable' if I wanted to leave. He'd finish up as quickly as he could and meet me at the gallery with a hot breakfast in hand. But I was craving a freshly cooked full English, so I opt to wait it out, enjoying the hour on my own with a bottomless coffee and not having to think about anything other than, well, *him*.

When Christopher finally walks through the door, ratty, paint-smeared T-shirt stretched over his shoulders and around his arms, phone pressed to his ear and hair fluttering in the warm breeze, my teeth stop grinding and the knot between my shoulder releases. He switches his phone off as he approaches.

'I am so sorry.' He smooths a hand over my hair and bends to kiss me. 'Things just didn't quite work as intended this morning.'

'That's okay,' I say, even if I'm not convinced of that myself.

'Brothers, hey?'

'Older or younger?' I watch him sit and fold his arms across the table. Ooft. Those arms. God, help me. It's not yet midday.

'Younger.' He watches me carefully for a moment. 'What is it with younger siblings being a pain in the ass?'

'How very dare you.' I chase his hand around the table and clap it between mine. 'I'm the youngest.'

'That explains so much,' he says with a mischievous laugh. 'How was the rest of your night?'

'You'll be pleased to know I spent most of the night gazing in wonder at my postcards.'

'And you'll be pleased to know there's something else for you in the back seat this morning.'

'You're such a tease.' I lift my mug to my mouth. 'What is it?'

'You'll see,' he says, getting the attention of our waiter. 'Shall we order? I'm so sorry, again, you're probably hungry.'

'Starving.'

He refuses to tell me what's in his car so, while we wait for our meals to arrive, we fill each other in on our mornings. Mine was writing up a few more of Lainey's new, improved menus. His, taking measurements to help build a set of bookshelves into his brother's lounge-room wall.

'So, what you're saying is you're good with your hands.' I circle a finger in the air.

He smiles. 'He's just moved into an old farmhouse in Barnsley with his girlfriend. It's a bit run down, but it's cosy.'

'She nice?'

'Yeah.' His head bobs. 'She's really lovely. Very quiet girl. Nursery teacher, so they're set.'

'What did Claire do?'

264

'She was an accountant.' His eyes drop to his food. 'Always got a bloody good tax return.'

'Can I ask you something personal?'

'You can ask me anything you feel like asking.' He stuffs some breakfast in his mouth.

'Have you been with anyone since her?'

'I have. Took a bit to get my head around it but, you know.'

'The hurdle?' I say.

'I just wanted it over and done with. Do you think that makes me terrible?'

'I think it makes you human.' I grimace as I watch a waiter trip, sending a stack of cutlery sliding across the floor with a glass-shattering screech.

'We're still painting today, aren't we?' He drops himself down into my line of sight as I scrape a mushroom from my plate to his. 'You were keen on christening the gallery.'

'If that's your idea of christening a building, we're going to have some serious discussion.'

He sniggers. 'Well, I've brought my easel all this way so I may as well use it.'

'I'm sure you don't get your easel out for just anyone.' I sink back into my seat.

'You're right, I don't, so make the best of it while you have access to it.'

I clap a hand to my mouth and cough on a mouthful of bacon. 'Stop it.'

'You started it.' He smiles down at his plate. 'You know, this meal would be perfect if it had tattie scones and black pudding.'

I gag and call for another coffee.

'And you're doing what while I'm painting? You mentioned stationery,' he says. 'Your friend's wedding?'

'Thank you for reminding me! I volunteered you for something.' I reach across and take his coffee. It's bitter and black, but

265

it'll do until mine comes. Funnier still is the fact that he doesn't flinch at the theft.

'Here we go,' he says through a yawn.

'Sorry, I'd completely forgot until now.' I cringe. 'Are you mad at me?'

'You haven't told me what it is, but please don't say you want to commission a wedding gift,' he says with a groan. 'They are the absolute worst. You know, I did one once. The bride hated it.'

'What? No. She's going to use disposable cameras on the table. I said that I, we, *you* could take care of developing the film.'

'I did say I wanted to learn.' He sounds surprised. 'Ask and ye shall receive, right?'

'Is that okay?' I shrink back a little.

'Fine by me,' he says. 'Though, if I may be blunt?'

'Are you ever anything but?' I pop food in my mouth and smile around my fork.

'That may be so,' he concedes, brows raised. 'Still, I've noticed you do a lot for Lainey but, from what I've seen, you don't get a lot in return? Even your father said she absconded the minute someone suggest she help the other day.'

'I'll give you that,' I say. 'I'm hoping it's only because of the wedding right now. She's busy, she's stressed. Fingers crossed life will go back to normal soon.'

He forks his pancakes. 'You went to London the other day to help her, yes? How'd that go?'

'Oh, you mean the great north–south divide?' I grin.

The mention of the dress fitting, knowing it threw *us* completely off trajectory, rankles me, stirs up an old irritation.

'Here's the thing.' I lean back into the booth.

'Shoot.' He puts his cutlery down and gives me his full attention.

It's so refreshing to be with someone who's not busily checking his diary, or tapping off a reply to an urgent email, or is looking generally distracted by a random fact of law that leaves a comet trail through his mind. It's a world away to how I'm used to being treated, and it's in this moment that I realise this and appreciate him so much more.

'So, it's a total thrill to watch your friend getting ready to marry the love of her life. Who doesn't want to revel in the happiness of others? It's beautiful. But something's been bugging me lately,' I say.

'What kind of something?'

'You know how, when you've done the same thing for so long and you're living in your own curated bubble, everything makes sense? There's a whole lot of confirmation bias and the world works as it always has and you're happy like that?'

'Isn't that most of us?'

'Then life changes and you step into a new arena. You form new habits and make new friends.' I gesture to him. 'Then, when you try and fit back into that old life it just feels wrong? All the problems and issues and things that you never saw before are being delivered in 4K HD with 7.1 Dolby sound?'

'That sounds like it was a huge success.' He glances away momentarily to look for a napkin.

'No, no, no. Look, I'm not saying it was awful. Far from it. I enjoyed seeing her. I've always loved spending time with her. I just, I don't know, maybe I realised things are changing, life is evolving, and some of those friends I thought would be around into old age are being left behind. Things just aren't quite how they used to be. It's hard to explain, and I realise it sounds rather apocalyptic. It's not meant to be.'

'In my experience, some friendships don't survive cataclysmic change,' he says. 'Or maybe it's just another evolution. Things will eventually settle into a new normal.'

'Maybe,' I say, though I immediately feel bad that I'm concerned about a wedding in the face of everything he's been through. 'A wedding isn't really cataclysmic.'

'Moving away, opening a new business, change of priorities?' He motions to the space around us. 'Could be the perfect storm?'

A fresh cup of milky coffee is placed between us. Christopher looks at it, looks at me, and looks back at it again before snatching it up and taking a sip.

Christopher opens the rear door of his Defender. It may be bruised and battered with questionable rust spots but, inside are six carefully wrapped and transported pieces of art. I bounce on the spot, race to unlock the gallery door and straight back to him as I try my best to see through the layers of bubble wrap.

'Are you kidding me?' I throw an arm around his neck and pull him down into a kiss. 'You. Are. The. Best.'

'Yes, I am,' he says proudly, calling to my retreating back, 'They're not all quite ready, but tomorrow I should have more.'

I pop my head back out the gallery door. 'They'll be worth the wait.'

'I'm worth the wait,' he argues, pointing at himself. 'Me.'

'I wouldn't know!' I shout. 'You went home last night!'

'Oh, boohoo.'

I can still hear the echo of his laughter as I slip into the main room. It's like Christmas all over again. I'm dancing in a snowfield of bubble wrap that's tossed all over the floor and trying to decide where each piece needs to be hung. Screw today's plans, this is much more inspiring.

When it comes time to unwrap five of his six pieces – the last one he wants to paint today – I want to burst with excitement. Among them is a still life of the front door of my father's shop, a tram that's almost as tall as I am, and a dazzling portrait of Joe Cocker.

'He's local,' he reasons. 'Someone will buy it.'

'I love them all.' I clap my hands. 'Let's hang them. I'll go get the fasteners.'

'What? Now?' he asks. 'You don't have them all yet. How do you know how they'll all fit together?'

I gawp about for a moment. 'Does it matter?'

'Katharine, you know the answer to that.'

'Please?' I clasp my hands in front of me. 'I thought you said you were good with your hands.'

'Oh, I'm *very* good with my hands.' He points to the portrait in front of him.

I look away and hope like hell he can't see me blush.

Slowly, he reaches across and tucks a lock of hair behind my ear. His finger draws across the tip of my ear with a featherlight touch. It's painfully slow, so much so I'm aware there's every chance someone will one day make a Netflix documentary about me entitled *The Spontaneous Human Combustion of Katharine Patterson*. Instinctively, I close my eyes and feel myself lean into the palm of his hand.

'Are you trying to distract me?' I ask, looking at his lips just as he licks them.

'Is it working?'

He tips my chin towards him as he bends to kiss me, tripping my pulse and chasing a thrill up my back. For all our talk, our jokes and innuendo, this is about as real as it gets. I brush my mouth over his, again and again, and, as he eases his tongue inside, it becomes fevered and desperate.

We manage to tumble up the stairs, knocking against the wall and gripping the bannister, listening to the scratch of a photo frame slip against the plaster.

'I have thought about this all fucking morning,' he whispers in my ear.

Despite the warmth of his breath, my skin prickles. I have, too.

Through jagged breaths and breathless promises, we grapple with zips and buttons, boots that won't unlace and fall about in laughter when that one pesky leg of my jeans just will not budge.

I feel the mattress dip and wobble between my legs as he snatches it away.

In that moment when it slips off the side of the bed and he's finally inside me, it's so easy to pretend like nothing and no one outside this room exists. We aren't cramped in the front seat of a car, nor are we rushed at the end of a long week. This is completely intentional, and we have all afternoon to prove it to each other.

When the sex is that good, once is never enough. It's late afternoon by the time we untangle the sheets and ourselves and decide that getting something done today isn't the worst idea in the world.

'You know, if you have one more piece to do, you could always paint me.' I bat my eyelids. 'Inspiring local icon that I am.'

'Oh, I could, could I?' He's standing about in bare feet, and I'm sure his shirt is buttoned incorrectly. 'Are you offering to pose for a life drawing class? I'm not sure what I just saw is family-appropriate, but I have been thinking of adding them to my already massive repertoire.'

'As impressive as your massive repertoire is, it would only be for you.'

'Only for me?' He smiles coquettishly. 'I feel so exclusive.'

Before I can draw breath, his hand swings out and I feel the cold wet swill of a paintbrush across my face. I draw my hand across my upper lip and look at the blue stain left of my hand.

I cough and splutter as the odour hits me between the eyes and burns up my nostrils. 'That is so pungent.'

'Just be thankful it's not something worse.' He grabs my chin to stop me from moving as he rubs at the colour. Judging by how hard he's rubbing, it's not moving. 'You look like a post-orgasmic Smurf.'

Laughter springs forth. 'Never have I thought of a Smurf in that context.'

'Here I am, bringing the weird and the wonderful experiences to you. Free of charge.'

'Katharine, are you ready?'

I just about jump out of my skin, turning to find my best friend, dressed up to the nines, standing in the doorway with her hand poised to knock.

'Lainey?' I look at her, surprised.

She frowns. 'What, don't tell me you forgot?'

Oh, shit. Her hen do.

Chapter 27

'Help me,' I mouth to Christopher.

'What?' he says with a laugh. 'No.'

'No?' I can hear Lainey approaching from behind. 'You have to come out with me. *Please.*'

I'm barely changed and looking only slightly less shagged when Lainey drags me outside to the waiting car and sighs heavily as she opens the back door of Frank's car. 'Katharine, this is Hunter. We thought you'd like to meet him.'

Not again.

The last thing I need is to be set up with somebody, anybody. Hunter's in the back seat, drawing his fingers through curly dark hair and waving nervously, and everybody is hoping I'll just slip right in beside him and cruise off into the night.

I glance at Frank in the driver's seat. I can't be sure, but I think he's pretending he can't see me.

'You've, er, got a—' Hunter gestures to his own face '—got a bit of a Violet Beauregarde thing going on there.'

Frank can barely contain his laughter. 'It's very becoming. Not sure it'll catch on though.'

'What?' *Oh shit*, the paint.

'I'll be just a second.' I dodge a delivery van that zings past and is almost launched from a pothole and scuttle back inside. I reach for the rag and bottle of thinners again.

'Give me five minutes.' Christopher stills me with a finger. It's then I realise he's washing his brush and he's not picking new colours; he's preparing to leave. 'I'll pack up and be out of your hair.'

'What?' I ask. 'No. Come with us. Leave that here and come with us.'

'Katharine, I don't think they mean for me to come with you.'

We both look outside to the car, to Hunter in the back seat, and to Lainey gesticulating wildly about something I feel might involve me. There no two ways about it; they don't want Christopher there; I do. I'm twisted like a pretzel trying to work out which obligation to fulfil.

I turn back to Christopher. 'Too bad. I'm asking you to come with me.'

He drops his head and lifts his eyes to mine as if to say, *Are you serious?*

'Christopher, please?' I try, rubbing at my face. 'Gah, look at me with all this paint. Am I just spreading it around?'

'To be fair, you were more beautiful five minutes ago covered in paint.'

My shoulders slip. Trust him to throw that word out at a moment like this.

'Are you coming with us?' I ask. 'Or at least give me an excuse to stay? Tell me I can't go because you're not done.'

'Katharine, it's your friend's hen do.'

'Combined stag,' I point out.

He shakes his head with an irritated laugh. 'How about if I just stay here and finish my painting and you go out and party?'

'Are you even listening to me? I want you there,' I say.

He shrugs, but something in the way he won't make eye contact tells me he's not as nonchalant about this as he makes out.

'What?' he says. 'Your friends have obviously got plans for you.

Heaven forfend *I* get in the way. Anyway, it'll do you good to get out of here for the night.'

'Oh, come on!' I laugh incredulously. 'Are you seriously upset with me? I forgot about tonight. And what if their plans aren't what *I* want anymore?'

'Yes, but you clearly did agree to this at some point.' He swings an arm towards the diorama outside. 'So a) you should go and b) I don't want to get in the way.'

There's no need for this. He's gone from spirited to solemn in five minutes flat and I cannot work out why. I feel like I could shout his name from a mountain top and he still wouldn't hear anything other than what he wants to. I'm so confused right now. More than that, I'm frustrated. I'm locked in a shopfront and banging on the windows to be let out.

'I have asked you to come with us because I want to spend time with you. But if that's not good enough, then just lock the front door on the way out.' I drop the spare keys on the seat beside him and walk out with nothing more than my phone, bank card and my own keys in my hand.

As I slip into the back seat, Hunter does a Dracula turn-out and does his best to hide the fact he's smothering his lips with Chapstick.

Good Lord.

'We thought it would be great for you to meet Hunter.' Frank hands me a Heineken. I don't love beer, but I'm not paying so don't complain.

Behind us, there's electronic music pinging and ponging about the bowling lanes, the clattering of pins scuttling into ball pits as another group of their friends cheer, and the smell of deep-fried food wafting through from the kitchen. My hired shoes pinch the bridges of my feet.

'He'll be on your table at the wedding and, since neither of you has a plus one, we thought you might like to get to know each other.' Lainey's voice trails off as she looks at us both hopefully.

While her plan is admirable, I've been trying to work out how to ask Christopher to be my plus one all day. Though, I'm not sure what his response will be after those last few moments in the gallery. Do I say something now and risk embarrassing poor Hunter, whose only role in this whole scenario is sitting there harbouring all the excitement of a cat with a laser pointer?

It's not his fault, and I doubt he knew any better, so I keep my discomfort to myself. The least I can do is have a few drinks and head home. There's no rule saying something *must* come of tonight.

'In that case, it'll be good to know another face there,' I concede, tapping my bottle against Hunter's and taking a long slug.

I hate myself for excusing this behaviour right now.

Hunter's not the worst person I've ever met. It's just that he's not the best, either. He keeps us entertained with stories about his work as court clerk while the four of us split a share plate of hot dogs and fries. When Hunter officers me a behind the scenes tour of the court house, I look at Frank like I might choke him.

'You look like you have a lot on your mind.' Hunter angles to get a better look at my phone screen as I check it. Not a peep from Christopher, not even a message to say he's left. Or stayed. God, I hope he's decided to stay.

I pull back and close the cover. 'Just really busy with work stuff.'

'Lainey said you were thinking about opening an art gallery, is that true?'

'That's where you picked me up from today.' I glare at Lainey. Has she not told him anything? Don't you at least give people the Wikipedia quick facts before setting them up? 'So, I'm not really thinking about doing it, it's happening. I open next week.'

'The day after our wedding, of course.' Lainey clucks her tongue.

'Wow, that's quick.' He rests his elbow on the table.

And that's the thing with people, isn't it? Nobody ever sees the work that happens under the surface; the late night and gnashing teeth, the bills that are piling up on the sideboard or the tears when you're just so stressed you have no other outlet. All they see is the glittering lights and free drinks that, *voila*, obviously appeared overnight.

'So, ah, do I get an invite to opening night? I mean, I don't know a thing about art, but it'll be a good party at least,' Hunter asks.

'It'll be open to the public, so I'm sure you'll be welcome.'

He smiles proudly, as if I've just given him the keys to the city.

'Anyway, how's all that going?' Frank looks at me. 'Under control? Do you need any help with anything? We didn't interrupt anything important today, did we?'

'It's going brilliantly, actually. And Christopher has been nothing short of amazing, from helping me into the local scene to making introductions, I'm not sure I'd be where I am without him pointing me in the right direction.' I don't answer the rest of the question because today was already planned, so it might be a little rude to answer in the affirmative.

'Really?' Lainey asks. 'That's an about-face.'

'Really,' I say. 'I tried to talk to you about it the other day, but you hung up the phone.'

Frank frowns at Lainey.

'Who's Christopher?' Hunter leans into the conversation again. 'That tall guy today? I saw him through the window, he looks like a barrel of laughs.'

I feel myself wriggle further away from him as I draw back in horror. 'He owes you a smile, does he?'

'Katie.' Lainey lays her hand atop of mine. 'I think what he means is that he just looks quite serious.'

'He can be, yes. I like that about him. But he has a wicked sense of humour once you get to scratch the surface.'

'So, what is he? A business partner or friend?'

'Yes.' I look at Hunter.

Frank covers his eyes and winces.

'He's just someone she knows,' Lainey excuses. I glare at her.

What happened to my friend who was ready to dismantle the patriarchy only weeks ago? The woman who sat in a pub and raged about the sausage factory has been replaced by someone who's trying to shove my square head into a round hole for the sake of what? Setting me up with someone who's so wildly inappropriate for me?

I feel so outrageously agitated that it's like the walls are closing in on me and the chequered floor is stretching out further with each step. Everything's *Alice in Wonderland*, and I'm suddenly too tall to squeeze through the door to freedom.

The longer I stay, the more desperately I want to go home, or to wherever Christopher is right now. Hell, if I had the money, I'd take an Uber out to Loxley and finish what we started in my bed this afternoon. But I have a table full of people staring at me, waiting for another answer. I excuse myself and head for the bar.

Standing on my own at the bar feels like a weight off my shoulders, like slacking off at work and hiding in the toilet from your boss when they're on the warpath. My fingers hover over a 'Please come and pick me up' message, but I'm not sure I want to be that person tonight. It's not that I'll be doing anything wrong, but I worry it'll be all too much trouble with Lainey and Frank. Then again, I don't love that I'm making excuses for that, because why should I? Once again, I slip my phone away and turn back to the table.

Hunter is on his way over and desperately trying to stuff his Chapstick back in his pocket again.

'I'll get this, you go back to the table.' He slips a fifty-pound note across the bar while I rattle around my pocket for the last of my change.

'No, thank you. I'll buy my own.'

'Really, it's fine. I don't mind,' he says. 'I need to break this note anyway.'

It's a moment in stark contrast to breakfast this morning and the two of us standing around emptying pockets to make up the last ninety-five pence of our bill. Twenty pence here, fifty there, and a final five pence that came tumbling out of my handbag at the last minute. I make eye contact with the bartender and roll my eyes.

Our bowling lane is ready when I return, Hunter hot on my heels and talking about a promotion at work, one that's going to skyrocket him up the ladder, or so he says. Lainey interjects that she has everything under control tonight, talking about breaking off into teams; her and Frank against Hunter and me, naturally.

I think I could also retract my statement about never feeling like a third wheel, because tonight I feel like the third, fourth and transmission box all at once. A week away from getting married and they're understandably handsy with each other. And it's not even that that bothers me. It's that it gives Hunter more than one idea and, while I manage to dodge him before his hand makes contact with my arse, he does manage a hip grab more than once.

'Aren't they amazing?' Hunter leans in as we watch our friends dance at the top of the lane. I shout at them that we aren't at the wedding reception yet and that they should calm down. 'I'll have what they're having, right?'

'Huh?' I offer him a cursory glance.

'I'm just saying, it would be nice to have what they have.'

I take a sip of water.

'You know, I'm not far from here. My apartment, I mean. It's in Kelham Island.'

I listen as he prattles on about the view from his balcony window. In fairness, it does sound like a lovely flat, an open plan red-brick converted warehouse. Thank the developers for triple-glazed windows, he says with a wink. When he asks where I live, I tell him it's a short tram ride away and leave it at that. I don't need him to know I live at the gallery. And then, I hear a sniff. Right. In. My. Ear.

'What do you say we skip off on these two and I can show you the butler's pantry? Maybe get to know each other a bit better?' he asks. 'It's been a bit loud around here tonight.'

I look at him. 'I'm quite happy here, thanks.'

'Oh, come on, I have it on good authority you're up for a good time.'

That cheerful façade I've done my best to maintain all night slides off the side of a cliff and sinks to the bottom of the ocean. 'What do you mean by that?'

'I mean I'm keen to keep things casual, too.'

'What did you say?' I glare at him.

'Just a one-night thing if you like?' He looks nervously to Frank, who's now watching all this play out. 'You know, if that's still what you do?'

'Now, you listen to me, you jumped up little shit.' My nose flares and twitches. 'Don't you ever, ever touch me again, do you understand?'

He peers up at me, wide-eyed and nodding as I stand and grab my coat. My heart almost physically up and throws itself on the floor as I look at Frank and Lainey, these two people who I thought were my dear friends. But best friends wouldn't have said something like that about me to another man. I'm certain I haven't done anything tonight to give Hunter such an impression. Lainey steps down from the lane as I grab my coat, mutter a few choice words, and disappear to the loos.

I hold my phone above my head but there's no service in the cubicle. I allow myself a pity cry, just enough to let the pressure off but not enough to make a complete tit of myself. Lainey shuffles in behind a few sets of feet.

'Katie?' She walks along peering under each door. I'm surprised nobody's telling her to sod off. She stops when she sees my shoes. 'Katharine, are you okay?'

'No,' I blub.

'Do you want to talk about it? Did he do something inappropriate?'

I scoff and peer up at the fluorescent lights. All they do is make my eyes water again. 'Are you kidding me right now?'

'No, I'm not kidding at all,' she says. 'Please tell me if he did something.'

'Have you been blind to all the unwanted touching, have you?' I yank the toilet door open and unwind a mound of paper around my hand. 'Or were you too busy telling him I was an easy lay?'

'What?' she shrieks, a dozen notches less snarky than she was hours earlier. 'No. Why on earth would I do that to you?'

'Well, somebody told him that.' I snivel, dabbing wet paper under my eyes. '"I have it on good authority that you're up for a good time." Who says that?'

'It certainly wasn't me.'

'Did Frank?' I grab at the basin and turn to face her. 'Because someone must have.'

'He wouldn't do that.' Her face is awash with sorrow, lips and the corners of her eyes turned down. 'Frank adores you, you know that.'

'You know, I love you like a sister, but I'm saddened to think that's how one or both of you speak of me when I'm not around.'

Two of the other toilets empty. There's a distinct, conspiratorial silence as the two women watch us nervously and we wait for them to clear out. I tear at the paper towel again.

'I'm so sorry he's made you feel like that, Katie,' she says. 'I just wanted to spend some time with you. It's not the same since you started this gallery thing. We don't see each other, it's just text messages, and it kind of sucks.'

'It kind of sucks because you kind of suck right now,' I bite. 'Every single time I've seen you lately, it's been you-centric. Your menu cards. Needing paper *right now*. Paper which you didn't even pay for, so thanks for doing that to my dad. You beg and plead that I have to be at your dress fitting, so I rush through a meeting to be there. Why? So your mother can insult me and I can listen to you talk about yourself all day.'

Her mouth gapes.

'Where were you when I desperately wanted to talk to you the other day? I wanted to tell you how things were going with the gallery, and about how I'd met somebody and that, despite a rocky start, I really, *really* like him. That I can see things with him I only ever imagined with other men. But, again, it was all about what you needed from me. The minute you had what you wanted, you hung up on me mid-sentence.'

'Look at you.' She's almost spitting as she speaks. 'What, you think you're amazing because you're opening some tiny gallery? And Kit? Well, Frank wasn't wrong in his assessment, was he? You've jumped straight on the first guy who looks at you.'

I toss the wad of paper in the bin and look at her. 'Delete my number.'

I'll bet any money you like that I look like hell right now. A crumpled dress, running mascara, and the stain of a blue moustache above my upper lip. I don't have enough credit on my travel card to get me home, nor do I have the money in my current account to do a top-up. The bus driver gives me a pitiful look as the door closes with a pneumatic hiss.

'Just this once,' she warns. 'We'll get you home safely.'

'Thank you.' I slink away to the back seat, embarrassed but grateful for the small mercy.

A chronic heaviness sits at the base of my spine. I'm rooted to the spot while at the same time desperate to run. I want to be as far away from tonight as I can possibly get. I want away from the discomfort and unwanted attention. I want to be left alone. I want Christopher.

The realisation is sudden and overwhelming, so much so that I miss my stop and continue staring into the night sky for a whole six stops afterwards. I finally race from the bus on the seventh stop and start walking the last of the trip.

Maybe Christopher was right when he said that this was the perfect storm. With my moving away and the both of us having less time on our hands, he had strangely become my closest confidant. I'm worried I left him upset this afternoon and hope he's still home when I get there.

Home. See how easy that rolls off the tongue?

As I make my way along dimly lit streets, I watch restaurants winding down for the night. Chairs are being stacked atop of tables, lights are being dimmed, and roller shutters are clattering down. About a block from home, a café is still frothing milk. I consider a late-night coffee but stop short at a couple making out in the front window. It would only serve as a diversion tactic, and I'm sure he will have gone home by now anyway.

Approaching the gallery from the other side of the street, I can see all the lights are out and he's locked and bolted the front door. He's made progress with his painting. Whoever his subject is, there's a chin and a Mona Lisa smile, and it fills me with nervous excitement to see it from this side of the window.

It's like seeing your favourite movie for the first time. No matter how many times you see it, you know you can never enjoy it quite the way you did the first time. He's even switched the new neon sign to closed. I imagine him walking around, shutting up for the night, and it sits warmly in my stomach.

I slip down the side street and into the car park where his car is still sitting silently. It hasn't moved all day. Unless he's had a few beers and caught an Uber home, but that strikes me as a very un-Christopher thing to do. He's always seemed so in control of it all, so I can't imagine him leaving everything behind. I find myself relieved at the idea that he's somewhere behind the door I'm currently unlocking.

A kick of breeze pushes the door shut behind me. I lock it as quietly as I can and tread carefully upstairs, avoiding steps five, seven and twelve. They all creak. When I reach the top of the stairs, all my answers are waiting there for me.

He's asleep on the sofa. An upright lamp glows a warm yellow, and a pad of paper rises and falls against his chest. I watch over him a moment while I decide what I'm going to do. Even asleep, he looks like he has the weight of the world on him. His brow is still knitted in argument and his bottom lip juts like a toddler on the verge of a tantrum. The thing is though, I can't think of any other sight I want to see more right now.

I am utterly done for.

He is why tonight was so awkward and squeamish, why I couldn't help but compare the rotten orange at the table to the crisp apple he is, if even just because of my cheap shampoo I can smell on his hair as I lean down to kiss his forehead.

I would much rather have been here at home with him, mulling over points of light and shadow, or listening to him natter about a podcast he doesn't quite agree with, or chatter with excitement over the latest artist he's discovered in some back-alley gallery I've never heard of.

When I've double-checked locks, plugged devices in to chargers and switched off all the lights, I settle in carefully beside him. It's a tight fit, but my back curves into the mould of his front and his arm becomes my pillow. Just as I'm about to slip off for the night, he shifts, pulls his other arm from between us and slips it over my waist. If you listen carefully, you can hear him take a slow contented breath. He stirs as I clutch his hand and decide to pull him over to the bed.

Chapter 28

He's the first thing I see through barely opened eyes the next morning, standing over a frying pan in yesterday's clothes with a spatula in his hand and blond hair at Picasso angles. As he moves about, I wonder how Christopher has managed to climb out of bed without waking me. It's the smelling salts of coffee that have done the trick. That and the buttery vanilla scent of pancakes cooking.

Though I'm certain I have none of the ingredients necessary to make breakfast, I don't question it. The fact is, he's still here. There are no notes, text messages or workplace excuses. A featherlight tickle curls my feet as I think about how I dragged him to bed when I got home, but that we barely slept. Hoisting myself up on my elbows, I yawn and stretch, feeling my body ache like the Tin Man after a humid night.

'Good morning.' He smiles, looking at me quickly. 'Finally.'

'Finally?' I croak, amused. 'What time is it?'

'Just gone nine.'

'Oooh,' I perk up. 'Lie in.'

Throwing the sheets back, I untangle my hair with fingers and shuffle past a dining table set for two. I even claim a glass of orange juice that's been placed out for me. He is just … *sigh*.

'Don't have you have class to teach this morning?' I ask.

He shrugs. 'They know how to let themselves in, I can be a few minutes late.'

Placing an arm around his back, I snuggle into his neck and enjoy his warmth while he lands a kiss on my forehead. If I weren't so hungry, I'd probably drag him back to bed. I reach over the stove, cracking the window above the sink and letting the world in. Sleepy city sounds waft in, and I consider that I could live this morning over again and be perfectly content with life.

'I'm glad you stayed.' I curl myself around him again.

His shoulders slip, only slightly, but enough to be noticeable. I brace myself for what I think might be an annoyed response, but he says, 'I couldn't very well leave a note when I'd gone and bought everything to make breakfast. I should at least get my money's worth.'

'Please, feel free to capitalise.' I pick a pancake apart and listen to laughter ripple up through his chest.

'How did last night go?' he asks.

Last night. The question jogs my memory in the same way flicking a switch illuminates a dark room, and I kind of wish he hadn't. Purposely, selfishly, I lost myself in him in the early hours of the morning. I just didn't want to think about the fact I'd tossed sixteen years of friendship in the bin. It hurt too much. Even now, I can feel my throat closing.

'Were you angry at me when I left?' I pull back and look up at him.

'Me? No.' He shakes his head. 'Did it seem like I was angry with you when you got home?'

'No, I just.' My voice crackles as it drifts off. 'Last night was balls.'

'Want to talk about it?'

I'm not sure people ever expect the avalanche of words that come after a question like that but, to his credit, Christopher listens as I step him through Lainey's grand plan of setting me up with Hunter. At least I can laugh about the Chapstick, even if I can't laugh at his assumption that I'd be happy to go home with him.

Christopher bristles when I gloss over his suggestive comments. I don't want to repeat too much or dig too deep into them; knowing my best friend at least helped those ideas fester was painful enough.

'Why didn't you call?' he asks, so gently that my throat gets all cloggy again. 'Hey?'

I shake my head. 'I thought you were angry at me.'

'No.'

'And, so, remember how we were talking about friendships that don't survive change?' I ask, my voice shaky. When he gives a slight nod, I continue, 'Well, this one imploded.'

He steps back from the stove as I walk around him. 'Katharine, I'm sorry.'

'Me too.' I give him a watery smile. 'I'm just going for a shower. I'll be back.'

Ten minutes is all I need to have a good cry, scrub last night out of my hair and pull myself back into some semblance of woman. Even if that involves not much more than wrapping myself in a bathrobe and towelling my hair dry.

I push last night into the back of my mind and tell myself I need to step away for a few days before calling Lainey. Space will be good for everyone. Right now, instead of wallowing, I want to concentrate on the man in my kitchen, the amazing breakfast he's made, and how he got on last night. There's the beginnings of a painting downstairs and I'm wildly curious as to what it will become. I step out of the bathroom, towel pressed against my crown and freeze.

He's gone.

In his place: John.

Both our brows twitch in something like confusion as he looks down at the dozen red roses in his hand. He's dressed down in slacks and a sweater with a T-shirt underneath. It's probably the most casual I've ever seen him since the day we met. My blood runs cold.

Not because I'm scared of him, but because, if I thought last night was bad, then I suspect it's about to get a whole lot worse.

'Katie,' he says.

'Katharine,' I correct him.

'Katharine,' he repeats. 'Can we talk?'

'Where's Christopher?' I ask, starting across my flat in a panic. 'Is he downstairs?'

'Oh, he's—'

I hold a hand up as a stop sign. As much as I hope to find Christopher sitting by his easel in the front window, wearing that barely there smile, I know the answer before I make it to the bottom of the stairs. He's gone, as is every trace of him being here yesterday and last night. I check every room before I throw open the back door and stick my head out into the car park, there's nothing there but gravel, weeds and rubbish bins.

'What did you say to him?' I blaze past John, pick up my phone and try to dial Christopher.

It doesn't ring out; he rejects the call. When I try again, his phone is switched off.

'Only what he needed to know,' he says. 'I didn't think it was—'

'Which was?'

'That we had unfinished business.'

'Oh, you are *kidding* me?' I shove my hands on my hips. 'John, we broke up. I get that the gallery is a public space and that it's the easiest thing in the world to find, but this is one hell of a Sunday drive.'

'Katharine, I want you back.'

My face crumbles and I let out a tired, stressed sob as I sit at my dining table. Yep, this is bad.

287

'I screwed up. I know I did,' he continues. 'And I'm sorry.'

I grab aimlessly for the elastic around my wrist, pulling my hair up into a ponytail just for something to do, something to make this moment feel real. 'You're sorry?'

'Letting you get on the train that night was the worst thing I have ever done, and God knows I've done some shady shit at work,' he says, peering at me from under his eyelashes, desperately hoping his joke lands. It doesn't. Not quite. 'I behaved like a complete twat. I know I was. I was awful and selfish.'

My brain is television static, too much happening to make sense of anything. 'I worked around you for months. I tried desperately to be okay with what little you could offer me, but it was abundantly clear you had no interest in changing.'

'I want to do better, Katharine. I want to do better by you and by us. And I know things aren't going to change if I keep doing things the same way,' he says. 'So maybe we should try things your way.'

He places the bouquet on the kitchen counter and reaches into his pocket, retrieving a … oh *shit, shit, shit, bloody hell no*. He's come prepared with a ring. The lid of the Tiffany blue box cracks open quietly, exposing a rock so big it looks like pulling it from the ground would collapse an entire Botswana diamond mine.

I'm speechless.

'I want you to know that I heard you.' His voice trembles. 'Loud and clear. I want a future with you. I want to make you happy. I do. All you have to do is say the word and I'll pull out all the stops. Pimlico will be on the market and we can find a nice family home to make our own. I don't know what you would want to do with this place, but we can work something out that suits you.'

'What I'm hearing is you think that giving me everything I ask for will make everything okay?' I ask, astounded. 'What about Christopher? Or are you just going to ignore him?'

'That's not what I'm saying.' He shakes his head slowly. 'I know this will take work to fix, a lot of work, and I'm prepared to overlook him because I love you. I do, and I want to give you the life you want.'

How very noble. All these promises, these things he's saying, it's everything I desperately wanted to hear before I left London, before that disastrous work function. I'm not sure it hits the mark.

'And what happens in six months when we slide back into old habits?' I ask. 'When I wake up and you're gone? Or you don't come home from work? Or you get cold feet? Again? It's happened before.'

'We had some fun though, didn't we?'

I sigh. 'We did, yes, but—'

'And we can get back to that, I'm sure of it.' He looks around the room. 'You're opening in a week or so, aren't you?'

'I am.'

'What do you say? Get through that and we can maybe go away and start working things out?'

'Are you in town long?' I ask.

'I'm here for the week, with Adam. We've been sent to scout for an office location.'

Does that mean he'd be open to moving north? Surely, if he's volunteered for the mission, then surely that's a possibility.

'I'm going to leave this here.' He taps the ring case against the counter, interrupting my thoughts. 'I've put forward my case. Have a think about what you want. I don't want to crowd or pressure you. Let's meet for dinner later this week.'

His words niggle. After everything, he still thinks he's in a bloody law court and can argue his way to a decision. I want to throw the box back at him, to lock the door behind him and scream at the sky. But something in the back of my mind stops me, and I hate myself for it.

It makes my stomach roil because, as angry as I am with him right now, he's not too far back in the rear-view mirror that I've completely forgotten just how good we could be together. We did have fun, and we lived carefree lives with weekends away and expensive dinners in plush surroundings. I wanted for nothing, at least superficially, while he was part of my life, and he's just offered me everything I've ever wanted from him. And, right now, with a bank account that's thinner than tracing paper, giving in to temptation doesn't seem like the worst idea ever.

Chapter 29

I wonder if this is how an orange feels as it's being juiced, breathless from being squeezed at every possible angle, but still heavy in a way that drags down heads and buckles shoulders. John hasn't even closed the door behind himself and, already, I know my answer.

There's no way I could possibly say yes to the dress, not with what I know now, with what I've experienced this past month of my life. It would be ludicrous, and it would be nothing short of rescinding everything I stand for, and everything I've achieved since I made the decision to leave London.

I don't want things handed to me. I want to feel the innate satisfaction of knowing that, while things can get hairy at times, I've worked for the results. I want to come home to someone who appreciates and understands what and why I'm doing the things I do. What does he even mean when he says I can come back and check up on the gallery occasionally? If his thoughts are in line with his words, then he likely still perceives art as a bit of a 'finger painting' hobby.

And I can't gel with that.

Look, I know people can change. Hell, my moving across-country involved a whole lot of bitter humble pie and changing my perspective on people and things, so I can't discount that he's genuine when he says that things need to change.

But he is a lawyer, and don't they just love a good bit of precedent? By that token, he's told me he's going to change before and done nothing about it. There's all the proof I need that this is never going to get any better. All he's doing is giving me what he thinks I want in the hope it'll calm me down and the carousel of life will continue. But it can't. My life has changed, and I don't think he has a place in it anymore.

I need to go to Loxley. I need to see Christopher, to explain all of this to him. I consider heading up there immediately, only he'll be in the middle of class and the last thing I want on top of this morning is to look like an unprofessional harpy in front of his class. So, I hole up in my flat for the morning and scramble to tidy the darkroom, anything to keep my mind off what's happening although, as it turns out, that's a fail, too.

Because the first thing I see as I walk through the door are our photos, still strung up where we left them the morning of that fateful lesson. They're full of playful smiles and knowing looks that spoke volumes at the time, but sound like the gaping hole of silence right now. God, I really have screwed this up, haven't I?

Lainey may have called me upwards of twenty times since I walked out of the bowling alley last night but, judging by the text messages that have accompanied them, she's calling to give me a backlog of my errors, and not because she wants to be friends again. It feels like a complete undoing of the last sixteen years of my life, and I'm bereft at the loss.

The only way to counter my confusion is to step outside and get some fresh air. I can't run, but I can get away from the moment and spend some time thinking about my next steps and what I want to say to Christopher when I see him.

So, how do I explain what he saw? I'm gone for what feels like hours, chewing over the idea that, yes, this morning looked bad.

Really bad. But it wasn't quite what it seemed. Actually, it really was what it looked like. I can't wrap this up any other way than to tell him the truth. I step into Sainsbury's for a chocolate croissant because, if nothing else, I'll get to enjoy something this morning.

DECLINED.

Huh? I frown at the chip and pin machine. That can't be right, I was sure there was *something* left in there. Not enough to get me home on the bus last night, but enough for a snack, at least on my credit card. Surely things aren't that dire? I scramble out the door and into the street with nothing more than the receipt in my hand and burst into tears. It's humiliating. When I check my banking app, a direct debit I'd forgotten about came in overnight and whisked away my last chance of buttery goodness.

That's it. I'm broke, my best friend hates me, the man I thought could be something won't answer his phone, and the one who could never work out what he wanted suddenly wants it all. For a breath, I consider calling John and saying yes. It's the simplest solution to every problem I have in this very moment.

It's an extremely fleeting moment, one that passes in the time it takes to walk past the Novotel, and I'm quick to remind myself why that's a bad idea. Because: everything. Don't be stupid, Katharine.

When I get home, I try Christopher's phone again. It's still switched off. I hate the idea that this might drag on, so I jump in my car and head out to Loxley. The least he can do is talk to me, even if it's to tell me I'm the worst person he's ever met. At least then I'll have something to work with.

My insides feel like a washing machine the entire trip out there. Thoughts go to battle with gut feelings, and I talk back to the radio, rehearsing everything I want to say to him. It's not quite relief when I find his car the only one parked outside, but I am glad he's here.

My hands begin to shake. Sitting here fills me with all kinds of déjà vu. Like the first time I was here, there's going to be little chance he wants to see me. But, unlike that day, I head straight for his front door and knock loudly. It's not like I've got much more to lose.

No answer. I'm not sure I expected one, but I try again. I can sense the odd electronic static of a television that's switched on and nearby somewhere. I don't want to sound like a crazy woman, but wouldn't it be better to come to the door and sort this out now? Because that's exactly what I want to do, I follow the veranda that circles the house, down the side passage, past a neat as a pin bedroom and, there he is, sitting in his studio.

For weeks, I've wondered what this room would look like, where his art originates. Now that I'm here, I can't quite concentrate to piece everything together. There's a worn green velvet chaise piled high with curled papers and books about art. An easel sits in the window facing the hills, but it looks like most of the work happens on an oversized table in the middle of the room. It's covered in jars of murky liquid, tubes of paint, brushes and spatulas. There he is, hunched over with his chin in his fist and dabbing at the canvas in front of him.

I knock on the glass bifold.

Startled, he topples from his seat, blinking up at me from the floor. As he stands, I get a better look at him, at the filthy paint-covered apron that's knotted around him, at the smear of dark paint by his temple and the dot on the end of his nose. He crosses the room and cracks the door barely enough to breathe through.

'What do you want?' he asks.

'You're home.'

'Where else would I be?' he grumbles. 'I do live here.'

'Can I come in?' I ask.

'No.'

'But I need to talk to you.' I wring my hands and chew my lip. 'Please?'

He tries to close the door, so I stuff my foot through the gap. My nervousness is quickly replaced by anger. At least give me a chance to explain, I think.

'Why do you do this?' I demand.

'Do what?' he asks, annoyed, giving in, letting go of the door.

I take the opportunity to push past him into the room. 'You reel me in like a fish on a lure. You dance around and dangle your big, beautiful brain in front of me and then you vanish. You don't answer emails, phone calls, messages, nothing. Why? Why can't you just talk to me?'

'Oh, so this is a *me* problem?' he says with a laugh. 'I mean, sure, it's completely my fault you ditched me for another man.'

'I haven't thrown you over,' I say quietly.

'I take it you turned down the engagement ring he flashed about before I left then?' He lifts his eyes to meet mine. 'Rock of bloody Gibraltar.'

My head snaps back and I stare at him. 'What did he say to you?'

'Tell me you told him no, Katharine,' he says, this time a little louder.

'I haven't told him anything,' I say.

'That's not the same thing.' He runs his brush through a rag that hangs from his apron. 'What is it? You're waiting to see how this pans out before you give him an answer?'

'Listen, I know that you're angry.' I hook my hands together. 'It's okay to be angry. In fairness, I probably would be, too.'

'Angry?' He looks up. 'Katharine, I'm furious.'

'And that's okay, Christopher. It's okay to feel like that.'

'Of course it bloody well is!' he shouts. 'I wake up after a night with a woman I think might be my girlfriend, though I'm not entirely sure yet because we haven't talked about it yet, only to find her *other* boyfriend on the doorstep ready to pop the question and crack open the champers.'

'But it's not like that.'

'How can it possibly be any different?'

'Because we broke up,' I plead. 'This is what I'm trying to tell you. We broke up before you and I ever met. To my knowledge, I was single when I met you and I've been single the entire time I've known you and been with you.'

'So he just woke up this morning and thought today was the day he was going to drive three hours to propose marriage?'

I nod and shrug. 'I can't explain it either.'

'When was the last time you spoke to him?'

I shrug. 'I don't know, maybe the week I moved here?'

'You mean you don't remember?'

'It was the week I moved here,' I repeat. 'I'd been here a week, he hadn't stopped calling, and I hadn't answered because I wanted a clean break. I wanted to move on, so I rang him and asked him to leave me alone.'

'He certainly seems your type.'

'What's that supposed to mean?' I snap.

'Flashy suits, fast cars, Pimlico apartments.' He looks at me from the corner of his eye. 'Drama.'

'Sorry, what?'

'I've known tons of people like you. As long as they're the centre of attention, that's what matters. Not happy with the fancy London job? Didn't get the promotion you wanted? That's okay, you can quit and walk out because there's always Dad to pick up the pieces. I mean, even the stuff with Lainey last night, all of this, this trouble and drama comes back to you being the common denominator, doesn't it?'

'How dare you use that against me.'

He stops on the spot, Simon Says, before throwing his hands up in the air. 'Do you even care about the art, or is it just about the fame and glory behind it? Is it all just status?'

I try cutting in over the top of him. 'I know you're upset, but you don't have to be cruel.'

'Sometimes the truth hurts, Katharine,' he utters, his eyes wet.

'It certainly did when I found him on the other side of your front door down on one knee.'

'I didn't know that. I'm so sorry.'

'Do you remember the day we met? You had no interest in me whatsoever. None at all. You knocked me back at every turn. Didn't even know my name.'

'Excuse me?' I say with a laugh. 'Are you actually serious? You openly mocked and insulted me in front of my own family. If all you're worried about from that day was the middle-aged equivalent of "Don't you know who I am?", then maybe you need to check your priorities. You want to rail on me about my name in the spotlight? It's exactly what you did that day. It is exactly you. You're just as bad.'

'You wanted nothing to do with me until you found me online. Not a damn thing,' he says. 'When you found out who I was, I couldn't get rid of you.'

'Couldn't get rid of me?' I scoff. 'That's rich, considering you seemed to be everywhere I went.'

'Prove me wrong,' he says.

'But it wasn't like that,' I plead. 'Okay, so maybe I did turn you down that first afternoon, but I'd just left Webster so I couldn't do anything with your art if I wanted to. I couldn't. You know that. Then, when I decided to open my own place then, yes, I chased you. I thought you'd be good for the gallery. You are a phenomenal artist and a wonderful person.'

'I've made a decision about what's happening this week.'

'Please don't do this.' I can feel myself turning to water. He's going to cancel; I can feel it. Every single thing I've built up will vanish in less than a heartbeat and I don't know what I'll do if that happens. 'Please, no.'

'When I agree to do something for someone, I follow through. No matter the cost, so you can have your artwork, but I won't be there on the night. I refuse to be wheeled out like some draw four card for you to show off to your friends.'

'But I want you there, you have to be there,' I plead. 'This is just as much your show as it is mine.'

'No. This is about the students. I told you that from the start. Clearly, again, you weren't listening.' He purses his lips and looks away. 'If my work doesn't sell, then your father can drop what's left back here, but I don't want to see you, talk to you, or hear from you again. I'm done. Go and marry your uptown boy and leave me be. I was happy as I was.'

Chapter 30

Without another word, I leave his studio feeling like everyone on earth knows just how awful I am. From our very first meeting, he's always had this way of making me feel completely exposed. It's not always the worst thing, especially when I felt it pushed me to do better, but this is beyond even the worst of that.

My legs have been blown hollow and I've been shown for the fraud he's always known I am. I slip on gravel as I approach the car park, a fence post and new splinter the only thing saving me from a muddy backside.

Looking back at his house, I freeze and consider pushing my way back into his studio and pleading with him again to please listen to me. But there's so much anger hubbling and bubbling inside me that the best I can do is sit in my car and cry. Again. It's all I've got left at this point.

My hand trembles as I shove my car into gear because I realise there's every chance this could be the end of my dream. Packing up my life, upending everything I've known will have been for nought. And why? Because I hedged my bet on him, the big drawcard for the exhibition.

All the online traffic and chatter has been about angling for a spot at the front door just to get a look at the glorious, reclu-

299

sive Kit Dunbar. Sure, there are other artists, people I believe to be just as important, but I can't deny that he's the main attraction. Without him, will anyone show up?

And I don't mean merely spectators at this point. The closer I get to home, the more panicked I become about the future of the entire exhibition. Regardless of his own beliefs about seeing plans through, I can't be certain that any of the other artists won't start pulling their work once they realise Christopher won't be there. After all, they're his friends first and people take sides. I've seen it happen in every single relationship breakdown I've ever witnessed. It's human nature, for better or worse.

At some point though, I'm going to have to tell people he won't be attending the opening night. It's the right thing to do, even if it risks losing both visitors and artists alike. Not telling them will only make me look like a liar because, while they might be there to see his art, there's no doubt that people will want to see him, talk to him, share the night with him.

Perhaps I shouldn't have been so quick to say no the other night when Dad floated the idea of selling his shop to me. The nine-to-five of customer service would be so much easier than this right now.

When I get home, I shut myself off from the world. I slide down the wall and settle myself on the floor, away from prying eyes, and drag my laptop towards me. Opening up all the social profiles I've set up for the gallery, I start writing a lengthy post about scheduling conflicts and deep regret, and all that flouncy corporate jargon that, to the naked eye, is a very fancy way of saying: 'Oops, I done fucked up.'

'It's with great regret …'

'Due to unforeseen circumstances …'

'Unfortunately, a scheduling conflict has arisen …'

In the end, I write what I know: from the heart. Though he won't be there, I assure people his art will still be on display as planned. It's a hard post to write. It feels like I'm unravelling with each touch of a key, but I don't have a choice. I hit 'Post' and sit back and wait for the fallout.

It's quick, I'll give the internet that much. I read the first few comments through a gap in my fingers, barely wanting to see them at all. I'm surprised, and slightly relieved, when many of them are supportive. Then, there's a knock at the door. It's Adam, standing there looking dishevelled with a bottle of cola pressed against his hand.

'What on earth have you done?'

He shakes his hand out, opening and closing his fist. 'I suspect, dear sister, that I may have just lost my job.'

'Why?' I say slowly, watching as he climbs the stairs to my flat.

'Let me tell you a thing.'

As he begins digging about in my freezer, looking for a something to replace the warming bottle, he explains that John volunteered for the law firm's Sheffield sojourn at the last minute. So last minute that Adam didn't know John was going to be here until he arrived this afternoon to find him in the hotel restaurant.

'Hey, if they're paying for the fancy room, I'm going to stay,' he says when I ask why he's not staying with Dad and Fiona.

'Fair enough,' I say.

'And, look, I knew something was up the second I saw him. He doesn't just volunteer to come north for the fun of it. He's so city oriented I'm surprised he knows anything exists outside his own postcode.'

I snort. 'Evidently, he does.'

Adam continues to explain that, over a drink at the pub, John admitted to having been out here first thing this morning, to having proposed, and to being totally thrilled to see my latest post on social media about how Christopher had stepped aside from the exhibition. Apparently, all of that equated to me coming to my senses. All John had to do now, he boasted, was wait for me to accept his proposal.

301

'And, so, I might have punched him, it might have been in his smarmy face, and it might have been in the middle of my favourite pub which I am now, subsequently, banned from.'

'Oh, Adam,' I say with an exhausted sigh. 'Why?'

'Because a) he deserves it, b) I'd been wanting to for years, and c) he's been baiting me for weeks.' He looks around. 'Is this it?' He nods at the engagement ring box on the bench.

'Yup.'

'Christ, that must be worth a fortune.' He gawps as he cracks it open. 'Look at it.'

I scoff. 'Christopher's words were "rock of Gibraltar".'

'Ahhh,' Adam says knowingly. 'I thought there might have been something between you two after dinner the other night. Once upon a time you couldn't spit his name out quickly enough and, suddenly, he's offering to drive you home.'

I blush wildly. 'Well, his finding John grovelling on my door-step this morning may have put the kibosh on that.'

'At least he grovelled.' He sits next to me on the floor by the sofa and shoves it in my face. 'You'll be well on your way to a Chelsea Tractor with that thing.'

'I wasted so much energy thinking that's what I wanted,' I say. 'Although it would certainly solve all my problems right now.'

'Please don't tell me you're thinking about—'

'What? No.' My face cinches in disgust. 'I meant it would also solve my problems if I sold it, which I'm not about to do because, while I am broke, I'm not a complete jerk.'

He leans back to get a better look at me. 'You're what?'

'I am broke.' My chin crumples. 'Couldn't even enjoy an exotic butter croissant for breakfast this morning. I've got nothing left, drained my accounts and credit card completely. I have a loaf of bread, some butter and jam to get me through opening night. But, now, Christopher hates me and has decided he's not coming to the opening night, and I'm terrified people are going to start pulling their art.'

'I don't think he hates you,' he says quietly. 'I think his ego may be a little bruised, but hate is a strong word.'

'He thinks I was leading him on.'

'Were you?'

'No! No, of course not.'

'Have you told John no?' he asks.

I shake my head. 'You know what he's like, just goes on and on until you're bamboozled and then disappears.'

'All right.' Adam crossed his legs and wriggles himself into a more comfortable position. 'Firstly, the money thing? It's not a problem. We can fix that. Really, it's not such a big deal.'

'But, Adam, it is. I'm a thirty-five-year-old woman, not a teenager looking for an allowance. I don't want other people turning around and saying "Yeah, but he paid for that" or "She'd be nothing if he didn't buy it for her", and I certainly do not want to be indebted to a man. I was supposed to do this on my own.'

'If that's the case, why are you losing sleep over either of them?' He elbows me. 'Hey?'

I drop my head down onto his shoulder. 'Why? Because it's supposed to be a massive exhibition. This was my chance to prove to everyone I could do this, that I was right about leaving London. Everything I have went into it, and I've ruined it,' I say. 'Also, I could really use the commission.'

'But Kit's a *man*,' he says. 'You just said you don't need to be indebted to a man, so toss them both into the sea.'

'I don't want to toss Kit into the sea,' I grumble.

'As for your exhibition, I think you're being way too fatalistic. The pieces you have will sell, you'll make some money and, when that's over, you'll hold another one. On and on it goes in the great big circle of art.' He stands and drags me to my feet with him. 'Come on. Chin up. Put your big girl pants on. We've got things to do.'

'We do?'

'What are your big problems right now. List them.'

'Kit.' I count on my finger. 'John. Exhibition. Money.'

'You know what? I think we can kill all those birds with one stone. Kind of.'

I give him a quizzical look. 'How? Have you got the winning lottery ticket?'

'Are you telling John no?'

'Yes.'

Adam's eyes widen. 'You're telling him yes?'

'What? No. I'm going to tell him no.'

'All right. So, what we're going to do now is we're going to go shopping. You need food.'

My words come out in fits and spurts and, for the next few minutes at least, we revert back to what feels like childhood arguments.

'Kate … Kate … stop … no … listen to me,' he says forcefully, all the while I'm shaking my head and talking over the top of him. 'This is not a negotiation, this is a necessity. You need to eat. Let me help you with that. There's no shame in this. None.'

I'm silent.

'And, anyway, I'm sure I owe you for more than a few tanks of fuel,' he says. 'So, let's do this and call it square, hey?'

'I feel like an idiot.'

'Yeah, well, that's something I'm well versed in lately,' he says. 'Let me do this. Then, when we're done there, we're going to show Kit you're serious about him by doing a drive-by at the hotel and you can lob that stupid ring at John's head. Maybe you'll hit the other side of his face.'

Whenever I've walked around town with a wad of cash in my pocket, I've been wildly nervous about being mugged. Not because anyone had watched me take that extra rent money from the cash machine, but what if they had? Maybe there's something written on my face that says: mug me, I have money. And, if money made

304

me feel like that, you can guarantee that bloody ring made me feel worse.

It was a neon sign above my head daring people to look into my bag. What if I lost it? What if it just slipped right out in the middle of the fruit bins at the supermarket? Maybe a sticky-fingered thief would decide against my purse and go for the small blue box instead.

'Want me to come with you?' Adam calls to my back as the front doors glide open.

'Is that wise?' I ask, disappearing inside.

Reception is bright and airy, sofas in one corner, armchairs and coffee tables in the other, I'm not entirely surprised to feel myself trembling, as if I've just been set to high alert. I walk towards a handful of sleek reception desks against the back wall.

'Can I help you?' The concierge grins as they hang up the phone.

'I'm here for a meeting with John Harrison. Could you let him know Katharine is here for him, please and thank you?'

Minutes later, I hear the ding of the lift and the squeak of overly polished shoes on linoleum. I flash a quick look to Adam, who's waiting outside, coffees in hand to save him trying to mount the counter and strangle him. I turn back as John approaches. He leans in for a kiss, but I take a strategic step away from him.

'Kate.' He flinches in pain as he attempts a smile. The corner or his mouth is red and raw. 'It's good to see you.'

I swing my handbag around and riffle through for the ring box, my heart flopping when I think I can't find it. But it's there, buried beneath a grocery receipt and box of tampons. I place it on the reception counter between us and push it towards him.

'It's a no from me.'

His brow creases like he can't quite believe what he's hearing.

'What you did this morning was grossly unfair. We had broken up. Last we spoke, I asked you to leave me alone. Yet, here you are thinking this is going to solve all our problems. You're right, we would need to work on them, but they run too deep for a ring to fix.'

'Oh, Katharine.' His shoulders slide down towards his pockets. 'This isn't a court case; I've told you that. Repeatedly. You can't argue your way out of this. You can't remind me of a handful of good times and think that makes a good marriage. It doesn't. You need to listen more and talk less. And there's every chance your stunt might have ruined something very precious this morning. So, thanks for that.'

I don't wait for a reply I don't want. Instead, I turn and walk away. This time, I don't look back. Adam's where I left him, standing by the doors, coffees stacked and frowning into his phone screen.

'Yeah, so.' He turns his phone screen to me. 'I've definitely been sacked. Rad.'

'Can I talk to your boss? Would that be okay?' I ask.

'Nah. Pretty sure decking a colleague is against company policy, no matter the circumstances.' He wrinkles his nose. 'Total L'Oréal moment though.'

'Hey?'

He puckers his lips. 'Because you're worth it.'

Chapter 31

After clearing out his hotel room, Adam comes back to my flat. He stays long enough for me to cook a slap-up pasta dinner, one of those foolproof fresh-from-the-pack ravioli and sauce meals. He could go to Dad and Fiona's, but he can't stomach the idea of telling them he's lost his job. I can definitely sympathise so, instead, we break garlic bread and drown our sorrows with a bottle of red. It hits the spot.

I'm starting to feel a touch less apocalyptic and more like myself as we natter about the week's litany of events. I even fire off a message to Christopher. I don't want to bombard him, I really don't, but some things need to be said. The message rambles a bit, but I tell him again how sorry I am, that I've told John no, and that I would love the opportunity to speak to him when he feels ready.

Even though it feels like John has won on a technicality, with a fractured opening night and an unemployed lawyer, I'm not sure I'm ready to back down quite yet. I've got a lot riding on the opening night next weekend and a lot of people I need to prove wrong. I've come this far, why stop now?

Sitting around the dining table, Radio 1 playing in the background, Adam watches as I write a list of everything that needs to happen between now and the crack of the front door on opening night. The further I dig into my brains, the more detailed the list becomes. With the exhibition still running and everything now resting on my shoulders, I want this to be so good that people can't ignore me or the real stars of the show: my artists.

First thing Monday morning, I start making phone calls. I check and double-check that people are still taking part in the exhibition, that those who haven't already are still planning on dropping their art at the gallery in preparation. Even though everyone is still wildly enthusiastic about participating, I won't feel calm until my walls are full.

The first work appears on Monday night, when someone named Teddy arrives, and I'm sure I fall over myself with gratitude at the sight of him.

More art is delivered over the next few days, culminating in the appearance of Fiona late Wednesday afternoon. I'm beyond excited to see what she's come up with for her contribution and, as she begins to unpack her car, I find myself laughing in pure delight.

She's produced a group of colourful paintings that at first glance look to be reproductions of classic canvases, but with mocking details of the present. Books are replaced with e-readers, fans with phones, and earrings with earbuds. They're glorious and I love them.

'I call them the plight of the modern woman, trying to get peace from the man for thirty-four seconds a day,' she jokes as she waddles in through the back door with a canvas that's taller than her. 'Sometimes, I think they can't even breathe on their own.'

'Oh, I think some of them are perfectly self-sufficient.' I reach for the canvas. 'Here, let me grab that.'

She gives me a look. 'You mean like Christopher?'

'Right, so, Adam's told you then, has he?'

'We have ways of making him talk.' She flutters a lead pencil by her mouth. 'Also, because Kit rang this morning to say I had better be turning in my piece soon.'

'He said that?'

Even when he's not around, the surprises don't stop. The fact he knows she hadn't yet delivered tells me he's still keeping a wary eye on our shared spreadsheet.

For a moment, I stand there in stunned silence. Christopher is possibly the only person I can think of who's kept their word when the chips are down. Not many people would be so gracious as to continue supporting something they were no longer involved in. How is it that, in the depths of this, he makes me want to do better?

'Do you want to talk about it?' Fiona leans into my line of sight, though she's a little fuzzy around the edges.

'I don't know.' My voice breaks. 'Do I?'

'It's up to you,' she says. 'I'm here if you need an ear.'

I shake my head. I'm not sure I'm ready. Instead, I ask for her help hanging the art. I should have already begun this part of the process but have found myself too preoccupied. Whenever I've had a moment to consider it, it's coming up to evening and the lighting hasn't been great. Now that I have help, though, we make quick work of it.

I've spent the last few days trying to work out the correct placement for each piece, and my paper bag heart fills out a little more with each artwork we hang. To see the gallery come to life with colour is beyond satisfying. Not quite in the same way it would have, had my week gone to plan, but this is what I'm left with and I'm determined to make the best of it, to love the here and now.

It had always been such a pipe dream to open my own gallery, something I'd talk about wistfully with Lainey while chowing down on another soggy sandwich on the South Bank. So, I embrace the frustration of trying to get things exactly right, my spirit level dragged up and down the ladder constantly. I'm so glad I've got Fiona here, hurling about her jokes and generally being the tonic I need.

I'm halfway up a ladder when a courier arrives in the early evening, so Fiona signs for the delivery and brings it over. With its carefully packed exterior, it can only be one thing: more art. And it has to be from Christopher because we're almost done hanging everything else and his display is still one painting short.

'Looks like one final piece.' She turns it over. 'Oh.'

'Christopher?' I step down. She nods.

I want to tear at it to see what it is, to see how it places with the other pieces he's offered. When it's finally free of its protective layer, I feel a quick stab somewhere delicate.

It's me.

I'm staring at a portrait of me, complete with dark hair and bright eyes, with a blue smear above my mouth. I'm bathed in light, and I don't know what to do with what I'm feeling. Everything begins to bubble up through blurry eyes.

'Oh, Katharine,' Fiona gasps, taking the canvas from me and walking it into the back room where his work is displayed. 'It's like looking in a mirror. He's even captured that mischievous look that hides behind your eyes. Whenever you wear that look, I know I'm in for a cheeky joke or ten.'

'I think I love him.' I bury my face in my hands. 'And it's so scary because I didn't think it would feel like this.'

'Like what?'

'I thought it would be all-encompassing, lovely and soft like a Cupid-infested toilet paper ad, but I'm so distracted all the bloody time.'

'That is the utter definition of all-encompassing.' She takes my hand. 'You can try and think about something else, but he'll be front and centre, like a lifetime's worth of pass-the-parcel, except it's inside your head, which is on fire, and you never get to the middle of the parcel.'

310

As I watch her hang the last piece of the puzzle, I have a sudden, overwhelming urge to tell Fiona everything. She's been around, she's seen things, so I'm sure she's got more than one or two pieces of advice handy for the way I feel. At the risk of sounding like broken record, I invite her upstairs for coffee.

I lay everything bare, the last few weeks of my life in painstaking chronological order. We chat about men and commitment, what it was I needed from the future and how that sat with how I felt about Christopher.

'Do you want to know when it was for him?' she asks, her eyes sparkling with all the secrets she's bursting to share.

'When what was?' I plonk a teapot in the middle of the dining table.

'When he fell for you?'

'Oh, no, he does *not* love me.' I roar with laughter. 'He made that abundantly clear when I went out to Loxley the other day.'

'Bulldust.' She barrels on. 'It was the moment you walked into our house that afternoon with Adam. I watched him as you stepped outside to greet him. It was all very flowers from the sky and soft vignetted edges.'

'Stop it.' I snigger.

'I watched it happen!' she squeaks. 'He looked at you, his back straightened and, bam, he clutched at his solar plexus because you just went straight in for the kill.'

'Oh, please,' I say with a groan. 'He did not clutch his solar plexus. He looked for his nearest exit.'

'You know, he wants to think he's this ultra-broody, mardy arse painter, but he's a terrified boy who doesn't know what he wants half the time.' She hides behind her teacup. 'Or, he does know, he's just being a boy and dawdling to the conclusion.'

'Don't tell him that,' I say with scandalised laughter. 'He'll argue you out of town with a pouty lip and big old frown.'

Talking to Fiona is always illuminating. I love how she refuses to bury herself in worries and, instead, takes things at face value.

When I ask for her advice on the situation with Lainey, her answer is again simple and to the point.

'There's no competition in friendship,' she says. 'You aren't going to win a prize by being the last to apologise.'

'I know,' I murmur. 'I just don't know what to say to her.'

'Do you have to say anything?' she asks. 'I know when I see my best friend, Dottie, we don't generally have to say anything. We just know. With best friends, you just know.'

'Her fiancé told his friends I'm easy.'

'Katharine.' She fixes me with a serious look. 'You have never been an easy woman.'

I laugh and blush and hide behind my hands. 'I don't think he was talking about my temperament.'

'Then it wasn't his business to be talking about, and your beef is with him, not her.' She grabs for the last of the Jaffa Cakes. 'So, what do you do with that knowledge?'

I clear my throat and sit up a bit straighter. 'I'm going to go to the wedding.'

'With?' she asks.

'The menu cards?' I try.

'And?'

'A smile on my face.'

'Why?'

'Because she's my best friend and I told her I would do something for her, so I'm going to follow through on it,' I say. 'And I'll deal with Frank on my own.'

'Good girl. So, what we're going to do now is make sure everything here is one hundred and ten per cent.' She leans into the conversation. 'That way, you can give her a call, do what you need to do in London, then come back here to enjoy the party.'

Chapter 32

Friday morning finds me jittery with nerves as I board the train to London. It's not quite 10 a.m., I'm wearing the best dress I own, and I have thirty-seven perfectly presented eggshell blue menu cards tucked safely in my handbag. I know Lainey only asked for thirty, we ordered enough paper, so I just kept going.

And if I could just stop sweating, that would be great.

As I gaze around the carriage, playing my old university game of picking out the Monday-to Friday-commuters, tourists and other students who all look plucked from the confines of sleep, I wonder if today isn't a dumb idea.

We haven't spoken yet. Truth be told, I haven't been able to work out where to begin. What I do know, however, is that it's not a conversation that needs to happen over the phone. We've been friends long enough and had enough minor disagreements for me to know that speaking to her in person is best. And way too much gets lost in the ether of messages and emails, no matter how heartfelt they may be.

Fiona stayed until the early hours of Thursday morning, insisting we go over everything one final time. We mopped and vacuumed, laughed at the photos we found in the darkroom, the ones I'd developed with Christopher, and I sent one final confirmation email to the caterer. Getting the place as ready as possible on Wednesday night meant I could spend Thursday finishing Lainey's menus, making London seem like a far less rushed effort.

Not that I'm expecting a warm welcome when I arrive. I'm not quite that silly. In fact, I wouldn't at all be surprised if I arrived at the reception centre to find my name has been scrubbed from the seating list. It's that reason alone that prevents me showing up on Lainey's doorstep; I couldn't bear the thought of upsetting her while she's getting ready for her big day.

When I step off the train at St Pancras, it hits me how quickly I've adapted to life in Sheffield again. London is all a little too loud, too exhaust-y, and I sure as hell haven't missed the push and the shove of the Piccadilly line. There are so many people.

Arriving at Twickenham Road is a breath of fresh air. I walk the rest of the way to Syon Park, stopping for a bite to eat on the way. The last thing I want is to draw attention to myself with a growling tummy in the middle of a wedding.

The ceremony will take place in a garden full of colourful blooms, and it's decorated the only way my friends could. It's tasteful and minimal, but with the air of sophistication they share. Plain white chairs sit in rows facing the altar, which is an arch of linen white blooms. I take a seat at the rear when friends and family start arriving.

I can do nothing now but wait. I spend what feels like an age checking my phone, digging through my bag and inspecting my fingernails, before rolling back through the cycle again.

'Katharine, God am I glad to see you.' Frank appears at my side, squatting beside my chair and reaching for my hands. He looks gorgeous in his suit and bow tie, hair slicked back and clean-shaven. 'I owe you the world's biggest apology.'

'Hey, you,' I say quietly. 'You look incredible, by the way.'

'Don't scrub up too badly, do I?' He takes a moment to enjoy the compliment, as he should. 'But, how are you? Is the gallery coming along well?'

I smile, realising I'm enjoying spending the day away from the place – even if it does mean having the tough conversations. 'I am ready to rock and roll tomorrow night. Everything is up, I just need to open the doors.'

'You know it's going to go off without a hitch, right?'

If only that were true.

'If I can say something, though, I am so sorry about what happened. I can't—' he taps his hand to his forehead '—I truly can't believe the night ended like that. What I told Hunter was not what came out of his mouth.'

'What did you tell him?' I ask, remembering Fiona's words yesterday. He's the source of the trouble, so he must be the source of the solution.

'I told him that you were, *are*, a dear friend, that we'd love to see you meet someone just as wonderful as you, and that you'd had enough of quick flings,' he says carefully. 'When we were on the way to pick you up, I did mention how much he might like you because you were always up for a good time, in that the three of us would go out and have a literal good time. I certainly didn't intend to give him some mental image of, well, you know.'

'That might have given him an impression though, don't you think?'

He nods. 'I can see that now, and I take full responsibility for that. I am so sorry.'

'I appreciate that, thank you.'

'Are you still joining us for the reception?' He grimaces. 'Please say yes. We'd hate for you to miss it.'

I pull the top of my handbag open to flash the menu cards at him and he smiles.

'Lainey's going to be thrilled.' He leans in and kisses me on the cheek. 'As am I. You are incredible. Don't let anyone tell you any different, okay? When this is all done and dusted, we'll catch up for a night out. My shout. You can bring that guy, too. Is it Kit?'

315

I nod as he makes his way towards the celebrant to wait for Lainey.

She arrives fashionably late, making it seem like the breeziest thing ever, as only she can. Now, if I thought her dress looked beautiful on her in the bridal shop, it looks a million times better today. Her hair is swept up in an effortless ponytail, and her make-up is so flawless you'd think it was her natural skin. She looks incredible and, far from being jealous, I'm thrilled for her.

Like all wedding ceremonies, which seem to be months of planning boiled down to a twenty-minute timeslot –a terribly unromantic view – it goes past in such a flash. Frank kisses his bride, the register is signed, and they're bounding past everyone at a rate of knots on their way to have their photos taken.

I can't be sure Lainey even knows I'm here yet, but it doesn't matter in the slightest, because today is not about me. I follow the crowd to the Conservatory where there's a framed seating chart awaiting our perusal.

I'm glad to find my name is still there. Not only is it there, I've been shuffled over to one of the family tables, on the other side of the venue from Hunter. I duck inside and, after a quick chat to staff, replace all the bubblejet printed cards with my handwritten menus. Everything matches now, eggshell blue and white place cards and menus in a spidery yet precise font, just as it should have been.

While I'm relieved that I've spoken to Frank, I can only hope Lainey is happy to see them. And me.

Hunter steers clear of me, a nervous look thrown my way as I scuttle past his table and up towards my new one. If he stays on that side of the room tonight, everything will be fine. But I'm still nervous as I join everyone in standing for the bride and groom. They're both beaming beyond what I ever thought possible for two human beings. It's gorgeous, and it makes me so happy.

They work their way through the centre of the room, waving

and mouthing thanks to parents who leap out to hug them again. When they reach the bridal table, I stop and hold my breath as the look on Lainey's face changes. She goes from beaming bride to something close to sobbing in no time flat as she picks up the first of the menu cards from her table.

As soon as she's able to, immediately following the first toast, she makes a beeline to my table, scooping me up from my seat and clutching me so tightly anyone would think this was our farewell. But it's okay, because I'm holding her just as tightly. We don't have to say anything, we just know: it's okay.

'Frank told me.' She smiles. 'Thank you so much.'

'I wasn't sure if you wanted me here or not, but I really wanted to be here,' I say. 'If that's okay.'

'It's more than okay.' She looks at me.

'You look beautiful, just so you know.'

'I haven't stopped thinking about you all week,' she says in a teary whisper.

'Likewise.' I look around the room. 'I really regret what happened.'

'Did you bring someone with you?' She looks around me. 'We left the spot next to you free.'

I blow my cheeks out. 'Boy, do I have a story or two, or ten, for you.'

'What? Really?' she asks. 'What happened?'

We're back in our impenetrable huddle. People are trying to get her attention, wanting to drag her away for photo opportunities, so I don't get to tell her much right now, but that's what the dance floor is for later on.

Chapter 33

A champagne cork pops behind my head, bubbles frothing and spilling over the mouth of the bottle and directly onto the freshly mopped floor. I'm not even the least bit concerned because, seconds later, the fizz is joined by laughter and the clink of glasses. Finally, I'm having a party – the Katharine Patterson Gallery is open for business!

There was a small crowd waiting to get in the door. Mostly students with a smattering of family and friends, their excitement palpable. And contagious. I'm carried along on a cloud of introductions and handshakes as we make our way to the middle of the front room. That's where we stay, a dozen of us, huddled in discussion for the next thirty minutes. Eventually, one person breaks off and the rest follow, dispersing around the gallery.

It was a long, late trip back from London last night, but I was wired from the buzz of seeing Lainey married. We had the quickest of reconciliations and debriefings on the dance floor where, I think for the first time, I openly gushed to someone about Christopher. She almost brought the place to a standstill when I told her about John and the fallout from that, offering to call Christopher herself by way of verbal referee.

Getting back on the train, and before the night had officially wound down, was difficult, but not as difficult as not attending her wedding altogether. I'm relieved and proud of myself for taking charge. Because of that, I barely slept a wink. But I can't possibly think of yawning when I see excited faces cramming for space by their own art.

Cameras flash and selfie sticks are whipped out, the notifications on my phone start rolling over like the arrivals ticker at Heathrow, and all I can do is wait for the night to play out. The work is done, all that's left to do is enjoy the night. A little like the wedding yesterday. So much planning and, if I don't pay attention, everything will be gone in the blink of an eye.

Local press filter in and out, and I'm chuffed to see a few critics have made the trip up from London. They're armed with their phones and busily taking notes as they walk the room and chat to artists. When a group of colleagues from Webster arrive, we laugh about the last time we all saw each other and pop another bottle in celebration. I delight in regaling them with stories of paint pots, floorboards and broken toilets; the trials of the new business owner.

The first sale of the night whisks me away from them just before 9 p.m. A collector who's driven down from Edinburgh with their chequebook ready looks primed to buy Fiona's set of prints. So excited am I that I grab her by the arm and drag her into the far corner of the room to meet the buyer, where we talk numbers and sign contracts. It's one of the best possible things that could have happened tonight. For both of us.

I watch as she races back into the crowd, searching out an ebullient Dad, who bursts into tears at her news.

I slip away from the crowd and hide away upstairs for a few moments so I can fish my phone out of my bag. I'd love to say there's a message waiting for me, or even a quick voicemail from Christopher, but there's nothing, and the realisation hurts. Even more so when I consider that my phone is full of messages from random strangers, all wanting a piece of the action. Even Lainey, who's busy packing for her honeymoon, has sent texts demanding pictures.

When I dial his number. It goes straight to voicemail.

'Hey you, it's me. Don't really want to leave you another rambling message into the abyss, so I'll make it quick. Tonight has been, it *is*, amazing. You'd be so proud everyone. We've just had our first sale, so we're not quite there yet, but I'm hopeful. Anyway, I just wanted you to know. I wish you were here.' I stop. 'And I'm sorry for everything. It was utterly my fault and I would love to sit and talk about it if you'll hear me out. Anyway, I love—'

I reach the time limit and the phone cuts me off.

'—you.'

Back downstairs, Adam has arrived and is already deep in conversation with Lolly, the red-headed girl from Dad's shop. There's a lightness about them that fits effortlessly, and every time he makes her laugh, she blushes a bit more. I skirt past them with the offer of a fresh drink and search out Fiona.

When she hasn't been busy selling paintings, she's been doing her best to be my personal assistant, walking and talking with any member of the press who stands still long enough to warrant a hello. If she's not doing that, she's latching onto the catering team, wandering around with trays of drinks and nibbles and making sure I get my share of food.

'Come with me.' I wave her over as she whizzes past for the third time in fifteen minutes. 'I want to show you something.'

'Me?' She exchanges a look with Dad, who ambles over, as well as Adam when we brush past him.

Dad's wearing the best suit he owns, bless him. His shoes are polished, he's had his hair trimmed and his tie is straighter than a die. He's a minor celebrity in his circle of customers, not that he'd ever admit it. I do a quick lap of the room, clocking the front door opening in the corner of my eye, before excusing myself.

There's one more thing I want to do tonight, and it involves the small room that currently features Christopher's art.

'What a lovely painting.' Dad stands right up close to the portrait of me. 'Not as handsome as me, obviously, but the blue is an interesting touch.'

I blush nervously, knowing full well what that afternoon signified. Gosh I miss him. In all the time I had to think last night, I came to the unsurprising conclusion that he is everything I've ever wanted. Someone I can talk to, work and celebrate with. What happened between us was entirely my fault, I get that now. In the rush to bury my past, I hadn't told him enough to be prepared, if there was such a thing as being prepared for John.

'He really is amazing, isn't he?' Fiona looks on in wonder as if she's seeing it again for the first time over. 'I wish I had half his talent.'

'You've got his talent and more,' I interrupt her thoughts. 'Fi, I want to offer you this room.'

She looks around, confused. 'But it's full of Kit?'

Oh, how I wish that were true. 'Yes, but what I mean is after that. Once this first exhibition is done, if you'd like to hold a permanent display here, this space is yours.'

She makes a noise not unlike a startled mouse and looks to Dad like she's not quite sure she's heard right. Dad's heard, and he's dabbing at his eyes with the end of his tie.

'What do you think?' Adam creeps up from behind and hugs her. 'I told her she'd lost the plot, that you should have the big room because you're amazing.'

'Oh, my heart,' she says with a jittery laugh. 'I would be thrilled.'

'Really?' I clap my hands to my face. 'I didn't want you to think I was being—'

She leaps forward and hugs me like she never has before. 'I've tried for years to get into a gallery. I think I'm a little too left of centre for some people, so this is just … it's everything I've ever hoped for. Of course I'll accept.'

I pull back and hold her by the shoulders. 'You are absolutely perfect; you've been the most amazing help these last few weeks and I love you more and more every time I see you. Don't you ever change.'

'Oh, you.'

'You're like Mum two-point-oh,' Adam adds. 'Mum squared? No, that's not right.'

Fiona wipes at her eyes and laughs. 'I don't know, if I keep eating those canapés you've got on offer tonight, I might end up mum cubed.'

'Mum to the power of pie?' I try.

It may be that I'm feeling a little peaky from the champagne but, damn I love group hugs. The four of us hold tight in the back room while Fiona has a sobby moment, Dad has a sobby moment, and Adam tells us he's moving home to open his own law firm. Apparently, I made upending my life look easy.

I really didn't.

When we gather ourselves, they leave me alone to collect my thoughts before I head back out into the fold. They're wild and scattered, but as I stand in front of this painting of me, I know that I'll be heading out to Loxley tomorrow morning. I'm going to tell him how I feel and let the chips fall where they may.

'Would it help if I begged you not to marry him?'

There it is, that feeling, that bump that says: here he is. I turn to find Christopher standing there, hands in pockets, shoes sparkling and suit freshly pressed. As I hope for a moment of peace, we're greeted by the steady stream of shoulder pats and backslaps as people walk past the small room. One forceful thump pushes him forwards into the room.

For the first time all week, we share a knowing look.

'What would help is if you checked your messages.' I reach forward and take his hand.

'Oh, I heard them,' he says. 'And saw them. I just want to be sure that, if you marry anyone, it's going to be me.'

I thread my fingers with him and pull him closer. 'Are you serious?'

'Scarily enough, yes.' He smooths a hand over my head. I love it when he does that. 'Katharine, I was done for you the second we met.'

'That, sir, is a lie,' I say with a snigger. While twelve-year-old me, who flipped through bridal magazines and traipsed downstairs Homer Simpson-style with a bouquet of garden variety rosemary, is screaming that is a for real proposal, my adult brain is trying to temper this with reason. 'I got the distinct impression you found me insufferable.'

'Not quite insufferable.' He narrows his eyes and I copy. 'Challenging, absolutely, but that's what I love about you.'

'You love about me?'

'Well,' he starts with a shrug, 'one of the things, anyway.'

I go to speak again, but he stops me with a look.

'Katharine, I have been completely unfair to you,' he says. 'I should have stayed. I should have listened to you.'

'Yes, but I could have, I don' t know, warned you about him,' I say. 'I'm sorry, too.'

'Did you know that he was coming?' he asks.

'What? No,' I say with a disbelieving laugh. 'Absolutely not.'

He rolls his eyes and sighs. 'I am absolutely filling my pants right now because I don't want this to come out the wrong way.'

'There is no wrong way.' I reach up and hold his cheek. 'Just spit it out.'

'You drive me bloody insane. You are brilliant and smart and funny, and you are so unbelievably beautiful, and you are the only, only person who can hold a decent conversation with me about art, who can take me to task in the most wonderful way. And I was so determined to keep you at arm's length.'

'No,' I mock. 'You?'

'Worked well, didn't it?'

323

'Slipped through.' I pinch my thumb and forefinger in his face. 'Completely accidental, I assure you.'

'Maybe you were an accident, but I'm so glad you were. I don't connect with many people.'

I chuckle and clutch at the lapels of his jack, eventually slipping my arms around him and, boy, is it good to hold him again. He's warm and solid and totally real. There's nothing loud or flashy about him, it's all genuine. I've either just wet myself, or that's the warm flood of affection that's filled me from head to toe.

Love, huh. How good is it?

'Fancy that, you being difficult.'

'Another fun fact.' He leans down and pops a kiss on the tip of my nose. 'The school was actually struggling before you came thundering along. I just couldn't find my groove, class numbers were low, and then you arrived and saw through every stupid excuse I had. Now with this exhibition, because of you, I can't keep up. You are a challenge and you challenge me and, God, I love you. I do. Maybe that's too much, I don't know, but I know how I feel.'

'So do I.' I reach up and kiss him. 'And I love you, too.'

It doesn't take long to get used to him all over again, his touch, the feel of him against me and the soft curl of his hair between my fingers. I don't think I could ever, ever be sick of this.

'Hey.' He pulls back. 'Do you like your painting?'

'Like it?' I look at it over my shoulder. 'I love it.'

'Good, because the original is still at home.' He presses a finger to his lips. 'I liked the original too much, thought I might keep it.'

'You did?' I smile and bite my lip.

'But I need to keep you, too, matching set and all.'

'You're not joking about the marriage thing, then?'

He shakes his head. 'Not joking, no. I'm not wasting a moment this time around.'

'Do I get to pick my own ring.'

'How did I know that was going to be the next question?'

'Can I?'

'Is that a yes?'

I nod as I kiss him again. 'A big, fat, loud, not at all accidental yes.'

We're interrupted by a cough at the door. Dad's head slinks away. Busted.

'See, I told you! I told you I was right,' he calls to Fiona, who's already dragging people back to look at her small new art space. 'I told you they were perfect for each other.'

If you fell accidentally in love with Kit and Katharine's story, don't miss *Lessons in Love,* a laugh-out-loud romantic comedy from Belinda Missen. Available now!

Dear Reader,

We hope you enjoyed reading this book. If you did, we'd be so appreciative if you left a review. It really helps us and the author to bring more books like this to you.

Here at HQ Digital we are dedicated to publishing fiction that will keep you turning the pages into the early hours. Don't want to miss a thing? To find out more about our books, promotions, discover exclusive content and enter competitions you can keep in touch in the following ways:

JOIN OUR COMMUNITY:
Sign up to our new email newsletter: hyperurl.co/hqnewsletter
Read our new blog www.hqstories.co.uk
🐦 : https://twitter.com/HQStories
f : www.facebook.com/HQStories

BUDDING WRITER?
We're also looking for authors to join the HQ Digital family!
Find out more here:
https://www.hqstories.co.uk/want-to-write-for-us/
Thanks for reading, from the HQ Digital team

ONE PLACE. MANY STORIES

If you enjoyed *Accidentally in Love*, then why not try another delightfully uplifting romance from HQ Digital?

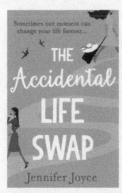